Also by Nadine Gordimer

None to Accompany Me

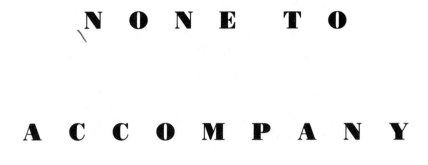

NONE TO

ACCOMPANY

ME

Nadine Gordimer

Farrar, Straus and Giroux ||| *New York*

Library of Congress Cataloging-in-Publication Data
Gordimer, Nadine.
None to accompany me / Nadine Gordimer. — 1st ed.
p.   cm.
1. Women lawyers—South Africa—Fiction. 2. Man-woman
relationships—South Africa—Fiction. 3. South Africa—Race
relations—Fiction. 4. Marriage—South Africa—Fiction. I. Title.
PR9369.3.G6N6 1994   823—dc20   94-7553 CIP

Fic.

For Roland Cassirer

We must never be afraid to go too far,
for truth lies beyond.

— MARCEL PROUST

•

None to accompany me on this path:
Nightfall in Autumn.

—BASHŌ

seventeenth-century Japanese poet

BAGGAGE

And who was that?

There's always someone nobody remembers. In the group photograph only those who have become prominent or infamous or whose faces may be traced back through experiences lived in common occupy that space and time, flattened glossily.

Who could it have been? The dangling hands and the pair of feet neatly aligned for the camera, the half-smile of profile turned to the personage who was to become the centre of the preserved moment, the single image developed to a higher intensity; on the edge of this focus there's an appendage, might as well trim it off because, in the recognition and specific memory the photograph arouses, the peripheral figure was never present.

But if someone were to come along—wait!—and recognize the one whom nobody remembers, immediately another reading of the photograph would be developed. Something else, some other meaning would be there, the presence of what was taken on, along the way, then. Something secret, perhaps. Caught so insignificantly.

Vera Stark, lawyer-trained and with the impulse to order that brings tidiness with ageing, came upon a photograph she had long thought thrown out with all she had discarded in fresh starts over the years. But it wasn't any print she had overlooked. It was the photograph she had sent to her first husband in his officers' quarters in Egypt during the war—their war, the definitive war, not those following it which spawn without the resolution of victory parades. He must have kept the photograph. Must have brought it back in his kit. It was a postcard—the postcard—she had sent when on a trip to the mountains; a photograph of the little group of friends who made up the holiday party. What she had written on the back (turning it over now, the lifting of a stone) was the usual telegraphic few lines scribbled while buying stamps—the weather perfect, she was climbing, walking miles a day, swimming in clear pools, the hotel was as he would remember it but rather run-down. Best wishes from this one and that—for those linking arms were their mutual friends, there was only one new face: a man on her left, a circle round his head. He was identified by name in a line squeezed vertically alongside her account of the weather.

What was written on the back of the photograph was not her message. Her message was the inked ring round the face of the stranger: this is the image of the man who is my lover. I am in love with him, I'm sleeping with this man standing beside me; there, I've been open with you.

Her husband had read only the text on the back. When he came home he did not understand it was not to be to her. She defended herself, amazed, again and again: —I showed you, I ringed his photograph next to me. I thought at least we knew each other well enough . . . How could you not understand! You just refused to understand.—

But yes, he must have brought it back in all innocence with his other souvenir knick-knacks, the evidence of his war, brought it back and here it was, somehow hadn't been torn up

or thrown away when they divided their possessions in the practical processes of parting in divorce. After forty-five years she
was looking at the photograph again and seeing there in its
existence, come back to her and lying on a shelf under some old
record sleeves, that it was true: the existence of his innocence,
for ever.

•

Vera and Bennet Stark gave a party on one of their wedding
anniversaries, the year the prisons opened. It was a season for
celebration; sports club delegations, mothers' unions and herded
schoolchildren stood around Nelson Mandela's old Soweto cottage queueing to embrace him, while foreign diplomats presented
themselves to be filmed clasping his hand. The Starks have been
married so long they don't usually make an occasion of the
recurrent day, but sometimes it suggested an opportunity to
repay invitations, discharge all we owe in one go, as Vera says,
and on this year of all years it seemed a good excuse to go further
than that: to let themselves and their friends indulge a little in
the euphoria they knew couldn't last, but that they were entitled
to enjoy now when, after decades when they had worked towards
it without success, change suddenly emerged, alive, from en-
tombment. There were her Legal Foundation colleagues, of
course; and white men and women who had been active in campaigns against detention without trial, forced removals of communities, franchise that excluded blacks; student leaders, ganged
up under a tree in the garden drinking beer from cans, who had
supported striking workers; a couple of black militant clergymen
and an Afrikaner dominee excommunicated for his heresy in
condemning segregation; a black doctor who hid and treated
young militants injured in street battles with the police and army;
black community leaders who had led boycotts; one or two of

the white eternals from the street meetings of the old Communist Party, from the passive resistance campaigns of the Fifties and rallies of the Congress Alliance, the committees of any and every front organization during the period of bannings, who had survived many guises. And there were some missing. Those who were Underground were not convinced it was safe to come up, yet. Negotiations with the Government on indemnity for political activists were not decisive. One of their number made a surprise appearance—a late-night cabaret turn bursting into the company in a purple-and-yellow flowered shirt, gleeful under the peak of a black leather cap. There were wrestling embraces and shoulder-punching bonhomie from his brothers-in-arms Above Ground, and the hostess reacted as she used to when she didn't know how to show her son how moved she was by the pleasure of having him home from boarding school—she brought her best offerings of food and drink.

The occasion was already marked by the presence of that son—Ivan, on a visit from London, where he had made his way to become a successful banker. With his aura—he wore what Jermyn Street called leisure clothes, silky suede lumber jacket, Liberty cravat and tasselled loafers—he seemed an unacknowledged yet defensive embarrassment to his mother (his father never showed his feelings, anyway) in the illusion that he was one of the colleagues and comrades; that coming home meant the matter of taking a plane. If the party was supposed to be for him as well as to celebrate an enduring marriage (and who would remember, of that extraordinary era, what occasioned what) it became a clandestine welcome for one of his mother's mysterious friends. Music began to shake the walls and billow out into the garden; political argument, drinking and dancing went on until three in the morning. Ivan danced wildly, laughing, with his mother; it was as if their resemblance to one another were a shared source between them. When the man who had come up from Underground was found to have gone as he had come, from where and to where, no one would ask, it was as if the music stopped abruptly. He left a strange hollow silence behind; the echo chamber of all those years, now closing, silence of prisons, of disappearance, of exile, and for some, death. Over? The guests driving away to sleep, the hosts collecting dirty glasses, could not answer themselves.

•

Vera opened the door to a ring at ten o'clock at night—no fear of muggings back in those days of the Forties. He stood, still in his uniform, come to see if he could find some keys missing in the possessions he had packed up and taken away to the hotel where he was living. —Can't lock my suitcases, damn nuisance as everything's still lying about stored here and there.— He didn't have to apologize for turning up unannounced at that hour because, of course, he knew her habits, she stayed up late, sometimes even after he had gone to bed he used to wake from first sleep and feel her sole sliding down his naked leg.

She kept him standing a few moments in the doorway as if he were a travelling salesman, and then stalked before him into their old living-room, now hers. He rummaged through the desk; she stood looking on. He might have been a plumber mending a pipe. She made a few offhand, low-voiced suggestions of where the keys might be. He had come prepared to meet, in the civilized way already established between the three of them, her lover with the thick smooth black hair like the coat of some animal, a panther, maybe, and the clear ridged outline of turned-down lips—how was it he hadn't taken notice of these striking features in a photograph? Poor stupid trusting bastard that he was! But the lover wasn't there, or he hadn't come 'home' yet.

—They just might be in the (he didn't say 'my') old tallboy in the bedroom—I left some stuff I thought you might still want. D'you mind if I go in?—

He turned to her politely.

Suddenly she peaked the stiff fingers of her hands in a V over her mouth and couldn't suppress snorts of laughter.

He smiled, the smile broadening, sending ease between them like circles from the broken surface of water.

They entered together. She behaved as if their bed weren't there, walking past it as something she didn't recognize, and pulling out drawers for him. —I haven't got round to going through this—

He held up papers. —Your old school reports, believe it or not. I thought you might want to keep them.—

—Good god, what for? I'm sure I would have thrown them in the bin, it must have been you who stuck them away.—

She made a gesture of refusal, not interested.

—Maybe I did rescue them from you some time. You still want to become a lawyer?—

Her chin jerked vigorously towards her sternum, with the vehemence of a child whose determination is beyond words. And at once she casually deflected this intrusion of past confidences. —Why are you still in that outfit?—

—Not yet demobilized.—

Perhaps the remark was not so casual; a subconscious rebuttal of unease she had never admitted to herself—'that outfit', referred to as if it were some form of affected fancy dress, had never been taken on by her civilian lover.

There grew between them the silence of nothing left to say. Nothing of their boy-girl love affair, their clumsy assumption of adulthood together, when she was seventeen, in a marriage interrupted by war. Absently he took off to toss to a chair the jacket with its epaulettes and insignia, its strip of campaign ribbons, and got down on his hunkers, searching through the lowest drawers of the piece of furniture. She opened a window to establish that the closeness in the room was lack of air.

Arms crossed, she stood there, watching as he set aside papers in sorted piles, and his back with its muscles moving under the stretched cloth of the shirt, the unawareness of her expressed in the nape grained with sunburn and clipped pale hair bared before her, the warmth of the flesh releasing the smell of a clean, creased shirt—she could not believe the sensation this was bringing her. She fled from it to the kitchen and poured two glasses of fruit juice, but as she was lifting the tray went to the living-room, took a bottle of whisky, came back to the kitchen and in two fresh glasses poured the liquor slowly over ice. She returned to the bedroom with harmless words ready: I think you need a drink. But she approached that warm and redolent back, forgotten, familiar, discovered anew, and touched the shoulder with the hand that held a glass. He turned at the nudge and lifted eyebrows in acknowledgement of the welcome drink, getting to his feet with weight supported on one palm.

They drank.

Nothing to say.

She tried to let the distraction of alcohol in her blood over-come the insistence that, clear of circumstance, unwanted, un-reasonable, her body urged to her. She could not stop it from reaching him from her, as the flesh and soap smell of his shirt came from him to her. It took him by surprise; his face changed, resistance or pain passed across it, but swiftly. He took the glass out of her hand and put it down behind him. They stood, arms helpless at their sides, looking at each other in restless contra-diction. He took her against his chest, her face pressed into the odour of the shirt. They made love for the first time in two years, on the floor among the papers, not on the bed where she belonged with the lover, now.

And what if the lover had walked in on them, he must have the key of the door, what change in direction would have happened then?

•

Vera was awarded the house in her divorce settlement and her lover Bennet Stark became her husband the day after her divorce was final. She gave up the wartime job she had had as secretary to someone in the set she had mixed with in her previous life, got herself articled to a legal firm and registered as a part-time law student at the university. There were no children of her previous marriage and, having lived with her lover in confident anticipation that they would be able to marry soon, she entered the second marriage already pregnant. The child—it was Ivan—grew inside her, her lover was secured as her rightful possession, she was working and studying to fulfil the ambition she had been deflected from in the rosy feminine submissions of a first marriage, but that had been hers since she was a schoolgirl. She sang as she lumbered heavily about the house. At night between the arms of her chosen man, with all the possibilities of her life envisioned in the dark, refrains of precise legal formulations she was learning ribboned pleasingly through her mind on the way to sleep. She saw her happiness as conscious and definitive. Once, in the first months when she was appearing in public with her lover as husband, a woman she did not know turned to her girlishly: 'Who's that terribly handsome guy talking to the woman in the red dress?'

He—hers. Sometimes when she woke before he did she would raise herself carefully on one elbow to gaze at his profile, the red bevelled scroll of his closed lips, the delicate hollow scooped beside the high bridge of his beautiful curved nose, the clear black shape his hairline cut against his white brow and temples, and, as if reflected, its blue shadow, the dark beard that was growing under the skin of the finely-turned shelf of jaw. If he stirred and the eye opened, black diamond mined from the depth of the subconscious, unfocussed, she suddenly was able to see him as the woman stranger had, existing in the eyes of others, her adoration—her luck—compounded by this. And there were times when, in the release of love-making, after the marvels he had first introduced her to in the mountains, caresses that had singled him out for her with an inked circle, Vera sobbed and huddled as if ecstasy were remorse or fear. Despite the extreme sensuality of his looks and the fascination it had for women, Bennet had not had much to do with them, inhibited by fastidiousness until he met this woman who, although so young, already had had the experience of marriage, abandoned a life, another man, chosen him. He understood that the passion she roused and they shared might find unexplained outlets of emotion through her; he would soothe her gently, unquestioningly. But she would take and roughly thrust his hands here and there on her distended breasts and swollen belly and between her legs so that he lost his head and they coupled wonderfully again, while he feared for the child tossed so wildly inside her.

The baby was born strong and healthy. His mother's gaze during his gestation had been so concentrated on his father that he might have been expected to be imprinted with his father's Celtic or Semitic beauty; but he came out favouring his mother, exactly, from his infant days; in Vera's image, alone.

·

Mrs Stark is a fixture at the Legal Foundation. Although she has refused to take the executive directorship which has been offered to her, preferring—selfishly, she says—not to spend time on administration, no one can imagine the Foundation running without her. Her quiet acerbity at meetings, when she disagrees with aspects of policy (and the fact that she's so often proved right), her ability, sitting back with her head in its close-cut cap of white-streaked dark blond hair held immobile in attention, the left corner of her mouth sometimes tucked in (the cleft could be expressing impatience or understanding) to recognize and separate the truth, or as she would qualify, the facts from the fantasies born of poverty and powerlessness in applicants for the Foundation's intervention—these combine to make her the colleague to whom everyone from the director to the telephonist turns for the last word.

Nobody can con Vera, her colleagues agree with satisfaction. The Foundation is not a legal aid organization in the usual sense, it does not provide legal representation in the courts for individuals who cannot afford to hire lawyers. It came into existence in response to the plight of black communities who had become so much baggage, to be taken up and put down according to a logic of separation of black people from the proximity of white people. A logic can be made out of anything; it lies not in the truth or falsity of an idea, but in the means of its practical application. As part of their schedule of work for this week or that, Government officials commandeered the appropriate personnel from the appropriate department and went off to bulldoze the homes of a community, pack the inhabitants and their belongings onto trucks drawn, like any other government equipment, from the State's stores, and transport them to an area designated by the appropriate department. There they were supplied with tin toilets, communal taps, and sometimes, if these could be drawn from the stores department, tents. Sheets of corrugated tin might be supplied for them to begin building shacks. They might be allowed to bring along bits and ends left intact by the demolition of their houses—a window-frame or some boards—but cows and goats had to be left behind; what would the beasts feed on, in a stretch of veld cleared and levelled for the barest human occupation?

All this process was perfectly logical, Mrs Stark would remind her colleagues; we have to come to terms with the fact that in the Foundation we are not dealing with the only real means to defend these people, which is to defeat the power that creates and puts the idea into practice—we are not tackling that at all, at all, let's not kid ourselves—we are only grappling with its logical consequences, looking for the legal loopholes that will delay or frustrate or—occasionally—win out over that logic. They would smile in appreciation of her hard-headed sense of proportion, quite difficult to keep when confronted with the sort of trusting wretchedness facing them in supplicants every day.

Now that the Act that put the Idea into practice has been abolished by the beginning of political defeat of that power, the Foundation has not, as might be expected, become redundant. Mrs Stark was not entirely right—or rather she and her colleagues, absorbed in pragmatic strategies while the Act was in force, had no time to think how far beyond its old promulgation and logical enactment, beyond its abolition, its consequences would become yet new consequences. Now communities whose removal the Foundation had been unsuccessful in stalling are coming to present the case for having restored to them the village, the land, *their place*, which was taken from them and allotted to whites. The same old men in stained worn suits, taking off hats in hands that seem to be uprooted from earth, sit on the other side of the interviewer's desk. There is the same patient alertness needed to listen to the tale and, while it is being told, assess where, out of desperation and guile, it is omitting something the emissary thinks might prejudice his case, where it is being exaggerated for sympathy, and where the facts and their truthful interpretation are the strength of the case, something to work on.

Although Mrs Stark is the one who prepares the yearly report for publication—it has to be both comprehensive and persuasive, because it goes out to existing and prospective donors—and she sometimes travels abroad as a fund-raiser, she does her share of interviewing and investigation. Nobody can con Mrs Stark, no. To some she seems forbidding—and what white person, who among all those whites who still have to be approached and convinced before you, a black, can come into what you are now told is your own, is not forbidding, still there, on the other side of the desk, just as before? But although with her discouraging coldness she doesn't patronize these applicants struggling to express themselves in English—the language of the other side of the desks—and although she doesn't try to ingratiate herself chummily, as many whites feel obliged to do, with the blacks among her colleagues, she has—how to categorize this?—connections with some of these colleagues that have come about rather than been sought and even, over the years, with individuals who to others would be scarcely distinguishable from any in the endless trudge of dispossessed in and out of the Foundation's premises. The young clerk named Oupa will saunter into her office eating from his lunch packet of chips or takeaway of curried chicken, and sit there, sometimes in easy silence while she reads through notes she's taken in an interview just concluded, a silence sometimes broken by talk between her bites at an apple and sips of yoghurt. He's studying at night for a law degree by correspondence and started off by coming to ask her for an explanation of something he didn't grasp; it was her very reserve itself that in his naïvety made him think she would be

better qualified to give him the right answers than any of the
other lawyers on the premises. She was the figure of the school-
mistress missing in his lonely self-education, she was the abstract
image of authority that, resented all your life or not, you had
to turn to in your powerlessness. Then he began to talk to her
about his four years on Robben Island, seventeen to twenty-one.
It was everyone's prison story, of his kind and generation, but
he found himself telling it differently to this white woman, not
censored or touched up as he was drawn out to tell it to other
whites eager for vicarious experience. He broke off and returned
to it on other days, remembering things he had forgotten or not
wanted to remember; not only the brutality and heedless insult
of walls and warders, but also the distortions in his own behaviour he now looked back on. Sometimes with disbelief, talking
to her, sometimes with puzzlement, even shame. There was the
comradeship, the real meaning of brother (as he put it). —But
you suddenly hate someone, you can hardly keep your hands
off his throat—and it's over nothing, a piece of string to tie your
shoe, one time a fight in the shower about whose turn it was!
And the same two people, when we were on hunger strike, we'd
do anything for each other . . . I can't think it was *me*.—

What did she say? He was a gentle person forced, too young,
to see another version of himself that it needed only violence
against him, degradation in suffering the lack of humanity in
others, to bring to life. She didn't console, didn't assure him
that that individual, that self, no longer existed. —It was
you.—

He reached for a tissue from the box on her desk with a
gloomy tilt of the head and the answering tilt of her head said
it was not necessary to ask. He was wiping chicken-wing-greasy
fingers. She passed him the waste-paper bin, dropping her apple
core into it on the way.

Oupa doubled as driver of the Foundation's station-wagon battered by the lawyers' trips into the backveld to consult with communities under threat of removal. One day when Mrs Stark's car had been stolen he gave her a lift home, and the theft revived something else. Before he went to the Island, he was awaiting trial on the mainland in a cell with criminals. —Murderers, man! Gangsters. I can tell you, they were brilliant. Nothing to touch them for brains. The things they'd brought off—robberies, bank hold-ups. And they'd play the whole show through for us. Exactly how they did it. Prison means nothing to them, they had the warders bribed and scared of them. Even whites. They had all their stuff waiting for them outside, for when they'd done their time. I tell you, those guys would make top-class lawyers and big businessmen.— He grinned, chin lifted as he drove.

Again Mrs Stark was comfortably silent, if she noted, she made no remark on what he had just innocently confirmed: something of the unacknowledged self that came into being in prison still existed within him, a pride in and defiant community with anyone, everyone, who had the daring to defy the power of white men, to take from them what was not theirs, whether by political rebellion or by the gangster's gun; silent because this was a self that, by nature of what she was, could not exist among her selves.

—You ever come across any of them again, outside?—

Oupa pressed his elbows to his ribs and brought his shoulders up to his ears. —Those people! Man! Je-ss-uss! I'd be terrified.—

Vera left her promising position in a prosperous legal firm after, when she had failed to conceive for twelve years, her second child was born, Annick.

She has never known whether her first child, Ivan, is the son of her divorced husband or of Bennet Stark, her love of whom was ringed indelibly on a photograph. No one else will ever know that she herself does not. He of the sun-grained, fair-skinned nape is now living in Australia, retired from something to do with shipping, and has nothing around him to bring to the surface that last visit he made to the house they had once shared; and if, in the mood of male camaraderie on a drinking evening there is an exchange of confidences about the unpredictable sexual behaviour of women, he contributes the example of an ex-wife who gave him a better hour than she'd ever done during the brief marriage, he is unlikely to think there could have been any consequences—she was accustomed to see to that. Perhaps he might feel a momentary stab of betrayal, despite her complete betrayal of him, at mentioning her more or less in the context of the one-night stand, but it was all so long ago . . . As for her present husband, it's unthinkable that ever there could be between them one of those terrible, embattled stages of marriage when she might thrust her hand down into their life to seize a weapon to wound him mortally.

Ben was almost embarrassedly dismissive of the fact that his daughter had inherited his beauty; part of the quality of that beauty was that he was not aware of it, he was brought to see it only by remarks upon the beauty of the baby girl as the image of her father. Ivan—because he reproduced the face of his mother?—remained Ben's favoured child.

When the girl was born, with the marvellous markings of her father's black hair and double fringe of lashes, even the bevel-edged lips, Vera could have been looking in a mirror where her lover from the mountains was preserved as he was as a child. A tremendous gratitude gushed from her along with the expulsion of the afterbirth. For a year she stayed at home taking care of the baby with the tender emotional fervour of one making amends—for what, to whom, was diffused in maternal energy; from which she looked up, only now and then, at the newspaper headlines announcing arrests, trials, bans, finally the outlawing of political movements. Physical fulfilment is a temporary withdrawal from the world, a sealing-off from threat and demand, whether directed to oneself or others. At the time, it seems the other world, all extraneous, is jabber and distraction, a crowded station passed through, train blinds drawn and compartment door locked. The self-absorption was pierced only by the fact of the baby shot dead on its mother's back at Sharpeville—an infant like her own, like Bennet's. Her life was all touch: during the day the smooth plumpness of her small daughter damply warm against her hip, the hands of her leggy son, roughened and scratched in tussles at play; the caresses of love-making. There could have been a biological explanation for the strong resurgence of eroticism between Bennet and her. Some theory that after giving birth women experience fresh sexual initiatives and responses. They had been married for twelve years; whatever the reason, the feast of sex begun as a picnic in the mountains again preoccupied her and her lover-husband as it had done. Intelligent people as they were, while they discussed what was happening around them he could be distracted by the bare cup of her armpit showing in a sleeveless dress, and she could be conscious of the curve of his genitals enticing under his jeans.

Bennet Stark carved wood and modelled clay but while recognition for his work in this vocation seemed long in coming had had to make use of a conventional degree he had earned when too young to know what he wanted to do. Bennet Stark was known, behind his back at the Department of English in the university where he worked, as Our Male Lead; as if he were responsible for his looks and the mixture of resentment and admiration these aroused. From the point of view of advancement in an academic community it's a bad sign to have some advantage that is simply a gift of nature, not earned and not attainable for others by any amount of hard work, lobbying or toadying. He remained in a junior position and the ambitions the lovers had for him as an artist when first they exchanged confidences beside a mountain stream were in abeyance while they concentrated on each other and the extension of themselves in their children. He still modelled in clay occasionally over a weekend—the heads of the children, which were growing, changing, even as the clay hardened the image of one stage or another, and the naked torso of Vera, anonymous female body to anyone other than himself, who supplied the beloved head in his mind. But married to the woman he had captivated and captured and the father of a family, he had given up the idea of becoming a sculptor. Vera, at least, had attained her easier ambition of qualifying in law. Lovingly, he felt no jealousy; hers was a practical goal, not dependent on the imponderable mystery of talent, of which, protected by sensual happiness, he came to accept he perhaps did not have enough.

When Annick began to wriggle out of her arms and Ivan distanced himself from the need of her touch on childish wounds, Vera appeared restlessly displaced. She told Bennet she was going back to work.

They could certainly do with the money.

—I'm not going back to the firm.—

He did not know what to make of a sudden announcement that overturned all assumptions.

—I don't want to fight their insurance claims when they lose their jewellery and Mercedes. Or dig the dirt in their divorces.— He looked at her tenderly, patiently. —Set up on your own?—

—I don't know.—

Vera read newspapers and reports, White Papers, was drawn to people who were spread-eagled between their private attachments and those other tentacles, the tug of others' predicaments, the tangle of frustration and misery; women, as she was a woman, lifted out of the humble ramshackle of their lives and dropped, destitute, in the veld, men, as hers was a man, endorsed out of a town where they might find work, driven off farms where their fathers had given their labour; children unlike hers because there was no childhood for them, begging and sniffing glue for comfort in the street. She did come to know. She went to work at the Foundation, not out of the white guilt people talked about, but out of a need to take up, to balance on her own two feet the time and place to which, by birth, she understood she had no choice but to belong. This need must have been growing unheeded—seed shat by a bird and germinating, sprout-

ing, beside a cultivated tree—climbing the branches of passion-
ate domesticity.

Population removals were being fought everywhere to the
limit of the Foundation's resources; she was working until midnight at home as well as all day at the offices; Bennet had left
the university and, with a partner, opened a market consultancy
in the city. Alone in the house in bed at night, they talked over
for hours the disappointments, worries, resentments and com-
pensations each had gathered during the day, giving one another
advice, putting together the context, from his experience of one
level of society and her experience of another, their life.

.

Mr Tertius Odendaal had three farms, one inherited from
his grandfather through his father, one that came as his wife's
dowry, and one that he had bought in the agricultural boom
times of the early Eighties. With America and the British—even
the Germans who had once been supporters of the war in which
his grandfather was a Boer general—interfering in the affairs
of the country, embargoing oil supplies, boycotting sports tours,
encouraging the blacks to make trouble so that even his ignorant
farm boys were no longer reliable, he began to think about
looking to the present, if not the future. With the old stern
President pushed out by one of his cabinet who smiled like a
film star and was said to be having talks with blacks, no one
could be sure what that would be. Not twenty kilometres across
the veld from his homestead there was a black homeland. He
had had to put an electrified fence round his kraal to protect
his Holsteins from thieves, after one of his watch-boys had been
slashed in a panga attack. Even the old President had dumped
blacks too near white farms. On one of his other farms—the one

bought when there were good rains for his maize crop and beef prices were high—that he used only for seasonal grazing, he found squatters, although the herd-boy who had his women and umpteen children with him in his outpost of mud and thatch huts lied that these were just his family, visiting. He told the herd-boy to clear out, get off the farm and take his hangers-on with him. But next time he drove to inspect the place with one of his other boys there were fluttering sheets of plastic and lean-tos of cardboard, tin roofs held down by stones and old tyres, thrown up on his veld like worm-casts. Only women and children to be seen; the men would have been away at work or loafing somewhere, even as far as town. He got his boy to warn these people with an harangue in their own language: what were they doing there, they must pack up their rubbish and get off his land immediately, if they were not gone by tomorrow he'd bring the police. A tiny child clutched his penis in fear and drew up his cheeks to whimper. The women stood unblinking or turned away. As the farmer's bakkie lurched and swayed off, one screamed something the herd-boy didn't translate to the farmer. The cry trailed in the wake of the vehicle.

Mr Odendaal decided to move with the times; whatever they might be. What the Government had done, was doing, could not be undone by one Afrikaner alone. Fighting its betrayal of the white farmer was something for which political action would be found. In the meantime, farmers would have to—in the businessmen's way of speaking—'diversify resources', yes, that's it, get up to the tricks that make those people rich. He applied to the Provincial Administration for permission to establish a black township on one of his holdings. He would convert the farm into cash as a landlord; he would divide it into plots for rent to blacks. He was going to turn their invasion to profit.

During the year pending the Administration's decision—the application appeared in the Government Gazette and there were ponderous objections from farmers in the vicinity—1,500 squatter families representing approximately 26,000 people took possession of Portion 19. These figures for the Odensville squatter camp (it must have got out among the squatters that Odendaal had thought to commemorate the family name in his township) were ascertained by a field-worker of the Legal Foundation, to which a man who presented himself as the spokesperson of the squatters had appealed for investigation. A station-wagon with a tide-mark of dust and a windscreen dashed with splattered insects drew up at the Odendaal farmstead. Odendaal sensed at once it had been through the squatter camp that had been meant to be his township. A woman with white-streaked hair cut like a man's, speaking the usual badly accented Afrikaans of English-speaking townspeople, introduced herself there on the stoep as a Mrs Stack or Stock from the Legal Foundation.

At the pronouncement of that title his body shifted in reflex to bar the front door; that body would not let her past into his house. She actually had with her the man he had refused to meet, whose existence was a matter for the police to deal with —the black bastard who put up that crowd of criminals, drunkards, and won't-works on his land to talk about 'rights' they never would have had the nerve to think of. She introduced the man and even the driver, also a black, as if she expected that the two blacks would be received as part of her delegation and greeted as visitors.

She ignored that the farmer did not respond. *Mr Odendaal this, Mr Odendaal that.* Polite and talked so you couldn't get a word in to stop her. —We've come to discuss the situation down at Odensville, which must be distressing for you, don't think the people there don't realize this. I'm one of the Foundation's lawyers and—we know from experience—the worst aspect of this sort of situation is when the farmer feels he's accepting it if he should agree to talk to the other parties concerned. The Odensville people have a spokesperson, Mr Rapulana, and I can assure you that neither of us is here to deny your position (changed to English, not knowing how to put that sort of sly lawyer's phrase in Afrikaans). We've come because it's in the best interests of everyone . . . believe me, I've seen it, solutions can sometimes be reached where there has seemed no possible way out while the only communication is the threat of police action . . . Mr Odendaal, I hope you're going to talk to us, Mr Rapulana and me—oh this morning or whenever it suits you—we're going to hear each other out without prejudice to either side.—

This was the kind of woman who produced a revulsion in him. To him, in fact was not a woman at all, as he knew women, even if she had been young he could never have believed a man would want to touch a woman like that, would never have thought there were breasts you could fondle in the marital bedroom dark, the mouth asking questions and addressing him without the respect and natural deference due to a male, yet offensively quietly, could bring the sensation of a woman's tongue in your mouth.

He made her wait. He was looking over her head as if she were not there. He spoke in Afrikaans, since she thought she would make herself acceptable by trying to speak his language.

—*Daar's geen Odensville se mense nie!* Odensville is my township that's not yet declared, nobody is living in Odensville, nobody! All those people are trespassers and the only thing I'm going to tell you, lady (the term of address emphasized, and in English), I'm going to get them run off my land, I'm going to burn down their rubbish, and you can go back yourself and tell

them I'm not just talking, I'm not talking at all to you, I've got
the men to do it with me, we know how to get it done, all right,
and if they want to get in the way, that's going to be their funeral.
Running to you won't help them. There are no Odensville 'people', so you can forget about calling them that. They're nothing,
vuilgoed.—

This meddling woman—lawyers, they call themselves!—
stood calmly, even the twitch of something like a smile at the
side of her mouth, as if waiting for a tantrum to spend itself.
He began to breathe heavily at the insult.

The black man he would never speak to—never!—looked
at him unavoidably as the dark aperture of a camera aimed.
This was a country black, brought up where his parents and
grandparents, share-croppers and labourers, spoke the language
of the farmer they worked for, and the school for blacks where
he learnt to read and write taught in Afrikaans, not his black
language. The man's Afrikaans was Odendaal's, not Mrs Stark's
pidgin.

—Meneer Odendaal, don't be afraid. We won't harm you.
Not you or your wife and children.—

The woman lawyer touched the man's shirt-sleeve (dressed
up like a gentleman, jacket over his arm). Before she led the
way back to the station-wagon she paused persistently. —Mr
Odendaal, I apologize for turning up without telephoning. I'll
be writing to you and probably will be able to explain the Foundation's assessment of the situation more acceptably than I've
been able to do now.—

The farmer turned his back. He opened his front door and
slammed it on them behind him. In the optical illusion of blotchy
explosions that comes with leaving the glare of sun for a dim
hallway, he, too, paused a moment. He listened to hear the

station-wagon leave his property. As if he had just stopped running, his leaping, bursting heart slowly decelerated to its normal
pace.

·

For a long time—how many years?—Vera still told her
husband everything. Or thought she did.

Meneer Odendaal, don't be afraid. We won't harm you.

This reaction, response, whatever you like to call it, lay
between her husband and her like a gift. Of what, to whom,
their faces showed neither could decide. Back in the blueish
domes where his black eyes always stirred in her the strange
attention they had attracted against the thudding of a waterfall
she and he had climbed to at the beginning, she looked for his
answer. Once he had been the answer to everything; that was
falling in love: the end of questions. But she was finding an
answer within herself. The gift of the squatter leader's tolerance,
forgiveness—whichever it was—was something the farmer didn't
deserve.

And it was unclaimed! Rejected. —Don't you see, he isn't
able to be aware of it.— A further explanation, coming from
one whose familiar symmetry of features juxtaposed the harmony
of life with the discord she had not only witnessed, but been part
of in this experience and was part of routinely in many others.
How could these contradictions exist in one species, the human
one? How could such beauty be achieved in the composition of
this man's, her chosen one's, face, and such ugliness distort the
ability of human response in that man's, the farmer's, spirit?

—Who's the fellow, anyway—from Odensville—d'you
know anything about him?—

She opened and shut a hand in the gesture of her limitations.
—About as much as I do about all the others who come to us.

Only difference, he's apparently the one all the squatters trust
to represent them. In many of these places there's so much
rivalry, different factions saying theirs is the man. Often we find
the person we're working with isn't accepted by this group or
that. Little power struggles going on even among people you'd
think too desperately busy trying to survive, to have the energy
. . . He seems well-educated, not like most rural schoolmasters.
But I don't know if we're going to get anywhere with this case.
If the Administration does give the farmer permission to declare
a township there, he'll be in a position to say to the people, pay
up or get off. He'll zone such and such a number of plots, and
that won't be enough for even those who possibly could pay.
There's no minimum living space in a squatter camp, you
know!—

—He could charge what he likes for his plots?—

—I've seen farmers rent a piece of ground half the size of
this room for a hundred rands a month. Rural rack-rent, and
we've no legal recourse. Exploitation is the other name for the
law of supply and demand, my darling.—

—Maybe. Maybe. In the situation of people with nothing.
When it comes to land. Pocket calculators, deodorants, vodka
brands . . . the stuff I'm consulted about—the greater demand
you create the greater the competition and the less chance of
getting away with exploitation.—

He spoke in irony but without resentment. A contradiction
between the purpose of Bennet Stark's occupation and the purpose of Vera's was something that, as with other couples of their
kind, of their place and time, was unremarked in their intimacy,
part of an accepted ambiguity. For so long this had been a place
and time when integrity in many matters could be maintained
only by dishonesty, when truth had to survive by lies. If Security
(itself a euphemism for threat) came to ask where so-and-so was

living, you said you did not know, and, out of necessity to protect yourself as well, might even put Security off on a plausible false trail. If you were going to be a conduit for letters addressed to certain destinations that risked being intercepted by agents at the post office, you hired a mail-box under a fictitious name in a suburb far from where you lived. If there was a rumour that this one or that among acquaintances was suspect as a police plant, you smilingly dissimulated before the person but no longer talked in that company about anything you believed in. You lied by omission, and warned others against association with someone who perhaps was innocent, a name smeared by yet others to cause dissension in your ranks. These were the only ways to defend at least something of the truth against the ultimate lie, the only way to defend the principle of life struggling against death, which is the ultimate, forgotten etymology, not to be found in any dictionary or political speech, of that embarrassing word, freedom. So while Vera's Foundation upheld the right of land and shelter, the object of Bennet's market research consultancy was to discover for his clients the enticements that distract people from what they really lack.

But—again, wait!—isn't there another, everyday, pop-freedom, broadcast everywhere in shops and elevators and the combis which transport everyone in cities and on country roads, an easy-to-use freedom in the choice of buying the beer that champions drink or the hair-relaxer beauty queens advise? Must people forgo the pleasure of the unnecessary, as well as every-thing else they don't have? If Bennet had stayed on as Our Male Lead at the university, he would have been teaching a curriculum devised for the level of general education and Western cultural background of white students, difficult to attain for the black students who satisfied entrance standards nominally but came from township schools where boycotts were their history thesis, running battles with the police their epic poetry, and economic theory that of a home where there wasn't enough money for bus fare, let alone books. So what was the difference, whichever way a failed sculptor might earn a living?

In some blessed peaceful country, existing far away, an obvious moral contradiction in the activities of a man and woman might destroy the respect that goes with love. But here, for these two, while the great lie prevailed, it was part of a shackle of common experience of what was wrong but aleatory, could not be escaped. They were scarcely aware of its chafing.

·

When Oupa had driven two or three kilometres from the Odendaal place the little party from the Foundation stopped on a side road for tea under a tree. Mrs Stark always took along on such trips a flask and a packet of biscuits, sugar in a jar, and a stack of plastic cups. Most welcome, the Odensville man said several times, sitting with his knees neatly together, on the grass. Young Oupa crunched one biscuit after another and every now and then, irresistibly, shook his head and laughed on a full mouth at the encounter they had left behind them. —I know that man. Yoh-yoh! I know him! That kind from the Island, warders just like him. There was one commandant—stood there like a bull in front of you when you came up for interrogation. Never spoke himself, let the other one question you and rough you up, but just standing there he was in charge. If he hadn't been there, they couldn't have done the things they did to you. And every time I thought, now it's coming, now he's going to start in on me, too. Yrr-ah, man. But he didn't need to, he just had to be *there*.—

Mrs Stark ran her fingers through her hair, a commonplace sparrow ruffling its feathers, and yawned, the yawn turning into a smile, the pleasure she always took in the young man's ebullience, his awesome way of dealing with his terrible experiences in the indiscriminate narrative style in which he would gossip of something pleasant or funny. The soft red road was empty except for a distant stick-figure zigzagging on a bicycle just below the horizon. The tea was hot and sweet. Beyond a barbed-wire fence where wispy beards of sheep's wool were caught, veld grasses and weeds streaked in undulations of green woven to bronze and rust where a declivity in the ground had been swampy in summer. Black-and-white plover flung themselves up out of the grass as if they had been thrown, crying out on a single note at human presence. After the battering of responses and emotions in the exchange with the farmer, the irritation and exasperation repressed—and who knows, neither Mrs Stark nor Oupa, what else the Odensville man was experiencing?—calm and quiet fell upon the three as a common bond. After this one unremarkable manifestation of that conflict which rang and babbled about them, in them, a constant garbling of their different lives— suddenly the swallows of hot sweet tea were their only awareness. The paper-flutter of white egrets lifting the sky, the gauzy sleeves of water trailing from irrigation faucets in a vast field of something barely there, barely green; the three rested on the land: this was what it was, not a wrangle in a cross-fire of saliva on a stoep, not folders of documents citing deed, claim and proclamation in the files of a Legal Foundation. Oupa wandered off to pee behind a tree. Mrs Stark, unconcerned about the dignity of her maturity, climbed through the spiky fence with the skill of one used to improvise and found a bush for herself. As she squatted there so privately, the flit of insects in the sun above her head made her drowsy, as if they were some pleasant drug taking aural effect. In an instant measured by the flick of transparent wings, there/away, she felt she was about to lie down on the damp rough grass and dream something she had forgotten. She came back to herself and through the fence again. The Odensville man was still sitting as if at a church meeting. —What about you?—

But if he understood the brisk reference to the humble call of nature he perhaps thought it an embarrassing familiarity on the part of this woman, from whom he expected the formulations of the law. He dusted the elbows of his jacket as he rose, asking whether she would mind dropping him at a store nearby, he had to see someone. He got out of the station-wagon there, taking off his hat.

—I'll be contacting you when I have any news, good or bad. You have my phone number? Yes, keep me posted if there are any developments. One of us'll come out again some time next week to take statements—if you could get some people together.—

It was the same sort of professional formula she had used for the farmer, a lawyer must not identify with the anxiety of a client any more than a doctor can function effectively if he begins to feel the pain of his patient.

·

A day or night when Vera heard, like a phrase recurring from a piece of music once listened to and out of mind: *Meneer Odendaal, don't be afraid. We won't harm you. Not you or your wife and children.*

She separated the three statements.

Meneer Odendaal, don't be afraid.

(Meneer Odendaal) We won't harm you.

(Meneer Odendaal) Not you or your wife and children.

She thought that she had not heard them aright on the stoep that day. The farmer heard them and Rapulana the Odensville man heard them the way she did not, they understood what was being said. The words of tolerance and forgiveness so strangely coming from the Odensville squatter dweller, shaming her for the crude aggression of the farmer, were not tolerance and forgiveness but a threat. Remember, Meneer Odendaal, we are thousands on Portion 19, our Odensville. We are there across the veld from you, every night. You have dogs, you have a gun, but we are thousands, and we can come across the veld to this house, this house where you and your wife and your children are asleep, and, as you said about us if we don't go from Portion 19, that'll be your funeral.

TRANSIT

You don't know who this is?

On her way in the city, coming up to the street from the underground garage where her car had its regular booth, a creature within its range of burrows walking the block to the Foundation from the bank, a coffee bar where she might have joined a friend or the Italian restaurant where occasionally she and Ben, in the observance of a forgotten retreat for clandestine lovers, met for lunch, Vera sometimes found herself stopped by someone who was searching for recognition to come from her.

You don't know who this is?

The chestnut satin skin of a young black woman now darkened and puckered beneath the eyes, the saucy jut of dancing buttocks now built into a monument of solid, middle-aged flesh; a figure of a man with one tired shoulder lower than the other, shining pink dome where Vera would have recognized only the lost blond curls, another whose belly-fat, straining gaps between shirt buttons, had swallowed the slender black Jonah (that really happened to be his name) she and Ben had hidden from the police in Ben's office before he fled the country—who would suspect a market research consultancy of harbouring one of the leaders of the uprising in '76. Some had come from their years in prison, some were the first of those returning from exile. As they talked, hands grasped, sometimes embracing, the double embrace first clasped round this side of the neck then that, which everyone in the liberation movement forgot was derived from the embrace of dictators, Vera and these old acquaintances and friends were giddy with discovery, the past set down on the streets of the present.

You don't remember me?

The past is known to be irretrievable. But here that proposition is overturned.

In the euphoria of being back, of presenting themselves alive, resurrected from the anonymity of exile, of these who have returned, and the eager desire of those who have stayed at home to make up, in welcome, for the deprivation of exile they have not suffered, people who had had reason to distrust or simply dislike one another and people who once had been close as brothers and sisters are all greeted in the same way as cherished returning heroes. It is something of the same phenomenon as young Oupa's lively accounts that do not discriminate between terrors he has experienced and the everyday gossip of the Foundation's personnel. A convention came instantly into being, as conventions often do, to serve where it seems established patterns of behaviour don't. Yet beneath it, under the disguise of flesh, behind the sunken eyes, within the clothes of a foreign cut, the black leather caps of East Germany, the dashikis of Tanzania, the Arab keffiyeh worn as a scarf, the old events and circumstances exist; standing there in the street, the old dependencies, the old friendships, the old factional rivalries, the old betrayals and loyalties, political scandals and sexual jealousies were not gone for ever but persisted in evidence of traceable, ineffaceable features, visible cell structure, still living. The past was there.

Perhaps because of the break in continuity this was so. If the satin skin had been seen slowly bruising dark with age and heavy drinking, if the blond curls had been observed, in the course of ordinary encounters, thinning, if Jonah had been heavier, maturing each time he dropped in for talk and a beer with Ben, the changes would have wound away naturally in the reel of years. But there was no tape running between the state of being they had been in when they left for exile or prison and their sudden reappearance back here where they had left: the weight their lives had was the weight of the past, out of storage and delivered to those who had stayed behind.

The man whom experiences had bowed to one side and shorn of his hair turned up at Vera's office to see if there might be something for him—a research job, anything; he had been back three months and could not find work. He had been a journalist on an often-banned small paper when they knew one another long ago. While she tried to make some suggestions, where he might find employment and—she had to offer—she would be able to put in a word for him, there lay between them the knowledge that he was—had been—suspected of being a police agent at one time, and when he fled the country, although apparently cleared of this suspicion, he was mixed up in some schismatic defection. This was what he was, to her; she did not know whether he had been reinstated among the exiles abroad and whether or not he had returned with the status of one fully accepted within the Movement—knowing him only in the persona of the past, she saw that that persona might have inveigled by some subterfuge the status to return under indemnity, supposedly vouched for by the Movement.

But if there were ambiguous feelings subsuming the enthusiasm of welcome and the obligations it carried, there was also the overwhelming sense of good times impossibly restored.

Among the people who were returning were some the sight and sound of whom, their very mannerisms and turn of phrase, were proof that such times are carried along within the self.

When a railway line is abandoned, the tracks aren't taken up. Under weeds and grass, they remain, marking a route. For the Starks, with Sibongile and Didymus Maqoma suddenly sitting in the Starks' living-room again after more than twenty years, there was the unexpected warmth and understanding, across the conditioned inhibitions of colour, between couples sharing youth and the ties of children. Now again, in the presence of Sally and Didy, the Starks were the lovers in an affair continuing in the protection of domesticity, expansive towards others in the bounty of sexual happiness. Vera had not seen Ben as the woman at a party once had, his male allure, for a long time, had not even been aware, in her familiarity with him and her preoccupations, of not seeing him. He, Bennet Stark, was still there, with only the deep lines from the corners of those lips to that fine jaw to mark him, as if in the conduct of his life he had sculpted his own face.

She exchanged again with him the side-glance smile of complicity, displayed the coquetry of joking reproaches that claimed him as hers, the recognition of his judgment in quoting him on this matter or that, which was the atmosphere the young couples used to generate between them. The class difference set by white privilege had been rather less than was usual between whites and blacks. Didymus was an articled clerk then, in a law firm, as Vera had been a few years before, Sally ran a black co-operative and ambitiously attended the extramural classes Bennet taught at the university, moonlighting for the money. That was how they met—through Bennet, and made the discovery that there was a link in that both their partners had chosen law. Of course, Vera had the house that had come to her with divorce, and the Maqomas lived in Chiawelo, Deep Soweto; Didymus carried a pass. But the Maqomas, both politically active, even then had open confidence that they would be among those who would destroy white privilege sooner or later, and pragmatically made use, as of right—and this was recognized unembarrassedly by the Starks—of the advantages the white couple had. It was more pleasant to pool the children in the Starks' run-wild garden on a Sunday than to have the Starks over in the two-roomed Chiawelo place, although the Stark couple enjoyed breaking the law of segregation, from the comfort of their side, by coming at night into Chiawelo to listen to jazz recordings—Didymus was a collector and himself played the trumpet in those days!—and drink and perhaps dance, bumping into Sally's well-polished furniture.

Sally and Didy now back in the same living-room in the same house where the four of them had been together so many times, talking across one another in the same animation. The Maqoma boys might have been there, in Vera's house, as they often used to be, come to spend the weekend, Ivan might have been there, sharing his schoolboy room with them, and, down the passage, the disdainful small girl, Annie, against whom they ganged up.

It was not nostalgia Vera was experiencing on such occasions, but something different: a sense of confrontation with uninterpreted life kept about her, saddled on her person along with the bulging shoulder bag always on her arm, her briefcase documenting inquiry into other people's lives.

·

Didymus Maqoma, whose whitening curls sat like the peruke of a seventeenth-century courtier worn stately on his black head, and Vera Stark with the haircut of a woman who has set aside her femininity, in this joyful reunion of friends gave no sign, even to one another, that it had not been twenty years since these two had seen each other. One Saturday morning five years ago Vera, alone in the house, had answered a ring at the door. A black man with a scanty peppercorn beard round lips and chin, wearing thick glasses and the collar of a clergyman, stood there. He did not speak, or before he could, she gave her usual response to anyone in the racket of purporting to collect church funds. —Sorry, I've nothing for you.—

The man smiled. —How mean of you Vera.—

It was long before the encounters in the street where people waited to be reassured by recognition, to have confirmed the claim that they were back. There were no indemnities, there was no lifting of bans on political movements. The last thing the man looked for was to be recognizable. To be recognized was to be hunted. Didymus, he said.

As if she had dropped up to the neck in a pit alarm for him engulfed her. She took his arm and pulled him inside, kicking the door shut. She did not need to be told that he somehow had been smuggled into the country, and that he had a purpose about which she must not ask. Her nervous amazement broke hysterically. —*Umfundisi!* You look so funny! No—no, you look dead right, that kind of Sunday suit, and the collar frayed, where did you get kitted out so perfectly—

They were both grinning with emotion. —We have our network in the shops down Diagonal Street. One week I'm a labourer with cement on my shoes, torn overalls and a woollen cap down to my eyes, next week I'm in a three-piece blue with a white cap, a soccer promoter from Jabulani.—

They were walking through the house, weaving about each other, she was out of breath.

—Are you all right? Do you think they know—

—No, so far it's okay. But I can't stay in the same place too long. I can't stay with anyone who has any connection . . . As soon as neighbours want to be nice to me, I have to disappear. Move on.—

—I'd heard you were ill, you had something awful—leukemia?—you were being treated in Moscow.—

—Yes, that's right, I'm out of action sick in Moscow. I've been here six months.—

She was looking at him, head on one side, thrilled by the audacity. —Six months!—

They were in the kitchen, she was distractedly picking up cups and putting them down, turning on her heels to rummage in a drawer for spoons, forgetting whether she had or had not switched on the kettle.

She talked fast at him, as if the house were surrounded and at any moment there would be a hammering on the doors—and what would she say? Where would she hide him? She tugged the kitchen curtains across the window. —D'you need money—how do you manage, I mean. I haven't much in the house, but I could go quickly to the bank—oh god, no, they close early on Saturdays—but how stupid, I can use my card at the machines—

—Money is one thing I don't need. That's taken care of, thanks, don't worry.—

—Does Sally know?—

—That I'm not dying in Moscow, yes. But not where I go. And other comrades in London believe I'm sick.—

She was shaking the coffee jug to make the liquid drip more quickly through the filter, she didn't know whether she wanted to get rid of him or take him and hide him away. —Ben'll be home soon. Wonderful for him to see you. Can't believe it! But I'm so afraid for you, what they'll do to you if they catch you

—you could just disappear, you know that, they keep infiltrators in solitary for months under interrogation, months and months before they piece together enough to bring them to trial. If they ever do.—

He looked as if he really were an old preacher, tranquilly breathing in the aroma of coffee steam, adding another spoon of sugar like a poor man making the best of luxury. But coaxing irony surfaced from his own identity: —You'll defend me, if I come to trial, Vera, I count on you.—

—Lot of use I'd be.— What would she do if the police did come, what if they were waiting somewhere hidden in the street, sitting in a car, ready to take him as he walked out of her gate? —I hope Ben won't be long.—

—I must go before Ben comes. Vera, there is something I do need. I've got things here I want you to send overseas for me. But not by post. If you have someone, if you know someone who's flying out and won't ask questions—they can post them somewhere in Europe, doesn't matter, anywhere.—

She took the letters and a package, claiming trust, not necessary to add any assurances. As she saw him to the door, a rush of rejection of fears swept her, she walked out with him into the street, they were ambling together in full view of neighbours, police, anybody who might be witnessing them from watching houses, the eyes of windows, crossing and rounding the corner in the middle of the street where they could not fail to be seen, arm in arm to where, for discretion so that it would not mark her house, he had left a car. And there they embraced goodbye: the open stare of the street fixed on them.

If no one finds out, it's as if it never took place.

It was not the first time Vera had experienced something she never revealed. Only five years of silence had passed this time; but Ivan was more than forty years old. So it comes about

that the precedent of lying by omission becomes a facility that
serves a political purpose just as well.

·

Sibongile and Didymus Maqoma regained their names when
they came back. In exile they had had code names; there would
always be many people in the outside world who would know
them by no other. Addressed by these names, they would
react—answer—to them as they would to the names given them,
attached as an umbilical cord to the location outside a coal-
mining town (Sibongile, daughter of a Zulu mother and Sotho
father) and the steep hut village folded in maritime hills (Didymus, in the Transkei) where they were born and first answered
to a name at all.

They did not go back to the little house where they were
young—probably a slum by now, with the crush of people
doubling- and tripling-up for somewhere to live—unthinkable
to live in Chiawelo, anyway. They spent the first few weeks in
a Hillbrow hotel that had been taken over as a reception centre
for returning exiles. It had been a drinking-place for working-
class white toughs and their women, and the cheap orange car-
peting was stained with beer and pitted with cigarette burns.
Stretched tapes on the music diffusion system repeated themselves through twenty-four hours, day and night. Sibongile
stripped the beds to look for vermin. She felt them on her skin,
sleepless, although they were not there.

The plane-loads of returning exiles who were arriving every
few days were awaited at the airport by chanting and dancing
crowds; when they came through the automatic doors that closed
behind them on the old longing for home, when they emerged
pushing squeaking chariots charged with the evidence of far
places, carrying airport store giant teddy-bears, blind with ex-

citement in the glare of recognition—not, at once, of who they were individually but of what they stood for, the victory of return—a swell of women's ululating voices buffeted them into the wrestle of joyous arms. Children seen for the first time were tossed from hands to shoulders, welcome banners were trampled, flowers waved, bull-horns sounded, the hugging, capering procession of transit to repossession, life regained, there outside the airport terminal, was a carnival beyond belief it would ever be possible to celebrate. Home: that quiet word: a spectacle, a theatre, a pyrotechnic display of emotion for those who come from wars, banishment, exile, who have forgotten what home was, or suffered not being able to forget.

The Maqomas of course had not come on one of the crowded charter flights and their reception was less flamboyant though no less emotional. Didymus was a veteran of the inner circle in exile, one who for all those years had been involved in international missions and certain other important activities, and they were met by comrades equal to him in rank within the internal organization. A car was waiting for them, driven by one of the young returned Freedom Fighters now deployed as Security men. Home. They slept, that first night, in what used to be a forbidden white suburb at the house that had been acquired for one of the most important leaders. But it was understood they could not stay; the room would be needed for other transients in the to-and-fro now established between representatives from the Movement's missions in other countries. A comfortable room with the niceties of bedside reading lamps, a supply of Kleenex, a television set, a room where bags were never unpacked. Until a house or flat could be found they would have to live in a hotel—there was, in fact, a hotel provided for just such an unavoidable interim.

Sibongile came to Didymus with a blanket held draped over

her raised palms. He had no idea what for, but was always
patient with her sense of drama.

—I can't live like this.—

—What is it?—

A crust of something whitish-yellow dried in a smear on the
hairy surface.

—What is it!— Her rising laugh, a cry. She thrust the evidence at him.

—Oh. That. Yes.— Semen, someone's seed.

—I can't live like this, I can tell you.—

—Sibo, you've lived much worse. It didn't kill us.—

—At the beginning, years ago, yes. It was necessary. In
Dar, in Botswana. But now! My God! I'm not running for my
life. I'm not running from *anybody* any more, I'm not *grateful*
for a bit of shelter, political asylum (the blanket dropped at her
feet, her hands lifted, palms together in parody of the black
child's gesture of thanks she had been taught as a little girl).
This's not for you and me.—

—What can they do about it? They can't find accommodation for everyone overnight. Give it another week or so . . . —

—*Accommodation.* How long can we be expected to carry
on in this filthy dump, this whore-house for Hillbrow drunks,
this wonderful concession to desegregation, what an honour to
sleep under the white man's spunk.—

—What about all the others living here . . . it's no better
for them.— He was confronting her with herself, as she was
every time she entered the foyer of the hotel or walked through
the room smelling of cockroach repellent that was the restaurant,
embracing unknown women, men and children in the intimacy
of shared exile and return.

She had a way of screwing up her eyes and opening her
mouth, lips drawn back, mimicking the expression of someone

straining to hear aright. —If you're happy to come back to this from your meetings of the NEC, your big decisions, no complaints . . . —

—How can I have complaints when so many have come back to nowhere at all. At least we have dirty blankets.—

She ignored the smile. —And how does that help them?—

It was Vera Stark to whom she suddenly felt she could unburden herself; the farce of self-sacrifice when it was not necessary might have to be kept up with the wife of the leader in whose house she and Didymus had spent the first night, but Vera, while counted upon to understand perfectly the necessity for such tactics within that circle, was outside it. There were whites who had been in exile, but Vera had not; there were whites who shared the wariness of return, Vera was not one of them. Unburden to her and, by implication of a grant of intimacy, place responsibility on her.

When Vera answered the telephone with the usual cheerful how-are-you, there was a pause.

—Lousy.— And then that cry of a laugh.

Vera, good old Vera, didn't make the usual facilely sympathetic noises. —Let's have lunch today. Have you time?—

—I just have to get out of this place.—

On the site of the small restaurant where young Vera and her wartime lover had sat longing to embrace, the place now transformed into a takeaway outlet with additional vegetarian menu and tables open to all races, Sibongile was first to arrive. Her crossed legs were elegant in black suede boots draped to the knee.

—I love those boots. London boots.—

Vera had the generosity, towards women who still make their appearance seductive, of a woman confident that she was once successfully seductive herself and now knows she may only

occasionally, and in an abstracted way, herself be merely
pleasing.

The two women kissed and each gave a squeeze to the other's
arm as men greet one another with a mock punch.

—Do you? Yes, London. I suppose they give me away.—

They ordered a meal. Vera, whatever was the special for
the day; her guest reading up and down the menu and asking
for what was not on it—fish, was there no fish? The waiter
smilingly patient, addressing her respectfully as mama, persuasive in what he somehow correctly divined was their shared
mother tongue that this dish or that was (back to English) very,
very nice, tasty.

Vera read the message of the fish. Lousy; everything lousy,
not even possible to get what you wanted to eat.

With the waiter gone the required time had passed for her
companion to be able to speak. She described the hotel—the
'accommodation' she kept calling it, by turns derisive, angry,
disgusted, despairing, and—being Sibongile, Sally—giggling
sharply. —But Didy! I don't know, he seems ready to accept
anything, he's *meek*! Like a rabbit, quiet, nibbling at whatever's
given to him.—

That veteran of prisons and interrogation. That fox at infiltration, raiding under the eyes of the police and army. They
laughed at the notion.

—I'm telling you! He seems to be living in the past, a time
warp, we're still some sort of refugee, we must suffer in noble
silence—for *what the cause doesn't need any more*. While he's
meeting members of the Government, for God's sake! The Boers
fawning all over us, inviting us to official dinners, getting themselves photographed with us for the papers! But he won't tell
anyone on the NEC, straight out, we must have something decent
to live in if we're to function properly at that level. They're

never going to find anything, that I know. We'll have to do it ourselves . . . *I'll* have to do it . . . but in the meantime! That flea-pit, I wouldn't put a dog in it, and you know I don't like dogs. I never dreamt I'd think back on our basement London flat and the one we had in Stockholm, those grey days—my God, I do.—

So Sibongile and Didymus Maqoma regained the personae of Sally and Didy, the code names of their old concourse with whites. They came to stay with the Starks. —Ben, you should just see the Hillbrow dump! Not just the dirt Sally goes on about . . . people sit around in the bar lounge watching television all day long, sprawled there sucking Coca-Cola, nothing to do and nowhere to go. She's years from that kind of slum atmosphere, even though they're her own people . . . she and Didy have moved away from that cheek-by-jowl existence they were at home in, the old days, Chiawelo.—

Ben defined the element exile had, at least, brought into the Maqomas' life. —Privacy; they've had it in London for years, now.—

There was no reflection between the Starks that their privacy was invaded for the five weeks Sally and Didy lived with them. Their own relationship was at the stage when the temporary presence of others was revivifying. They had an extra bathroom; that was the only condition of middle-class existence that had any importance for them.

Sally and Didy's late-born daughter, Mpho, arrived from her school in England. She stayed indiscriminately, a weekend here, a week there, between her grandmother's house in Alexandra township and the Starks' house, sleeping in the bed and among the curling pop-star posters and odd trinkets that had survived their daughter Annick's adolescence and absence. The Maqoma daughter was a sixteen-year-old beauty of the kind created by the cross-pollination of history. Boundaries are changed, ideologies merge, sects, religious and philosophical, create new idols out of combinations of belief, scientific discoveries link cause and effect between the disparate, ethnically jumbled territorial names make a nationality out of many-tongued peoples of different religions, a style of beauty comes out of the clash between domination and resistance. Mpho was a resolution—in a time when this had not yet been achieved by governments, conferences, negotiations, mass action and international monitoring or intervention—of the struggle for power in the country which was hers, and yet where, because of that power struggle, she had not been born. This schoolgirl combined the style of *Vogue* with the assertion of Africa. She was a mutation achieving happy appropriation of the aesthetics of opposing species. She exposed the exaggeratedly long legs that seem to have been created not by natural endowment but to the specification of Western standards of luxury, along with the elongated chassis of custom-built cars. The oyster-shell-pink palms of her slender hands completed the striking colour contrast of matt black skin with purple-red painted fingernails. Her hair, drawn back straightened and oiled to the gloss of European hair, was gathered on the crown and twisted into stiff dreadlocks, Congolese style, that fringed her shoulders. Despite all this, Mpho did not have the aspirant beauty queen's skull grin but a child's smile of great sweetness, glittering in her eyes. Out of her mouth came a perky London English. She could not speak an African language, neither the Zulu of her mother nor the Xhosa of her father. —Oh but I *understand*, mother dear, I can *follow*— And she would open her eyes wide and roll her head, appealing to high heaven in exactly the gesture of the mother with whom she was arguing.

—Yes, but who knows you *understand* when you never

answer, people will think you're an idiot, my retarded child. You're going to have lessons.—

—Well, that's pretty humiliating for you, ma, isn't it—have your daughter taught our language as if it's French or German or something.—

Sally appealed to their hosts, Vera and Ben —Listen to that. My girl, that is exactly what has been done to our people, you, your father, me. We've been alienated from what is ours, and it's not only in exile. Your father's descended from a great chief who resisted the British more than a hundred years ago—you have a name to live up to! You were robbed of your birth—that should have been right here. Take back your language.—

The schoolgirl gave a smile of complicity with the witnesses to her mother's emotionalism, dealing with it in harmless insolence. —I'll learn from my *gogo*.— She giggled at her use of at least one word in a mother tongue, but was too shy or perhaps defiant to admit that she was serious about the intention. It was of her own volition that she left the guest room so well suited to her age and comfort and often went off to stay with her grandmother in Alexandra. After the first duty visit of respect required of a son's child, Sally had not expected the girl to go back again soon, let alone pack her luminescent duffle bag and spend days and nights there in the house with its broken-pillared stoep and dust-dried pot-plants, battered relic of real bricks and mortar with two diamond-paned rotting windows from the time when Alex was the reflection of out-of-bounds white respectability, yearned for, imitated, now standing alone on ash-coloured earth surrounded by shacks, and what had once been an aspiration to a patch of fenced suburban garden now a pile of rubbish where the street dumped its beer cans and pissed, and the rib-cages of scavenging dogs moved like bellows. How could a child brought up with her own bedroom, fresh milk delivered at the front door in Notting Hill Gate every morning, tidy people who sorted their newspapers for recycling, be expected to stand more than one night in such a place, *gogo* or no *gogo*? Going out across a yard to a toilet used by everyone round about! Heaven knows what she might pick up there! A return to a level of life to which Sibongile, Didymus, had been condemned when they were their child's age—what did a sixteen-year-old born in exile know of what it was like when there was no choice?

The distress is something that can be conveyed to someone other—Vera—but a kind of pride or self-protection would prevent Sibongile from acknowledging to the child herself the dismayed humbling of the mother by the worldly child's innocent level of acceptance: the sense that she knows what home is.

Mpho moved between Alexandra and the house that came from Vera's divorce settlement with an ease that charmed the Starks. At the Starks', along with her parents, she met and mingled with the Starks' friends, Vera's colleagues from the Foundation, the protégé Oupa and the lawyers. The young people got on well together, Mpho was carried off to parties with these youngsters her relieved parents knew were decent, no drugs or drunkenness; through a contact of one of the lawyers, the Maqomas found exactly what was needed, a small house in a white suburb near the school where, again with the help of someone met in the Stark circle, the girl was accepted to complete her A-levels. The day after they moved in with nothing but borrowed beds, Sally, taking the car the Movement provided for Didy, drove along the street of local shops to look for secondhand furniture, and reversing into a parking place was held up by a municipal cleaner, a woman sweeping the gutter-muck into a drain. She didn't know that women did this work, now. Well, any job was better than nothing, these times. It could be that some of those she had known in exile, the fighters in the training camps, might end up sweeping streets; the probability gave her an internal cringe, the drawing in of her stomach muscles that was involuntary when she confronted herself with the responsibility in which she was engaged: she had just been appointed deputy director of the Movement's regional redeployment programme, at present a collection of research papers emerging at the pace of stuttering faxes. As she locked the car (forewarned since the day of arrival of those for whom theft was better than nothing) she saw that the cleaner had not moved on, was leaning on her broom and looking at her, a woman dressed ridiculously in the handout of bright protective overalls, football stockings rolled round her calves, flat-footed in men's shoes, a fisherman's hat complete with slots for flies crammed on her head. Begging? She would give her a greeting, anyway: *Sawubona, sisi.*

The woman did not approach but spoke excitedly. —Sibongile, when did you come? I'm Sela's child, your mother's cousin, you remember? From Sela's house, you used to see us there, in Witbank.—

Wakened suddenly, shaken alive into another light, another existence. Sally is drawn over to her other self, standing there, the one she started out with, this apparition with a plastic bag tied over the hand with which, deftly, it picks up dirt the broom misses. Home.

In the streets of Johannesburg, on your way around the city, *You don't know who this is?*

•

Even Oupa managed to move into a white suburb.

Why did his white colleagues at the Foundation use, to themselves, the prefix 'even'? Because once the legal restrictions they campaigned against were lifted there remained an older, even (yes, again) greater restriction to be addressed: poverty.

The clerk was decently paid by the decent standards of a Foundation that was non-profit-making not only in the money sense but also the human one, providing the same benefits of medical care and pension fund for all who worked there, from the director to the cleaner. But the rent of apartments in the area where he wanted to live was beyond his means. In one way, he was like any other young man in training for a professional career; a stage when it is assumed the youngster has as yet no responsibilities, has emerged from school, free, to a few years of chasing girls and enjoying himself with his male peers. *Starting out in life*, the saying goes. But of course this one's start had been delayed so long, he had queued up unable to get into schools, dropped out into political action, spent four years on Robben Island, that before he could start on the lowest rank of a career he had acquired the responsibilities of maturity. Oupa was a man, not a boy. A burdened man, at the same time as he was the Foundation's bright protégé. For him the business of growing up had not been, could not be, followed in recognized chronology. Of course Oupa had a wife, somewhere, of course he had children. His decent salary was diminished by the rent, the food, the clothing to be provided out of sight, for the anachronism of his life. The wife and children lived in another part of the country, with relatives who were dumped by the Government in some resettlement area. The eager apprentice was in fact an adult already trapped by adult desires, conflicts and responsibilities.

The Foundation was more than tolerant of the time he took off from work to find a place, a bachelor home among them in what had been the streets where only whites could live. They feared for him on his daily journeys to and from Soweto by train; he could be knifed by gangsters or thrown out of the window to his death by political thugs. Mrs Stark was remiss in being too busy, at the time, to telephone around among friends who might know of vacancies or have influence with estate agents who were wary about letting to blacks; it was someone else in the office who found a lead that resulted in the young colleague getting what he wanted. He was elated, although the rent was too high for him to afford; untroubled, although he had signed a lease restricting occupancy to two people, and he was going to split the rent by sharing the place with a couple and their two children.

Oupa planned a house-warming for everyone from the Foundation. Mrs Stark, to compensate for not having been any help to him in finding somewhere to live, offered to contribute home-made snacks and left with him a little early on a Friday afternoon to help with preparations.

—Where do we go?— Oupa had mentioned enthusiastically to everyone an area where there were numerous apartment buildings but had given no further details. He named a street and chattered on. —It's an old building, man, but that's why it's so nice, big rooms and everything. Here we are—here it is. 'Delville Wood.' (Look at that real marble entrance!) Something to do with a war, isn't it?—

The car came to a standstill neatly against the kerb. —Delville Wood.— Walking up the steps under packages loaded between them, Mrs Stark turned to him, an odd smile accompanying the banal scrap of information she was giving. —Yes, it's a battle. Where it happened.—

He thought there was some unhappy connection with the name he'd ignorantly blundered on. —Someone you knew died there?—

But she laughed. —That war took place before I was born.—

He led her along red-polished corridors. Her eyes counted off the numbered doors as they passed.

—That's it!—

In his proud moment, she pronounced before his doorway: —One-Twenty-One.—

He rapped zestfully on the number and echoed her. —One-Twenty-One Delville Wood.—

In the living-room two junk-shop chairs covered with nylon velvet shaved by wear, a one-legged stand topped with a fancy copper ashtray, and an old box trunk covered with a piece of African cloth. Everything faced the glaucous giant eye of the television set.

—Of course it's not fixed up yet. Pictures and so on. I need a desk and something for my books. I'm going to do a lot of work here, man! But nice, aih?—

—A desk over there at the window . . . Ben might have one you could use. Yes, this is a lovely room.—

He had switched on the television, it was a children's programme with the squeaky voices of anthropomorphic animals but he did not notice, it didn't matter, the gesture was that of possession, he was at home in these walls where only whites had lived before.

—Come and see the rest.—

Talking expansively, he led her to a room with a double bed made up under a fringed bedspread with three cushions propped diamond-shaped against the wall. —I might put the desk in here, because the others use the sitting-room as well. Better for work.— He was assuring her of his seriousness about studying; after all, although she was a motherly friend, she was also one of the seniors in the Foundation that employed him. The second room: a chaos of clothing, toys, pots and pans, hot-plate standing on a triple-mirror dressing table, cot filled with jumbled shoes. —They're moving in.—

Oupa went to fetch from the car the folding chairs borrowed from the Foundation and when he returned Mrs Stark was in the kitchen unpacking what she called the goodies. He stood about: —I haven't got the hang of the stove yet— But she had opened the oven door and taken out fat-encrusted shelves, she tried the plates one by one, knowing exactly how everything worked, I'll show you, she said, just as she calmly and quietly would explain to him some legal question he would bring to her from his correspondence course. He was flattered that she concentrated on the preparations for his little party as if it were of great importance to get everything right, to think of nothing else until this was so. He felt Mrs Stark knew what this occasion meant to him, even if to others it was just another office party.

The extended family of the Foundation arrived. Husbands and wives, permanent lovers of this sex or that, the other half of unexplained attachments. There was the bonhomie of the special set of relationships between people who work together and find themselves at play, their joking in-house references that others might not follow but which raised the general level of celebration. Somebody's boy-friend had brought a guitar and he sang his compositions in a mixture of Zulu, English and Afrikaans to a group that stood about or sat with their drinks on the fringed bedcover in the bedroom, while in the living-room nobody was listening, the talk and laughter at a higher volume than the music. Mrs Stark's hot cheese puffs ran out. She and several others from the Foundation were back in the kitchen opening cans of Viennas that seemed to be Oupa's sole food supply, when her husband arrived late and had brought along a carrier of wine and beer. With a knife in one hand and the greasy other hand held away from contact with his jacket, she dropped what she was doing and went over to kiss him for the thought. He almost backed in surprise, then held her shoulders a moment; it was so unlike her to make a show of affection public. His contribution to the party hardly called for any special mark of gratitude; perhaps she'd had a few drinks—well, why not?

The promised desk was picked up from the Starks' house and delivered to One-Twenty-One Delville Wood by a friend of Oupa who borrowed a bakkie from another friend. Oupa bought a computer, on credit, to complete the equipment; the only problem, he remarked to Mrs Stark some weeks later, was that the friend who transported the desk had moved into the flat with him, the couple, and the two children. —He's got no place to stay. His place is in Sebokeng and now he's working here in town.— Soon this friend, who had agreed to contribute to the rent, was joined by another, workless and penniless. This came out when Oupa, bringing his lunch as usual into Mrs Stark's office, relieved by talking to her his anxiety about not having fulfilled that month's correspondence-course assignments. —He also slept in the living-room, with my other friend. On the floor, but better than nothing, aih? But now the other people are fed up, they say they're paying for sharing the sitting-room and he's always there, lying around. And doesn't pay. So now he stays with me in my room and when I want to study at night he's talking to me all the time. Man! Till midnight, one o'clock.—

What could she be expected to say? 'Tell him to find somewhere else.' Where else? Weren't she and the young clerk surrounded by the papers, right there under crumbs from their lunch, of people who had been sent somewhere else, over years, and still had nowhere. She offered what she knew was useless, indignant at exploitation of him by his peers; he could have been her son. —Oupa, you have to be firm. You're too soft. If he could move in with you, there must be someone else he can go to in the same way. You can't be expected to live like that. Now you've at last got a place—

The young man swallowed a mouthful and sagged in his chair, blowing out his cheeks. He shook his head, again and again, in denial of the pressure of her attention. —He was with me on the Island.—

He bit again into his chicken leg and chewed.

She held her cup in both hands and gulped tea.

—Oh god. Wha'd'we do. What's his line of work, can't we find something for him.—

—Worked in a dry cleaner's, a box factory, I don't know . . . he hasn't got skills.—

She threw up her hands, then rattled a pen against her cup. —Why do I have to open my big mouth! Why do I have to open my big mouth!—

assing.

Passing down the street. Driven by countless times so that the destination it once meant has been obliterated, layer upon layer, by errands taking that route. At first, for months, halted at a traffic light, staring up at the closed windows of the flat as if into the eyes of someone who gives no sign. Then there was someone else's washing on a laundry stand on the balcony. A dartboard hung on the wall below where the bathroom fanlight looked out. That was when the letters stopped; or only now did the image seem as signalling that other dispossession; the end of such experiences in reality comes much more slowly, the drama of parting, repeated in variation—the end of touching, the end of talking on the telephone, the lengthening gap between letters—it's over-rehearsed and so the final performance is not recognized.

An old actress in many positively last appearances.

Here we are.

To stop outside the entrance, to hear the name spoken by a stranger to the site, is simply the quiet ripple of a smile: Delville Wood. This is it. Walking along the corridors, same concrete slippery-polished ochre red, a mixture of fascination and a sort of dread. After all, the mail-boxes in the foyer are numbered through six floors, the new kind of tenant could have been leading along another corridor to another number. Even on this floor it surely must be another number. But no, more and more impossible, a coincidence against odds of six floors of flats, One-Twenty-One. The door opening on locked feelings; the coming to life as fascination and dread is the old sexual anticipation of walking along the red-polished corridor to enter One-Twenty-One. Amazing: the sensations are pleasurable, as if the one who had been there at the desk before the window will get up to press himself against her or in the sleepy surprise of an early-morning visit lift back his bedclothes for her to slide in, shivery-naked beside him—as if he were going to be there, was there, in the return of the desire he had created in this living-room where the great eye of the television set sees nothing, in this bedroom where a new, poor young tenant makes his bed. The motherly friend is helpfully surveying the needs of the new kind of tenant. She is briskly preparing the dirty stove to warm up her provision of snacks. The evidence that she knows her way about this kitchen as if she lived there is attributed to the general familiarity of women with the domestic domain: I haven't got the hang of the stove yet, the new kind of tenant says, apologetically male.

·

What you have done once you will do again. Sometimes Vera had reminded herself, sneered at herself, jeered in reproach; but this did not stop her. She felt resentment at self-confrontation with this evidence of what, when she was a child, her mother termed 'behaviour'—which implied only transgression. Bennet was her lover, he was the one with whom she had slept while her young husband was fighting a war, expecting to come home to her. Bennet therefore would be for ever in the category of lover, the one chosen above the sexual bond and moral ties of marriage, even when he became husband. That was how it was for how long? Again, the reality comes at an unnoticed pace, in the brief human time-span of one life the equivalent of the smoothing of the thumb on a holy effigy by centuries' homage of those who kiss the hand. Bennet became Ben. The skill of his love-making became satisfaction to be counted on. She could not believe she was being strongly attracted to another man; Ben, Bennet *was the other man.* Yet in a way it was he who made another man possible, wanted, because he it was who had shown her, up in the mountains with those friends of a group photo-graph, what love-making could be, how many revelations of excitement and wild sensation it could mean beyond what she had thought was its limit, with the husband who was out of the way at war. If Ben had taught her that the possibilities of erot-icism were beyond experience with one man, then this meant that the total experience of love-making did not end with him. The understanding of this, in her body, must have been there for years—logically, ever since she first was made love to by him? But it remained unaccepted or dormant until, somewhere in her forties, oh when her hair was still abundantly glossy, not a single broken vein showing a red spiderweb on her legs, a man came to the Foundation to film an interview on its work for a documentary he was making about forms of resistance in the country. He left his card to join those of other visitors to the Foundation who imagined they might be contacted again, though what for, politeness forbade asking. Otto Abarbanel. The sur-name was one she had never heard of; he worked for an Austrian television network and spoke with a slight—to her—German accent. He was solemn going about his filming and formal in manner, like Germans she had met. He telephoned her several times and came back to the office, apologizing for disturbing her, wanting to verify this information or that, and when she realized these were pretexts she was at first amused to find she did not find him a nuisance. Then, that afternoon, without any transition from formality, he grasped her fist where it was resting slackly on her desk, covered it tightly in his own. She placed her other hand over this grip. And so suddenly, there was a covenant of desire.

Will you come and see me, he had said, to make it possible to seem that some professional appointment were being discussed, there in the office where anyone might come in upon the atmosphere the gesture had created. —For coffee on Saturday afternoon.—

Vera and Ben were busy people who did not need to account to one another for every movement. He had invited for lunch an old schoolmate who had become a successful painter. She was tranquil, serving at table, unbelieving of what she was going to do, and in the same state of mind went to the bathroom after lunch and fitted into her body the rubber device that had prevented her from conceiving since the birth of Annie. She left Ben and his visitor with an apology—she had to put in some duty appearance at a political gathering. She had many obligations of this nature and her husband looked up from his preoccupation, giving the goodbye-go-well salute that was their customary private signal before other people.

And when she came home later in the afternoon it was as she could never have imagined it could be, what had happened in the three hours' interim was something that concerned her alone, her sexuality, a private constant in her being, a characteristic like the colour of eyes, the shape of a nose, the nature of a personal spirit that never could belong to anyone other than the self. Bennet Stark stood in a doorway once, admired by some woman who did not know he existed in a relationship with the woman to whom she remarked on his male beauty; that unknown woman was demonstrating a truth Vera now euphorically believed she had only just discovered; sexuality, in his case displayed guilelessly by nature in the sensuous allure of his face, was a wholly owned attribute, could not be claimed by the naïve bid: He's my husband. Now Vera saw herself in that doorway. She lay beside Ben that night with a sense of pride and freedom rather than betrayal.

During those two years there was no yoghurt and apple lunch eaten over papers at the office. She fled, whenever there was an interstice in activity there or at home, whenever her absence would not be noticed or when there would be some reason for it plausible to her colleagues, her husband, her adolescent daughter (Ivan was already living in England); fled to number One-Twenty-One. The duplicate key she was equipped with hung with her car and house keys on the ring with the bluebird medallion, a birthday gift bought for her with pocket money saved by the daughter. She let herself in. He was there or was to be anticipated. Sometimes he arrived with the kind of food he liked—herrings or smoked sausage or cold Kasseler ribs—and they ate together in that kitchen before or after making love. They bathed together before going back to other people, soaping each other—why was it no one, least of all women, would admit the tender pleasure of handling like this a man's slippery soft tube, pressing it a little, playfully, to make it grow, palpating, rounding out the shape of the two eggs, often uneven in size, in the pouch that keeps warm and alive the seed of the young, akin to the physical attribute that belongs, in the animal species, to the female kangaroo with her pouch of unborn young, quaintly reversed in the human species to the other sex, the male; the pouch that is anciently wrinkled, as if about to atrophy, even in a young man.

Otto was fifteen or more years younger than Vera. Vague about his age perhaps because he wanted to forget the age of his lover. But when, in talk, she made references he was too young to remember, the attempt to catch up, the momentary blankness in his expression, was obvious. He had a high forehead tight, anxious, shiny-skinned, like that of a rosy apple, was not good-looking; in fact, Vera did not know what he really looked like, if the face is what one is; she knew the body, the cruciform male body with its line of light brown curly hair branching up from the navel into a crossbeam at the nipples, following the dominant shape from the narrow hips and widening with a splendid thorax to the shoulders. His face was the disguise that bearded men all wear; dark shaggy-blond growth curled round his mouth and gave its own shape to whatever his chin and jaw might be. Thick-rimmed glasses protected the expression in commonplace blue eyes as if they were seen through the distancing of binoculars. His mouth was the soft one, upper and lower lip the same full-ness, she associated with dissatisfaction with self, and generally found unattractive in other people. In him, surrounded by that seaweed beard, it was to her one of those fleshy creature-flowers in rock pools, sensitive to the temptation of the slightest touch. Not only had she thought she never could be attracted to another man; she had been sure she would never be attracted to another blond man. So it was this foreigner who exorcised for her some residual resentment—and resentment remains always damag-ing—that must be surviving against the first blond, the wartime husband. She wanted to tell Otto this odd fact, a confession surely endearing if not flattering to him, but didn't because she sensed that references to that war, at the end of which he was

a child, made him uneasy—for herself, she had no embarrassment at being so much older than he; verifying critically in a
mirror, she knew there was no mark of ageing to be found on
her!

But she had said after the first few times she had visited
One-Twenty-One, This won't last long, you know.

He misunderstood what she was telling him: that he couldn't
count against Ben, although she was free to choose both of
them. He thought she was referring to the limit of his working
assignment in the country. —I've got a surprise for you—I've
applied to be stationed here, the channel's correspondent for
the region.—

They were getting dressed. He did not know what to make
of the way she dropped her hands at her sides. He came over
and bound her arms with his, bending his head to bury it in her
neck.

Alongside the success of managing clandestinity there was
in her a wish to take her foreigner home, to introduce him to
her life, so that he might know her elsewhere than behind a desk
or in his bed. She rationalized: if he were invited to the house
occasionally, as both she and Ben would naturally bring home
a new acquaintance whom they liked, this would reduce the risk
of someone drawing other conclusions should she and Otto happen to be seen together somewhere.

Otto was reluctant to come to Vera's home, to enter her life
in which he had no part. But he acknowledged she must be a
better judge than he in the situation. There were other guests,
some of them blacks he had met in the course of his filming of
trade union officials and minor political figures, and there was
the husband, an impressive man, very skilful in pleasing the
guests in unison with his wife, the two of them managing the
gathering. The wife: that's what she was, in this house. He was

introduced, also, to her daughter, who quickly disappeared from the parents' gathering that no doubt bored her; beautiful, but exactly like the father. So there was nothing to trouble him as evidence, in a younger version of herself, that his lover had faded in the years she had lived ahead of him.

With the chat that accompanies clearing away in the wake of guests Ben mentioned he hadn't had much chance to talk to the young German, what was his name again? A strange name; giving it, she asked in innocent-sounding interest what its origin might be? Ben was so well-read, had a memory for all kinds of esoteric knowledge that never came her way.

—Abarbanel? But that's an old Sephardic name, must be a Jew, not a German.—

—I think he's Austrian.— She was enquiring.

—Could have been born there, I suppose. Jews've been dispersed all over, so long. Who knows.—

Who knows.

And so it was her husband who roused her curiosity. An erotic curiosity. In the dreamy confidentiality after love-making, she spoke to her lover. —So you're a Jew. Someone told me your name's Jewish. Sephardic. That's Spanish, isn't it.—

—It has a Spanish origin but the Jews were expelled from Spain in the fifteenth century.—

—I wouldn't have known you were a Jew.— Murmured laugh. —They're supposed to be circumcised.—

—I didn't have the usual sort of beginning and I was sent away quite young with other orphans and adopted, I grew up in Vienna with those people who took me. People of Sephardic origin, somewhere far back.—

—What about your own mother and father?—

He turned so that their profiles faced one another on the pillow. —Dead.—

She would ask no more: the Gestapo round-up, the closed
cattle-train, the concentration camp, the gas chamber; a prove-
nance she could be familiar with only from books and films,
documentation.

Vera was a gentile atheist gratified by the idea that her lover
was a Jew, orphaned by racism, without a name that was his
own—this linked him with the open, daily purpose of her life,
the files of displaced communities on her desk and, before her
on the other side of it, day after day, the faces of those who had
been made wanderers because they were decreed the wrong race.
She found herself paused, before the windows of expensive shops
selling men's clothing; she bought French shirts and Italian ties,
and because he was fond of a few Ghanaian gold weights he
picked up on assignments in West Africa, searched the art and
craft galleries to bring him additions to his collection. She was
making up to him for the deprivation of childhood, deprivation
like that of so many she knew in the veld settlements she investigated. She was giving him toys and sweets. Naked in bed with
her, he was also an infant deported, naked in the world.

Vera continued to make love with her husband, even if she
felt she had the delicacy not to initiate it. She thought of it as
part of a strategy, both to have her lover and not to hurt him,
Ben; for the credo she had adopted for the situation was the
well-worn one that anything was permitted her, was her right,
so long as no one was hurt. Otto had no woman she knew of;
there might be one he would go back to in Europe. And the fact
was that the love-making with Ben was strangely successful. Ben
must have been moved by her; instead of hurt. It was rather
like it had been long ago on the mountain holiday, and again
after the birth of Annick; she could not help being convulsed by
wave after wave of orgasm.

Bitch.

Bitch, greeted her face in the mirror.

And next day she went back to One-Twenty-One. There she felt it was her lover she was hurting. What lover would accept that a woman like her could enjoy making love with another man? With her husband?

She was not free at all, after all. There was a clause in their love affair—she had formulated the small print of it, through her work she was familiar with the importance of clauses that allow breach of contract. *This won't last long, you know.* But the clause was forgotten, buried in bedclothes and that other fabric, of the intimacy of a certain complementary pattern in their working lives. He witnessed: he was becoming filled with horror at what he recorded on film, the savagery of those who called their victims savages, the shooting of children, beatings, torture, and the savagery that this was beginning to bring forth in retaliation, the knifings and burnings in the revenge of the night. He was telling her of what he managed to film the previous day, before the police had threatened him with arrest unless he left the site of a school where they had thrown tear-gas into classrooms to drive out children who had stoned their vehicles. Dogs rounded up the terrified children, white policemen caught them at random and beat some as they were dragged to police vans, there were shots—the two children he saw fall screaming: he did not know whether they were dead or not, nor would anyone know, because at that point he and everyone there to record was ordered out of the area. Black kids, he said. As if expecting some explanation. —Black kids. A girl tried to hide behind me.—

—You haven't lived here long enough to know. The Nazis didn't end in the war where your parents died, they were reborn here.—

He stirred as if to ask a question and did not. He stared at the food before them. A plate of delicatessen smoked ham and potato salad she had provided to indulge his native tastes.

—There's something I haven't told you. I don't like to tell even myself. But it's true. You know what a Hitler Baby is?— His German accent became unusually pronounced.

He knew she did.

—I'm one. My mother was mated like a cow to produce a good German child for Hitler. I don't know who the Aryan stud was. She didn't know. Was never told his name when he was put on her. Artificial insemination for a cow is better, hei'm, it's a syringe, hei'm?—

If there is some form of love between people there surely must be something to say, always, whatever has happened. There was nothing. Vera listened to what was there but could not be seen, the transformation foretold in legend of a being into another, a woman into a tree, a god into an eagle; a creature of the unspeakable mythology of genetic engineering, the chimera of modern history.

—You want to know why she did it. I don't know. I don't know and you don't know what we call living was like then. But you want to know who she was?—she was an attendant in a—what d'you call it—a public wash-place, a lavatory, she came from Bavaria. She had nothing, the only boast she could have —she would tell me my father must have been a good Nazi, chosen to give me a better brain, a better body, a chance—I don't know—than any ordinary man.—

To remain in silence much longer would be interpreted as revulsion against him.

—The genes. I'm no Jewish victim. No Jew. I'm a German. That's where I get the only name that belongs to me, the good

German Otto my mother gave me. The genes are like the ones they have—the men who were beating up kids and shooting them.—

Vera said what came to her to be said. —Shave off the beard.—

And so there in the kitchen of One-Twenty-One the past was interpreted and shed, he clasped her fist as he had done that first time in her office, they returned to the beginning newly, over again, something based on a recognition so alien that it transformed the feel of his body, for her, and hers for him. There was no appropriate place for that curious passion to be enacted, and so it happened in the kitchen, she took him in through the aperture of clothes pulled out of the way, standing up where they had risen from the kitchen table, they were clutched like a pillar shaking in an earth tremor, and never before or after in her life was she, in her turn, transformed, and fused with a man in such blazing sensation.

That was the day and place of betrayal of Ben, Bennet, the chosen man.

·

Bitch.

Many years later, Otto Abarbanel has long left, and occasional meetings abroad, telephone calls from remote places, letters, have ended, and all sense of touch and feel associated with him seem to have returned to other responses as nerves regenerate after damage—that kitchen, One-Twenty-One Delville Wood, is still the day and place of betrayal, as a battlefield never loses its association. And that is why when Ben comes in with his offering of wine, Vera, spreading apart hands innocently soiled, a knife in one, suddenly drops her housewifely task, comes towards him, and embraces him.

Does the past return because one can rid oneself of it only slowly, or is the freedom actually the slow process of loss?

What she remembered while Ben uncorked the wine and joked with Oupa—come into the kitchen fondly steering a giggling young woman who protested in Tswana—was driving with Otto Abarbanel into the city one summer day and passing a restaurant where through the open doorway she saw Ben. In that moment before the traffic bore her on she could not possibly have recognized anyone but him, matching one whose unique features and bodily outline she carried within her.

He was bent over his plate, his dark head down and shoulders curved. He was alone. By the sight of him she was overcome with desolation, premonition like the nausea of one about to faint. How could he look so solitary? Did all the years together mean nothing? A childish fear of abandon drained her. His lowered head and bowed shoulders knew without knowing that he was no longer her lover. His aloneness was hers; not here, not now, but somewhere waiting.

Under banners on posters in the offices of Movement Headquarters, just opened in the city, on photographs in progressive journals and newspapers, Didymus appeared among others released from prison or returned from exile. Our leaders, our heroes. Who would occupy which office and in what capacity could not be decided quickly after so long a period when there had been leadership dispersed between a number of representatives in different countries of exile, leadership confined in prison, and leaders in the front organizations which had grown up and survived within the country. He did whatever was needed, as everyone must. Sometimes he found himself arranging protocol and press conferences; then he was off to fulfil the request of some provincial branch for a speaker, he was in one of the first delegations to talk with white businessmen, he gave a graduation address at a college where the rector had hoped for some better-known face too busy to attend. But this was while it was taken as understood that his legal training rather than the avocation of clandestine missions he had carried out so successfully in the days of exile and underground activity would decide what position he would hold on the national executive in

a time, now, when that formation was legal and the political
ethos was negotiation, the grinning face at receptions in place
of the disguised one moving in the streets.

—Jack of all trades!— Sally with her affectionately exaggerated shrug as a softener to her rising voice answered Vera
when her friend asked what position Didy held now. A rap
performer yammered into a microphone with the speed of a
tobacco auctioneer; the Starks were come upon at the opening
of an exhibition of painting and wood carving by black artists
whose work had become fashionable since city corporations and
white collectors had seen such acquisitions as the painless way
to prove absence of racial prejudice. —And what a mob this is
. . . all these *cultural workers* who're ashamed to call themselves
painters and writers. And the insurance bosses and bank PROs
showing how they appreciate our black souls. Now for Christ's
sake don't quote me, Ben!—I use that jargon around the office
corridors, oh yes I hear myself . . . but thank God to find a
businessman, dear Ben, among my friends in this crowd who
don't want to say what they are.—

Of course. The torsos are only part of the furnishings Sally
knows well in the Stark house. No one singles out the identity
—*sculptor*—of the one who shaped them, only he remembers the
identity of the missing head, the complex nerve-centre of the
woman he lives with and that he had given up (once, long ago)
attempting to capture in its material form.

So Ben laughs with her. Of course.

—You don't have any work going in your firm, do you?—

—Only the kind of thing you read in the Smalls. Some of
my clients are in the mail order business. Money in your spare
time selling from your own home—you know.—

—Most that we're dealing with don't have homes to sell
from. But seriously . . . I've been meaning to get in touch with

you, your advice about how we might set up some sort of liaison with business people, operating outside the usual employment-agency style, something more personal, tapping bad conscience . . . why not. I've been meaning to come round.—

The Starks and the Maqomas had not seen much of each other lately. Although Sibongile spoke of her job as if it were quite humble—it was the democratic vocabulary, hangover from exile with its brave denial of hierarchy—she was one who could not be reached except through a secretary these days. She had her offices and battery of command—computers, fax, assistants whose poor education and lack of skills she was attempting to tolerate while disciplining and training them. When there were complaints about her she said to her comrades in high positions what they themselves thought it better not to express. —I don't want to be told I behave like an exploiter just so someone can go on sitting around filing her nails or someone who was once detained thinks he's for ever entitled to disappear two hours for lunch. Comrades employed here are expected to have the will to work harder, not less than they would for some white boss. This's not sheltered employment.—

The furnishing of the house was completed, if too sparsely for her taste; she liked beautiful objects, and some of those she had collected with little money saved while moving around in exile had had to be left behind. The daughter had been fitted out with all her mother needed to supply for the new school. There was a microwave oven installed in the kitchen so that she could leave a meal to be heated when she had an official obligation that meant she would be home only in time to find Didymus and her daughter in darkness lit up by a television film, or to take off her shoes and move about without disturbing the husband who, asleep, left space for her at his side. Home was set up; but she did not have time to do the daily tasks that would maintain it; it was Didymus who took the shopping lists she scribbled in bed at night, who drove Mpho to and from her modern dance class, to the dentist, to the urgent obligations that schoolgirls have to be here or there, it was he who called the plumber and reported the telephone out of order. His working day was less crowded than hers. She would be snatching up files, briefcase, keys in the morning while he was dipping bread in coffee, changing back and forth from local news broadcasts to the BBC. Their working life was housed in the same building; sometimes he came to look in on her office: she was talking fast on the telephone, held up a hand not to be interrupted, she was in the middle of briefing the fieldworkers through whom she had initiated research into the reintegration of returned exiles.

She began to appear at many of the meetings he attended. Glided in, late, graceful with her well-dressed big hips, eyebrows arched when anyone was long-winded. She had a complaint about her director, who didn't want to attend and made a habit of asking her to do so in his stead. Let's have a post-mortem, she would say, at home. She and Didymus were the best of comrades, best for one another, of all others, at such times. The months she had gone about her work in London and taken care of their child without knowing or asking where he was, the letters—suddenly, sometimes, a love letter—that came to her unsigned through some country other than the one he was in, the strangely pure emotion of his returns—what other relationship between a man and a woman could prove such trust? The abstentions from adultery that 'trust' means to most couples are petty in comparison; this was a grand compact beyond the capacity of those who live only for themselves. They argued, they met in complicity over this issue or that, together in the line each would follow, she in her department, he at his higher level. They defended to each other a partiality for or lack of confidence in certain leaders. —We need someone tough and quick-thinking in that sort of negotiation. Sebedi's too much like— (she closed her eyes and thrust her head forward, pinching the bridge of her nose)—he's an old rhino, only one horn, only one tactic—

—But when he charges, aih! There's force, he knocks the hell out of government spokesmen.—

—Ah . . . how often? By the time he's got his bulk together to charge, they've slipped the issue to something else, out of the way.—

—Not always. Not always. I've seen him make a hit. And what you must remember is that he's impressive, these early days, he sits with his hands folded and his big head held back that way, and the government boys see he's really listening to them, he doesn't scratch himself and drink water and stub out cigarettes like some of the other comrades, the young ones who're only thinking what they're going to say next. He commands *respect*.—

She drew back in staring reproach. —Who wants respect from those people? Those bastards who've been mixed up in hit squads, who've sent their men in to murder our people at the funerals of people those same police have killed? It's the other way round—they have to be shown there's no *respect* due to them!—

—Then you don't understand negotiation. There has to be an appearance of respect, it's got to be there, it's like the bottles of water and the mike you switch on before you speak. It's a convention. It reassures those ministers and aides. And it traps them. They think if they hear themselves nicely addressed as minister this and doctor that, if they're listened to attentively, the whole smoothing-over process is in progress, the blacks have been flattered into talking like white gentlemen, they're nicely tamed. Why do you think we turn up in suits and ties instead of the Mao shirts and dashikis the leaders in countries up North wear? So that the Boers on the other side of the table will think there's a code between us and them, we've discarded our Africanness, our blackness is hidden under the suit-and-tie outfit, it's not going to jump out at them and demand! Not yet.—

Sibongile was twirling her hands in impatience to interrupt. —And out lumbers the old rhino! Where are the young lions?—

—Queueing up at your office, that's where—the only place they can be. They're the ones you're trying to find jobs for!—

Mpho watched her parents as if at a tennis match, sometimes laughing at them, sometimes chipping in with an opinion of her own. Sibongile and Didymus encouraged her, proud of a bright girl whose intelligence had been stimulated in exile by a superior education which perhaps also disadvantaged her by setting her apart among black youngsters. They were uneasy about the school they had been relieved to find for her; although 'mixed' most of the pupils were white, it retained the ethos and rituals of a white segregated school. They were grateful that in the early weeks when they were staying with their friends the Starks, Vera had introduced the girl to some decent young black people with whom she enjoyed herself. Her surprising attachment to her grandmother unfortunately did not mean that there were any suitable contacts for her in the dirt and violence of a place like Alexandra.

Didymus kept in himself a slight tautness, the tug of a string in the gut ready to tighten in defence of Sibongile—he was troubled that her frankness would be interpreted as aggression; her manner, sceptical, questioning, iconoclastic, would be taken as disrespectful of the traditional style of political intercourse that had been established in the higher ranks of the Movement through many years of exile, and would count against her advancement at the level to which she had, for the first time, gained access. Even the way she used her body: coming into conference, where she was by proxy rather than right, on high heels that clipped across the floor, no attempt to move discreetly. He was anxious; not looking at her, as if that would prevent others from being annoyingly distracted, then not being able to prevent himself from being aware of the stir of legs and seats as perfume marked the progress of her breasts and hips to her place. He felt that even her obvious undocile femininity would count against her; the physical disturbance she made no attempt to minimize prefigured the disturbance in the male appropriation of power she might seem presumptuous enough to ignore. He was sensitive to any response to her comments, sometimes hearing, as offensive proof of what he feared for her, undertones that merely made her laugh (the volume of her laugh was not moderated to the atmosphere of conference, either) or provided her with the opportunity of expounding a new point. He was familiar with the way things were done, always had been done, must be done, he was part of them; he could sense how others would feel towards a personality like Sibongile's; and a woman's. What he knew was remarkable in her could be misunderstood. He did not know how to give her the benefit of his own experience, teach her how to conduct herself if she wanted to realize the ambitions he saw were awakened in her. Home for her was the politics of home. That's how things had worked out. But she wasn't going about it in the right way. He feared the effect of failure on a person with such high confidence in and expectations of herself. God help me, and Mpho, and everyone else she knows, when that happens.

Didymus was against nepotism, but what is nepotism?—nothing more than putting in a word when this seems appropriate. He was one of the old guard, there were private moments when he could remark to a comrade with whom he had experienced much in so many situations and crises, that he scarcely saw Sibongile these days, she was working so hard, she was so dedicated to her returnees. And the permissible observation was always received with some such formula: Oh yes, she's doing a remarkable job of it. But whether this was a cautious assurance that her value was not unrecognized, and went no further, or whether it was to remind the old comrade that he should not think he could promote his wife, the response was dismissive. A brush-off.

Driving through an area where her work took her Mrs Stark's attention to the voice beside her and what she was seeing about her kept being diverted, as if by a seized muscle which will not be discernible to any companion. There was, among the documents in that loaded sling bag that was always with her, a letter found in her office mail that morning. Ivan's handwriting on the envelope, not addressed as usual by one of his typists and sent to his childhood home. She had opened it in the awkward privacy granted to the recipient of a letter in the company of others. Hardly taken in any details, any explanation; just the central fact her skimming arrested: Ivan was getting divorced. She folded the letter without reading the last page and thrust it somewhere in the bag.

The undertone of a shy young woman was speaking of brutality. —So you see, Mrs Stark, I mean they's upgraded Phambili Park, sewerage and that, and we all building, but now the men from the hostels is just coming to run all over, the women from the squatters' place is sitting in the veld right there by our houses—what can a person say to them? They frightened. Like we. We frightened, too. Last week two nights there was shooting, the men from the hostel was chasing someone—

How was it—'I've got Alice to agree to a divorce.' The sight of his handwriting on the envelope is already a signal of something unusual to be conveyed; a banker so successful that he is going back and forth from London to Poland, Hungary and Russia to negotiate new banking alliances doesn't have time to lick stamps personally. As if she were saying it to Ben now, she heard herself, when Ivan came back to South Africa and married his schooldays girl: He'll stay with her as long as he's not successful.

—so I was scared, I can tell you, I was so scared, and my mom, we just hid there without the lights while there was running and screaming, terrible, and then that noise, that noise! something falling hard, just like that, heavy at the door, so I thought what if it's Colin, he wasn't home yet—

Billboards on bare ground proclaimed the right to shelter elevated to middle-class status. Easy Loans Available, Protea Grove, Blue Horizon, Hill Park, you too can say you live in a place with a beautiful name like a white suburb, you too can feel you are making a claim for yourself when your address is Phambili Park—forward, let us go forward! Now on the horizon, a vast unloading of scrap without any recognizable profile of human habitations, now at the roadside, the jagged tin and tattered plastic sheets that are the architecture of the late twentieth century as marble was the material of the Renaissance, glass and steel that of Mies van der Rohe; the squatter camps, the real Post-Modernism: of the homeless.

—Oh sorry—turn here, no, left, sorry— Such an apologetic young woman, with her oval face, varnished olive by the mixture of races, in its corolla of springy black hair. Is she apologizing for existing at all, neither white and living far from the wrath that overflows from the black hostels into a fake suburbia nor black and fleeing into the veld from a burning shack? —and I heard someone groaning there outside and what can I do, my mom was trying to stop me, I thought what if it's Colin so even I get killed I must—

Ben was shocked. That's not the kind of attitude you'd expect to have towards young married people. Hurt. Ben, who had been Bennet, the young man who took someone else's wife while the man was away at war, had fear disguised as disapproval in his face, the withdrawal in his eyes in their dark caves. He did not want his son to suffer any complications in the search for sexual fulfilment and companionship that beckons from that other billboard: Happiness.

On a straggle of wire clothes were dripping, a woman flung a basin of water to the ground and looked up, a white flag on a dead-branch pole announced something to the initiated—a healer or some other form of counsel for sale, or maybe mealies to be bought—above a shack leaning like a house of cards. Business going on; straggling letters on board or wavering across the corrugations of tin, New York Gents Tailor, Dry Cleaning Depot, Latest Hairstyle Braiding Afro Relaxing, Mosala Funerals, Beauty Salon, a shutter propping up an eyelid of tin where a handful of cigarettes, a few bottles of bright drinks, twists of snuff and dice of chewing gum were ranged. Store. Coal Wood. Turn here. Turn there. *Oh Mrs Stark*. Combis have widened and channelled the dirt road to the passage of a river in flood, the Legal Foundation station-wagon is carried along, keeping track as the combis draw level so close the elbow of the driver out of his window almost touches the arm of the station-wagon's outside mirror; held back when the combis stop at speed, without warning, to take on or discharge a passenger.

—Oh Mrs Stark, I tell you a person can't go through that, he can't. When I saw it wasn't Colin, when I opened the door just a bit and I saw the head, the black man, blood, and the brains—

Crying, and all she has to deal with the shock and horror come back to her in the telling is a fancy handkerchief patterned with a pierrot's head, his two crystal tears printed tinsel: Mrs Stark sees as she turns in the gesture of acknowledgement that is all Mrs Stark has to deal with it. For the moment; the Foundation must not flounder in effects, it tackles causes.

—like at the butcher's shop, I never knew our brains was like that—

There is no stain on the doorstep. Neither blood nor the red-veined jelled grey displayed in shallow pans. All has been scrubbed away in the desperate upkeep of housewifely standards. A tall woman is waiting, bony in the way that often comes to African fleshiness from the mixture with European blood, and prematurely aged (she could probably give Mrs Stark a year or two) by the determination to defeat poverty by the virtues of fastidious cleanliness and decency believed to belong without effort to people with money, the rewards of being white. The door is not that of a house but the side-door of a garage; a stove, refrigerator, TV, beds, the family is living there. —Colin's doing the house on weekends, oh it's over a year now, a slow business!— The older woman insists on making tea, there's a granadilla cake with yellow icing, she breaks in for emphasis: —His brother-in-law, my other daughter's husband, he's in the trade, and there's others in the family comes to plaster and so on.—

—Sundays it's quite a party!— Distracted from her tears by the comfort of pride, the young one shows Mrs Stark over what will be her house one day, Sunday by Sunday, the breakfast nook, Colin's clever with his hands he's doing the table himself, the master bedroom (she calls it), the kids here, with an entrance to the yard for them, the living-dining's going to have a hatch counter to the kitchen, ma's room with a separate bathroom and that, this's the foundation for a patio and braai. The visitor is led outside again to admire the façade. There is no roof yet but on the unplastered wall where the window frames are paneless the replica of a brass carriage lamp is in place just as if it were standing to light the pillared entrance to a white man's driveway.

The assertion of this half-built house is so undeniable that both women feel an unreality in returning to the object of Mrs Stark's presence, which was supposed to be an inquiry into what happened in Phambili Park the night a man was murdered on the young woman's doorstep. This sort of investigation was not normally within the purview of the Foundation, but on this occasion, as increasingly lately, the connection between the people who had been removed from a site and squatted near Phambili Park because they had nowhere else to go, and the violence from hostel dwellers they were subject to, pursuing them, the disruption this in turn caused residents in a legally proclaimed, upgraded etc. township, was relevant to the Foundation's case against the removal. The young woman leads Mrs Stark up and down roads in the veld drawn by the rough fingernail of an earth-mover. Woodpecker tapping—building going on wherever you look—the veld an endless offering to the infinity of light that is a clear Transvaal sky, scaffolding standing out in the exaggerated perspective of bareness, de Chirico, Dali, thought they imagined it, Munch saw open-mouthed women fleeing in space from dingy, smoke-smouldering encrustation of shanties, there, over there. But where is Europe, what place has the divorce of a banker in the mind of anyone picking a way over rubble and weeds to the neat hallucination of small houses with their fancy burglar grilles, and flowered bedsheets hung out to dry, someone

speaking to families living in garages while the habitation that
has existed over years, in their minds, is slowly materialized in
walls rising at the rate at which money is saved and free Sundays
are available. The normality in these homes—camping out in
the garage is home, because it is the first occupation of what has
existed in mind—is also hallucinatory. So what is normality?
Isn't it just the way people manage to live under any particular
circumstance; the children who are teetering a stolen supermarket trolley under the weight of two drums of water back to
the squatter camp (one of the Phambili Park residents' complaints is that the squatters come over to use their taps)—the
children are performing a normal task in terms of where and
how they live. They yell and pummel one another, tumbling
about as they go. A carriage lamp is the blazon of aspiration,
fixed to the wall where a mob smashes a man's head in.

Mrs Stark put her notes into the sling bag, assuring that
she would find her way back to the city. Without the face of a
resident in black areas as escort beside her, she took the precaution of locking the car doors and closing the windows. Moving
in a capsule; neither what usefulness her notes will be to the
case nor the letter lying beneath the notebook dispelled the unreality of the place just left behind. She was accustomed to
squatter camps, slum townships, levels of existence of which
white people were not aware; the sudden illusion of suburbia,
dropped here and there, standing up stranded on the veld between the vast undergrowth of tin and sacking and plastic and
cardboard that was the natural terrain, was something still to
be placed.

She had an urge to pull over to the roadside and read the
letter.

But it was a resort to distraction; just as having to go about
her business to somewhere named Phambili Park had served as

a reason to thrust the letter half-read into her catch-all bag. And you don't stop for any reason or anyone on roads these days. With one hand on the wheel, she delved into the bag to feel for the envelope. *Ivan a frowning child her own frown of attention always looking back at her from him his habit of fingering his nose while he talked (don't do it, it's ugly) at the butcher's I never knew our brains was like that a carriage lamp to shine out over the grey spill—*

She found she was at the turn-off to the hospital where the soft-voiced witness had said people from the squatter camp had taken refuge. So she drove into the hospital grounds, waved on by security guards, and brought the car to a standstill. But not to read a letter.

She trudged over raked gravel between beds of regimented marigolds towards the wings of the hospital, dodging the hiss of the sprinkler system. Pigeons waddled to drink from the spray; a two-metre-high security fence under the hooded eyes of stadium lights surrounded this provincial administration's hallucination of undisturbed ordinance. All along the standard red-brick and green-painted walls of the hospital people were collected as if blown there as plastic bags and paper were blown against the fence. Women sat on the ground with their legs folded under skirts and aprons, small children clinging and climbing about them. Men hunched with heads down on their knees, in a dangling hand a cigarette stub, or stood against the walls; looked up from staring at feet in broken track shoes advertised for the pleasures of sport. She greeted some groups; they blinked listlessly past her. She made a pretext for her approach, Were there people living in the hospital? An old woman took a pinch of snuff and pointed while she drew it up her nostrils. Are you sleeping there? A woman tugged at the blanket tied cutting into the shape

of her sturdy breasts, needing to accuse anyone who would listen.
—They tell us no more place. Here! We sleeping here!—

Out of the stasis others were attracted. They didn't seem
to understand questions in English or Afrikaans—Mrs Stark
knew from experience how people in shock and bewilderment
lose their responses in confusion, anyway—but the woman in
the blanket spoke for them. —Five days I been here. What can
I do? That night those shit take eveything, they kill—look at
this old man, no blanket, nothing, the hospital give him blanket,
when he's run those men catch his brother, TV, bicycle, everything is gone from his place—shit!—

The man was coughing, his knees pressed together and
shoulders narrowed over his chest, folding himself out of the
danger of existence; the babies sucked at breasts, greedily taking
it on.

—And this woman, she try to go to her home yesterday, in
the night she come back again. No good, terrible—

The woman had the serene broad face that at the end of
the twentieth century is seen only on young peasants and nuns,
she will have followed her man from some Bantustan to the city
that had no place for her, but neither the squatter camp nor
the flight from it had had time to redraw the anachronism of
her face in conformation with her place and time. She didn't yet
have the tough grimace pleated round the eyes and the stiff
distended nostrils of the woman, a creature of prey, who was
displaying her.

She prepared herself obediently to speak. A hump under
cloth on her back was a baby. A small girl hid against her thick
calves. —Friday there by Phambili where we living they come
to get my husband. We run away but there's plenty people running, night-time, and I don't see where is my two children, the

boys children, I was running with the small ones like this—
(raised hands towards her back, carrying the weight)—now I
don't see my two children when I'm come to this hospital. Now
yesterday I think I must go back to my house and see where is
my children, my boys children, but when I come in the veld I
see those men again they by my place—

She looked to others, someone, to find words for this sight,
an explanation, what to do.

Were they hostel men, did they carry knobkerries, knives,
how were they dressed?

The woman pulled the baby's legs more securely round her
waist and took again the long breath of her panic as she fled
dragging her children into the veld, how could she be sure what
she saw, how could she know anything but the urgency of her
flesh and the flesh of her children to get away.

What about you—you get a chance to see who they were,
the men who came that night?

The woman with the blanket stood before Mrs Stark on bare
planted feet. —Me? You say what you see, your house is burn
down or they kill you. Better I see nothing.— A fly was creeping
round her cheek under the eye. Too much had happened for
her to notice so small a predator treating her as if she were
already a corpse.

And the letter. Lying at the bottom of the sling bag under
the notes, under the sign of spilt brains and carriage lamp and
the people staring for salvation, becoming dark clusters and
clumps along a wall as she walked away from them.

When she got home—it was too late to go back to the
Foundation—she came upon the letter. She was alone in the
house that was hers as the bounty of divorce, in an order of life
that could take for granted rights and their material assurances—her normality. It's always been her house; Ben moved

in with her, first as lover, then husband. It contains tables, lamps, posters and framed photographs, worn path on a carpet, bed—silent witness to that normality.

She leant against the windowsill, where there was still sunset light. The handwritten address directed to the Foundation was itself part of the text waiting to be read. Why does he tell me and not his father?

Why did he know—think—she would understand better? The envelope written in the well-rounded upright script she had seen form from his kindergarten alphabet, sent to a clandestine address like a love letter; a claim to share a secret that should not have turned up again at the bottom of a bag of notes. He cannot possibly know what she does not know herself: whether he is the son of love-making on the floor (in this very room where the letter is in her hand) one last time with the returned soldier, or whether he is the son of his mother's lover, Bennet.

He does know. Somehow he does know. She has an irrational certainty. It was always there, can't be denied; he doesn't only look like her, in the genes that formed him is the knowledge of his conception. If she has never known who fathered him, he does. The first cells of his existence encoded the information: he is the child of the childless first marriage, conceived after it was over on this bedroom floor in an hour that should be forgotten. The information was always there: when she and Ben took him into their bed for a cuddle, as a tiny child, and in the inner-focussed emergence from sleep his gaze would be fixed on her eyes; when, a grown man, a banker, he danced with her, each holding the other in their secrecy.

You might have been aware, I think you were aware the last time you were in London that things were not going too well. Alice made me promise we'd keep up the appearance and I gave in—mistakenly, I believe, but when you're what's known

*as the guilty party (that's my designation with the lawyers . . .)
you try to make small concessions in order not to seem too much
of a bastard. I should have known better, not so? Alice was
plotting, poor thing, I suppose, every kind of delaying tactic
she could think of. I sometimes wish you could be here now to
tell her what people like you and I accept, that if you didn't
exactly tell Annie and me, we somehow learned from you about
emotions—you can't fake love. If it's gone it's gone. She wants
me to stay with her, she says she doesn't ask me to love her.
She's grown to be the kind of woman who's content to be used
like a prostitute, I should go on sleeping with her for god knows
what—hygienic reasons, what she thinks of as the sexual needs
of men that have nothing to do with love. She doesn't understand
for a moment that the idea fills me with disgust. I don't want
a vessel for my sex. Vera, I've outgrown her, she's the little girl
I took to school dances. For a long time I've had nothing I could
discuss with her, not my work, not what's in the newspapers,
not my ideas about life. If it's not concerning Adam, his earache,
his school marks, whether he needs a new tennis racket, there's
nothing. I can't live like that and I'm not going to be party to
her weak choice to do so.*

*I have another woman. Have had, of course, for a long
time. She hasn't pressed me into divorcing Alice, I can tell you
that. She's not the type to go in for emotional blackmail. She's a
Hungarian redhead, if you want to know what she looks like (!),
half-Jewish, and she's very bright, an investment banker.
There's no messy tangle on her side, her husband died at thirty-
nine five years ago, a brain tumour. No children. I don't know
whether to contest Alice over Adam. He's almost grown up. She's
got a strong case for custody, but doesn't an adolescent boy
need a father, more? Difficult for me to judge, because I had
both. All the old clichés of what's best for him etc. Sometimes I*

just want to get out, I'd agree to anything. Other times, I feel bad about the boy. This is beginning to sound like one of the soap operas Alice watches on tele and quickly switches off when I come in, to pretend she doesn't. No doubt every divorce is a soap opera. And you get addicted to your own soap opera, never mind the important things that are happening in the world. I've just come back from Moscow, the refinancing of part of the arms industry to make vehicle components, the swords into plough-shares operation. But it's so much more profitable to sell arms, and they need money, no financial aid consortium can give them what can be earned by selling to the Middle East. I'm enclosing a photograph. We're at some dinner in Budapest a few months ago. She's the redhead next to the fat man standing up making a speech.

But there was no photograph. He must have thought better of it; had the instinct that a photograph, a face ringed, is no way to announce a betrayal.

When she heard Ben come in, his relaxed home-coming sigh as he paused in the passage at the bookshelf where the day's mail was always left, her concourse alone with Ivan's letter sank away; the reason why Ivan didn't write to Ben was because Ben is his father, of course, must be; he knows how deeply Ben loves him, and doesn't want to upset him with the sudden evidence of any unhappiness or instability in his son's life.

Vera threw away the envelope.

Who are the faces arranged in a collage round the great man himself? The posters are curling at the corners and some have faded strips where sunlight from a window has barred them day after day, month after month. Crowds who dance their manifesto in the streets are too young to recognize anyone who dates from the era before exile unless he is one of the two or three about whom songs were sung and whose images were kept alive on T-shirts. Didymus went about mostly unrecognized; disguised, now, as himself.

In the ranks of the entourage at mass rallies the cheers and chants fell pleasingly on him among other veterans as a category to whom this sort of valediction was due; it didn't matter who they were individually. The press mixed up the attribution of names and that didn't matter either. In a democratic movement the personality cult must be kept to a minimum, except in the case of dead heroes, who are an example to the people without any possibility of leading a tendency or faction that might be divisive. The time of welcoming posters was over; there were many new faces, or the unexpected appearance of known ones in positions they had not held previously. But these positions were interim ones—more or less on the level of his own adaptation to a variety of impermanent roles.

When the date was announced of the congress at which the Movement's elections for office would take place, lobbying began, of course. Among the strong group to which he belonged, those returned from prison and from experience as a government in exile, the concern—not to be admitted outside their own ranks—was how to concede positions to those who had earned them by keeping the Movement alive within the country, while retaining key positions for those who had surely earned them by conducting the Movement from exile or prison. Women's groups, youth groups, trade union groups were busy gathering support for this or that candidate; the old guard welcomed the influx as affirming a new kind of mass base after so many years of clandestinity. They had no need to fear they would not be returned to office—loyalty to the most militant is a dominant emotion in the masses; deserved; to be counted on. Meanwhile Didymus made it quietly but firmly known that on the new National Executive he would not expect to continue doing whatever came up. He would get the legal department, or at least something on that level; it was tacitly assured by his comrades on the outgoing Executive that this went without saying.

Among the possible newcomers Sibongile was nominated by a combination of returnees and a women's organization, neither very prominent as yet. He didn't think she had much chance but was proud of the recognition nomination, at least, brought her.

—They've put me up only because I'm a woman—I'm wise to that and I don't think it's a good enough reason. The women just want to see one of us there among you men.—

—Of course the women have. But not your returnees. They know what you're capable of, they know what you can do.—

—For them? Well, then they know more than I do.— Her theatrical, comic stare. —All I know is how we allowed the government to get away with giving us amnesties and passports and nothing else. All I know is we didn't hold out for training centres, housing—your executive didn't insist, it was up to you. In my office, with three raw youngsters and a pittance, I'm trying to deal with the results—and believe me, I'm not making miracles.—

Didymus had always appreciated her vehemence. He acknowledged the reproach, smiling. —I promise you I'll take it up in the new executive.—

•

What has been forbidden for so long—a gathering, any gathering—becomes a kind of fairground of released emotion, with its buskers, its symbolic taking, together, of food and drink, its garrulous decibels rising after long silence, its own insignia-banded marshals mingling as if already the unattainable evolution of humankind has arrived, where men and women discipline themselves. No more police, no more dogs, no more tear-gas, no more beatings on the way to the Black Maria. Even if it never comes, it is enacted here and now. And as always in the mix of human affairs the tension in the sense that the future of the country is being decided is combined with dissatisfaction with the catering and discomfort occasioned by a hopeless provision of too few toilets.

Didymus moved among old acquaintances, old comrades who had to introduce themselves with reminiscence of campaigns they had shared with him. He had the politician's flattering tactic of the hand on the shoulder, the grin of recognition even without knowing whom he was greeting. Every now and then he would excuse himself from his progression, called to confer with another of the outgoing Executive members—questions of protocol coming up, complaints from the press, requests from the groups that should have been settled in advance; in a country where it had been a criminal offence for people like those gathered in the hall to meet for any kind of political purpose, what are routine procedures anywhere else here were arcane secrets of power and privilege. While his conclave drew aside, their eyes glancing into and away from the throng as they sheltered within their half-turned backs, in the air thick with voices and the friction of movement, the sussuration of clothing, the echo of coughs, laughter, a slithering stamping of feet, the tremolo of ululating cries broke again and again into song. People sing on marches, they sing at funerals, they sing on the way to jail; it was their secret, all that time of the forbidden.

You can't toyi-toyi your way to freedom, Sibongile often tartly remarked in exile. He saw her, caught up in a sway and shuffle of women and young men. Her shoulders shrugged rhythmically and her head was thrown back; Sibongile was enjoying herself, or learning how to be a politician. He was amused.

The old guard sat on the podium through the announcement of nominations and process of voting, facing the people they had gone to prison for, gone into exile for—and died for: in their faces were those who were absent, who would never come back. Didymus, looking out at his people, had a strange realization, in his body, in his hands resting on his thighs, of his survival. He had moved among them as if dead; had he died under treatment in Moscow, the fiction, and walked among them those months as a phantom? Disguised, unrecognized, do you exist? And now they see him; back to life. It was a conviction of pure existence. He sat there; he was.

In this state he heard the results of the election announced. His name was not among those voted to the new Executive. The applause continued, the shouts flung about like streamers, the songs lifted, the list of names was somewhere beneath. *Sibongile Maqoma.* She was hidden in a scrum of triumphant supporters. He was congratulating his successful comrades, the clasp round the shoulders, the dip of the cheek to each cheek, ridiculous, as if he were a prize-fighter coming forward in defeat to embrace the victor. Nobody said anything, with the single exception of a comrade who had always felt enmity towards him: —It's crazy. That they dump you, man.—

He made his way to the chanting, dancing press around Sibongile, pushing to get to her until someone saw who he was and nudged to have him let through. His embrace was again a public one, the hug and hard kiss on the mouth from the comrade-husband; his presence before her bounced off the excited glare of her face like the flash of a piece of glass in the sun. But what could she say right then—he was eddied about with some sort of respect among those celebrating her, the husband congratulated by eager hands.

When the surface of the crowd began to be broken up like foam in a current she appeared drifting to him with Vera Stark linked by the arm. He was back at the podium gathering briefcase and papers to leave his seat vacant for a successor. Vera was one of the team of independent observers—lawyers were regarded as having the most credibility for the task—brought in to monitor the votes. Clasped chummily by Sibongile as if they were schoolgirls after a victorious match, Vera stood waiting for him to speak; knowing he wouldn't. —You'll be co-opted. So it doesn't mean anything.—

He patted her on the arm, smiling at the lie between them. —Let's go and look for a drink—we must toast Sally, man!—

-—Oh there's a party! We're all going to a party! Vera'll come in our car—who's got the keys, did I keep them or have you— Sibongile used this abstracted jollying tone when Mpho was little and had to be hustled off for an inoculation or an exam. After Vera had entered the back of the car Sibongile stood with her hand on her door, turned her head, close to him. —You're all right . . . ?—

—Of course I'm all right! What do you think! Now come on.—

At the party he took part in the noisy discussions that assessed the composition of the new Executive which ('on balance' was the phrase) had kept the key positions intact while pushing a few of the leadership upstairs under honorary titles, and bringing in new people with better contacts within the country. One would have thought him quite detached from the event; he succeeded in this: no one dared commiserate with him. Towards the end of the evening, when he and everyone else who took alcohol heightened the atmosphere of achievement (the younger comrades tended to find this a weakness of the old guard and drank fruit juice), he himself was in a mood to believe he felt that all that mattered was that the congress had established conventional political legitimacy for the long-outlawed Movement. You had your role, your missions, you took the risks of your life, you disappeared and reappeared, went into prison or exile, and there was no presenting of the bill for those years to anyone, the benefit did not belong to you and your achievement was that you wanted it that way.

The marital tradition of the post-mortem between husband and wife who were also comrades: one o'clock in the morning in the bedroom, the silence of weariness, stripping off shoes that have become constraints, opening waistbands that leave the weal of a long day—Sibongile burst into anger.

—Those sly bastards! They planned it! They wanted you out, I know that cabal, I've seen their slimy smiles. They've never forgiven you the time when you opposed them over the business of landings on the coast—

—Oh nonsense. It was a crazy idea, I wasn't the only one.—

—How can you say that? You *were* the one. You were the one who had gone inside and reconnoitred, you were the one who knew whether it was possible to carry it out or not. What you said had to be what High Command would listen to. And those others couldn't stomach to see themselves made fools of.—

He sat down on the bed. This seemed to make her angrier. He did not look into her anger. —All so long ago.—

—They slapped you on the back, they whispered with you in corners, I saw them, even tonight, right there! And all the time they had it all set up to get you out. It isn't long ago, for them. They don't forget they didn't come out of that business too well.—

She was pulling clothes over her head and flinging them across the room. Her straightened hair broke loose from its combs and stood up blowsily, her mouth was squared open, anger made her ugly.

—For God's sake, Sibo— He changed from English to their language, or rather hers, which was the tongue of their intimacy. —It's done. It's happened. I don't want to deal with it now. It's political life, we held everything together in exile better than any other movement did, now's not the time to start stirring up trouble. There may be a purpose, I don't know, something else planned for me.—

—Hai you! What purpose! You going to grow a beard and all that stuff and infiltrate—where? What for? Where can't we just get off a plane at an airport and walk in, now? We're not living in the past!—

—That's exactly what you're saying—we are—there was a plot against me because of something that happened outside, done with. For God's sake, let's sleep.—

She lay beside him stiffly, breathing fast. —I don't sleep. I can't turn over and forget about it.—

—Listen, woman.— He sat up with effort. —You are going to be there, now. In there. Here at home in the country. Keep your mind on what you have to do, you have to work with everyone on the Executive, don't make enemies for private reasons.—

She came back to English. —On principle. Ever heard of it, Didymus. *On principle.*—

—You've got a lot to learn. Let me look after my own affairs.—

—Your affairs are my affairs. Have I lived like any other woman, hubby coming home regularly from work every day? Have I known, months on end, whether you were dead or alive? Tell me. And could I ask anybody? Did I ever expect an answer? Could I tell our child why her father left her? *Our affairs.*—

—Not now. Not in politics, where you are now.—

Deep breaths snagged on a few sobs. She had always wept when she was angry. But was she also giving vent to the emotions of excitement and pride she had repressed out of consideration for him, when in the hall filled with delegates she heard that she was one of their chosen?

We don't seem to have much success with them.

All he said.

—What d'you mean? Banking may not be exactly what you or I would have chosen for him, but he's good at it, and Annie always wanted to be a doctor, she's doing good work isn't she, her heart's in it— But she knew what he meant. Annick, inheritor of his beautiful face, had brought many boys home when she was a teenager but since she had qualified and taken a post in community medicine in the Cape she appeared to have no man and in her thirties gave no sign of marrying; Ivan was getting divorced without showing enthusiasm for a new woman who evidently was as much business associate as lover. Arid lives, by Ben's hidden standards of high emotion.

—Well I don't suppose we were such a good example—at least to Ivan.—

—I've never been divorced.—

The forgotten heat of blush, called up by Ben in her cheeks: Bennet, who thought he had seduced someone's wife but had been seduced by her, and never since made love to another woman. That she was sure of, the certainty was there in the image bent alone over a meal in a restaurant that came back to her with blood in her face. I love you. That was in the blood, too, but she could not say it, what reason would he find for such a—declaration, at this moment? What reason was there? —Anyway, it's not whether or not *we* make a success of their lives. Nothing to do with us.—

His palms smoothed along his jaw-line, a familiar gesture in the language of their marriage, not, as it might seem, a physical response to the shadow of his dark beard that by evening always had appeared again, but a sign of disagreement. —Maybe we should take the boy if they're squabbling over him. Give him a stable home for a year or two.—

He went away to write a letter to Ivan, turning from what he knew was her alarmed silence.

Ben didn't show her the letter and she did not ask to read it. Perhaps he had not made the offer to Ivan. It was not mentioned when Ivan telephoned, as he did now and then, or they called him because there had not been time or thought to write to him. The idea that there could be space in their life for something more was mislaid like a document lost in the bottom of the files where the struggle for another kind of space grew up every day around her. On the western border people from a tribe that had been moved with the concession that they could come back to their land to tend the graves of their ancestors for one day a year did not leave at nightfall but began to build huts. The sullen silence of reclaim met the arrival of authorities to evict them; they were left there—temporarily, the Foundation was warned, when it took up the issue on the appeal of the tribe. Vera and Lazar Feldman, a young colleague, found themselves proceeding from instructions of two kinds: one, from their own training in secular law, that the owners of the land had been displaced illegally in the first instance; the other, from the people

who were thatching huts and surrounding them with fences of
thorned branches and hacked-off prickly pear plants, that the
instruction to return and take possession came from the ancestors.

It was easy to see this use of ancestor worship as a political
tactic shrewd peasants had thought of beyond the rational ingenuity of lawyers; but there were moments when, listening to
the people's spokesmen, she felt confusion and uncertainty—
not about them, but in herself; whether the only validity of their
claim lay outside the political struggle, outside the challenging
of laws made by governments that rise and fall, in the continuation of life itself from below and above the very ground that
sustained it. What other claim is there that holds? The wars
fought over land, the boundary proclamations, the paper deeds
of sale—each cancels the other. What was she—the Foundation—working for, if not for that claim? But it didn't look good
enough in legal plea—peasant mysticism can't be codified as a
legal right—it was *too good*, for that. With a shift in a chair or
a half-smile she and Lazar passed over the instruction from the
ancestors and took that which came from their own strategical
experience in opposing the law through its interstices, which
consisted mainly in delaying tactics. The action of re-evicting
the people would be held off—maybe so long that the present
policies of land ownership would be torn up. Who knows? Such
things are not discussed with Lazar; he is young, and would not
understand that doubts do not mean that belief in the necessity
of the work she does is abandoned. And even while this case was
occupying her, Oupa came with a favoured opening: they've got
a problem, we've got a problem, he's got a problem. The owner
of that apartment building where he was living was seeking the
eviction of some tenants.

—The problem is, rooms on the roof. There are many people living up there.—

—But who pays rent for the rooms?—

—Well, that's it. The tenants of the flats let them out to, say, one person or two. Then those people take in more. People who work in the day let the bed to people who work at night and sleep in the day. It's like that.—

Yes, it was like that; when the apartments were built for white people, for their occupancy, their way of life, for the white millennium, when they lived in the apartments, each had the right to one of the rooms to accommodate a servant.

—I didn't know about it. So I haven't got anyone up there.—

They laughed together at the missed opportunity.

But the 'problem' remained, between them on Mrs Stark's desk. Oupa had received an eviction order along with the other black tenants. The Foundation would have to look into it, take it up on behalf of them all. Oupa had been so proud, so happy to move in. Yet he was cheerful; she noticed he was wearing a new lumber-jacket, brown suede, and he asked his old adviser and friend something he'd never done before—she didn't know he went to the theatre—whether a current play was to be recommended? He had about him the confidence of a young man elated to find himself attractive to a chosen girl; well, circumstance kept his wife away in another part of the country, absence makes room for other attachments, and perhaps they were parted, emotionally, by reasons only absence makes clear. She filed at court an intention to defend against the eviction order; she had to find time to interview the other tenants. Along the corridors of Delville Wood the old, faint signals from One-Twenty-One were jammed by the static of complaint, voluble indignation that buzzed about her in flats she had never before entered, and by the sight of the cubicles on the windswept roof, water dribbling from the communal washrooms, spirit stoves beside makeshift beds that in her clandestine occupancy of the white millennium had existed above her head while she was making love.

Ben—Ben was negotiating finance for the new enterprise in which he had involved himself. Promotional Luggage. She made staggering, clownish movements of hands and head when, that evening, she heard the name, the term. What did it mean?

The gestures offended. He read scorn or ridicule into them, and she felt exasperation at having to deny these. He had to be coaxed to explain coldly. Suitcases and briefcases designed exclusively for executives, to their requirements and incorporating their logos in materials superior to some embossed stamp. Custom-made. Business has its jargon just as the test-cases of the Foundation have. After a bath to wash away the ancestral instruction from beneath the earth and the sense of lying, herself, buried in One-Twenty-One with reality windswept and forlorn ignored above her head (for if you deny any time, any part of your life, you have no continuity of existence), she dressed and perfumed herself to go with Ben to a business dinner. They agreed it was inexplicable that people in business seem to have no feeling for the privacy of leisure; apparently they are lonely after the occupation of the day and want to fill this vacuum with a continuation of the same company and the same talk over an extended taking of food and drink.

He looked at her in detail, a sculptor's eye for line and volume, her legs patterned in a filigree of lacey black stockings, her waist marked with a wide belt, her face made up sufficiently to conform with what would be expected of her. For her it was a calculation; for him it put something of the fascinating distance between them that had existed when he first saw her, unapproachable, somebody else's wife.

—You look lovely.—

—My old glad rags.—

In the car he took up what her banal show of modesty provided the opportunity to say. —Unless I do something about making some money now we're going to be without resources when we're really old. (My god, I'm beginning to use their vocabulary.) Hard up. That's what I'm saying. That's what Promotional Luggage is about.—

They had never talked about provision for some long survival. A country where there was so much death—why should you need to choose your own solution. —If you can believe we're going to live so long.—

—It's easy to think there's the option of dying before you run out of cash.—

—We'll always have somewhere, Ben. We've always got the house.—

She had taken him in there, into the booty from her relationship with another man; he had given up the idea of becoming a sculptor to provide for her through Promotional Luggage. She put out a hand and squeezed his thigh, a compact, one of the bargains constantly negotiated by marriage.

•

The restaurant is called the Drommedaris, after the ship that carried the first European to the country; it's fashionable for cartels that own hotels and restaurants to feel they honour history and claim patriotism with such names. History and patriotism implying settler history and patriotism. They are the clubs whose entry requirements are that the applicant shall be expensively dressed and willing to pay one hundred per cent profit on a bottle of wine. The password comes from the client's own cabalistic vocabulary—promotion—and is evidenced without being pronounced: up-market. Everyone's main course is served at the same moment by waiters who, taking the cue from the senior among them like members of an orchestra with one eye on the conductor, simultaneously flourish silver-plated covers from the plates. Revealed are not four-and-twenty blackbirds (she catches Ben's eye across the table) but attempts at culinary distinction and originality that combine incompatible ingredients in—fortunately—an unidentifiable mixture. Eat. It's expensive, therefore it's a privilege, she admonishes herself. It you don't like it, you're a prig. Between courses a fake silver egg-cup of watery ice cream is served that coats the palate it is supposed to clear for more eating; a ritual someone in the cartel has picked up in eagerness to claim elegance as well as history, patriotism etc.

The galleon decor is not inappropriate to the conversation, for the men frequently speak of this or that absent colleague being 'taken on board' some enterprise. And there are others referred to as small fry; the fingerlings in the sea of business. Women are expected to talk to other women, she knows that, and does not attempt presumptuously to engage the host, on whose right hand she has been placed (the position to be interpreted as recognizing a woman's husband having been taken on board). He assiduously signals a waiter to fill her wineglass and passes with surface attention friendly remarks suitable to feminine interests (Just like my wife, she's always removing those chunks of ice they put in the water. Where do you have your holiday house—Plettenberg?—do try some of this, looks exciting doesn't it oh I agree the Cape is too windy but I'm out in my ski-boat, that's my passion, Yvonne's a girl for winter holidays, game parks, you know, all that).

There's one exception to the contented dinner table purdah
in which women chat to one another under the vociferous competitive exchanges of the men. An Afrikaner, dressed, coiffured
and made up in the television-star style of an indeterminate age
that will never go beyond forty while at the same time adopting
every change of fashion, flashing her mascara-spiked eyes from
this speaker to that, clinking gold and ivory bracelets and neon-
coloured jumbo watch as she laughs in the right places, calls out
a tag punch-line now and then that reinforces attention to the
male speaker rather than draws it to herself. Some group's public
relations director, a prototype of how, in the choice of a female
for the job, the display of possible sexual availability may be
exploited to combine with suitably acquired male aggression.
Poor thing; she comes clip-clopping into the ladies' room on high-
heeled hooves and behind the door there is the noisy stream of
her urine falling, she's even taught herself to piss boldly as a
man. Or perhaps that's wronging her—she comes out and smiles,
My God I was bursting, hey, sorry.

At the table the host stands courteously to see his right-
hand partner seated again, they know how to treat a lady. There
are cigars and small fruits encased in glassy hardened sugar, as
Coca-Cola and buns are distributed at treats in the townships
whose workers are being discussed. A recent strike in the cardboard container trade is being compared with that in the tanning
industry. Opposite Vera a man keeps pushing his glasses up the
bridge of his nose and breathing heavily in readiness for an
opening to speak. At last: —We told them—called them all
together with their shop steward, I don't talk to those fellows
on their own, eh, you only get told afterwards he didn't have a
mandate—we said, look, you can bring your wives (hands
chopped edge-on to the table, then lifted) you can bring your
children (hands again) you can bring the whole bang shoot, we'll

give you blankets, we'll supply food, so you won't have to risk anything coming to work. Most of them said fair enough, you know? I feel sorry for them, we genuinely wanted to help, they can't afford to lose two days' pay and they can't risk being beaten up if they come to work—so it's a solution. But there was one guy who said no, he has to stay away. Not for political reasons, no, no. So he said. But because he can't leave his house for two days, in the township. He hasn't got locks on the doors . . . So I said . . . (waiting for the laugh) so I said, all right. Don't come to work Monday and Tuesday. All right. But then don't come back on Wednesday.—

Through muffled background music inescapable as a ringing in the ears a cry comes from farther down the table: —Hands in the till! Everywhere you look. I could tell you many more instances . . . this Government's become as corrupt as the blacks' states. If they're going to lose power, they're going to make sure they give over a ruined economy. Positively last sale. Everything up for grabs. D'you know what's happening in the pension funds—

There's another who sits back with the care of one who has drunk too much, but a rush of words upsets the balance: —I think I'm a damn fool to be negotiating labour deals with the black unions. I ought to be learning how to get *my* hand in the till and get out. First thing they're going to do when they get into power, you can own only one property. So bang goes my trout farm, no more invitations for you boys to come down and fish . . . —

How she sees them laugh it off, their confidence in themselves makes a joke of their fears, they will always find a way to dine on board the Drommedaris no matter what government comes, the power of being white has been extrasensory so long, they feel it within them like a secret ability to bend metal by looking at it. If they 'get out' they will come back; we shall ask them to. She is the only woman who has accepted a cognac (the public relations director made the approved female choice of a sweet liqueur) and she's joined the party on the ship of fools but (too much wine, as well) for her it's a listing oil tanker she's on that will spill its cargo to slick territorial waters round the new state.

Why do I drink on these occasions? Why does duty make me drink? She sat in the car beside Ben, going home. What have I done, to put him in such company, what have I done to him.

But why *me*? What has he done to himself?

In the morning, they were in the mood to laugh over the evening. 'Hand in the till' became itself a password between them for ironic judgments in their private language.

·

The pulsations of perception throb, and die down. Throb again. How, in the end, between the swirling newspaper and slimy drains of the roof-top hidden from the streets and One-Twenty-One, evidenced as testimony bared to the sky; the probabilities in London of fulfilment or unhappiness in attachment to a redhead whose photograph was not sent; the claim of the ancestors and its codification in a land policy paper that may deprive business associates of river frontage for weekend trout-fishing, *Better I see nothing, Don't come back on Wednesday*—how, between all these, will you know, will you recognize the beat: this is my self.

What happens, happens early in the morning, when the hand with the blue vein raised from outer wrist-bone to the base between first and second finger feels for the switch on the radio. Sometimes as he draws the hand back she takes it for the return to life, and closes her eyes again, waiting for the news; his hand and hers, the warm pulse palm-to-palm of a single creature who exists only while bodies are still numb in half-consciousness. The news is brought to you by this bank or that with its computer services and thirty-two-day deposit convenience at maximum interest. There are wars and famines too far away to stir response; there are coups and drought drawing nearer, there are the killings of the night, still closer. Some mornings, attacks on farms; a white farmer shot, the wife raped or killed, money and car missing. Taken. 'Taken' to mean the motive is robbery; as if robbery has a single meaning in every country at every period. Take cars, take money, take life. These mornings robbery means taking everything you haven't got from those who appear to have everything: money, a car to sell for money, a way of life with house and land and cattle. Otherwise, why kill as well as rob? Why rape some farmer's ugly old wife? No violence is more frightening than the violence of revenge, because it is something that what the victim stands for brings upon him. It is seldom retribution for a personal deed, of which innocence can be claimed. The rape has nothing to do with desire; the penis is a gun like the gun held to a head, its discharge is a discharge of bullets.

She lies in a body-warmed bed, the first refuge after birth and the last, for those fortunate enough to die a natural death.

What happened one morning was the sudden startle of the word 'Odensville' in the newsreader's bland recital. 'Nine people were killed and fourteen injured in violence at the Odensville squatter camp last night. The clash occurred when a local farmer, leading a group of armed supporters, tried to evict the squatters. Police report that it is unclear whether the bullet wounds sustained were the result of the group's action or of cross-fire from the squatters. An AK–47 and three Makarov pistols were recovered at the scene. The farmer, Mr Tertius Odendaal, said that he had called by radio the local farmers' defence commando when the squatters were spotted approaching his house under cover of darkness, carrying stones and weapons.'

The Foundation had been unsuccessful in keeping any contact with the farmer Odendaal. The day he shut his door in the face of its lawyer, her driver, and the squatters' spokesman, Zeph Rapulana, was the end of negotiation with him. Communication was with his lawyer. Rapulana came to the city a number of times to confer with Vera on the squatters' options in a course of action. It had become clear to her that it was best for the Foundation to be guided by this man, rather than the other way about. He read, enquired, informed himself of all the intricacies of legislation, so that her task was simply to formulate procedure; there was a zest in working together with a plaintiff rather than

taking over decisions for the helpless, which was her function
most of the time. He sat quietly watching her, in her office, while
she walked about going over exasperatedly her attempts to talk
to Odendaal. His alert patience had the effect of taking the place
of her own customary manner in that office; he was the one
listening to her without showing reaction, as she listened to others. It was a curious kind of release, almost a pleasure, that
created ease between them. He had ready what he was going to
say, but a natural respect for the views of others made him hear
out what might modify his own. There were homely colloquial-
isms in his command of English, a little out-of-date, with its
careful grammatical construction, in comparison with the spliced
improvisations—TV jargon, Afrikaans and tsotsi slang, mother-
tongue syntax, mixed with English—of city people like Oupa or
the Foundation's black lawyers. —Odendaal won't budge. We
can abandon any idea of that nature. Our only possibility is to
sup with the devil. Take a long spoon. Yes . . . The agents of
the Government who put us in our position are the ones we must
shame into getting us out of it.—

—Count on the Provincial Administration? Well . . . —

—Odendaal has threatened to bring the AWB* with their
guns to evict us. It doesn't look very nice, does it? In the present
political climate, the Government surely doesn't want too many
press reports of blacks being forced out of their homes. That
still going on.—

—Their hands would look clean. It would be the work of
the right-wing rebels.—

—Even so. They'd be asked why they didn't do something
about it. That's where we step in. Take the bull by the horns.

* Afrikaner Weerstandsbeweging. A white militant right-wing resistance movement.

He applied to the TPA* to build a black township on his land, we apply now to the TPA to appropriate the farm and declare it a transit settlement, for a start.—

—Worth a try. Our case would be that it's an initiative to avoid violence in an area of dangerous contention. I suppose we could lead with this.—

Making light of their 'conspiracy', they grasped hands that day; sat down together over the formulation.

That other clasp, two hands joined to make one creature, broke apart. Out of bed she stumbled to find the sling bag with the address and telephone book she kept handy when away from the office. She summoned the well-trained orderliness of her working mode in order not to think—anything—not to ask of herself the name of one of the nine dead until she reached the telephone and heard it answered. Zeph Rapulana was a squatter but he had given her the number of a relative in a nearby township who had a store and lived behind it; there was a telephone, whether in the house or the store she didn't know. It must have been in the store, and so early in the morning the store was not yet open. The telephone rang and rang. It seemed to her an answer: Rapulana would never reply again, anywhere. She called through the bathroom door to Ben in the shower, something terrible has happened, she has to go at once—he came to the doorway streaming. —What? What is it all about? What happened?— He naked, she dressed, it was an encounter between strangers. He called out after her, Don't go there alone! Vera, do you hear me!

But she was alone. He didn't know the man, Zeph Rapulana. He hadn't stood before Odendaal's anger, Odendaal's barred

* Transvaal Provincial Administration.

door, with him, made decisions affecting families with him, hadn't come to read the dignity, the shrewdness of confidence and intelligence in that calm black face of the man. She drove first to the empty Foundation—no one at work yet—to pick up documents relating to the Odensville affair. Well along the highway, she remembered she had not left a note, and turned off at a petrol station to telephone her office. The young switchboard operator could hear the voices of the petrol attendants, laughing and arguing over a game of cards set out on the ground, and the jabber from their radio. —Where you partying already, in the day, Mrs Stark!—

She drove; a mind caged back and forth between the witness of the empty office where Zeph Rapulana had talked reason and strategy, the desk from which she had sent the letter to the TPA, and the collage, made up of so many press photographs, so many leaping and falling, running figures on TV, so many burning shacks, so many dead slumped on the earth as so many bundles of blood-stained washing. There was no connection. Before a reply to the letter, hers and Rapulana's, could be received through the authorities, before bureaucracy had 'taken steps', the solution to everything had taken steps—deaths, again deaths.

The car door slammed behind her outside the district police station with the blow of sun striking her with dizziness of the long solitary drive. Dust, sparkle of the wire security fence; she passed under a drowsy-lidded gaze of a black policeman with his sub-machine-gun hitched on his stout thigh. Inside, a white policeman, elbows on the counter and forearms shielding his flirtatious face over the telephone, was engaged in one of those calls made up of sniggering silences and intimately curt remarks between young men and girls. Another policeman was standing before a filing cabinet, smoking and hesitating over papers. While she questioned him he continued to glance sideways at this sheet and that; shrugged without answering and called towards an open doorway through which someone of more senior rank appeared. He was a handsome Afrikaner with a glossy moustache and a Napoleon haircut, a well-groomed stallion of the kind with a special manner when dealing with women, since he felt himself to be pleasing to them somewhere under their complaint or distress, like it or not, in their female innards. Even to this *tannie** he extended the patronage, listening to her rap of questions with the air, yes, yes, he knew how to deal with over-anxious ladies concerned about their black servants. That business with the squatters last night; nine deaths confirmed but no names available, the bodies still to be identified —if the relatives can be found, you never know with them, they're spread around in these camps. He scribbled the name of the Foundation without reaction to her revealed connection with that trouble-making organization; yes yes they could phone and ask for him personally, yes yes ready to be of any assistance. He cuffed the head of the young man at the telephone as he passed to his office.

She drove to a complex of garage, chain restaurant and restrooms in a loop off the highway and found a bank of telephones. At the store, someone who sounded like a child listened, breathing gustily, and then put aside the receiver. Vera called loudly, hullo! hullo! possessed by a useless impatience with everyone, the police, the unknown storekeeper, the wild-goose chase of calling culpability to account, finding interstices in official obduracy and solutions to ignorance of the uneducated that was, had been so long, her working life. The gaping receiver at the other end of the line, the background noises lazily conveyed,

---

* Literally 'auntie' in Afrikaans. Originally respectful, became a way of referring disparagingly to any middle-aged or old woman.

ignoring her—this was nothing but another customary irritation, but it brought her to despair and destroyed the control within which she held the fact of nine unnamed dead. If that child had been within reach she would have struck it. Violence boiled up in her from somewhere. If Odendaals kill, kill back. If they killed that good man, why not deal back death to them—she understood with all her impatient angry flesh the violence that, like others, she called mindless. When the receiver was picked up she gave her name and business testily. A man's soft hoarse voice said no, it's all right, my cousin is well, everything it's all right, nothing is happen, if you want see him I can send someone—

She was given instructions to find her way to the shop. Lost, turned back by police road-blocks, she found another route—there it was, so that was it, she remembered dropping him off at that store the first day when they had left Odendaal's house.

He was there, standing, waiting for her, wearing a tie, right arm in a sling and, oozing through gauze, the pursed red lips of a deep cut drawn together by surgical clips on the black flesh of his cheek. Smiling.

She was overcome by a kind of shyness, because the man was alive. She began to shiver—not tremble—it was the quivering wave that comes when you give way to fear or are going to be sick. Certainty that he had been killed by Odendaal, that she had not allowed to rise in her, now struck at the sight of him.

—I'm so sorry. You were worried. My cousin told me.— A gentle and calm voice.

She stood there, someone dropped from another planet, the outer space of safety, in the dim little store's light moted by the dust of grain and spilt sugar, thick with the closed-in smells of the night, snuff, soap, sweat-dried secondhand shoes and army surplus coats, mouse-droppings and paraffin. He saw, came over at once and with his left hand strangely clasped her forearm above the wrist, held it there, between them. Tentatively, her other hand came to rest over his.

He tramped before her to a shed behind the shop. There were plastic chairs and a bed in disarray where someone had slept. He turned off a radio and gave some instruction to a child who brought cups of sweet milky tea.

She didn't ask whether the squatters had approached Odendaal's house armed with stones and weapons. She didn't ask if he led them. He told drily, now and then touching with a middle finger along the gash on his cheek, how Odendaal and his commando had gone through the squatters' shacks, firing, dragging people out. A pause, tracing the gash. A considering, rumbling murmur, expressive in his own language, that she understood from experience with blacks who have status in their communities as always some sort of warning or preparation for what was about to be said. —Now Administration will act. Now they'll have to buy his land. No more trouble for him. Lucky Odendaal. He'll get money, plenty of money, he'll be happy. And the land—

Their eyes held, and shifted.

—Nine dead, so we'll get it.— Now it was possible to say this to this man. —We'll have to make sure it's for occupation by your people there, no one else.—

—Quickly. When shall I come to the office? I'd better bring the Chief with me, it's always better for Pretoria if anything is backed by a chief. First I have to make the funeral arrangements.—

She had no preparatory murmur such as he could use. —Perhaps near escapes from death are always a resurrection. Perhaps that's how the whole legend of Christ rising from the tomb came about—I was thinking, they took him down from the cross and couldn't believe he wasn't dead, couldn't believe he was there, alive, in front of them . . . that was the resurrection, really. The whole tomb story, the miracle came from that.— Then she remembered he was probably religious. When they first met, that day they went to see Odendaal, the man had about him the kind of modest self-righteousness, prim bearing, an over-lay on the African spirit that regular church-going seems to bring about in rural people; at the roadside he sat circumspectly as if he were in a pew. This surface had burned off like morning fog in the heat of the events in which he was involved, as she had come to know him—or rather as he had come to reveal himself released by that involvement. Yet beliefs inculcated in childhood often remain uncontradicted by mature reasoning and experi-ence. He might be offended by a Christian heretic's doubts of Christ's divine powers.

He understood she was talking about—himself.

—I managed to drive. I took two of them to the hospital in my car. There's blood all over. The woman died before we ar-rived around midnight. Yes . . . The youngster may be all right. That's how I got this stitched up.— He moved his lower jaw against the stiffness of the flesh drawn together on his cheek.

In Vera's car they went to what had been Odensville.

A stunned aftermath of disaster slowed the pace of existence to its minimum; people were breathing, just breathing. Children with lolling-headed babies on their backs sat about, there was no way of knowing whether outside where they had lived—every element that could identify shelter and possessions cast in tur-moil. Dried tears were the salty tracks on the grey-black cheeks of women who must not be gazed at. Men wandered, turning over splintered wood, torn board, plastic burned black-edged into fantastic whorls and peaks like the frozen waves in Japanese prints. A sewing machine under kicked-aside crazy mounds of pots and clothing was an artifact uncovered from a destroyed culture. To Vera's eyes it had never seemed that the squatter camps she had been in could represent what anyone would be able to regard as home. Now in the destruction of the wretched erections of rubbish-dump materials she saw that these were home, this place had been home.

He talked quietly to people; he and she did not speak to one another, everyone ignored her, as if she could not be seen, the events of the night imprinted on their eyes, blinded to the day.

·

What happened.

There are always explanations expected.

—I can't . . . You can read in the papers what happened, you'll see on TV what the place looks like now. That's all. Who has ever explained what a war is like—everyone witnesses something different.—

Ben had a fingernail in his ear, something worrying him in the aperture; the private moment like an offended inattention.

She tried again. —When you're there yourself, it's not anything you've thought. And everyone who went there would know something else . . . it wouldn't be the same for you as for me, or for others as for you.—

—Isn't it that you didn't live through the night there.— The tone of one who assumes he knows the other better than she could know herself.

—No no. No no. That's obvious. It's not what I'm trying to talk about.—

—After the event: isn't that what your work is. Always the same thing, not something different: consequences. It's not the first time you've seen such things.—

In her office she dictated to a tape recorder an account of on-site investigation of the Odensville attack. It came back to her desk with neat margins and headings in the flat print-out of a computer. As she read it over for secretarial errors it seemed what Ben had annoyed, almost hurt her, by describing as having been a routine part of case work. The pain of catatonic inertia, yet another aspect of despair in addition to the many she already understood, was a terrible knowledge she would carry, because she never could be, never could wish to be inured to feeling by professionalism. That was what happened at Odensville; that she understood. The other happening was something she came to realize slowly, returned to as a distraction from work and all the preoccupations of her life, interrupting, like a power failure of all the main lines of consciousness and memory, seeking a new connection with responses untapped, as there are known to be connections in the brain that may go unused through a lifetime. At first, with a beat that was half-distaste, half-fear, it came to her suddenly that the gesture of the man, grasping her arm, and her automatic placing of her hand, for a moment, over his knuckles, was a repetition of the compact to begin a love affair with her Hitler Baby, Otto, years ago. Yes—that had been a sexual question-and-answer by sudden contact, but the advance of this other man towards her and his assumption of the right to touch her strangely, her hand placed over his, was something quite other. And yet again quite different from shaking hands, which also has as little to do with any kind of intimacy as greeting by the shoulder-bobbing accolade has to do with kissing.

Any kind of intimacy? She turned away from the problem of interpretation again and again. Certainly not sexual. She knew

without doubt from the impulse in the hand that had gone out
to cover his that she was not making or responding to a sexual
invitation. She knew, even in the tight warm grasp of his big
hand, that the gesture from him was not sexual; the nerves of
skin and flesh instantly recognize the touch of sensuality. Good
god, was she not too old? Wasn't it even ridiculous, a vanity,
that she should imagine this gesture could have been any repetition of the other? She had sometimes feared, in the want, the
involuntary yearning of her body for the man Otto, for One-
Twenty-One, after he had gone, that when she began to grow
old she would become one of those women who have a fancy for
young men, that she would dye her hair and undress in the dark
to hide drooping buttocks and sad belly from a lover paid
with—what? Gold weights and silk shirts are only the beginning.
Thank god, no sign of any taste for young men was occurring;
but the passing mistrust of self projected upon the commanding
outer reality of a community only just breathing under its own
rubble, nine dead, a man with a slashed cheek driving while a
woman was dying on the back seat—what meaning could the
mistrust of self have, what reality, standing against that! To
whom could she pose the very *inappropriateness* of any personal
preoccupation arising from a situation where all individuality
was in dissolution in terror and despair. Not the lover-husband
to whom she used to tell—or thought she had—everything. Only
to herself. First the schoolgirl confessional falls away, then the
kind of friendships with men and women where, the awareness
comes, confidences are regretted as weapons handed to others;
finally, the bliss of placing the burden of self on the beloved
turns out to be undeliverable. The beloved is unknown at any
address, a self, unlike a bed, cannot be shared, and cannot be
shed.

In the weeks that followed when Zeph Rapulana was back

and forth at the Foundation on the matter of Odensville she slowly came to understand—not so much thinking about it as accepting, unknowingly as a physical change or change of mood come about—that what had disturbed her as a mimesis of the past was the beginning of some new capability in her, something in the chemistry of human contact that she was only now ready for. This country black man about whose life apart from his place in the Odensville case she knew nothing (wife, children, web of relatives and friends) already had this capability. That was why he was able to claim her with what was neither a sexual caress nor an impersonal handshake such as they customarily exchanged. He understood her fear that he was dead was an indication that for reasons not to be explained, nor necessary to try to explain, he was not one more individual at risk in the course of her work. There was between them a level of knowledge of one another, tranquil, not very deep, but quite apart from those relationships complicated and profound, tangled in their beings, from which each came to it, a level that was neither sexually intuitive nor that of friendship.

The circumstances of the lives backed up behind them each had lived so far were an obstacle to the shared references of ordinary friendship. She a middle-class city woman—that was as much decisive as whiteness, ordering the services of her life by telephone or fax, taking for granted a secretary and a bay for her car at the office; his status in his rural community marked—it was not difficult to picture from experience of these places—by neat clothes hanging on a wire and the small pile of books and papers in a shack—what did they share of the familiar, outside the Odensville affair?

His sexuality in late middle-age was no doubt satisfied elsewhere; although it was clear, from the sense even of her reserved persona behind her office desk, that her whiteness would not be taboo for him, or his blackness for her, sex had no part in their perception of each other except that it recognized that each came from a base of sexual and familial relations to a meeting that had nothing to do with any of these. Vera had never before felt—it was more than drawn to—involved in the being of a man to whom she knew no sexual pull. And it was not that she did not find him physically attractive; from the first time he sat across from her desk, his face wide-modelled and firm as polished basalt, his heavy but graceful back as he walked out of a room, his hands resting calmly palm-down on his thighs as he spoke, brought her reassurance she had not known she no longer found elsewhere with anyone. It was as if, in the commonplace nature of their continuing contact through the Foundation, they belonged together as a single sex, a reconciliation of all each had experienced, he as a man, she as a woman.

Didymus's left eye flickered open while the other stayed gummed with sleep. In the artificial night when curtains kept out the early morning—she stood, a burglar caught in the act. The eye held her. But this was no intruder: Sibongile off an early plane, the swirl on tarmac coming up in the silence as the taxi that brought her home turned in the empty street.

She released herself. Put down the suitcase. He closed the bleary greeting ashamedly, better pretend to be asleep, drop back into sleep. She drew the suitcase on its wheels across the carpet, fluttered papers and clicked objects against surfaces. Then the waterfall of the shower in the bathroom. The bed dipped to the side as she entered. He knew she wanted him to know she was trying not to wake him: as if she were not there; or had never been away.

He spoke. How was it?

He couldn't dredge up in his mind where she had been sent, where was it this time, Japan, Libya, not the UN, no. Better not risk how was Qaddafi.

—Ex-tr-aordinary.—

She lay willing sleep, all she had heard and done alight

inside her, could not be extinguished, as he himself had felt when he returned from his missions about which she could not have asked, How was it.

The thick atmosphere of the world of discussion and negotiation came from her hair and skin as smoke clings to the clothing of one who has been in a crowded room. He scented it as a dog sniffs the shoes of its master to trace where he's been.

She was a stranger and she was as familiar as his own body; that must have been how he was for her, those years when he came and went; if he thought of it at all, he had thought that was how it was; something for women. She slept, suddenly, with a snorting indrawn breath. This body beside him invaded the whole bed, lolled against him. His own felt no stir of desire for it.

He must have slept. Both woke at the sound of the door slamming as Mpho left for school, and Sibongile was out of bed instantly, padding over in her slippery nightgown to the half-disgorged suitcase and packages on the floor. —Look what I found for you.— People are happy bringing the consolation of presents to those left behind.

It was a handsome staff (he saw at first), no, a walking-stick, ebony, carved with a handle in the form of a closed fist over a ring, and chased all down the shaft to a copper ferrule. —Isn't it great? Look at the work that's gone into it. I knew you'd love it. I'd looked everywhere in the market but I had so little time—and then there was this damned hawker pestering outside the hotel, one day the moment he held it up I knew, that's for you. See—all carved in one piece—

She loved it, she sat back on the bed as he received the stick from her and followed its features under her eyes, her feet with magenta-painted toenails waving, her thighs shaping shifting curves of shine on the satin that covered them (he always had been proud of her clothes, her ingenuity in devising the appearance of flamboyant luxury, even to go to bed in, even when they were poor in exile and this had to be contrived out of odds and ends). —And look at the grain, here, these lighter stripes going down the fingers—isn't that amazing—and feel how solid—

He duly held the object horizontally, raised from the pillows, weighing it on his palms. —Where shall I hang it? Above the desk, or here over the door perhaps.—

She slapped her thighs, sending the satin shivering. —It's not an ornament! It's to walk with! Keep your weight down! Don't think I bring you presents without a double motive, dear— Her voice climbed its scale of laughter. She swung herself off the bed and he could hear her going from room to room, inspecting the traces of her absence, closing cupboard doors in Mpho's little room, clanging the kitchen bin shut on something he or Mpho had neglected to throw away. The walking-stick rested across his chest. He opened his eyes. She appeared in the bedroom doorway, as she had from a distant country at dawn, but in her dressing-gown, her arms crossed under her breasts. —Aren't you getting up?—

—What's the hurry.—

—Oh come on. I'm hungry.—

So she wanted him there in the kitchen to deliver to him a lecture on the results of her trip while they prepared breakfast together. She was trying it out on him—he was a comrade, experienced in such presentations, after all—before she prepared a report. It has been an assignment in Africa—where else could that stick have come from—she'd been sent to negotiate the takeover by that country's Government of a school for exiles' children and various other buildings the Movement had had there. The National Executive left it to her diplomacy to see whether these assets, no longer needed, should be handed as a gift to a country that had given asylum, or whether it might be possible to expect some sort of compensation—the Swedes had funded the school and added living quarters for the teachers, so there was some improvement to the property since the host government donated the land. —Dinner with the President, flowers sent to my hotel room and all (I like it better when they send fruit, but only Europeans do that, aih, on our continent people don't think fruit's a treat). A lo-ong explanation from him on how we should run things here, my God, if you wrote out all the advice we get it would circle the world—not a word about any compensation deal for the property. The next day there was the great ceremony of the handing-over, President's guard, military band, more speeches, mine as well, but the best I could do when I got the Minister in his office was to get out of him the promise of an agricultural training project, quite small, they'd arrange for a few students we could send up there, tuition free but living expenses *our* responsibility. I don't think I can recommend that as worth taking up? Better that I come back with empty pockets than something we don't want.—

—And the camp?—

She signalled two slices of bread to be put in the toaster. She went into one of her repertoire of elaborate gestures, throwing hands wide, bringing them together with a slight clap that mocked the attitude of prayer, leaning elbows on the kitchen table with a slumping sigh.

—Did you see Matthew or Tatamkulu?—

—Who . . . —

—You know.—

—Not there any more.—

—So you did go.—

—I had instructions. Just delivering I didn't ask what—

some documents.— It was said as if this were to be the last word
on the subject. But he, not she, had once operated in that camp,
it was one of the periods when he disappeared from the exiled
homes they occupied in Europe and Africa. His was a right to
ask about that camp where spies who infiltrated the Movement
were imprisoned, although it was not a subject for general discussion. Recently there had been released by the Movement a
public report of things done there; unspeakable things. When
the report was about to come out he had thought he'd better tell
her what he had never told her: that for a time, a desperate
time when the Freedom Fighters and the Movement itself were
in great danger by infiltration, he had been an interrogator—
yes—a jailer, there. He'd told her the code names of others who
were running the place and how two of them had joined him,
eventually, in protest against the methods being used to extract
information. She knew, all right, about whom he was enquiring
when he mentioned those names.

—It's not closed down, then.—

She lifted her chin and blinked wearily. —In the process
of. I didn't see much sign of life.—

—Did anyone say what arrangements are made when in-
mates are released, who is it that brings them back here? Is it
the government agencies who sent them to infiltrate—or are they
just being abandoned, that sort of outfit wants to pretend it
never existed, these days. They seem to get here anyway, ready
to be used against us in other ways. Recycled . . . Well, we
couldn't think that far ahead; there were a lot of things we
couldn't think about in that place.—

—No one talked to me, I handed over what I had to. That
was that.—

—It's not like you to be satisfied to be a messenger.— He
put plates in the sink, his back to her; turned his head.

She was yawning and yawning as if her jaw would dis-
locate with the force and she wandered out of the kitchen.
Gone back to bed to sleep off the journey: but no, she
appeared, dressed, eyes made-up, briefcase and keys in her
hand, on her way to her office. He sat in his pyjamas over
the mug of coffee he had reheated for himself. Ashamed, was
that it? She was ashamed that he had ever been involved in
that camp where the methods of extracting information by
inflicting pain and humiliation learnt from white Security
Police were adopted by those who had been its victims.
Ashamed, even though he'd finally got himself out of the
place, refused to carry on there. Refused, yet understood why
others could do the terrible things they did; she was a woman,
after all, she could understand revolution but she didn't understand war.

He sat on in the kitchen aware of the irritating drizzle of
the tap he had not fully closed but unable to distract himself by
getting up to turn it off.

No. Not ashamed; wary of her political position, calculating
that since his code name had not been listed in the public report,
she was not tainted, through her connection with him, under the
necessity of leadership to discipline and perhaps in some cases
expel from the Movement anyone who was involved. *Unspeakable*: even the subject, for Sibongile. She does not want, even
in private, any reminders, any familiarity with names, from him.
She has her position to think of. He had the curious remembered
image, alone in the kitchen, of her frantically and distastefully
scraping from the sole of her shoe all traces of a dog's mess she
had stepped into.

She had made the bed and placed the walking-stick on the
cover. Mpho had ear-rings and trinkets from her mother's part
in delegations to a number of countries; he had this. *It's to walk*

with. A present for a retired man, who should be content to pass time pleasantly taking exercise.

•

Sally Maqoma chose the restaurant and is known to the waiters. She orders sole. —You know how I like it, grilled, not swimming in butter or oil, and plenty of lemon, bring a whole lemon.— She and her old friend Vera Stark have tried many times to get together (as they term it) and for once Sally has a free hour to squeeze between morning appointments and a meeting in Pretoria at two-thirty for which a driver will pick her up. They talk politics on a level of shared references—Vera through her work and connections is privy to most of the negotiations which go on while the political rhetoric suggests that there can be no contact—but Sally rarely lets slip any political confidences. Vera is aware of this and knows how to respect evasions while yet interpreting them. As they eat, and drink mineral water Sally has been advised by her doctor to take copiously, Vera is both listening to her friend and piecing together rumours to fill lacunae in the spontaneity of the discourse. What Sally doesn't say suggests or is meant to suggest that the delegation to Pretoria (Sally has spoken of 'the three of us' having hastily to go there) is to meet some Government minister on the education crisis, but it might well be that the meeting was one of those of the Movement rumoured to be taking place with right-wing groups at those groups' request. Vera tried to superimpose the bearded and side-whiskered outline of a figure in commando outfit over the lively, sceptical black face so voluble opposite her. She could try a general question. —Is there anything in the newspaper speculation that the AWB and their kind want to talk?—

Sally raised eyebrows and poked her head forward comically. —Sounds unlikely.— She took a long draught and, as she put the glass down close to Vera Stark's hand, let her touch nudge it. —Everything unlikely has become likely. That's our politics these days.—

In their laughter the side-current of family lives surfaced, the intimacy of the times in one another's four walls when they had pooled their children, danced to Didy's records; the weeks when, on return from exile, the Maqomas had moved in with the Starks. —Did I tell you, some changes. Ivan's divorced, and Ben's father's living with us now.—

—Oh naughty Ivan. Young people are not like us, no staying power. But I remember, she wasn't much of a personality, you said . . .? It mustn't be too good for you, having the old man in the house.—

—I've always got on all right with him but he needs time, from others. Us.—

—Get someone in to look after him, Vera, you can't do it, you mustn't. You've got more important things . . . I'm sure I can find someone for you, there're always people coming round my office, out-of-work nurses, nice elderly mamas, long-lost cousins, God knows what—I'll find someone who can live in, that's what you need.—

—I don't know. D'you know it's going to be awful to be really old, no one wants to touch you any more, no one likes the smell of your skin, no one ever kisses you . . . And Ben's never loved his father, it seems. Some sort of resentment from childhood, you know those mysteries no one but the one who was himself the child can understand.—

—Ben? Really? Ben's such a darling, such an affectionate man.—

The limits of confidences between two people constantly shift, opening here, there closing off one from the other. Vera Stark could not speak what she was saying to herself, Bennet loved, Ben loves, only me; loves in Ivan only me, and what shall I do with that love— The thought rising like a wave of anxiety trapped in voices at a restaurant full of people; no place to deal with it. —I hear Didy's commissioned to do a book. A history of the exile period, is it?—

—He's supposed to be researching. Don't ask me . . . Let's order coffee— Sally had the alert shifting glance of a bird on a tree-top, surveying the comings and goings of waiters. When the coffee came she arranged the cups and poured, measuring out words with the flow. —Half the time he doesn't even get up in the mornings. I go to work, I don't know what time he gets round to shaving and so on. Always some pain or ache. When I say in the evening, how did it go today—I mean, Vera, I'm showing *interest*, I'm talking about whether he's written letters to people who can give him material, whether he's organizing his notes— then he'll say something like, How did what go? To put me down. To imply I'm humouring him . . . Because of where I've been all day, at headquarters. Is what happened *my* fault? Can I help it? He's got to stop this wallowing in self-pity. I can tell you (her eyes shifted focus, round the neighbouring tables, where other people's talk and self-absorption made a wall of protection) I'm beginning to find it disgusting. He doesn't realize that; it disgusts me.—

This confidence almost alarms; to meet it means it should be matched, and Vera does not know, does not yet understand, what it is exactly that she needs to confide, or if that impulse is any longer something to be heeded. Who can give answers? A bearded man in a preacher's dog-collar stood in the doorway, *How mean of you Vera.* —He's become history rather than a living man. How can anyone be expected to accept that about himself.—

Sally made a fist above her cup, she was shaking her head

vehemently. —That's just the problem. He does *think* he's history. He's copping out because he's not centre stage any more, he sees himself as history and history stops with *him*. He won't accept that it goes on being made and we all have to make it, my part has changed, his part has changed. He's still a living man who has work to do even though it can't be what he'd choose.—

—Writing a history? That's the past.—

Sally leant on the table in silence but did not let it widen between them. —I came back from a trip—a mission—you'd think I'd never been away. He doesn't bring me home.—

They are not two young women, after all, exchanging bedroom secrets. Vera may take the odd phrase as some locution for welcome slipped in from an African language. And she's white, she has never known what exiles have, the return of your man from god knows where doing god knows what he had to do (Didymus's name as someone connected with one of those camps luckily hasn't become public). She may or may not have understood what Sally is saying. Didymus doesn't bring her home by making love to her, as she used to, for him.

·

When Didymus did make the approaches of love-making Sibongile felt no response. Mpho had appeared from her room one evening charmed—in the sense of talented, gifted—with youth. The clarity of the lines of her body in a scrap of a dress, of her lips and long shining eyes with their fold of laughter at the outer corners, the cheap, wooden-toy ear-rings in the shape of parrots hanging from the delicate hieroglyph of her ears— she was the embodiment of happiness. Waiting to be called for; where was she going? A party, there were so many parties parents couldn't keep up with the names of all the friends with whom she was apparently so popular. A girl-friend bustled in to fetch her, they chattered their way out. A thin chain looped through a pendant lay curled on the table where she had dropped it after lifting it from her neck over her carefully arranged hair when the friend pulled a face: the pendant clashed with the ear-rings. Didymus poured the chain from hand to hand, smiling. He came into the kitchen where Sibongile stood stirring a stew and, with the pretext of looking to see what was in the pot, leant his chin on her shoulder. His hand came round over her belly that was swelled forward as she moved the meat about with a fork, circled the navel in a half-humorous caress in anticipation of a meal, and then moved down over her pelvis a moment.

After they had eaten she seated herself at the computer they had bought for his work on the history of exiles. Staring at the luminous waver of the screen a moment, arrested, as if for some indication whether he had used it that day at all; she turned to him.

—Go ahead.— He chose to understand that she was asking whether he needed the machine now. She spilled out and sorted her papers exasperatedly. He switched on the TV, volume low in order not to disturb concentration on whatever it was she was writing. Swells of music and the exaggerated pitch of broadcast emotions emanated from where he sat, as she removed from and inserted words and phrases in a speech she was due to deliver in a few days. His back faced her every time she lifted her eyes from the juggled text swimming in phosphorescence; something about the droop of the head showed that he wasn't seeing, he wasn't hearing. Didymus was asleep, carried along, unconscious, like a drunk at a carnival, in the meaningless impersonal familiarity of the medium that invades everywhere and recognizes no one.

In their bed he took up the caress begun in the kitchen.

His hand slid from her hips pressing firmer and firmer, smaller and smaller circles over the mound of her pubis, working fingers through the hair and slipping the index one, as if by chance, to touch through the lips. She flung back the covers and swerved out of bed, the mooring of his hand torn away. She stalked about the room with the air of looking for something and when aware of him watching her went out into the other rooms.

She came back and offered: —Verandah light wasn't left on for Mpho.—

—I turned it on.—

—You didn't.—

—My memory, these days . . . —

She lay beside him, not saying goodnight in case this provided an opening for him to try to rouse her again.

•

That night, or another night, she woke in a tension of sadness in which she and he were lost together, bound, sunk. The sound of their breathing strung tight between them but the divide of darkness could not be crossed, the weight of fathoms could not be lifted. He had not forgotten the light for Mpho. The pain of repentance, so useless, for this stupid little spite was actual between her ribs, something conjured up from the religious pictures pasted to the kitchen walls in her grandmother's house in Witbank location, where she grew up. She seemed to be living simultaneously in the hum of the night all the images, the moments when she had been most aware of him, scattered through the years. Parted so often; what happens in these partings, his, now hers, in the one who goes away? Is the one who left ever the one who comes back? There are changes in understanding and awareness that can occur only when one is alone, away from containment in the shape of self outlined by another. Such changes can never be shared. Alone with them for ever. The images are postcards sent from countries that exist only in the personality of the subject; you will never visit them. She had to make sure that he was there, some version of himself, even as a shrouded bulk under the bedclothes. She hesitated where to touch him: on the forehead, the hand pressed against a cheek, the neck below the ear, where a pulse answers. She rested her spinal column back to back along the length of his and felt him break wind as he slept.

The old man occupied Annick's room, so she would have to take what had been Ivan's and the friend she was bringing would have to share it with her. Ivan's luxury had been a double bed across which he liked to stretch diagonally his adolescent sprawl. Vera bought a divan to move into the room to accommodate the friend. The old man's presence already had changed the balance of the house. Sally forgot or had been too busy to fulfil her offer but connections at the Foundation supplied a relative in need of work; the path of the old man's movements, on the arm of the woman who came to help him every day, intersected and deflected those of Vera and Ben. Vera's house had the transparent grids of various presences laid upon it—the brief comings and goings of the soldier whose military kit propped against her dressing-table left in the varnish a dent whose cause was forgotten, the clandestine movements Bennet brought in as a lover and established in usage as husband and father, the route the children used to take, out of the window in Annick's room and in through the back stoep door to get at potato chips in the kitchen cupboard without alerting parents, and the invisible trails of Vera herself, changing the function of

a space by bringing Blue Books and White Papers to occupy
what had held model plane kits and threadbare stuffed animals,
closing windows room by room in a storm, carrying, as if following back in footsteps that have worn grooves in the wood
floor of her house, an old photograph to the light. On her barefoot morning scamper to the bathroom the old man might cross
her path, wavering ahead with his paralysed hand dangling
curled at his side and the other held before him as a blind man
senses for obstacles. He was not blind but formed the precau-
tionary habit of keeping the hand in the position of one ready
to receive a handshake greeting, because even that side of his
body had not survived the stroke unimpaired and it took time
and effort to muster the appropriate muscles when the occasion
came. She had to remember to wear a gown, as she had done
when there were still children at home and a live-in maid coming
early from the kitchen to house-clean.

He wandered with a smile of strange sweetness from encounter to encounter, not that he had become simple-minded
but because he was reliving the sense of achievement a child has
when first it masters how to walk, and the house represented to
him territory daily conquered. He did not seem to mind the
wheedling patter of Thandeka, who winked and gesticulated behind his back in comment on his infirmity and pride in his
progress. How is he today, Ben would enquire of her in the
presence of his father; and the hand that he might have touched
sank uncertainly out of the way. He bought his father specialist
journals and newspapers that should be of interest—he had been
a chemical engineer—and left them on the table beside the old
man's chair in lieu of a visit. The woman attendant decided, as
part of her responsibility for the old man's care, what he felt.
—Mama, he's so happy for his granddaughter coming, I tell you,
mama! That time she is arrive he's going to be there, *there*,

mama! So happy! Mama, I'm going to put a nice suit he'll wear—

Brought forward on her arm with abstract joy expressed on his behalf as smiling nuns set themselves to beam radiance of the holy spirit and politicians display their amorphous love of humankind, he looked uncertain, for a moment, which of the two young women who arrived was his granddaughter. He had not seen her since she was a high-school girl; but the face, the face of his son, there in hers, was surely unmistakable. Vera and Ben had somehow omitted to mention to her that the grandfather was living with them—as often, with them, each thought the other had done something neither had. But Annick kissed him, took the old hand—cold scaly skin like that of a tortoise she'd kept as a pet as a child—placed it in that of the friend with her, using the childhood form of address. —Grandpops, this is Lou, she's in biology and she's just come from a month on your old stamping ground, wasn't it—Zaire—the Congo.—

His voice snagged on the effort to speak, but he turned the pause into a mock appeal to Vera. —Of course this young lady's in biology, we all *are* biological—what does that mean she does, though?— He enjoyed his little quip and the polite laughter it brought; Ben only smiled, his black eyes unreadable. The granddaughter cuffed her friend lightly so that the girl shook her drape of hair like a mare stung by a fly; both had long hair, but the straight black tresses Annick had from her father had been frizzed since her parents saw her last. —Grandpops she's a professor, she's been doing important research up there, fascinating, we'll tell you about it.—

—Don't you believe her, Mr Stark. When we're at home and I start to talk microbiology to her, her eyes glaze over, all she wants to know about Zaire is what tapes I've brought for her, what kind of drums and strings you can still hear there.—

Annick with their two carry-alls followed Vera to Ivan's room while the friend took her tea over to the old man and settled for a talk about Zaire. The timidity with which the relation with adult children—actuality defies the oxymoron—is taken up when they return from their lives, surrounded Vera. Each time Annick appeared after absence she was the sudden live manifestation of someone fixed in a painting. The static features in the mind were moving, the details of the texture of the skin, the glance—what is she apprehending, at once, about her mother, about us in this house where she was once one of us? Her scent—not perfume but the smell of her that vaguely reaches back to the odour of her hair when she was observed, sleeping, as a child, by one leaning to hear her breathe. Something missing in that beautiful face? Mustn't be seen to be gazing for it. Not a change in the line of eyebrows; these are never plucked, they are definitive, seal-smooth and glossy, each tapering at the temple's hollow. Ben's sperm made her like that, in his image. Not the frizzing, though that hair-style's a pity; it's nothing that's been altered: something that's gone. But the last opening with which to take up the relationship with daughter or son is to pass some remark about physical appearance.

Perhaps one should tell, not ask.

Offer, not request. Put oneself in their hands, the ex-children. Place there the mystery of the totally unexpected: *what am I to do with that love.* If a doctor and a professor between them could explain it. Or to place, putting down carefully, a container of secret calm come out of an exaggerated fear of the death of someone not lover, husband, child: what would this young woman who was surely closer than any other woman make of that?

And all the time Vera was talking in the usual flitting, lightly anxious and excited way of someone wanting to make sure guests would be comfortable. The cupboard was cleared for clothes, the old man would share the main bathroom so the second one was all theirs, the daughter's and her friend's. —Sorry the room's crowded. But with full house now, no other bedroom, it's all I could do, I bought the divan.—

Annick thumped the carry-alls on it. She gave a sigh of pleasure as she recognized some poster of her brother's era that was still on the wall. —Oh you shouldn't have bothered. We always sleep in a double bed.—

The androgynous harmony present in Bennet's male beauty, transformed in this girl's femininity, her breasts under a loose sweater shrugged together by crossed arms, her pelvis and hips shaped in tight jeans, distracted Vera, she was conscious of something impossible trying to come to her. Instead, a sudden distraction: she realized what was missing in that seductive face. The black punctuation of that beauty, placed exactly as Bennet's was, below the spread of eyelashes shading the left cheekbone. —What happened to your beauty spot?—

Annie laughed instructively. —The mole. I had it off. No beauty; moles should be removed, they can turn cancerous, Ma.—

•

The usual party to celebrate a son's or daughter's visit. The usual people, Legal Foundation familiars—Ben's new associates in the luggage business remained business acquaintances he didn't particularly want to bring home—the old friends, once-banned political activists now turned politicians at negotiating tables, and the addition, among the returned exiles, of those whom definitive indemnity at last allowed to disembark without fear of arrest or to emerge from the subterrain beneath home, half-home. A few diplomats of middle rank, useful conduits to overseas funding, now appeared, a member of one of the UN commissions sent to monitor violence in the country; and there was a presence perhaps no one except young Oupa could place, a man introduced by Vera as Zeph Rapulana. He sat all evening in the same chair, while groups formed and broke up in and out of the garden and living-room; coming and going with drinks and food she was aware of the shine of the planes of his features sinking into the gathering darkness like the natural outline of a landscape, part of a view she could always expect to see from her house. But people came to that dark unknown figure, drawn in some way; she noticed them, Didymus, a consul-general, the UN woman whose professional qualification surely was to be enquiring. Annie and her friend Lou, shoes kicked off and feet on the grass, sat on the steps in rising and falling chatter and laughter with Oupa, Didy and Sally's daughter Mpho, and Lazar Feldman, the young lawyer from the Foundation.

Ben and Vera cast glances over the gatherings in and out-doors as an airline attendant walks down the aisle of a plane discreetly checking whether seat-belts are fastened. They were with every group and no group, and encountered one another apart from others. He put his hand on her shoulder. The night opened a soaring space above them, dwindling the voices and shapes of the human company they had gathered to a low hum-ming horizon, a thin and distant huddle of life stirring under a vast gaze. Was this all they could muster to set against the trajectory of people thrown off trains that morning; in the house an old man with limbs atrophying; a ship full of nuclear filth prowling round the shores that night with death at a twelve-kilometre limit? How far is a twelve-kilometre limit, for death, when this great engulfment of sky cannot be held off? They didn't speak but drifted together down the steps, past the backs and legs of those sitting there with their daughter, to the garden. The

neglected grass licked dew on their ankles; she knelt a moment
to bury her hands in it, ants crept up her wrists, crickets filled
their ears ringingly, restoring the earth's scale. They strolled on
away from their party. —Lazar seems pretty taken with Annie.
I can foresee us being left to entertain the girl-friend from now
on.—

Vera became conscious of the hand on her shoulder as if it
had just descended there. —I don't think so.—

—He's the kind of man who'd be right. Appeal to her,
surely. He isn't living with some woman, is he? You usually know
what's happening outside the Foundation.—

—No one permanent, far as I know. Girl-friends, passing
affairs.—

—I've got a hunch they'd get on. She hasn't some big affair
going all this time in Cape Town, has she? What about that
doctor she once introduced us to, Van der Linde? Would she
have told you? This schoolgirl-sharing-a-house, going about girls-
together—it's all right for teenagers but she's over thirty. I can't
believe it isn't a smoke screen for something—some love affair
with someone who's married, probably.—

—She's living with this girl. She seems happy.—

—That's why I think there's some complication with a
man.—

They walked on. There was a stutter of music from
the house, a cassette starting and stopped. Vera halted,
and he turned, thinking they were about to return to the
house.

—Ben, they sleep together. In one bed. The other girl
doesn't use the divan. Annie said when I took her to the room
the day they arrived, they always sleep together.—

—My god, what an idea. Childish. She's a doctor and thirty-
something years old. Why not a teddy-bear, as well.—

They were approaching the steps, the young people there, the house full of others drinking and eating.

—Would you ever share a bed with another woman.—

—No. But you know that. We can't talk now.—

•

The party goes on. In the kitchen plates pile on left-over food, Vera washes glasses because Ben's supply has run out. One or the other, they join this group and that. In a corner of the living-room the stab of interrupting voices vies with the music. A heavy young Englishman in a catfish-patterned dashiki is using the height from which he projects his voice to dominate a discussion on conditions in the liberation movement's prison camps, which have been the subject of a newspaper exposé. —You can't make such sweeping generalizations. Things differed from camp to camp. I myself can say—

A head was dipped disparagingly. —As a journalist, from outside.—

—Yes, a journalist, poking my nose where it wasn't welcome. But I wasn't doing so in the capacity of my work. My brother-in-law happens to have been held in two of those camps so I have the picture from outside and inside.—

—Your brother-in-law?—

—Yes, my brother-in-law, my wife's brother Jerry Gwangwa.—

A small black woman wearing the Western antithesis of her white husband's outfit, satin trousers and a string of pearls in the neck of her tailored shirt, stood by looking up now and then to others in the manner of one watching the impression he was making. —But at first they wouldn't tell you anything, you had to—

—Why do you talk of things you know nothing about—

His soft thick throat throbbed like a frog's. He did not look at his wife as he spoke. —My own brother-in-law was beaten on the soles of the feet, he was strung up, in another camp these methods were not used, it was no five-star hotel but . . . all depends on who was in command. I had some contact with him . . . what I know is not secondhand. Jerry's not bitter although how he happened to be subject to all this—that's another story, he should never have been there, while there were plenty who certainly deserved to be.—

Didymus was in the group, a good listener who, Vera saw, contributed nothing. He turned away with her as she moved on, and Tola Richards, the journalist's wife, joined them.

—I didn't know about your brother.—

She stood, stranded, before Didymus; before Vera. She gestured with her glass as if about to tip its contents in someone's face. —Oh haven't you heard it from Alec before? It's his party piece. Whenever there's someone who doesn't know us, he produces his punchline about the brother-in-law so they can be impressed he's married a black. Don't you know I'm his passport? I'm his credentials as a white foreigner. Because he can produce me, it means he's on the right side. That gets him in everywhere.—

Best thing was to assume she'd had too much to drink; Didymus put his arm round her in a hug and said something to her in their own language. The three of them laughed it off. *We can't talk now.* Someone was waving and beckoning to the young woman and she broke away. Didymus and Vera had nothing to say to one another but were comfortable together at a distance each understood the other could not cross. It was, at least, their distance; like a place they had once been to, together. He had lied by means of an ambiguous sentence. What he had hidden by it was: I didn't know Jerry Gwangwa was your brother. But

I do know he was a plant, a South African police agent, nineteen years old, he was sent with a false record of being detained and escaping to make his way to Tanzania to present himself for military training with Umkhonto. He was to encourage dissatisfaction among the trainees, homesickness and drug-taking, and to inform other agents of the movements of military commanders, so that assassinations could be carried out. He was bloodied before he left home; he had killed two youth leaders in their beds and planted a car bomb that killed three others and took the legs of a fourth. He was interrogated by Maxi, code name for Didymus Maqoma. He survived, confessed, and having convinced the Americans he was a Freedom Fighter, was studying for a Ph.D. on a scholarship at one of their universities. Vera could not know what Didy's preoccupation was, in the eye of silence he and she occupied briefly in the late-night animation around them, but she acknowledged it instinctively. In a long life there are many different pockets of collusion that form with different people out of different circumstances and, although generally forgotten, occasionally jingle there a kind of coinage, a handful of tokens good for re-entry to a shared mood.

Ben was approaching with an arm round either girl, his daughter and her friend, forced by him into a dancing trot. —I'm telling these two, either we get everyone going with some hot music or it's time to send them all home.— But he looked deeply tired, the skin around his eyes so dark it seemed each had been struck by a fist, the lines from nose to mouth chiselled heavily, thickening what had been his beautiful lips into drooping coarseness. Once again at a party—as she had seen him as if with the gaze of another, at a party when first he had become lover turned husband—she saw him without the lens of her image of him. Annie, smiling under his arm, was the bearer of that face, now; on him, it was no longer there. Weariness revealed

him in spite of or because of the youthful energy he was summoning. —Come, let's show them.— In the mountains, with
muscles lightly trembling from the day's climb, the love-making,
fresh from the shower, they stood together at the invitation of
music. There was the same readying slight movement of his shoulders before he took Vera to dance. The others laughed and
applauded his expertise, egging him on. The warmth of his body,
private in his clothes, was the warmth of the bed they shared.
People were looking around for the hosts to say goodbye; she
broke away to go to them, trailing his hand for the first few
steps. Behind the straggle of Oupa, the Maqomas, Lazar, the
Richards and the United Nations envoy, Zeph Rapulana was
leaving. She had not had a chance to talk to him the whole
night. Sally was embracing her with her usual formula, en-
thusing —You know just how to do things, what a good time,
we must get together— and she saw Zeph Rapulana over Sally's
shoulder. His was a calm she could not reach. He was shaking
hands with everyone in his countryman's courtesy.

What is a party? For Vera tonight it is a mass of distraction
hiding everyone from themselves, a dose of drink and noise that
blocks what you don't want to think about.

We can't talk now.

•

That night there was another party. When Ben in pyjama
shorts (still had the figure for them) went down through the
garden to fetch the Sunday paper from its slot in the gate there
was the headline. A wine-tasting in a golf clubhouse had been
attacked with hand grenades and automatic rifle fire. Four rev-
ellers were killed, others injured. He went slowly back to the
house, reading the story, aware in peripheral vision of avoiding
a couple of plates and a beer glass with its dregs filled with

drowned insects, left on the grass by his guests. He sat on the bed, where Vera still lay, staring unseeing at his fine dark-haired legs as he listened to the radio report of reactions to the attack. Horrible, horrible, said a black bishop; cowardly murder of innocent people, commented a Government spokesman; savagery due to the Government losing control of blacks, according to the white right-wing. And the whole outcry merely because the victims were white, stated the Movement's rival organization, neither confirming nor denying responsibility for the attack.

—Dorp connoisseurs.— Ben ran fingers up and down through hair on his thigh.

—And they don't know how it came to happen, do they. Wine-tasting and a terrorist attack! Ben—it's as if something contrived exactly what would show how out of the incongruity in our lives comes the horror? That's just it! *Innocence*, they say. I don't know what that means, any more, if it means we don't know what's happening outside a golf course. If people can sit sipping and spitting some Cape vintage 'innocent' of the existence for others of guns and bombs. How far away from one another they were, for the clash of incongruity to be so awful.—

—Further than we were.—

If it was a question she didn't seem to hear. Across mown greens and raked bunkers, across veld farmland, the man's reassuring broad back is leading them, the farmhouse door slams shut. —If you were to put that clubhouse in some film, some agitprop film, everyone would say it was too contrived, too obvious, too symbolic. Wine and blood. But with us, it happens.—

Sometimes picking up a garment as if not recognizing it, they dressed. The radio recounted the attack. —Thank god that crowd has taken responsibility—if you don't deny you're confirming, aih? That won't give anybody the chance to dump blame on the Movement.— Ben worked his feet into worn moccasins. —Not a noble satisfaction, I know.—

—How would the Movement be thought to go in for that kind of tactic? With what purpose? It's not exactly an act to reassure whites and win their votes when the time comes.— Vera was making the bed.

—Exactly. That's why it would be useful to the government, if suspicion could be planted. But once responsibility's boasted elsewhere—with a nice racist ring to it—you heard what the APLA* man said: there's outrage only because the victims are white.—

—But that's true, you know it, Ben. Last week a whole family was gunned down in their sleep. But in a black township not a golf club. Four or five lines on an inside page. Even I only now remember reading it . . . And no statement from the ones who're outraged now.—

—You know what my partner would say if you told him that? 'What if you'd been in that clubhouse? Your wife?'—

—So we keep the pretence that's forced upon us by this killing among so many. That everyone deplores, condemns unequivocally etc.—

—Yes, yes! You can't support any part of the views of that man, can you—

At breakfast the young women appeared languidly tousled, their yawns rapidly silenced by the news. —Imagine, could you possibly imagine how terrified they must have been, for a moment thinking someone was playing a sick joke, and then the person beside you blown to bits . . . better to be killed at once than to know you might be next.— Annie drew in her lips and hunched

* Azanian People's Liberation Army.

her arms. —Think of us all last night.— The two women held hands resting on the table, Annie's the spatulate-fingered, much-scrubbed hands of a doctor, the friend's large and dirtied with nicotine on skin and nails. In a skimpy T-shirt and shorts Lou was seen to be very thin and muscular, the nipples of breasts like a preadolescent's nobby beneath the clinging shirt, a concave chest between round posts of shoulders. The linked hands were laid out before Ben and Vera; their eyes drawn to them as the talk went back and forth.

Annie was persistent. —D'you think it could have been us?—

—The bishop said it could have happened in the middle of his service.— Vera directed herself to the girl Lou; it was as if she had something to ask her other than what was being said. —I don't suppose the fact that we were blacks and whites would make much difference if the object is to create terror. Stop negotiations. But think of the international hullabaloo if the UN representative were to have been killed. Now that would have been something to wake up the outside world to this Government's failure to deal with violence.—

Lou gave an aghast laugh. Annie assumed responsibility, perhaps admiringly, for her mother. —You do take things coolly!— She cocked her head to touch Lou's, it was the foal's butting gesture with which as a child she would claim affection and comfort from Ben or Vera. —Well . . . will you excuse us? That rather nice Lazar's asked us to come for a walk on a farm, he's due to pick us up.—

Ben was wheeling through stations on the radio for one that might be giving further details of the attack. —Where'd they say they're off to?—

—Lazar's invited them somewhere.—

—Lazar? Oh.—
We can't talk now.

•

He's sitting in her office against the light; the still solidity
of him. She gets up from her desk to lower a blind and his
features emerge, watching, listening. What is it about that face?
The eyes—the eyes in repose always have that line of fellow-
feeling, a slight lifting crease of the lower lid; that's the only way
she can define it to herself. Where does it come from, that expression that is not a smile, that self-assurance that is not concealed
arrogance? There is nothing in her experience of other people
to explain this man. Whatever she tries does not fit. Yet she does
not need to enter his life with personal enquiries that would
become a burden to both, each having to take into account
circumstances with which, unlike the Odensville affair, she has
nothing to do.

   —You once said something. 'We won't harm you or your
wife, your family.'—

   —Yes. Yes.—

   —And then he came with his commando and people in the
squatter camp were killed.—

   —Yes. He did.—

   —Now what about this attack, the night we were all together
at my house. When we talked on the phone you said you were
shocked, it was a cruel and terrible thing—you said. Just as
everybody else, we all did. I know you mean what you say. I
said the same. But I don't trust myself.—

   Patient for understanding, he never was waiting to jump in
with his own opinions.

   —What reason have you not to trust yourself, Vera.—

—The same reason I have not to trust any of us.—

They smiled.

—We all pass deftly from hand to hand the assumption that it's human life that's sacred, it's an unblinking pact, we look each other in the eye and say, it's the killing of human beings we deplore, we don't have any other considerations, no matter who does it or why.—

—Isn't that so?—

—Isn't it the conventional wisdom of whites? And what's that to us? Blacks don't believe it. When I heard that APLA man on the radio saying there's outrage only because this time whites were killed, I agreed with him. He shocked people because they see him as racist, but what he said is more than fact, Zeph, it's true, it's right inside, deep in whites who own newspapers and the TV and radio stations. But we can't say it because we're not racist, we can't say it because we have to demonstrate we don't stereotype, we don't use racial categories in the worth of human life. Killings are killings. Death is death. Blood and wine mix. All we can produce is this cover-up.—

—People don't believe what they're saying.— Her proposition put before her.

—The people I know. And the people you know, blacks?—

—There are some who believe.—

—How can they! They know Odendaal wanted to kill them. What were their lives, to him.—

—This thing—what you call it, conventional wisdom, it's a kind of law, isn't it—what's right, what's wrong, that everyone really knows. If we find the people who speak it don't mean what they're saying, the law's empty, there's only one thing left.— He stopped, claiming his time. —We have to take the law into our own hands.—

Her mouth changed in bewilderment.

—Because *we* mean it: killing is killing, every life is one of ours. So we have to become a law unto ourselves.—

She was moved, and blurted with awkward flippancy —Well why not, there are many who have done so for other reasons.—

He had come to the city because there was to be a further meeting with a provincial official over application to have the land purchased from Odendaal declared a site-and-service settlement for the people known as the Odensville squatters. The Chief was expected to accompany Vera and Zeph Rapulana to Pretoria; apparently he had stayed over the weekend with friends not known to Rapulana, since their arrival in the city together. As Vera and Zeph walked into the Foundation's lobby, he entered with an attendant a few steps behind him. He was the son of the first of his father's wives, a young man who held his head tilted back so that he looked down with half-closed eyes at those who greeted him. The hand, when Vera shook it, was the coldly damp one of someone who has had a drinking night. Zeph Rapulana in all his mature dignity placed his palms together, bowed with knees stiff, and pronounced a formal greeting in the terms of traditional obeisance. Yet both knew the Chief would be saying to the official only what Rapulana had coached him to say, only what Rapulana and Mrs Stark of the Legal Foundation had decided upon. Rapulana had said as if to himself —His interests are elsewhere. He wanted to come to Johannesburg and learn to play in a band, but his late father wouldn't allow it . . . Perhaps he was wrong.—

Vera stood by, as an unbeliever before any ritual. Zeph was his own man with masters and slaves, yet he knew how to dissemble; but whether it was to the Chief or whether to show that he himself, his own man, was definitively a black man, her observation of him did not easily reveal. At the same time, she was beginning to have an inkling that her sense of connection with this man was that she had something to learn from him, as all unbelievers secretly hope to appropriate a value without adopting a faith.

•

Their daughter is back sleeping, breathing in the house as she did when she was a child.

Ben turns off the light above the bed where he and her mother lie.

—I still hope she'll fall in love one day.—

—She *is* in love.—

We can't talk now.

•

He didn't have a name any more. They spoke of him as the old man; he had had a second stroke and lost the power of speech. He was incontinent and Vera had the impression that the whole house smelled like the primates' cage at a zoo, although Thandeka's care was supplemented by a trained nurse brought in on night duty. Ben saw Vera's nostrils pinching and felt anxious for her—this was his father, after all. It was as if he himself were in danger of becoming repulsive to her. He suggested it would be best to put the old man in a private hospital where he'd be well cared for. It was Annick who objected. —He's quite adequately cared for here, there's nothing more to be done: it's a massive stroke.—

—So it doesn't make any difference where he is, Annie. And this house really isn't geared to hold nurses and all the paraphernalia—it's just distressing for everyone to no purpose.—

But Annick was a doctor, she did not need to remind her

father. She had taken over from him the necessary contact with the old man's doctor, since colleagues can be more open with one another, even if they may be mistaken in their perceptions, as the doctor was when he told Annie he did not want to cause pain to her father by telling him that this stroke was terminal and the sooner life ended the better. —It does make every difference. He may not be able to move or speak to you, but he's not unconscious. He knows where he is. He knows he's at home.—

—Hardly that. He had to give up his own place, as you know. He's been with us only a few months.—

Annick opened her clear-lipped mouth and touched the tip of her tongue to her teeth, his mannerism inherited along with his beauty; so often, in her presence, it seemed that nature was mocking him in his own image, a reluctant Narcissus. She spoke gently. —Home where you are, Dad.—

She came out to the stoep-study and hitched her hip onto the table where Vera was doing some weekend work for the Foundation. —Would it be better for you if Lou and I cut short our stay. Don't be worried about saying so.—

—My god Annie, no. It's better for us that you're here.—

—But we're occupying the second bathroom . . . —

—It doesn't matter. You know how to see that the nurse and Thandeka are doing what they ought to.—

—Lou would like to take over the cooking, you know. She's damn good, at our place she does it all, I don't have to boil an egg.—

—Is that a fair division of labour—you both work.— Vera did not lift her head from her papers.

Her daughter's gaze drifted relaxedly out of the window for a moment, where the sheen of a hadeda's back took on peacock colours as it dug its beak-probe into the grass. —What about you and Ben? I remember when we were kids, he did most of the fetching and carrying to school and so on.— She smiled, for admittance. —Hasn't he always indulged you—quite in awe of your career, you're his priority, and yours . . . well you've always been available to so many other people. Is there ever a really fair division of labour, as you call it, between couples?—

The sense of approaching some move that would change what they were, what they had been since Vera had wept with the joy of absolution when the girl child was born in the image of Bennet, grew between them, a supersonic hum only they could hear. Instinctively—the Foundation papers were under her hand—Vera took on the impersonal openness of her professional manner: Mrs Stark spoke.

—Ben can't believe you are a couple. He refuses to see it.—

—You mean, accept it?—

—But also to see. He doesn't interpret what he sees.—

Annie wriggled her way more comfortably onto the table, pushing papers aside. —What does he think he sees.—

—Well, when I told him you were sleeping in one bed, that it's your choice, he took it as a sign of some sort of immaturity. He said why not a teddy-bear.—

Annie laughed. Clients often laughed when they were about to defend themselves from some real or imagined accusation. —But you have gay friends, you and Dad, there were gays at the party. Some of your Foundation people.—

—Men. Not his daughter. He just can't believe it. He was matchmaking with Lazar, he saw that Lazar was attracted to you—you are beautiful you know, men could be mistaken into thinking . . . can't blame them—

Vera had emerged, looking fully at her daughter, and the girl was amazed to see her eyes trembling with tears. To help

her, Annie was casual. —Poor Lazar, my guess is he's a bee
that bumbles into any flower. Anyway, he didn't object to us
both going walking with him. I suppose he'd invite a girl to bring
her mother along if he thought that would help his pursuit.—

—Perhaps he saw, but he thought it worth taking a chance
that there could be a man who'd convert you to men. It's surely
natural, if you're a man.—

—Their arrogance.—

—Not really. Maybe there's a chance, always.—

—That's Ben, not you! That's what Ben really believes,
doesn't he? You know I've had men. I used to bring them home
to my room occasionally.—

Somewhere in the house lies an old man who has lost the
power: here, it's time to talk. Vera overcomes the urge to touch
her daughter, place a hand on her cheek, trace her features.
It's as if over thirty years she has missed the times to do so, she
has always been looking elsewhere, turned away, while the girl
grew and changed and moved into another self.

—That's why I don't understand. My darling, how can you
do without a man?—

A plea, a cry.

—Oh perfectly well, Ma! I can look after myself!—

—I don't mean that. Anyway, I don't think you do, you
have someone who looks after you, doesn't she? Husband, wife,
whatever she is. You've just said there's never a fair division of
labour.—

—All right. Granted. Of course *you* can't know of the other
dependencies, how that works between her and me, just as it
does between your kind of couple.—

Vera was hearing her out with the gathering silence of a
determination to speak, against reluctance to reveal oneself.
—I mean the love-making.—

—The love-making!— The amused, coaxing tone; her mother might have been an adolescent timidly seeking information.

—I have to tell you, Annie, I can't understand how you can prefer it without a man.— Vera got up and went to close the glass doors that led into the house. In privacy she turned passionately. —Without a man!—

—It's wonderful. Let me tell you. A woman is like you, she knows what you feel, what makes you feel, and so—she does—instinctively she does what you want, she's feeling what you're feeling, at the same time. It's not like that with a man, who wants his kind of stimulation while you want yours. Oh I suppose you've never made love with a woman, for all your independence—

—Never felt in the slightest attracted to one. Though you know, you've seen, I'm affectionate with a few women friends—

—But it's men you like. Always men— There was an edge of judgment, the twinge of an old injury in the smile. —I suppose you've had a few more lovers I don't know about. You've experienced nothing but men, men.—

—Yes. I love men. I mean exactly what I'm saying: how can there be love-making without the penis. I don't care what subtleties of feeling you achieve with all those caresses—and when you caress the other partner you're really caressing yourself, aren't you, because you're producing in her, you say, exactly what you yourself experience—after all that, you end up without that marvellous entry, that astonishing phenomenon of a man's body that transforms itself and that you can take in. You can't tell me there's anything like it! There's nothing like it, no closeness like it. The pleasure, the orgasms—yes, you may produce them just as well, you'll say, between two women. But with the penis inside you, it's not just the pleasure—it's the being no longer alone. You exchange the burdens of self. You're another creature.—

Annie was fascinated by and yet moved to retreat from her mother. —The beast with two backs.—

Vera looked at her with a flash of anguish. —Annie, what did I do to put you off men?—

—What makes you always think what I am is determined by you! It's against all your principles vis-à-vis other people, isn't it.—

It was not only the door that closed them off from the house and its familiars, their separate existences. They had moved into a territory that might never be re-entered, never found again. As voices that come out of the mouth of a medium, they spoke with the dreamy groping of the subconscious, silences aloud between them.

Coming into the kitchen—the woman with wet tendrils of hair fresh from the bath at One-Twenty-One taken to disguise the roused flush of love-making—startled, because she was so far out of mind, to see the schoolgirl at the table with a mug of cocoa, doing her homework: —Did I disgust you?—

—No no. I was sorry for you, I don't know why. I wanted to comfort you. Seeing you come home, fucked out. I thought you'd come to the age when you'd need peace instead of what you were doing. What age! At seventeen anyone over forty seemed old to me.— The sense of a conspiracy unacknowledged in the past; neither brought up the name of Ben. —Tell me. We disgust you—Lou and I.—

—Of course you don't.—

—No 'of course' about it. Tell me.—

—Not disgust—

—'So long as I'm happy', mnh?—what all the parents deprived of grandchildren swallow bravely and say.—

—No—I don't disapprove, I don't consider what you do is wrong. It's just the penis. I have to say it. I regret for you—no penis.—

Annie gave the smile that acknowledged: you mean well, and they both laughed. —What about Ivan? With the penis, and the grandchild, it still didn't work out.—

—Ah, it doesn't solve everything, I'll admit—

—But it's the essential.—

—For me, yes.—

—So you see— Someone was rattling at the glass door, the eager black face of Thandeka was distorted through it. Annie thrust in quickly, their eyes already on the door: —You really have the same view as Dad, for him that thing's also the essential, because *he has it*, he can't bear to think of any woman rejecting what's gained for him the treasure of his life, you, you— Thandeka burst out onto the stoep, her face the standard-bearer of the old man's presence back in the house, and the lifeline between Annie and Vera fell before alarm that some crisis in his state had occurred.

But it was only that Vera was wanted on the telephone. Thandeka, so close to the drama of death, seemed to transfer a disproportionate sense of events to everything, even a telephone call.

Sally Maqoma: she stuttered interruptions through Vera's expressions of pleasure at hearing from her again after many weeks and cut short the exchange of circling civilities by which friends excuse neglect of one another. She had something to speak to Vera about, it could not be discussed over the phone. Vera felt the valves of her heart exposed, her blood vessels lying open from the time and place with Annie from which she had just emerged. Sally's voice came as a disembodied assault loud in her ear. She recoiled, distrait. She explained that her father-in-law had had another stroke, nurses in the house, confusion —could whatever it was possibly wait a day or two?

•

Without a man.
Bereft.
To imagine that state.
Why, if Renoir could say he painted with his prick, has no woman ever had the guts to say I live by my vagina? Love affairs as a neat motif, a sprig recurring woven in the textile of her life—it's been nothing like that. She is the one who, she understands, sent her soldier husband a photograph ringed in revenge—that was it; she has never forgotten or forgiven him premature ejaculation. That's the fact of it. The only time he didn't end up by himself like an excited little boy was after they had parted for divorce. A lover only in name; a father who has never known he is one. Wasn't that the real reason for abandoning him, never mind all the others more acceptable she gave to all around her: his conservatism, his love of sport that she didn't share, the mistake, for which neither was to blame, of wartime marriages between people too young to commit themselves.

Wasn't that the real reason for the passion for Bennet; not his remarkable beauty nor his attraction as an artist, a creator in clay, but his ability discovered on the mountain holiday to sustain what the other had failed at, to stay within her and exchange the burden of self.

Make the beast with two backs.

The emblem under which her Hitler Baby remains with her is that of the first image that drew her attention to his flesh. As he sat in her office one of his gestures brushed against a wire letter basket and loosened a scab from a scratch; he ignored it while she was aware of a trickle of blood below his rolled-up sleeve tracing a hieroglyph down his forearm—a warm message to her.

Spending on silk shirts and gold weights while the schoolgirl is kept short of clothes and once from a school camp wrote a pleading note because she hadn't had money to buy toothpaste and was ashamed to keep using other girls'; she must understand her parents are not rich, she must not be indulged.

And then to come home fucked out.

The shower in One-Twenty-One, the dousing with perfume, the careful rearrangement of the hair (still so long, then, she could caress his breast with it)—nothing could disguise sexuality. A sign of life. Without knowing it, she had ringed herself just as she once ringed a photograph.

•

Mrs Stark at her desk was working on the Foundation's yearly report and clerks and colleagues came in and out with documents she requested or advice she sought. The tension between tenant-labourers and white farmers had come into prominence alongside that of the old squatter removals and their consequences. The Foundation had had successes in overturning eviction notices farmers served on tenant-labourers for fear these might make a claim to their share-crop holdings under a future majority government, but already in one case success ended in tragedy. Philemon Maseko—in this very office he had spoken through an interpreter—was shot dead by a group of white farmers a few days after his case was won. There were no arrests, no names of the farmers published; the Foundation was to prosecute on behalf of the man's family. Whether it was a general disturbance, with doubts about the apparent consequences of some of their work, that produced a distracted mood among

Foundation people, or whether this was something she projected from herself, it was present. Even Oupa seemed inattentive and distant. There was agreement among senior colleagues that they ought to publish some sort of 'crisis' paper in addition to the report, urging that a drastic revision of property and land laws was necessary to forestall disaster in the growing conflict between white and black over access to land. She worked at night, at home, on a draft. Annie's Lou shopped and did the cooking. Ben entertained his daughter become a guest, and her friend, taking them to the cinema or one of the so-called clubs where they could hear black groups play the kind of music they enjoyed. The night nurse creaked heavily up and down the passage to make herself tea.

No arsenal of repressive laws, no army, no police force can stabilize the situation—catch herself out in the jargon officialdom used to abstract and distract, draw the shroud of order over the body of Maseko with his bit of legal paper in his dead hand. *No laws, no army, no police force can protect white farmers from the need and right of people desperate to find a place to live.* She wrote and rewrote. Who will read what is happening on the farm Rietvlei, Mooiplaas, Soetfontein, Barendsdrif, at Odensville? The newspapers paraphrase a paragraph or two, even those who read the original will be those who do not know, have never seen Odensville or lived, neither as farmer nor tenant-labourer paid once a year when he harvests his crops, on the 'pretty farm', at the 'sweet fountain' or the river-crossing Barend claimed for himself. Who, understanding by 'land re-form' the loss of his weekend fishing retreat, you chaps won't be invited down any longer, will be interested to hear that without reform tenant-labourers are losing the mealies and millet they have worked the land for, every day, for generations? How far from one another. The commissions in session, the politicians promising, the Foundation challenging the law by means of its interstices and the great principles of justice beyond it: these stand somewhere between. Through the will to formulate the Foundation's understanding of the meaning of land, her own life was gathered in. She had no thought, no space in herself for anything else. When she stood up a moment to place her hands at the small of her back and arch it, face upturned to the ceiling, to ease tension, with the slight dizzy lurch there came the presence of Annick, Annie, about the house, although the girl might be out at that particular hour: the fact of her.

You've always been available to so many other people.

The seventeen-year-old schoolgirl alone in the kitchen over those textbooks she used to cover with fancy paper and stickers of film stars. She looks up from the conventional wisdom of adults she's been taught, parents love one another, that's the goal of sex children are taught, for parents their children come before everything and all others—her mother walks in warm from the body of another man. Fucked out. How can that schoolgirl be expected to know the family never was the way she's been told families are, to accept that her own father was 'another man', her mother's sexuality something that made a claim above the love of children?

There came to Vera, as what had been a long time waiting to be admitted: it was because of her that Ben's daughter was a lesbian.

•

During the night she went into the room where he was dying. The black nurse was dozing in a chair, her uniform ridden up her thick thighs. Her stockings were stretched so tight over the flesh that they shone, catching the light silvery from the shaded lamp.

She looked at her father-in-law. His hand lay palm up out-side the covers. She looked a long time. She knelt at the side of the bed and said close to his poor flabby ear, with prurient curiosity: What's it like?

He couldn't hear; or he heard only as an echo in an empty chamber. His head stirred, she thought—imagined?—as if he were somewhere shaking it. The side of his mouth twisted. It was the way a baby's did when it was too young to smile—could be mistaken for a smile.

The Egyptians took with them furniture, jewellery, food, wine and oil, and attendants who must finish their lives in the next world. Even his false teeth had been taken from him. His watch, his time run out, had been handed to Ben for safekeeping. His attendant, as usual for whites in this country, was a black woman, caring for the failing functions of the body without sham-ing him. This black face crumpled with weariness, a deep division of effort frowning between the eyes, as if in perpetual anxiety to catch the crammed minibus that brought her back and forth from Moletsane or Chiawelo or Zondi to be with him on the last threshold.

There was no one else.

When the nurse saw he had crossed she would replace her knitting in its plastic bag, pack up her cardigan and tube of lip salve, collect her pay and maybe a gift of oranges from a box bought thriftily in bulk by Lou, and leave.

Vera was sorting the clothes to give to charity, taking the opportunity of one of the public holidays renamed like the streets under successive regimes to reflect shifts in the ethos of power: Dingane's Day, his victors oddly conceding the force of the black warrior-king's name, changed to Day of the Covenant, commemorating his defeat by the Boers' hard bargain with God, and become for the present something presumed semantically less offensive to blacks sold out by God: Day of the Vow. It was the first time she had handled a dead person's clothes; life shed like a skin. Different garments marked the ambivalence of the species to which the old man could be ascribed. Why two dress suits and a white dinner jacket as well, whereas the shirts were so worn they were not worth giving away, and there seemed to be only three pairs of misshapen shoes. A silk dressing-gown with satin revers was folded in tissue paper in its presentation box, apparently never worn, and of a style (she shook it out) that suggested it must have been very costly, even in the Thirties in which it must have originated. The awareness of a survivor that one knows so little about the other and there will be no opportunity to know more, is usual; an accompaniment to death. Only speculation on the evidence of relics: one of the few known personae with which the old man could be identified was as an Englishman among expatriates of various roving nationalities in corporate outposts and Belgian colonial clubs in the Congo. There (Bennet had picked up only the barest outline of his own origin, with which to fascinate her in the mountains) the liaison with the half-Spanish half-Lebanese wife of a dealer in wild animal skins had led to his marriage to his mistress's daughter. The dressing-gown had no place in the category of charity clothing for refugees or drought victims. But Ben wouldn't wear it, it was hardly for him, either. She was just thinking that the one person she could imagine it on, to his pleasure, was young Oupa, she would take it to the Foundation and offer the gift in such a way that it would not be a hand-me-down—when the phone rang. There was Oupa's voice. —Telepathy! You were in my mind—

Agitation made him hoarse. —Mrs Stark, please come over. To the flat.—

A call from Oupa on a public holiday? If he had been in her mind putting a living form into the dressing-gown that, for some reason, the old man had never brought to life, his immediate self had been placed by her, far removed, in however a young man like him would be spending a day at leisure. What on earth—an accident, a mugging, police raid, eviction—all the ordinary hazards that surrounded his life—she thought instantly of what it would be necessary to bring: money and a demeanour to pull rank with the police.

—Mrs Maqoma says you should come.—

—Mrs Maqoma? But what is all this about? Why Mrs Maqoma?—

She heard he was being interrupted by voices in the background. His hand must have cupped the receiver and lifted again. —Please, Mrs Stark, come.—

—Oupa, who's crying there, tell me what's happening— But the call was cut off; she had the impression someone had taken the receiver from him and replaced it.

In the living-room Ben was listening to his favourite Shostakovich piano concerto while reading. She stood about a moment; under her own sense of alarm was the serenity he had regained for himself, alone with her, now that his father and daughter were no longer in the house. —There's just been such a peculiar call from Oupa.—

He looked up over his glasses. —On a holiday? What's he want.—

—God knows. He said Sally says I must come to the flat— (she corrected)—his flat. *Sally.*—

—What's Sally doing there?—

—How would I know?— All she did know was that she had forgotten her promise to call Sally back when she telephoned just before the old man died.

—D'you want me to go with you . . . what's that you've got— The glasses slipped, his strange deep eyes rested on the dressing-gown lying over her arm; the eyes belonging along with the garment to some unexplained aspect of the old man's being, perhaps even belonging together?—the mistress's gift to her lover, and the son her daughter had borne him—in the double liaison out of which Bennet emerged.

—No . . . no, I'd better do as they asked.—

Oupa belonged to her Foundation responsibilities, Ben had no obligation to get up from his chair, his books, his music. She lifted her arm: —Grandpops's finery.— Annick's childish name for the old man.

—When would he ever wear it.—

—Of course not. Someone must've given it to him. Long ago, it's old-fashioned luxury.—

The son put out his sallow hand, as he could do now that her house was theirs alone again, to touch hers as she left, spoke drily. —Some woman.—

Oupa must have been hanging about at the door waiting to open it to her. There he was. His curly-lashed eyes were lowered sulkily as if to ward off reproach and his tongue comforted dry lips before he spoke. —Sorry. It's her mother made me call you here.—

—And what is this all about?— But they were already entering the room where her voice invaded a silence so charged she might have been shouting. She had the sudden impulse of distaste—premonition—to turn and leave: what am I doing here? What were they all doing here? Sally sat upright, thrust forward on the single armchair; Didy stood with his back to the television set against images without sound; and on the floor, shockingly, face hidden on her knees and arms shielding her head, was the girl, Mpho. Now Vera, with Oupa a step behind her: all might have been thrust by a stage director—you here, you there. Each waited for someone to speak. Only Didy flicked a blink of greeting at Vera's presence.

Sally's face was that of a stranger confronting Vera, broad with hostility and accusation. —Ask your favourite, ask the man you introduced her to, the one she met in your house, the one you liked so much that we let her go around with him and his friends. Ask him.—

Didy dropped back his head and expelled a breath of distressed embarrassment. He made some sort of appeal to her in her own language.

—No, let Vera ask him!—

—I don't know why you have to drag Vera into it.—

—Well if there's trouble . . . among friends . . . we're all in it.— Vera lied against the impulse to back out.

—You knew he was married, you know she's a child, why did you let us believe he and his crowd would be nice company for her, safe? Why didn't you warn us—

Vera turned from Sally's assault to Oupa, uncertain whether to defend or accuse. —What's happened with you and the girl?—

—He's been sleeping with my child, my daughter. I take her to a doctor and I find she's pregnant. That's what's happened. That's the result of the nice people you introduced her to! Not a word from you, Vera, not a word of warning, you must have known she was running around with him—

—I? I knew nothing, I had no idea. I don't have anything to do with the private lives of the people at the Foundation—

—Oh yes you do. You had him in your house. You said nothing to me when she went to parties and they were not parties, he was bringing her back to this place to sleep with her! You had him and the other nice friends in your house, you and Ben.—

The girl began to wail, twisting her feet one upon the other. Everybody looked at her, nobody touched her.

Vera did not turn to Oupa, who slunk out to fetch a kitchen chair for her, a gesture Sally read with a despising glance as a call upon his employer-friend's support.

And did the companionable lunches in her office count for nothing? The years of deprivation on Robben Island, did they not make understandable a weakness for the pleasures of affection and love-making, the temptation of an enticing girl? But a schoolgirl. Sally and Didy's daughter.

He placed the chair. —Oupa, you idiot.— The moment the aside came from her she realized it would be taken by Sally as a dismissing insult to her. And to say to him, is this true, would be worse: doubting Sally. She looked at the bowed head of Mpho, the dreadlocks falling either side of her pretty ears dangling ear-rings large as they were. Likely that this girl had made love with others, as well, and Oupa was the one named as culpable, unable to prove he wasn't. This lovely child—she saw now what should have been evident while the girl lived in her house—had all the instincts of her sex Annick never had had. She wanted to put out a hand and stroke her head, but there was in Sally a forbidding authority against anyone making such a move.

Vera addressed Didy as if he stood once again in the persona she had not recognized at her door. —How was I to know? Do you think I wouldn't have done something, I would have spoken to him . . . —

Sally wrested the attention away. —But you should have told us your nice young man was married, his wife wasn't here, he was running around like any man . . . and look at him, ten years older than a schoolgirl, and no respect for her or her parents. Parties! She lied to us. When a girl-friend came to call for her, it was him! That pig. He sent a girl so we wouldn't know he was waiting in this place.—

Vera knew it was pointless to question Oupa but could not ignore that this was expected of her. Their gaze met apart from the others, he was cornered by her, counting upon her. —How

did you let it begin.— He understood this signalled *You knew
I trusted you, there are plenty of other women for you.*

—It was nothing, quite okay, we all went to Kippies together
to hear the music, poetry readings, and that. And then one time
she said she wanted to see a play, she used to go to plays in
London and—I even asked you, you remember . . . what was a
good one . . . and she said her parents mustn't know she would
go out alone, she was only allowed if there were other girls, she'd
tell them she was going to a party. So after that, we saw each
other.—

—And the wife?— Sally rang out. —The wife and children,
and now he makes my child, under age—does he know that?—
a criminal offence—he gets my child pregnant? He'll go to jail,
does he know that!—

—Your child is not under age, don't talk like that Sibo.
Sixteen is not under age. She's an adult by law. And what's the
use of threatening? You want him to divorce his wife? You want
Mpho to get married at sixteen, not yet passed her A levels? Is
that how we want to see her end up before her life's begun. Is
that what you want? Of course you don't. Then what's the use
of all this, blaming this one, blaming that.—

—We should never have brought her from London. She
should have been left at school there. You wanted her home;
'home' here, to get pregnant at school like every girl from a
location.—

—All right. You also wanted her here. Blaming again, blaming doesn't help.—

—That's how you can count on these people.— Sally spoke
of Vera as if Vera were not summoned by her to be present.
—Same as it always was, eager to help so's to be on the right
side with us. And making a mess of it. Bringing us harm.—

—Sibongile, stop it! You're talking nonsense, you don't

know what you're saying. It's my fault, it's Vera's fault—what's the use, what we need is to talk about what we're going to do, have you forgotten about Mpho, she's sitting there on the floor, she's our daughter—

—*I* don't know what we're going to do about her. I only know she's got herself into a mess.—

—What we're going to do has nothing to do with this young man. We shouldn't be in this place of his at all. He's out of it now, the whole matter. What happened between Mpho and him is finished. That's all he needs to know. Finished and *klaar*. This child will not be born. Over and done with. Vera will help us—

How could they all keep the girl grovelling before them on the floor—her mother, her father, Oupa, herself? Vera, shamed, spoke roughly. —Mpho, get up, come on, you're not alone—

Usually so quick and graceful, the girl lumbered to her feet, her tear-bloated face had the withdrawn expressionlessness Vera was familiar with in accused brought before court without hope of being found not guilty. Still the wrong thing: making her stand there. Perhaps she was in love with Oupa; but she knew, young and inexperienced in the judgments of the world as she was, that this was no plea.

—You mean Mpho should have an abortion.—

Didymus was used to doing what had to be done. —Yes. And we're new here, now. It must be without danger to her. You're the one who'll be able to make sure of that for us, we know.—

Sentence passed. The girl went over to the arm of the chair where her mother was sitting and picked up a duffle bag decorated with the iconographic names of pop groups. She ignored her mother and took out a handkerchief, blew her nose.
FUNK DOGS HIPHOP ROCK ELECTRIC PETALS INSTANT KARMA

An intense discomfiture filled the room as if the temperature were rising. The girl was disposed of like a body. She *was* a body, in the solution that had been found; nothing else. The other aspects of the situation that had brought them together had been withdrawn—emotions, motives and responsibilities nobody knew how to deal with. Didymus gathered his wife and daughter; the girl walked out before him without glancing at anyone except—a moment—up at Oupa; Vera saw the movement of the head, from behind, and could not tell whether the look was in compact or defiance; but she saw no responding change in Oupa's face. Didymus gave a nod to Vera: —We'll call.— Oupa was imploring her with his eyes and his stranded stance not to leave with the Maqomas. In sudden distress Vera wanted to waylay them —Don't treat her as if she's a criminal, put your arms round her, hug her, she's your daughter— but the girl, walking alone before her parents, was gone down the corridor. Vera slowed to keep to the hesitant pace of Oupa accompanying her, urgent to speak. —I wasn't the first one she'd been with.—

—Oh what does that matter. Why tell me. It's not the point.— Vera was impatient with him for burdening her with the confusion of excuses, if they could be accepted as such, she had thought of already.

—Not to you. But it would matter to her parents. I didn't want to make more trouble for Mpho, if I'd told them.—

They walked a few steps. —So you love her. You think you were in love with her.—

—I don't know. How can I be in love, I've got a wife.— He closed away from the intrusion.

—You mean you don't think you have the right to.— She smiled. —That doesn't prevent it coming about, you know.—

—When I say I don't know . . . she's such a kid, the time

when I might have a girl-friend like that, I was inside, those young years. But also she's seen, she knows, so many things I never have—London and Europe and so on . . . sometimes she even laughs at me, the things I don't know about. In one way she's too young, and in another way she's ahead of me. So I don't suppose we could ever get it right.—

·

As she drove home she realized she had not once, while there in the flat, been aware that this was One-Twenty-One. Otto's One-Twenty-One. With that unawareness, everything that place had been to her and her lover slipped out of grasp; no retracing of walls and footsteps along a corridor would bring it back, once let go, overlaid, it was disappeared for ever. No part of her was occupied by it.

That flat was now the scene where she, whose daughter would never have a child, was appointed to arrange to abort the child of someone else's daughter. The procuress. On the day when the Maqomas were to come and talk to her about arrangements, Didymus, once again, stood alone at the door. —Sally doesn't want anything to do with this.— He revised what Sibongile had said: Just get rid of it.

—She's still angry with me?—

—She has the idea you ought to sack the man.—

—How could she possibly expect that! Even if I had the power to, which I don't.—

—Of course. It's just that she's in such a state. I can tell you. It's not easy. After all, Mpho is our only daughter, we'd given up hope of having a girl and then she came along . . . Sally brought her up on her own, you know I was away most of the time. And Mpho just shuts herself off, she won't speak to her mother, she won't even speak to me, though I don't reproach her, I'm prepared to forget about the whole business once it's been dealt with.—

Didymus looked so different, so—battle-weary, in comparison with the man in great danger who had smiled and said, *Vera how mean of you*; so isolated, in contrast to the man who lived in the solitude of disguise. She had the instinct to offer some sort of exchange of unexpected situations, as people who feel attachment for one another do; something private out of her own life. —You know Didy, Annie has become a lesbian.—

He glanced away, clucked his tongue bewilderedly. After a moment, an African exclamation: —Yoh-yoh! What makes you think that?—

—I didn't have to think; she's told me. That woman with her you met at the party, she's the other half of the couple.—

—I don't know what to say—I'm sorry? Does it worry you? D'you mind?—

—I think I do, but not morally; from my own point of view, you know, because I'm a woman.—

—I've never thought much about it—among our people, about men of that kind, I mean. They're around. Of course, it'll be part of our constitution that there'll be no discrimination against any sex . . . but that doesn't cover about your own child becoming—d'you have any idea what made her?—

—At present just . . . I suppose we believe we're responsible for what we think has gone wrong with our children and in their judgment hasn't gone wrong at all.—

—Sally and me, with Mpho.—

—Maybe. The villain of that whole business said something to me about Mpho and him. He supposed they couldn't 'ever get it right' (he meant even if he wasn't married with kids), they've both been displaced, their relative ages don't tally naturally with their actual experiences, there's a dislocation that couldn't be corrected. He missed out her teenage stage, in jail; she has a worldly sophistication beyond her years, because of European exile.—

—And our generation created both circumstances . . . well, it could be. Man, I don't know. But they wouldn't apply to Annie?—

—No.—

He saw that this was the limit of her confidences, for the time being; his old Underground experience in being alert to moods when people reveal themselves remained sensitive to the dropping and raising of barriers.

They discussed, as if the itinerary for a journey or the agenda for a meeting, the doctor Vera had managed to persuade —playing on his left-wing sympathies and lack of open activity in liberation politics—to salve his conscience, do his bit by removing an embryo from the daughter of an eminent couple who had suffered for the cause much disruption in their lives. A date and place were set.

Vera walked with Didymus, once again, to his car, this time there openly outside the gate. She hesitated at the window after he was seated. —Ben refuses to believe it—about Annie. He pretends not to know.—

The radio alarm clock Mpho had not been able to resist, duty-free, as she left London airport, woke her with its Japanese version of Greensleeves at the hour she had set. She lay with her fists at her mouth, feeling on them the soft double stream of breath from her nostrils. To awake in the very early morning when everyone else is unconscious is to be alone in the world.

She got up and went to the window, carefully pulled the curtain. All was blurred with mist and, set back on a hill, only the glass façade of a towering building glistened out of it, mirror to the still hidden sun. She took off the Mickey Mouse T-shirt she slept in, her breasts dragged up and bouncing back; threw the shirt on the bed and then picked it up again, rolled it and put it in her duffle bag. Naked, she packed some other clothes and a goggle-eyed toy cat. She went to the window to see one more time the radiant face witnessing her. As she pulled in her stomach muscles to zip up her jeans a sense of fear and wonder and disbelief at what was there, inside, held her dead still. A lump of panic was suppressed with a swallow of saliva. She put herself together as she always was: frilled elasticized band circling her dreadlocks like an open blue rose on the crown of her head, another T-shirt with some other legend or logo on it, bright socks rolled round the ankles, black sneakers, the crook'd wires of one of her collection of ear-rings hooked through the soft brown tips of her ear-lobes. Mpho. That's Mpho. The mirror on her dressing-table caught her as the sun did the face of the building; there she is, nothing's changed. In her trembling sullen unhappiness, something overturned: she felt gaily released for a moment; nothing had ever happened, she had just got off the plane from London to meet the admiring glances of this country called home.

Nobody heard, nobody saw her close the front door behind her. In this white part of the suburban city only joggers were about, hamsters working their daily treadmill. She took an empty bus to a city terminal where blacks arrive from the townships to go to work. Street children lay in doorways as drifts of cartons, paper and banana skins lay in gutters. Women were setting out rows of boiled mealies, the venders of watches, sunglasses, vaseline, baseball caps, baby clothes, were unpacking their stock. A shebeen on a packing-case displayed litre bottles of beer and half-jacks of brandy, and before this altar a man still crazed from the drinking of the night danced round her to *mbaqanga* music coming from the stall-holder's cassette player. The freshness of the morning brought the smell of urine as dew intensifies the scent of grass. She passed through it all with an untouchable insolent authority beauty creates, going against the stream of workers, agile among the combis cornering, stopping and starting racing-circuit-style, smiling in response to remarks made to her in the language no one who made them would believe she didn't understand.

·

There is dread at the sight of an empty bed.
Gone.
Gone, it says.
Where?
The contractions of fear; people kill themselves if they have been made to feel ashamed of their lives. From that comes the extreme of fear: what should have been done to avert the sight of the bed, there, empty. What has been done to bring it about. Sibongile knows—he doesn't have to say it, doesn't have to conceal—Didymus thinks she has been too harsh and judgmental towards the girl.

An appallingly reasonable conviction strikes her; of course. —She's gone to that man.—

He bunched his mouth. —Unlikely. He'd be scared. I think he's a weak character. Never mind his record as a comrade. I don't think he'd take her in, now.—

Sibongile rummaged again for some clue—no note, of course, if the idea is to punish your parents you certainly don't leave a note. Didymus followed her into the room, a place mute and accusatory. The odour of Mpho was there, the mingle of perfume and deodorants and skin-warmed clothing, sweaty sneakers, the mint-flavoured gum she liked. She could have run away to people they didn't know she knew, people picked up at those places young people frequent, Kippies, discos. Now something really terrible could be happening to her, rape, drugs.

They stood about in her absence.

—Why do you think she's done this?—

—Scared. She's scared of what's going to happen to her. The operation.—

—For heaven's sake. It's hardly an operation. I've told her, she'll be asleep, she won't feel anything. I even told her *I've* had it, so I know.—

A change in his face. —Why d'you do that.—

But Sibongile—Sally—belonged to the generation and the experience that saw emancipation in burdening their half-adult children with the intimate life of their parents. —Why not? So she wouldn't be scared.—

—But if you put yourself in the same boat—why should she feel there's anything wrong with her adventure with the man, why that whole business in the flat, her having to hide her face from us . . . you get pregnant, you have an abortion, doesn't matter, it's nothing to worry about.—

—Oh you make me mad. Isn't what's happened enough without you . . . d'you think she shouldn't be allowed to know what our life was like sometimes in exile, how hard up we were, couldn't even keep the boys with us, how could we have another child those days in East Germany! You always want to protect her from everything, and then look what she brings on herself . . . As if what I *had* to go through has anything to do with her playing around with someone else's man and getting herself pregnant!—

He spread and then dropped his hands: not prepared to argue. —I'm going to his flat to see if he knows where she is.—

Sibongile was due to take part in a press conference—it would be that very morning the child chose to run away, God knows where. She was dressed for public exposure. In her distraction and anxiety she had put on as a general does his uniform her tailored skirt and jacket, her accoutrements of small gold

ear-rings (nothing showy), her carved wooden bracelets—as roy-
alty is expected to wear garments and jewellery designed and
made in their own country, a walking billboard for home prod-
ucts, she always saw to it that she included on her person some
example of African craft. It's understood—and she exacted this
from her co-workers—that personal obligations must be sub-
ordinate to the cause, always had been in exile and clandestinity
and were no less now, round conference and negotiation tables.
Public exposure may be an armour within which trembling flesh
is hidden. Photo opportunities (that's what the press asks for)
are the victim's obligation to wear a persona separated by duty
from self.

It simply was not possible, for Sibongile; not possible, if she
was what she had taken responsibility to be in the Movement,
for her to telephone and leave a message that her chair would
be vacant—because? Because a foolish child had got herself into
a mess and punished her mother by leaving a deserted bed. When
she was ill and alone, in London, with a baby to care for, could
she expect to call her husband back from wherever they might
have sent him, another country, another continent?

She stood there, looking at Didymus, unable to leave. All
the partings and reappearances, the arrivals and departures,
the climates and languages, the queueing for rubber-stamped
entry and exit were present between them, as a wind gathers up
a spiral of papers in dust.

He released her. —Go on. I'll call. I'll leave a message for
someone to slip to you.—

•

The lift did not move; he stabbed at each button in turn.
A beer can rolled into one corner had dribbled its dregs and
caked dirt on the floor. He climbed stairs and walked corridors

to number One-Twenty-One, passing napkins, T-shirts and underpants hung to dry over the burglar bars of kitchen windows, doors with their sections of stippled glass replaced by cardboard, bags of trash in doorways, a bicycle frame without wheels he had to step round: our people moving into the shell of middle-class life without the means or habits that give it any advantage. So they inhabit it and destroy the very thing they believe they wanted. It becomes the ghetto we think we've escaped. Only it costs much, much more. The white landlord cuts the water supply because ten people in a two-roomed flat, multiplied by ten storeys, strain the sewage system beyond the capacity it was installed for; the rent falls into arrears and the electricity supply is disconnected. This building with its mirrored foyer and panelled lifts hasn't got there yet but it's on the way, it's on the way. Isn't this what our 'education for democracy' is all about, after you've learnt to make your cross on a bit of paper, after you've learnt not to allow yourself to be bribed or intimidated to vote for someone you don't trust to govern your life: it's about not occupying the past, not moving into it, but remaking our habitation, our country, to let us live within the needs of space and decency our country can afford. And that's what the whites have to learn, too. Luxury's a debt they can't pay. A good thing he wasn't called upon to make speeches any more; something more easily recognizable as rousing than this would be required.

Unlikely the bell worked. He struck the stippled glass with his knuckles and waited; if the answer were to be a long time in coming, he supposed she was there; he felt a curve of sorrow wash over him, as if he had come to fetch his little girl from some misdemeanour at that English school she had attended paid for by white fellow-travellers, and was about to meet her humiliation. Bloody fucking bastard: suddenly he joined Sibongile in anger against Vera's nice young man. But a watery dark

outline had appeared on the other side of the glass door; it
opened and he was there, barefoot, in running shorts, a thick
slice of bread with a bite out of it, in one hand; at once showing
in his face that he felt foolish caught like that.

Didymus spoke Zulu—it was Sibongile's, not his own language and he didn't know what this man's was, but every black
in Johannesburg at least understands Zulu, he needed a lingua
franca other than English for this occasion. Was the girl
there?

No.

He was not asked to enter but saw at once that it was
unnecessary.

You know her friends, your friends. Do you know where
she might be.

Uncomprehending: She's not at her home?

She's disappeared since last night. You know some friends
. . . where she would go?

The young man slid a glance at the piece of bread he could
not drop, came back with an open face, upper lip faltering before
he spoke confidently, no doubt at all: Her grandmother. There
in Alex.

•

Mpho.

That's Mpho.

Their girl was ironing on the kitchen table in the Alexandra
house where her father had come to live as an infant when his
parents left the Transkei. So many countries, cities, rooms, hide-
outs, personae—and now his daughter was ironing sheets on
that same table in that same kitchen, a doek tied over her fancy
hair-style. She said as if they were unwelcome neighbours
dropped in, Hullo.

The old lady was peeling potatoes into a basin on her spread lap.

They spoke in their family language, Xhosa. —Why should I phone you? She often comes, doesn't she? I thought you knew—every time. Why must I phone?—

—But Mama, didn't Mpho tell you?—

—What should she tell me, my son. You say.—

Sibongile's elegance, the hound's-tooth tweed suit and knotted silk scarf, high-heeled patent shoes and sheen of matching navy blue stockings emphasizing her stance before all that was familiar to him and his mother within the four walls; the old grey-painted dresser with its display of enamel plates, mugs on hooks, three-legged alarm clock ticking, the refrigerator with wadded newspaper under one lame leg, the enormous scoured aluminium pots on the stove, his childhood reassurance against hunger through many lean times, the calendars illustrated with pink blondes and fluffy puppies, the framed Last Supper and blurred certificates of children's prowess, long ago, at bible class, Didymus Maqoma's matric certificate—these powerful inanimates stood back from Sibongile's presence.

—I think Mama knows what her granddaughter told her. We don't have to go over it.— Sibongile spoke a mixture of her own Zulu with what she knew of Xhosa, not to be seen wanting in respect. But English was the medium for Mpho, English was the reminder to her that there was no running away from what she was, what circumstance made of her, a girl who had to have lessons in order to claim a mother tongue. Once home, the new world had to be made of exile and home, both accepted. In the vocabulary Sibongile herself had absorbed unconsciously through the circumstance of exile in London she found this next escapade—Alexandra—what the English called *tiresome*—yes, plain tiresome, mixed with a concealed hysterical relief that the girl was alive and safe. —Mpho, why did you have to go off in the middle of the night or whenever it was, not leave a note or anything. Nobody would have stopped you if you'd said you wanted to spend the next few days with *gogo*. It was just silly, darling.—

At the end of 'the next few days' was the appointment with the doctor Vera had found.

Ah, so it was still silence: the girl didn't look up, was expertly folding the sheet in four, testing the iron with the hiss of a finger first moistened by her tongue, and then running the iron over the neat oblong. But the old lady was ready to speak. —Our people don't do this thing. Our children are a blessing. We are not white people. Didymus is my son. Mpho is my child. This child will be my child. I will look after the child here, in my house. I have told Mpho.— She stood up, put aside the basin of potatoes.

Didymus rose, too, from the plastic chair whose screws on metal tube legs he had been turning in patient forbearance. He went over to Mpho and put his hand gently on her nape, the gesture of love familiar to both his women, wife and daughter. —One day Mpho will have children she'll care for herself. That's the way it's going to be for her. But it can't be now. Thank you, Mama, Sibongile and I, we thank you for looking after her so well; we'll come back to fetch her at the weekend.—

Careful that the movement should not be interpreted by him as a rejection of his hand on her neck, Mpho slowly looked up, untied the doek from her head, laid it on the table, and turned, ready, to her father.

A lawyer and a clerical assistant, both of the Legal Foundation, were attacked this week while on an investigative tour of State-owned land the Government proposes to sell off to private ownership in advance of the installation of an interim government. The Foundation has criticized the Government's intention to 'offer this land to speculators and developers when a future government expects to use it to solve the enormous land and housing crisis existing in the country'.

What play of inference and preconception, this way or that, comes between the news item on an inside page and what has happened as an interruption of or, maybe, the culmination of certain directions. In the context of newspaper headlines, the nightly sheet-lightning of violence, psychedelic entertainment darkening and flaring on the television screen, this must be an attack by black hatred on a white foolish enough to think she had any reason to be in areas whites themselves had declared fit only for blacks; or it could be an attack by white hatred of white collaborators with blacks' intention to seize land—the land!—for themselves. Either way, serve the victims right.

And the third possibility. Created as climate creates con-

ditions, accepted like the lack of rain—the couple could have
been robbed because they didn't lock the doors, they didn't keep
the gun handy, they should have had the sense to stay at home.
Stay out of it.

Mrs Vera Stark sustained a bullet wound in the leg and Mr
Oupa Sejake was wounded in the chest.

What were they doing on a road far from the site of any
State land on their itinerary? To know that would be to have to
enter their lives, both where they touched and widely diverged,
to be aware of what they knew about each other and what they
did not know; where they had expectations, obligations operating
covertly one upon the other. To know at least that much.

Vera could not know whether, by acting as procuress of an
abortion for Oupa's girl, she was someone to whom he felt he
owed gratitude or resentment. The old woman said—Didymus
had told her—We are not white people. Didymus dismissed this
smiling, in passing. But maybe Oupa would have liked to have
a child, somewhere, souvenir of the beautiful girl who was not
for him, out of his class, speaking and moving in the manner of
cities he had never seen, yet at the same time a black girl, sharing
the precious familiarity, the dangerous condition of being black,
for which he had dredged seaweed and broken rocks on a prison
island. Oupa didn't have his wife and children with him in One-
Twenty-One; what difference if there were to have been another
child, likeness of hours of love-making and virility, to be visited
with gifts at the home of some grandmother?

He didn't bring his plastic container of pap and curried
chicken-leg to keep company in Mrs Stark's office. He didn't
discuss problems of his legal studies with her. He was in and out
with papers and messages and talk on Foundation matters continued between them as usual, but there were no lively asides
from him, he kept his eyes on papers or unfocussed, to concen-

trate on what was being discussed; only occasionally, from the door, as if he had forgotten something, in what was barely a pause: his smile.

This—to her—self-punishing attitude became more and more unnecessary; she found herself increasingly impatient with the idea that he should have to feel exaggeratedly contrite, to the extent that this was carried over to his demeanour at work. If he thought it was expected of him *by her*, she didn't know how to convey to him that this certainly was not so. The image of Mpho, brought to mind by his behaviour, changed outline, developed, on reflection. That charmer was fully aware of, became completely in control of her attraction; quite as much capable of seduction as a man; this young man. There was never any suggestion that she'd been raped, or even found herself innocently in a situation where submission to unwelcome desire was difficult to repulse. Sly little miss lied to her parents, made friends collude with and cover up for her when she went to make love in that flat; the love-nest of two generations.

On the three-day drive around the country the atmosphere between Mrs Stark and Oupa was easier but still was created only by exchanges of reaction to what they saw and to whom they talked in relation to their task. They spent a night in a Holiday Inn where Oupa swam in the pool and she, drinking a beer on the terrace, saw no objection, from the party of white farmers at the next table, to his presence among their splashing, shrieking children. Even at the dorp hotel they slept in the second night, a place where the proprietor and his wife slumped before the television set in the bar lounge while a receptionist-cum-barman took the guests' particulars, their arrival was accepted with listless resignation. The dorp was dying; local farmers who used to fill the bar had abandoned their farms and moved to town during the years when they feared for their security from

groups of black guerrillas infiltrating from over the border; those
farmers who had formed commandos and stayed, then, were now
trying to sell their farms before blacks reclaimed land under a
majority government. But in the meantime without the patronage
of black drinkers in the public bar the hotel would be abandoned,
too. From his armchair the proprietor called out in Afrikaans
—Show *mevrou* and *meneer* to their rooms, Klaus, show where
the bathroom is.—

They laughed together over this as they had not laughed
since Oupa summoned her to the flat. The factotum dragged
back and forth serving a dinner of mutton, mealie rice and
pumpkin they ate with satisfaction, as people retain a taste for
the dishes of their country others would find dull and unappe-
tizing. In his high-collared white jacket moulded in sweat-dried
contours like a plaster cast containing his body, listing on shoes
cut out on the uppers to ease bunions, the old black man brought
Oupa's third can of beer.

—Didn't your *baas* see me when he told you to show the
meneer his room, Baba?—

In the black face darker-streaked with age the mouth gaped
on a thick pink tongue. He looked slyly, comically round the
empty dining-room before answering in his language. Oupa,
clasping the old man's arm, laughed as he translated for her:
The white man doesn't want to see nothing. Nothing any more.
Nothing nothing.

In the quiet of an early-morning start in another part of
the country, an empty road, hornbills taking off from cowpats
they were pecking at as the Foundation station-wagon approached, Oupa spoke as if to himself —This's only about fifty
kilometres from my uncle's place. Where my wife stays with the
kids. The turn's just over there at the trees.—

She was watching the approach of the stand of eucalyptus;

they neared; she could see long swathes of swaddling bark peeling from their white trunks.

—Let's take it.—

He turned his head to her. —We go there?—

—Yes.— Mrs Stark authorizing transgression of one of the strictly honoured rules of the Foundation: the Foundation's vehicles are not to be used for private purposes. And Vera added—Why not. It makes no sense for you to be so close, and drive on.—

So that day when they should have been heading for the city and the office she offered him a joy-ride; not in the usual sense, of aimless pleasure, but the joy of restoration, union, in some—tentative—compensation for the sundering that outcast him, in his sense of self, in what she knew of him in the city.

He asked no questions. That he didn't was in itself a dissolve of constraint and a return to the old simple confidence between them. He opened his window to let the morning air gush in wide, he slotted a Ladysmith Black Mambazo cassette into the player, he drove faster; it was as if he had downed a couple of the beers he enjoyed so much. —You give me the green light, okay. I'm going to stop at a store. Get some sweets and things.— As they neared the settlement there were roadside venders selling mounds of sweet potatoes and onions and an Indian store into whose dimness he disappeared in skipping strides. He came out with chips and Jelly Babies, clear plastic guns filled with candy pills for the children, and packets of tea and sugar, the gifts poor people offer adults the way rich visitors offer flowers.

If there had been somewhere for her to wait for him while he made his visit she would have suggested that he leave her there so that she would not intrude. She hung back as two small children threw aside the cardboard box in which one sat while the other pulled it through the dust, and leapt to fling themselves

at him. The younger had him by the leg, the elder hung from
his neck. Hampered with joy, he staggered through the gap of
a fence that had been shored up with strands of barbed wire
and off-cuts of tin roofing, and approached the small, sagging
mud-brick house, as much part of the features of the country
as anthills in the veld. One of the children broke loose and ran
inside shouting. There was some exchange; a woman came out,
a plump young face screwed up, hand shielding her gaze. She
greeted—her man? her husband?—respectfully, distantly, in the
manner of one expecting an explanation. In their language, he
introduced Vera. Shaking hands, brought close to her: the tender
roundness of the neck with the gleam of sweat-necklaces in its
three circling lines.

These shelters provided for by men absent in cities fill up
with women; in the all-purpose room were several and a baby
or two, flies, heat coming from a polished coal stove. The sweetish
smell of something boiling—offal?—was swallowed with tea flur-
riedly made for the white visitor; the children brought her their
school exercise books. Perhaps they thought she was some kind
of teacher or inspector. In her familiarity, through her work,
with homes like this one, scatterings of habitation outcropped
along with the trash-pits of white towns, she was accustomed to
being regarded as someone to whom it was an opportunity to
address a demand, attention. She and the children chattered
and laughed although they had no common language, while she
admired their drawings and painstaking calligraphy. Time
passed—some idea the visitors were to wait for the eldest child
to come home from school. But he did not appear, and his father
was not surprised or perturbed. —It's far. And they play on
the road, you know how kids are. Sometimes I myself, I used to
be the whole afternoon, coming home, forgetting to come . . .—
From the cajoling, laughing tone of his voice he was telling

the mother not to be angry with the child, but she jerked her head in rejection. Such movements of self-assertion surfaced from the withdrawn placidity with which she kept her place. Sitting at the kitchen table, she might be any of the other women murmuring there. Her man from the city talked and she responded only to questions, now and then giggled when others did, and covered her mouth with her hand. The sun shifted its angle through the window barred with strips of tin; he decided, turning to his fellow visitor —Time to get going, hei— And while the farewells were being made to all the women, the children hung again about him. Their heads caressed under his hands storing up the shapes, he asked—undercover—whether his employer could help him out? —The loan of twenty rands or so.—

Only then did he and his wife have a few minutes alone together; he put his palm on her waist to guide her to the only other room of the house, where through the door, in a mirror, a crocheted bedspread was reflected. The door was not closed behind them but their voices were so low they could not be heard in the kitchen. Whether they embraced, whether they said to one another what could not be said in the company in which the visit had passed, no one could know. They were soon back. He hugged his children, he joked again with the women: a man, a lover, a husband, a father. His wife stood aside—displaced by an arrival without a letter, without warning in the life she held together by herself; in her stance, the way her full neck rose, she alone, of all the other women, in possession of him; lonely. That was how Vera saw her and did not know she would never forget her.

Driving away. To say he was so happy: how to explain what this was. He might have expected to be sad. Depressed, at least, at taking up with the road the split in his life. But he was talking about his children, boastful of their excitement at seeing him, he was drinking deep of being loved. —Man, I wish you could've seen my big boy, last time, he was nearly as tall as I am—right up here to my ear. And he's clever, there he's already bigger than me, I'm telling you . . . He can do everything. At Christmas, one of my other uncles was here at their place with his car, so this kid says, *Ntatemoholo*, I bet you I can drive, so his uncle gets in next to him and hands over the keys. And off! That kid manages the clutch, gears, everything. Just learnt from watching people.—

To say he was happy: it's to say he was whole. He'd accepted himself again; husband, father, Freedom Fighter, womanizer, and clerk at the Legal Foundation. At that moment when, glancing at his profile, she found the definition, he saw someone flagging him down on the road. A black man was waving a plastic container. A good mood overflows in openness to others; the Foundation station-wagon slowed and pulled up level with a brother in trouble, run out of gas. He leaned from the window and spoke to the man in the language of the district. An arm thrust through and snatched the keys from the ignition. She heard the gurgle as the forearm struck against Oupa's windpipe in passing and saw the mound of a ring with a red stone on a finger. *Tswaya! Get out!* A voice that of a man giving routine orders.

All the muscles in Oupa's body gathered in a storm of tension that sucked into a vacuum his shock and hers, she felt it draw at her as if he had had his hand upon her. He burst out of the door knocking the man back with its force. The scuffle and animal grunting and yells of two men fighting. She saw another man run from behind the decoy car with a gun and she jumped out of the passenger seat hearing a woman's voice screaming screaming and ran screaming, another self, screaming, to where the two men fought on the ground. The keys were thrown, the hand that had held them struggling to get something out of his pocket as he fought. She and the third man were racing towards the ring of keys shining in the dust; she was terrified of what she was converging with, thumping tread like hooves making for her, there was a loud snap of giant fingers in the air—! and then another that gave her a mighty punch in the calf. She lost herself, more from lack of breath than whatever had happened to her leg. The first thing she was restored to was the ordinary sight of a man picking up a ring of keys. He came over and not looking at her face, tore off her watch and grabbing her left hand, pulled at the ring on her finger. She put her finger in her mouth, wet it with saliva and gave the hand to him. He made a disgusted face and signalled her to take off the ring. She worked it over the knuckle and handed it to him; she didn't know what had happened to her leg, she didn't know if she could get up, he was there above her ready to strike her down if she did. The sling bag—her money, the Foundation's money, all her documentation—was in the station-wagon, was his, taken possession of without any further effort necessary. As feeling came to her leg in the form of pain making pathways for itself, she saw as he left her that he was not like the other, he was a puny man and the thumping tread that had pursued her had come only from the pump-action of jogging shoes below skinny legs.

The two vehicles were driven away. He—Oupa—lay gasping over there. There was a tear in her jeans, quite small, some ooze of blood, she did not want to roll the pants leg and see more, she had the desire to sit up and wrap her arms tightly round the leg but she moved, squatting on one leg and supporting the other, to where he was. They clasped hands, dumb. Tears of effort, of the violence with which he had fought, were finger-painting the dirt on his face. He patted his ribs on the right side to show her where: blood was blotting out the face of Bob Marley printed on his T-shirt. They were castaways in the immensity of the sky. They were abandoned in the diminishing perspective of an empty dirt road, leaving them behind as a speck to be come upon as hornbills come upon a cowpat. They helped each other somehow to the side of the road.

Tears and blood. It was a country road, it was miles from anywhere. But they are everywhere, the violent. To meet up with them again: *Je-ss-uss! I'd be terrified.* He carefully rolled the leg of her pants and found —Oh my God, there's a hole on the other side, the bullet went right through . . . it should've been there, where you were standing, did you find it . . . — But neither had the strength to go back and search. She lifted his shirt and saw the hole, like the socket where an eye had been gouged; on his back there was no exit wound.

—It's still inside?—

—I don't know too much about anatomy. But it's far from your heart.—

Their watches were gone. They did not know how long after but it must have been quite soon that a cattle truck loaded with beasts huddled together for the abattoir stopped and the driver, calling out in his language, came over with the face of dismay and curiosity with which a man meets a disaster that could happen to himself. The cattle jostled to the bars of the truck to stare and low, giving off the ammoniac stench of their own instinctive fear of their last journey. Under the panicked whites of the beasts' eyes he and she were helped into the cab. She was a leg, her whole being stuffed down into a leg, a concentration of pain filled to bursting down there. Blood trickled from her; she kept her gaze on a vase with its branch of artificial carnations hooked above the windscreen. Oupa and the driver talked in their language; although short of breath he was fortunately in less pain than she, the bullet inside him perhaps was lying in some harmless space of the mysterious human body.

.

Oupa had his bullet on the cabinet beside the hospital bed between the bottles of orange squash and bunch of bananas his friends at the Foundation brought him. No longer any segregation of black and white sick and injured, but the elegant Indian lady who shared a ward with Vera rang for a nurse to come and draw the curtains round her bed when Oupa, in a dressing-gown, came to visit Vera; on crutches, she went to visit him. Animatedly they pieced together over and over again the details rescued from the confusion of the dog-fight blur in which the attack happened. —You noticed that big ring with the red stone— —Oh I can see his hand as the back of it hit your throat, I don't think I'd recognize the face but I feel I'd know that hand anywhere— —I heard you screaming, I thought my God they're killing her— They shuddered and they laughed together: lucky to be alive.

Oupa's bullet had been removed cleanly through an incision just below the ribs. It had missed both lungs and liver, merely chipped a rib and lodged in muscular tissue. He was proud of this form of resistance to the attackers. —I think I got so tough on the Island, you know, and I've done some weight-lifting, well, I used to, so I'm sure that's helped me.— He took his bullet back to One-Twenty-One with him in a cigarette pack. Vera's wound at the point of entry of the bullet became infected and she was kept in hospital a few days after his discharge.

Ben telephoned Annie with daily bulletins and requests for professional advice, insisting she keep in touch with the hospital surgeon. He related Annie's reassurances with a lack of con-

fidence in doctors' judgment, sitting through long silences at
Vera's bedside looking at her as if piecing her together, out of
destruction, from images in his mind. When she came home he
returned from Promotional Luggage at odd hours of day to make
sure she was following doctor's orders for healing to be established. —We ought to take a break somewhere.—

She was reading documents from the Foundation, sent by
messenger, strewn on the sofa. —I must get back to work. It's
piling up there.—

—Just three or four days together.—

She tried to give her attention to understanding the need;
his need or hers. —Well, where.—

—To the sea . . . —

—I don't suppose I should put this thing in water yet.—

—To the mountains.—

The mountains.

Ah, so there was no practical reality to be understood, she
was obtuse in objecting to the sea because she would not be able
to swim in it just as she would not be able to climb—these were
not mountains for climbing, they were the site in themselves,
herself and Bennet, proposed to return to. —I ought to get back
to work.— No more assertive than a murmur.

The words fell from him with the clatter of a weapon concealed on his person. —I couldn't live without you.—

A jump of fear, of refusal within her.

He began to straighten and stack the sheets of paper lying
haphazard as fallen leaves over the outline of her legs under a
rug. In her appalled silence his continuation of the senseless
task, picking up sheets that slithered off the sofa, putting an
order into documents whose sequence he did not know, understood the rejection.

She could not see the violence at the roadside as evidence

of her meaning in his life. She could not share the experience with him on those terms. She was not responsible for his existence, no, no, love does not carry that covenant; no, no, it was not entered into in the mountains, it could not *be*, not anywhere. *What to do with that love.* Now she saw what it was about, the sudden irrelevant question, a sort of distress within herself, that came to her from time to time, lately.

When he had gone back to his office she lay, holding off confusion and resentment, stiff, head pressed into cushions. She rose slowly and pushed back the rug, rolled up the leg of her track suit to the place on her calf where the punctured flesh, still an outraged blotchy purple, had been secured by metal clips.

The sacred human body is only another object that can be patched together, like a tyre. This is one meaning of what had happened on the road. Something to be traced with a forefinger. There are many. Violence has many: now, in this country, as the working out of vengeance, as the return of the repressed, for some; the rationalization for their fear, of their flight, for others. But the experience of violence is for the victims their conception of a monster-child by rape; only they share its clutch upon their backs. Only they, in the privacy of what has been done to them, can search through the experience for what they should have done differently in resistance, where there was a failure of intelligence, of courage, of wiliness, of common sense; of how much they were influenced, even in panic, by the conditioning of the rules of the game, their society's game. Never stop for anyone on the road. Let them die there. Break the rule for a brother, Oupa, and you stop a souvenir bullet. You admired the criminals you were forced to share a cell with—but to meet them outside —Those people? I'd be terrified. The attraction of power predestines us as its victims. And if I hadn't been wasting my breath screaming I might have reached the keys, run over the bastards. Oh easy to swagger in retrospect. While you were fighting, while I was screaming, weren't we conscious of getting what we deserved, according to the rules? If I had stayed home as a white woman should in these times (what other times have there been in the efficacy of a country run by fear) it wouldn't have happened, serve you right. There's someone there at home who can't live without you. What were you doing about that when you got yourself shot in the leg?

She leant to pick up the phone and ask him, Oupa, already back at work, to come by when the office closed, and then remembered she expected Sally that afternoon. Sally had put her hostility to Vera aside, as people do when its object encounters some sufficiently punishing misfortune, but it was unlikely that this clemency would be extended to the young man, if he were to arrive before she left. The experience of violence on one's person also makes one self-absorbed and forgetful of other people's preoccupations—Vera had failed, while she was in hospital, to ask if all had gone well with Mpho. —I've brought Didymus!— And there were flowers. Vera got up and went to fetch drinks. —Don't let her hobble about for us, Didy! You do it— But Vera was already in the passage, he followed her. —The young man?— A clatter of ice cubes he was releasing covered the question in that same kitchen where an *umfundisi* had drunk coffee behind closed curtains.

—Back at work. And Mpho?—

—The whole thing's never mentioned at home. She laughs a lot, girl-friends in and out, very busy. It's what we wanted, I suppose.—

Vera looked round into the pause. —Well, what else?—

—It seems a bit callous, the way she is. But I don't believe it's forgotten, inside her. In a way, we gave up her confidence in us. I don't think Sally realizes we're not going to get it back.—

As they were leaving the kitchen he blocked the way. —The doctor told me, it was a boy. Apparently you could see already.—

—He shouldn't have done that!—

—Of course she doesn't know, neither of them does.—

Vera was careful to enquire again, of Sally. —How are things with Mpho? Were there any problems?—

A momentary coldness, in admonition, flexed the muscles in Sally's face. —She's working quite well. She's been given a leading part in the school play. The school accepted she was away for a week with flu—that time.—

Everything can be patched up. Everything knits somehow, again. Souvenirs are the only evidence: a bullet in a cigarette pack, a half-formed blob of flesh dropped in an incinerator.

I couldn't live without you.

Her visitors had gone and the threat returned. She lay listening to the inanimate counsel of the house, creaking in its joints with the cooling of afternoon. The hand of a breeze flicked a curtain. The blurt of an old rubber-bulb horn announced six o'clock; as every day at this hour the black entrepreneur on his bicycle was hawking offal from a cardboard box, her gaze on the ceiling saw him as always, lifting portions squirming like bloody spaghetti into the basins of backyard residents who were his clients. Attackers take everything. The sling bag of documents. Address book. Wedding ring. She feels the place where it was, as she investigated the other scars of the attack. The place where the ring was is a wasted circle round the base of the finger, feel it, frail, flesh worn thinner than that of the rest of the digit. Documents, address book—ring; on the contrary, to live: without all these.

Until the man on the road forced her to do so, she had never taken off the ring since Bennet placed it on her finger. She had worn it while making love to Otto. Her finger is naked; free.

They went to Durban for a week. The break fitted in with an opportunity to have a look at a trade fair where Promotional Luggage was displayed.

The ring has never been replaced.

Mrs Stark returned to her office on Monday morning and was told Oupa was back in hospital. It was early, the story vague. Only the receptionist at his desk: Oupa had sat about 'in a funny way' last week, he was bent and couldn't breathe properly. Then he went to the doctor and didn't return. Someone phoned the doctor and was told he'd been sent to hospital. And then? What did the doctor say was the matter?

No further sense to be got out of a young man who didn't pay attention to what he heard, was incapable of reporting anything accurately. No wonder messages received at the Foundation were often garbled; irritation with the Foundation's indulgence of incompetence distracted her attention as she called the doctor's paging number. She reached him at the hospital. Slow internal bleeding, the lung. Well, it was difficult to say why, it seemed there was an undetected injury sustained when the bullet penetrated, perhaps a cracked rib, and some strenuous effort on the part of the patient had caused a fracture to penetrate the lung. It was being drained. The condition was stable.

At lunchtime Mrs Stark and Lazar Feldman went to visit their colleague. What should they take him? They stopped on the way to buy fruit. At the hospital they were directed to the Intensive Care Unit. Whites habitually misspell African names. Mrs Stark repeated Oupa's: wasn't there some mistake? The direction was confirmed. As they walked shining corridors in a procession of stretchers pushed by masked attendants, old men bearing wheeled standards from which hung bags containing urine draining from tubes attached under their gowns, messengers skidding past with beribboned baskets of flowers, unease grew. The community of noise and surrounding activity fell away as they reached the last corridor, only the squelch of Lazar's rubber soles accompanied a solemnity that imposes itself on even the most sceptical of unbelievers when approaching a shrine where unknown rites are practised. She shook her head and shrugged, to Lazar: what would Oupa, his bullet in a cigarette pack, recovered from what had happened to him and her on the road, be there for as she pictured him, sitting up in bed ready to tell the story to his visitors?

At double doors there was a bell under a no entry sign. They rang and nobody came, so Vera walked in with Lazar lifting his feet carefully and placing them quietly behind her. Cells were open to a wide central area with a counter, telephones, a bank of graphs and charts, a row of white gowns pegged on the wall. A young black nurse in towelling slippers went to call the sister in charge.

Was the place empty?

Is there nobody here?

The wait filled with a silence neither could recognize; the presence of unconscious people.

The sister in charge came out of one of the doorways pulling a mask away from nostrils pink as the scrubbed skin pleated on her knuckles. —Ward Three? We're pleased with him today, gave us a smile this morning.— The nurse was signalled to take

the packet of fruit from Lazar. —Nothing by mouth.— They
robed themselves in the gowns.

On a high bed a man lay naked except for a cloth between
the thighs, a body black against the sheets. Tubes connected this
body to machines and plastic bags, one amber with urine, another dark with blood. The sister checked the flow of a saline
drip as if twitching a displaced flower back into place in a vase;
the man had his back to them, they moved slowly round to the
other side of the bed to find him.

Oupa. A naked man is always another man, known only to
a lover or the team under the shower after a match. Friendship,
an office coterie, identifies only by heads and hands. The body
is for after hours. Even in the intimacy of the injured, on the
road, bodies retain their secrecy. Oupa. His fuzzy lashes on
closed eyes, the particular settle of his scooped round nostrils
against his cheek; his mouth, the dominant feature in a black
face, recognized as such in this race as in no other with an
aesthetic emphasis created by highly developed function, since
we speak and sing through the mouth as well as kiss and ingest
by it—his mouth, bold lips parted, fluttering slightly with uneven
breaths.

—He's asleep, we'll come back later.—

The sister stood displaying him.

—No. Unconscious. It's the high fever we're trying to get
down. Speak to him, maybe if he knows your voices they'll rouse
him. Sometimes it works. Go on. Speak to him.—

With these gentle calls you bring a child back from a night-
mare or wake a lover who has overslept.

Oupa, Oupa, it's Lazar.

Oupa, it's Lazar and Vera, here. Oupa, it's Vera.

She took the hand that was resting near his face. It felt to
the touch like a rubber glove filled to bursting point with hot

air. His eyelids showed the movement of the orbs beneath the
skin. They talked at him chivvyingly, what do you think you're
doing here, who said you could take leave, man, my desk's a
mess, we need you . . . Oupa, it's Lazar, it's Vera . . . And his
head stirred or they imagined it, under the concentration they
held on his face.

—There, he hears you. You see? Now nurse's going to give
him a nice cool sponge-down.—

In the reception area Vera waylaid the woman as she strode
away. —Why is he in a fever like this—what's the reason for
the high temperature?—

—Septicaemia . . . the blood leaked into the body's cavity,
you see.— The lowered tone of confidential gossip. —Of course,
he should have had himself admitted the moment he had symp-
toms. Dosed himself with brandy instead . . . But I'm telling
you, at least he hasn't gone down, he's fighting, we're pleased
with him.—

The nurse came to Lazar with the packet of fruit. It was
become evidence of their foolish ignorance, his and Mrs Stark's,
of the nature of the ante-room in life to which they had been
directed; of this retreat for those upon whom violence has been
done, where their colleague had entered as one enters an order
under vows of silence and submission. By contrast, the unini-
tiated are clumsy and intrusive and have only the useless to
offer. —Oh no, keep it, won't you.—

A giggle of pleasure. —Oh thanks, aih. Lovely grapes!—

·

There was an official roster of Foundation colleagues taking
turns to visit the hospital every working day. At weekends others
felt they had a right to disappear into their private lives; Mrs
Stark was older, there were surely no urgencies of family de-

mands, love entanglements, waiting to be taken up, for a woman like her. She joined the trooping crowds of relatives and friends who filled the hospital on Saturday and Sunday. Out-of-works, beggars and staggering meths drinkers officiously directed cars and minibuses searching for parking, sleeping children were slung round the necks of fathers, there were girls adorned and made up to remind male patients of their sexuality, Afrikaner aunts in church-going hats, bored young men gathered outside for a smoke, Indian grandmothers sitting in their wide-swathed bulk like buddhas, popcorn packets and soft-drink cartons stuck behind the pots of snake plant and philodendron intended to distract people from bleak asepsis, the smells and sights of suffering, the same plants that stand about in banks to distract queues from their anxiety, in the power of money.

The first Saturday and Sunday, and the second. Oupa, the body that was Oupa identified by the mute face, lay as he was placed, on this side or that, sometimes on his back. And that was something to stop the intruder where she stood, entering the cell that was always open. No privacy for that body. On his back, totally exposed. Once she asked if there could be a sheet to cover him and was dismissed with impatience at ignorant interference: he was kept naked because every bodily change, every function had to be monitored all the time, nurses coming in to observe him every fifteen minutes; he was kept naked to fan away the heat of infection raging in there, see the flush in his face, the purplish red mounting under the black. When she was alone—with him but alone—she carefully (he must never know, even if he were to be aware of the need for the small gesture it would humiliate him) drew the piece of cloth between his legs over the genitals that lolled out, ignored by nurses. Sometimes he seemed asleep as well as unconscious. The breathing changed; the men she had slept with breathed like that deep in the night. She wanted to tell him she—at least someone—was there yet it was a violation to touch him when he seemed so doubly, utterly removed. At other times she stood with her hand over his; it was the gesture she knew from other circumstances. She fell back on it for want of any other because nobody knew what he might need or want, they believed he had no thirst because salt water dripped into his veins, they believed he did not feel vulnerable in his nakedness because fever glowed in him like coal. Whether or not the people he shared One-Twenty-One with came to see him she did not know. And moving away from the black townships he had lost touch with neighbours and friends there, most did not know where he lived, now, in a building among whites. Very likely they would not have been allowed in to see him if they had come; the sister in charge made it clear that visits were to be restricted to his employer since it seemed he had no family.

Of course he has a family—but who knew how to get in touch with the plump young woman sitting among all the women who are left behind in veld houses put together as igloos are constructed from what the environment affords, snow or mud. No one had an address; as an employee and as a patient Oupa had given his permanent residence as One-Twenty-One Delville Wood. The only way to reach her was to retrace the journey from the turn-off at the eucalyptus trees—could someone from the Foundation be spared to drive there? Mrs Stark knew the way but her husband, supported by her son out from London on a visit, absolutely forbade her to revive the trauma of the attack in this way.

During the week Lazar Feldman and others tiptoed in and stood a few minutes, afraid of closeness to what the familiar young-man-about-the-office had become, the grotesque miracle of his metamorphosis. One of the clerks who had meekly suffered because she was too plain to attract him, wept. They went away and some found excuses not to come again; what did visits help a man, said to be Oupa, who did not know there was anyone present, did not know that he himself was present.

Vera glanced at her watch and set herself the endurance of twenty minutes. But she forgot to look at the dial again. What was a presence? Must consciousness be receptive, cognitive, responsive, for there to be a presence? Didn't the flesh have a consciousness of its own, the body signalling its presence through the lungs struggling to breathe with the help of some machine, the kidneys producing urine trickling into a bag, the stool forming in the bowels.

An insect settles on a leaf and slowly moves its wings.

She sat and watched.

The Fat Nurse and the Thin One, the Chinese and the Black (nurses are known by rank and the most obvious features, they seem to have no names) came and went, marking the passing of time ritually as the tongue of a church bell striking against its palate where traffic is not yet heavy enough to break the sound waves. How ignorant, how far away from this, she had been curious: *what's it like. This* is what it's like; an anatomical demonstration that spares nothing. When, in church between her mother and father, she heard about that moral division, the soul and the body, and grew up unable to believe in the invisible, what the priest really was talking about and didn't know it, was this: what he called soul was absence, the body was presence. It was swollen now, not only the hands: one day when she walked in there was the young man's flat belly blown up, the skin taut and shiny, a version in a fun-fair distorting mirror. To look for identity in the face was to be confronted by an oxygen mask. The Chinese gave it a touch to make it what she judged would be more comfortable, if one could feel. The Black used a little blood-sucking device to draw specimens from a huge toe pierced again and again. The Fat One cleaned the leaking anus. If one could feel? The dumb creature that is the body cannot tell. It is an effigy of life ritually, meticulously attended. Outside, in between times, the acolytes eat grapes, arrange on the counter flowers left behind by dead patients, and whisper forbidden telephone calls to children home from school and boy-friends at work.

Vera no longer imagined the plump young woman down the turn-off from the eucalyptus trees and phrased what she ought to be saying to her. Ivan, back at the house where he was conceived, disappeared from her awareness as if he were still in England. The wheeze and click of machines that now breathed for the body and eliminated its waste chattered over its silence. Remote from her, within that awe, a final contemplation was taking place—isn't that what it is—what it's like?—the years on the Island, night study to be a lawyer in what the politicians promise to be a new day, freedom the dimensions of a flat in a white suburb, a box-cart pulled through the dust by children— who knew what the final contemplation must be? In that silence she saw that the certainty she had had of death, Zeph Rapulana's death among nine at Odensville, when he was, in fact, to appear before her alive, was merely a mis-sort in time, a letter first delivered to the wrong address: the certainty belonged to her where it reached her now, in this place, in this presence.

•

Among the casualties of violence listed in the newspaper is a clerk in the employ of the Legal Foundation, Oupa Sejake, who has died of complications resulting from an injury received when the Foundation's vehicle was hijacked.

It was only decent that the Foundation be represented at the funeral. Because the poor young man had been more or less her assistant, Mrs Stark would be the obvious choice. Lazar Feldman volunteered to accompany her and do the driving, since muscles torn by the bullet's passage through her calf felt the strain of depressing a brake pedal. But the day before they were to leave he developed that perfect alibi for opting out of anything and everything, virus flu. While other colleagues were avoiding one another's eyes and suggesting someone ought to take his place, she said—without having any idea of whom she might have in mind—no need to worry, she would not have to go alone. Perhaps she had been thinking Ivan might come with her; it would give them a chance to talk, reopen the secret passages between intimates that have to be unsealed each time after absence. The first week of his visit had belonged entirely to him and Ben—between meetings at the Foundation with major funders from Sweden and Holland and running to the hospital, she barely had had time for a meal with her son. Ah—but she remembered Ben mentioning, with pride that drew down the corners of his mouth, that Ivan was so well thought of internationally

in the banking world that the Development Bank had invited
him as a special guest to participate in talks with a representative
of the IMF, to take place next day.

Another claim of life while the process of dying was moving
to its close was the hearing in the Supreme Court of the farmer
Tertius Odendaal's appeal against a judgment allowing an in-
formal housing settlement to be established on the land known
as Odensville acquired from him by the Provincial Administration. Zeph Rapulana was present when the judges dismissed the
appeal; one of the Foundation's lawyers who had accompanied
him while she was preoccupied with the Swedes and the Hol-
landers brought a note: 'Vera, we've won, this time we've shut
the door in his face.'

This other conclusion, of a process that had seemed to have
little chance of success, bubbled a clear spring through her
preoccupations. Zeph Rapulana had a base in the city, now,
backyard cottage in a suburb—his success with the Odensville
affair had brought him to the attention of a housing research
project which employed him as adviser. On the telephone they
both talked at once: Vera wanted to know exactly what the judge
had said, how Odendaal reacted—and it became quite natural
for her to go on to suggest, look, why don't you come with me
tomorrow, we could talk. He knew about the death of the young
man who had been shot, as she was, on the road: —If it'll be
any help to you.—

The stand of eucalyptus. Then approaching, a face awaiting,
demanding recognition: it happened, it happened, it happened
here, the death began here—the place on the road where Oupa,
sitting beside her as this other man, Zeph, sits beside her now,
drew up and called through the window, Brother.

—This is where they were.—

Pointing out a landmark, that's all. The only being with

whom what happened there is shared has disappeared. But there is a counter-balance in the presence beside her; with him is shared something else, living, that could not be shared with anyone else. From the day Odendaal had closed the door in their faces; from the statement, the threat (never to be discussed between them) Don't be afraid, Meneer Odendaal, you won't be harmed, your wife, your children—to the nine dead, to the judge's words dismissing Odendaal's appeal, the door shut in Odendaal's face—this single return of land to its people was their right, Rapulana's and hers, to quiet elation. Like the feeling between lovers continuing in the presence of the pain of others, it showed no disrespect to the dead. Out of companionable silences she let her thoughts rise aloud now and then. —Why is it that more can be done for the dead than the living? I'm on my way to his home, his wife, now, but neither I nor anyone else went to fetch her while he was at least still alive, although he might not have known she was there. There was no proper address to send a message, a telegram, no telephone, no one knew how to get in touch with her short of driving there, but once he died—suddenly someone at the office knew someone else who was a friend of his, the Soweto grape-vine was followed, there was a way found to get a message to her: Oupa dead. Just that.—

—You don't think he'd let her know about the attack.—

—I don't know. And would she read the papers? Unlikely. Of course, someone might have heard from the driver of the cattle truck and passed the news on to her. Who can say? It's hard for someone like me to imagine the feelings of a woman like her—living as she has to. You've known so many . . . I suppose it doesn't strike you . . . She gets his body back. And that seems so important. The dead body? She didn't show much enthusiasm when he walked in that day. But someone came specially—from

her—to arrange the transport, the money for the funeral. All
the things that distance and poverty and . . . I don't know—
acquiescence in the state of things?—couldn't manage before
become possible when there's so little purpose left. But I suppose
it's your custom.—

He watched the mealie fields approach and turn away,
cleaved by the road. —We have too many graves and too few
houses for the living.—

Vera followed the ritual of the funeral without understanding any comfort it could bring to the wife. She was dressed in a
polka-dot skirt and jacket that she endured like a tight pair of
shoes (an outfit bought by her husband from a street vender in
the city?), the skin of her stunned face peeled raw by tears. The
children were wearing white socks and polished school shoes.
The gangling boy who (that day, that day) hadn't returned from
school held the hand of a two- or three-year-old who stared down
curiously into the pit of dank-smelling earth ready to receive his
father. There was singing, of great beauty, from these women
left behind, and when they wept one of them took Vera's arm
because with the bullet that passed through her leg she was part
of the son they mourned and she wept, with them, for the horrible
metamorphosis revealed by Intensive Care.

The company trooped back to the house. She felt impatient
with herself, confused. —Oupa. Why was he named that? Grandfather, old man, and he's dead before thirty. Why do you name
children 'old man' for god's sake?— Zeph smiled down at her.
—Something to do with authority. You take the Afrikaans word
for a respected man and it gives—wha'd'you say—confers power
on the child. You give him the strength of a *baas*.—

At the Washing of the Hands in tin basins set out by women
he told her she was expected to say a few words to the wife and
company. But apart from their own language they understood

only Afrikaans, the language of the whites they worked for in that district, and hers was court-room Afrikaans; she did not have the right words for this occasion. —You speak to them.—

A mild reproach. —How do I know what you want to say?—

—I want to say I don't know what to say.—

—No, come on.—

—Really.—

—They want to know how he died, of what sickness, what happened at the attack, that he was a soldier in Umkhonto, that he was well-thought-of at work, that he was a good man who cared only about his family although he was far away—

—There, you know it all. Tell them you're saying it in their language for me.—

He became again as he was when he was among his own people at Odensville; the cadence of his voice, his gestures, transformed a fragmented life into wholeness, he knew exactly how to do it, it came to him from within himself in symbiosis with the murmuring group gathered. They understood the tradition and she understood, without words, without tradition, their understanding. It was not true; the son and husband of this place left behind did not think only of his family, he yearned for a girl who had seen things and possessed knowledge he would never have, he did not die peacefully, his body, in attempts made to keep it alive, suffered tortures his interrogators in prison had not thought of. It was not true, in fact, but this stranger she had brought with her made it so beyond evidence. Who was Mrs Stark, herself to some the forbidding eminence of the Legal Foundation, to others the procuress of convenient abortion, to know what was between the young man and the clumsy-bodied young woman with her peasant stance and the classical three lines of beauty round her neck? Who was to know whether or not the sister in charge was right when she said, finally, he doesn't feel what we're doing to him?

Vera had cleansed her hands of death, with the others. In the car driving to the city she reflected differently, now. —At least we saw him come back. At least he's home.—

The sonorous, lyrical, stately persona created by the company in which Zeph had found himself had retired somewhere within where it had its place and would never leave him. He spoke out of what he had perfectly reconciled with it, in his dealings with laws made to manipulate him, and the entry into relationships for which there was no pre-existing formula of hostility or friendship, suspicion or trust; combinations thrown together by compatibilities discovered, side by side, in conflict and in change. —He didn't want to go *back*, did he.—

How did Rapulana know? He'd seen him only a few times, first at Odensville and then at the Foundation, and, of course, at the party in Vera's house. —He'd had something to drink that night . . . yes . . . he told me he was going to do what he thought about when he was in prison. He was going to disappear and travel the world, he was going to Cuba—to England, China, specially Cuba—everywhere.—

The end of the joy-ride.

Lucky to be alive.

Ivan paid the courtesy visit expected of a son's interest in his mother's work and the assumed interest of her colleagues in her family; the Foundation is not a business, where directors and staff have no connection outside the purpose of making money. The very nature of their work, concerned with the condition of personal lives in communities, influences their own sense of community. One or two of the older lawyers remembered him as a schoolboy or youth; others, such as Lazar Feldman, exchanged ready-made friendliness established by proxy through their familiarity with his mother. That he looked so like her made this oddly easy. Chatting with him, Lazar remarked how sorry he was to have had to let Vera down over the trip to Oupa's funeral, he really would have liked to be there.

From the Foundation, Ivan took Vera out to lunch. Just the two of them, the son's treat, she walking before him to the table he had reserved in the quietest corner of a good restaurant, the succession to clandestine lunches taken with a lover.

—Is this the time when we compare notes?— She was con-

tentedly flippant, using the phrasing he would remember from
the days when he came from boarding school and the right moment suddenly arrived for wariness to dissolve, so that they had
no age, either of them, moved into knowing each other as an
element common to them.

—I was thinking all the time I was there—(he read up and
down the wine list, looking for something special) you're lucky,
with the Foundation. They're such a good crowd, so absolutely
dedicated but intelligently tough—you know what I mean? None
of the feeling that it's a refuge for the well-meaning who can't
face the kind of world I work in, can't face that you have to
deal with it, with the Haves, if you're going to achieve anything
for the Have-nots. And the way they value you and you're so
completely absorbed in what you do . . . lucky.—

—Are you thinking of yourself?—

—Myself? How, myself?—

—Oh I'm not suggesting you haven't been successful, exceptionally so. But that doesn't always mean you don't sometimes
think there could have been something else. Something you didn't
know about at the time; time of choice.—

He said it for her: —There's always something you didn't
know about at the time. Are you going to have meat, then, with
that wine? D'you still like calamari so much—we could have a
small starter, and a half bottle of white, first.— The habit of
discretion in their working lives—his in banking, hers in the
confidentiality of the law—tacitly guarded their tongues while
the waiter stood by.

—I was thinking about Dad—Ben. What he's doing. It's
marginal in his life, somehow. He laughs about it. But I wonder.
No . . . I actually see.— At once he sensed intrusion: leaning
on the table his mother linked her hands in a single fist and

covered her mouth against it. —I don't know what the centre is. He says this luggage thing is to provide . . . for the two of you. That's all.—

—All this concern, it's something new, with him; age syndrome, turning in on himself. If you live here, the future—not the one you can provide for with suitcases—the future's more like a pile of bricks. You can only opt to help sort out a few.—

—According to a plan you believe in.—

—Yes. Pretty much.—

—And you've got the satisfaction that whatever goes wrong with it, at least what you're doing now realizes something of it, in advance.—

—Oh— she lifted her head, fanned out her hands —So little, such a dab of cement filling in a corner. Typical that I'm using the old image of a building, while people have nowhere to live.—

—They were telling me, Odensville, what are the others— is it Moutse?—people with the right to live in these places, now. Of course it must be a satisfaction, it's there with you, in your busyness, your preoccupation—I don't mean that as a reproach—I see it in your face, everything about you since I've been here. But him. In him. None of that, in him. And I'm in London, Annie—well he mourns for Annie, d'you know that, you'd think she'd died—that's another story. What has he got apart from his damn suitcases?—

She looked up at him to see what he knew.

—Me.—

The waiter arrived with plates ranged along his arm. Another hovered with the censer of a giant pepper-mill. The wine was uncorked, Ivan lifted his glass and mouthed a kiss blown to his mother across the table; —Where are the Indian waiters there used to be when I was a kid? They're all African now.—

—Moved up a rung on the ladder. They've taken the place of whites who used to serve in shops—men's outfitters and so on. You're like an old man, reminiscing! That's what happens when you exile yourself.—

They ate and drank, in the charm each invested in the other during absence. In this variation of meals both had eaten as the opening act of a love affair, there was the same calculation going on of how presumptuous each might be, approaching the other. He judged he had cajoled her sufficiently, in the persona of her small boy become an attractive man, out from behind the line of intrusion set up by her. —You didn't tell us Feldman didn't go with you to that funeral. You know you shouldn't have gone alone.—

—I didn't go alone.— Head cocked at him.

—Oh. That was sensible. But how is it you didn't mention Feldman was ill and you were going with someone else? Ben thought you were with someone he trusts, back on that road again.—

—I took along a friend he knows, the man who's just won the Odendaal case, there couldn't be anyone safer to be with.—

—But Vera.— He tapped a dance between a knife and fork. —You puzzle me.—

—My darling, how do I puzzle you?— Her face thrust towards him in a smile.

He wasn't to be turned aside by any ploy of motherly af-fection. —Why didn't you let him know it wasn't Feldman? He thought you were safely with one person, you were with another. When you talked to us about the funeral you didn't mention Feldman wasn't there. It's childish.— He has the right to be critical with her; that's the kind of edgy relationship both are aware exists between them.

—I don't know. It's the usual form of evasion, to say so. Perhaps I'll find out now you've mentioned it.—

Fascinated, he hesitated, sat back in his chair, and then righted himself. He spoke with an intense curiosity. —Do you often lie to him?—

—Is keeping something for yourself lying.—

—I suppose so. Even if you manage to put it that way.—

—And do you?—

—Who to?—

His mother rounded her eyes exaggeratedly, pulled a face: what are the limits of what you will tell me, what can we divine of one another. —Well, the Hungarian.—

He laughed, and then shook his head, down, down, at what had been come upon. —*Well yes.* As you say, the Hungarian. She wants a child. From me. For instance, there's that. I tell her no, it'll spoil what's between us, I want her to myself. But that's not what I want. There's Adam, one hostage enough between me and a woman I couldn't go on living with.—

—So you don't envisage going on living with the Hungarian.—

—She's got a name, Mother!—*Eva.* No, we get along well but I'm getting old enough to realize what you don't know at twenty; life isn't going to end with the catastrophe of hitting the forties, you're very likely going to have to continue for a long stretch ahead with what—with whom—you take on now. Eva. It's not like with you and Ben, something for life. I'm not like him—alas, I suppose. He took you away from that first husband of yours, at least that's what he's sure he did, I think it's the basis of his feeling that he belongs to you entirely. You've always been and you are all that he has.—

—You can't belong to someone else. It's love-making gives the illusion! You may long to, but you can't.— She stopped, as if the mouthful of wine she swallowed were some potion that would suffuse them both with clarity. —You see, Ben made a great mistake. Choice.— A flick of a glance returned her conspirator to the earlier remark: *something not known about at the time.* —He gave up everything he needed, in exchange for what he wanted. The sculpture. Even an academic career—all right, it didn't look brilliant, but he might have been a professor by now, mightn't he? What d'you think? That wouldn't have been marginal? He put it all on me.— She was excited to continue by a sense of approaching danger, saying too much; doing exactly that, herself: putting the weight of all this on a son, a grown child. There is a fine limit beyond which a son or daughter may turn away in revulsion. Parents must be defined as such.

—What on you?—

—The whole weight of his life. That love he had. I love him but it's hard to remember how much I was in love with him. That love affair that started on a holiday in the Drakensberg, it hasn't moved, for him. It hasn't been taken up into other things. Children born, friends disappearing in exile, in prison, killings around us, the death of his father in the house, the whole country changing. It hasn't moved. Not even his confusion over Annie has shifted it, not even your divorce, because both he's understood only in relation to his own feelings in the Drakensberg, he hasn't any other criterion. The violence that was always there, pushing people out into the veld, beating them up at police stations, and the gangster violence that's taking the opportunities of change, now, that's killed Oupa Sejake—even that he understands now *through me*, it's because it's something that happened to *me*, it's the bullet that went through *my* leg. Love. There's been so much else, since then. Ivan, I can't live in the past.—

—I wish I were nearer. For him. Because I always loved you best, as a kid.—

An offering of complicity she did not choose to see, held out to her.

She was examining him lingeringly. —Yes, so far away. You are his favourite. His only child, now. That's how it turned out.—

Theirs was the last table still occupied but they sat on unnoticing, accepting coffee, more and more coffee, like lovers reluctant to part.

—You don't need anything, Mother.—

In the clatter of waiters clearing tables he touched her cheek to soften what she might take as judgment.

—On the contrary, I'm finding the answer presents itself before the need. I know only then that it existed.—

They went out into the street roused with wine and confidences, laughing.

•

'Do I lie to him often?'

How alike we are, it doesn't end with the mask that is the face. He knows me because he himself was the first lie. One day I'll be so old we'll even talk about that. And he will say, I knew all along, although he couldn't possibly know except through the code of genes and the language of blood.

Every time Vera leaves Ben out—isn't that simply a different kind of unfaithfulness? Different from leaving him out by making love with someone else, that's all. And just as after those times of love-making in One-Twenty-One, she 'makes it up' to him. Not by repairing the omission of telling him Rapulana instead of Feldman had accompanied her back along that road where she, too, could have met her death and left him to live without her—the trivial omission, as it could have been presented, of one name for another. When Ivan went off to London she asked Ben to come with her to Cape Town, where there were problems for her to solve at the Foundation's branch office. Ivan was gone; —We can see something of Annie.— If he was lonely, he must be reminded that he had a daughter.

Annie insisted that they stay with Lou and her. Vera and Ben had never been in this common household. It was everything Annie's parents' was not. Vera's house, that Ben had entered to live among the wartime makeshift provided by her first husband's parents, donated beds and mismatched chairs, was aesthetically unified—if it could be called that—by coffee-stained newspapers and journals where fish-moth scuttled, grotesque woodcuts and figurines bought at charity sales of African art, photographs of the children who once lived there, poster souvenirs of travel, bureaux lacking handles, box files and old utensils that were meant to be thrown away but might come in useful. From this collage of hazard Annie had taken what had been consciously created within the house, the female torsos Ben had sculpted years ago. They were encountered in a Victorian house balanced on a steep street, one at the archway into the living-room and the other at the centre of a small patio created by knocking down a wall, Lou explained. Old Cape furniture with the patina of acorns smelled of beeswax. There was a single huge abstract painting that suggested the sea. Flowers filled the fireplaces and plants trailed in the remodelled bathrooms. The kitchen was ranged like a surgery with glass-fronted and steel-topped equipment. Indolent cats slept, hetaerae on a velvet chaise-longue, in the room Ben and Vera were allotted. Whisky in a cut-crystal decanter and ice in an Italian-designed insulated bucket; bedside books, Thomas Bowler views of the nineteenth-century Cape, and a collection of poetry by black women writers.

The Bowler, presumably, was a guess at what Ben would appreciate, and the other, for Vera, chosen by Lou on the principle that the lives of blacks were Vera's particular province and that women ought to be, if they weren't.

Ben was alarmed to notice that Vera limped slightly going to bed up the narrow staircase with its perfectly restored brass stair-rods. —You were all right at home, what's gone wrong—

—There aren't any stairs at home, are there!—

Annie was called to examine her mother's leg while he stood by ignoring dismissal of his alarm, his frown turned away to ward off the example of the young man who had been with her on the road and died of injuries from which, like her, he was supposed to be recovered. —There's probably some slight shortening in the tendons, really nothing. It's inevitable, Daddy, the human body replaces, repairs, and in some instances it can adapt one function to substitute for another, but nothing's ever quite the way it was.—

—I'm not even aware of it, I told you, Ben. Thank god I'm not a ballet dancer and I'm too old to enter a beautiful-legs contest, eh. I haven't worn anything but trousers for years— nobody sees those scars.—

In the bedroom, naked, she smiled at him as he lay in the bed. —Nobody but you.— Nakedness in men and women who have lived together a long time is clothed by familiarity, a garment of self. Now she presented her body before him as nude again, consciously so. If that body was damaged by births and time, so that vanity would save her from presenting it before anyone else, for him (there's the advantage) it took the beautiful form of its known capacities, the flesh remembered everything between them. Vera seduced Ben again, for all that she withheld from him, she flung herself into his embrace, took the force of his entry into her body as a diver plunges to emerge unharmed

from under a high surf. They were making love the way a man
and woman do, in this house where, on the other side of a wall,
two women lay enlaced. The awareness became a kind of excitement, a defiance for her, an assertion for him.

In the early morning they stood against the wooden bal-
ustrade of the verandah outside the room. The black velvet
curtain of mountain held back the day, breathing smoke from
its folds. As the sun splayed over the top it rounded up in light
a flock of pines huddled like sheep on its flank. —When did
Annie take those torsos from the house?—

—Oh, the last time she came. After the old man died, don't
you remember? She had them packed and sent down by road
transport.—

—I know nothing about it.—

—But she must have asked you?—

—She asked you?—

—Of course, and I understood you'd agreed, I thought
you'd given them to her.—

—I would never have given those to her.—

—I can't believe she'd do that.—

—Can hardly ask to have them back now.—

—No don't. It must have been because she wanted them so
badly, she thinks your work was so good.—

Do you lie to him often. Vera knew that Lou had admired
them, Lou had thought they were—how did she put it—exceptionally explicit. Lou was the one who had chosen the paintings,
collected the old furniture, designed and put into effect the adaptation of an old house to express a chosen way of life without
disturbing the shell of its style, formed to contain a way of life
the women lovers rejected. The quaint wooden valances on the
verandahs and the white-painted wrought-iron fence were in
place, but the nursery was some sort of private retreat the two

women shared and where others were never invited; the family bedrooms, with the exception of a single guest-room, had been knocked into one grand space, the room where the heart of the house stood, a great low Oriental bed under a canopy mounted on carved posts adapted from Zanzibar lintels.

Ben had created Vera for himself as body, a torso without a head. As such it was (indeed, connoisseur Lou had observed) exceptionally explicit of the power of the body. It had no identity beyond body, and so the body that was Vera, that Ben could not live without, was transformed into the expression of desire between woman and woman. In Annie's house the headless torsos were become household gods.

A R R I V A L S

Not now, not now. The day would come—no need to be a prophet, a little political nous is all that's needed—when Didymus would be resuscitated from beyond his lifetime as one of the band of Jacobin heroes who had done terrible things to save liberation in a terrible time. But for the present his greatest service was for him to be forgotten. The chroniclers of history are not those who make it; sufficient honour is being done him in giving him the task of writing the history of struggle in exile. A university press in the United States would publish it and advertise it in literary journals among other books of specialist interest, black studies, women's studies, homosexual studies, theses on child abuse, drug abuse, holes in the ozone layer. Friends like Vera Stark asked how the book was getting on as if showing attention to a child by enquiring about its progress at school, and when he encountered members of the multi-party Forum on which Sibongile served they absently, looking past his head at someone who interested them more, shouted 'That's great, that's great' before he could finish answering their enquiry.

He attended sessions of a Patriotic Front Conference as an

observer. He certainly could observe Sibongile at her official seat while she could not always have made out where he had found a place for himself. Being there gave him the opportunity to take aside someone with whom he needed to arrange a meeting— hardly call such exchanges between old comrades an interview —to gather or verify information for his writing task. He listened to the speakers with a supplementary decoder of his own running behind the words. He knew where the vocabulary, the turn of phrase of the Communists and nationalist radicals had been revised, by closeness of accession to power, to moderation in provisions of state control, and where the cautious thought of the moderates assumed boldness in sensing that, with power rising under their feet, advocation of half-measures would topple them. Sincere words? If sincerity calls all compromise into question, what (Sibongile had been right) had he been doing, when first he came home and was still on the National Executive, wining and dining, that's the phrase, with the Boers? What then was the whole philosophy, the *business*—yes—that's what it is—of negotiation about?

Sitting there, the observer experienced drastic shifts of response, his body suddenly warmed or drew into itself coldly with the proceedings. After tea break, when men who had blown up power installations joked among themselves, hailing each other as terrorists, and Anglican churchmen ate cake with an imam, the Chair was taken by a man who, during the period when the *umfundisi* called on a white friend for coffee, had apologized to the Government for sitting down in a train on a seat reserved for white people. From behind his disguises in the person of the *umfundisi* and others, the observer had followed in the newspapers of the time cartoons depicting the man's craven apology: *Ag sorry my baas Mr Prime Minister Mr President*. And followed the scorn of the liberation movements towards this man who

had grovelled so that his white masters, poking at him with the
toe of a shoe, could let him get up and continue to serve as
Government-appointed representative of the people in his particular region of the country. Now he smiled the blind smile of
church ministers, before the assembly of men who had survived
guerrilla war, men and women who had endured prison and
exile, and he spoke of 'our struggle'. He spoke of 'the significance
of this great assembly', of 'my comrades in the struggle of the
past, now sharing the heavy responsibility of the future, and
bringing to it the same courage and dedication we roused in
ourselves when we were fighting the evil of the regime. My Brothers, so we go forward . . .'

Didymus gazed from the man to those grouped around him.
Men with whom Didymus had been in detention, known the
clandestine contacts of living as moles; with whom he had barely
escaped being blown up in Safe Houses; at his wife, with whom
he had moved from exile to exile on different continents. A
disbelief twitched dully in his hands and legs. Distress; he looked
about him for someone to blurt out at: the shit, that shit. What
was that man doing up there among people he had shamed by
grovelling before the white man?

Didymus knew: what he could not accept. A constituency.
That's what the man was. A community of people we can't do
without, in this conglomerate we call unity. But every time he
looked at him disgust rose and had to be suppressed.

If I could clear my head as you clear your throat.

Others were speaking and he had not heard.

His attention drifted back to them. A white man held the
microphone curiously, as if this were a gesture of allegiance, a
raised fist or the hand that rests on a bible to testify. Didymus
knew him, of course, although he was a strangely fat and hairless
version of himself, now. The result of some drug. He had been

ill—some said an incurable illness—and often absent from his place on the National Executive.

He was saying—what? He was answering the unheard Didymus. —We've made many compromises with the past. We've swallowed the stone of many indignities. We have formed relationships we never would have thought possible or necessary. (There was a fidget of alarm along the row of delegates.) But if we really want to serve our people, if we want to convince them, in every hut and shack and hostel, if we want to convince them that when they make their cross on a bit of paper in our first one-man-one-vote elections they really may have the chance to be led by and represented by honesty, by men and women who are not seeking power to sleep in silken sheets, to grant themselves huge salaries, to take and give bribes, to embezzle and to cover up for others who steal, to disperse secret funds of public money buying contracts that are never to be fulfilled—if we're going to ask our people to put trust in a new constitution we have first to put our lives on the table to vow integrity, we have to swear publicly, here and now, and entrench this in a constitution, that we will not take up with power what the previous regime has taken.—

Of course Didymus knew him well. He was a man in whom there were depths Didymus knew in himself, dangerous depths it was difficult to believe, knowing their history, a white man in this country could occupy. And yet there had been some, and what they had gained, for whites, was something most white people would never acknowledge because they would never understand. It was through such people that whites had gained acceptance for the future in spite of their past; it was through such a man that colour and race could count for nothing and the delegates in their seats were of different skins, instead of all black. Would the whites ever realize that? Such a man sets a

precedent others like Didymus's good friends the Starks find
spirit enough to follow, whether they're conscious of this lead
or not. Such a man wakes what has been buried by fear and the
deliberate function of custom, called, as if humans were dogs at
obedience class, conditioning.

—. . . we are not going to pay for private planes to take
our ministers on holiday overseas. We are not going to foot hotel
bills for their families, their lovers and mistresses. We are not
going to give our members of parliament allowances to run
Mercedes-Benzes. We are not going to disguise, cover up, label
'top secret' spending of public money the public won't know
about. They had their Broeders, let us not use our Brothers the
same way. Let us tell our people, and mean it—we shall not lie,
and cheat, and steal from them. Without this, I tell you, all the
provisions of a constitution we are debating so carefully are
meaningless!—

He ended with a sudden simple gesture, as if remembering
himself, passing his free hand over the dome of his skull, where
the pale spores of chemically blasted hair were a fuzz of light.

Such a man has been dangerous because in the depths of
self—his and what Didymus knows as his own—is the idea of
necessary danger. And this implies wiliness; the man has lied,
prevaricated, denied the facts when there was something to be
gained in struggle: but never for personal profit, never that!

This morality will remain a mystery for ever. It is the morality, beyond the old justification of ends and means, he and
Didymus knew rather in the sense the bible uses of 'knowing' a
woman: they knew it from entering it completely. But what the
man was saying now seemed to have nothing to do with all that.
What he was saying now was—terminal, yes. He spoke from
beyond his politics; but it was not his terminal illness that spoke,
it was the final conclusion beyond politics. It came up from a

depth dredged by a whole life, beyond the one he and Didymus
both knew. Pragmatic, clever, he would never have spoken like
this before. This was not his rhetoric, it was his message.

Whether the assembly of his peers, whether the observers
round Didymus knew that—there was applause because his status as one of the heroes always drew applause, and the new
heroism, of his resistance to illness, merited it anew. But no one
picked up the microphone—the public amplification of his voice
from the Mount by which he had sworn testimony—to take up
what he had said. The assembly passed on to other matters.

•

Didymus wanted to go up after the session and say to his
old comrade-in-arms—what? But the man was apart from the
general throng, apparently drafting something in a corner with
two others. An approach looked like curiosity. Or envy. Once
there has been rejection, nothing is certain, even between old
intimates.

•

The giant sky cracked its knuckles far off in an approaching
assault. Under the bedroom lamp Sibongile was sewing back the
loose metal catch on the neckband of his black tie. Her eyebrows
were lifted stoically at the last-minute task; he was to accompany
her to a reception given at the close of the Patriotic Front Conference by one of the new embassies opened in Pretoria. He
looked at his feet, shiny in black shoes acquired along with
homecoming. —What a loud silence when Dave spoke this morning. What did it mean?—

Sibongile had a way of breaking off whatever she happened
to be doing and staring into a statement she found suspect.

—What should it mean?—

—I expect someone to stand up and support a speech like that, I'd expect enthusiasm for it, coming from everyone there.—

She went on sewing. —There was plenty of applause.—

—For *him*. It's always done—applaud Chris, applaud Joe, applaud Dave. They're hailed for what they *are*—whatever they might say.—

—Of course the applause was support for what he said! You're getting morbid.—

—But not a word of comment, not a word, not a single reference, as if he'd never spoken at all. As if no one wanted to hear.—

—Because everyone's committed against corruption, no need to jump up and shout 'I agree', everyone believes it, every-one takes it for granted. Except you.—

—Except Dave. He thought you ought to hear.—

At the open window the sky thickened as if with inky murk expelled by an octopus. The drawn breath of the coming storm stilled birds, crickets, everything; the breath was cold against summer's surfaces—leaf, cloth, metal, skin. It seemed, in the small room, to be created by Sibongile, it was her chill of an-noyance, the presage of the storm came to him as the realization that she took 'you' to be directed at her instead of, as he had spoken it, the entire assembly. In place of hastening to reassure her he was overcome—with the sweep of a sudden gust that ran before the storm, slamming the window—by resentment. A lit fuse-wire of lightning racing across the sky struck and the house lights failed, providing a domestic diversion; Mpho stumbled in from her room with a shriek. She giggled and nuzzled her father. They hugged. He reassured her teasingly in Xhosa; Mpho had learnt something of an African language by now but she would never get accustomed to African storms like an African-born girl.

On the slow drive tunnelled through rain where their headlights poked a direction, tapes of old Dizzy Gillespie recordings, the kind of music that had accompanied their life together wherever they were, repaired fragility between husband and wife; an old remedy—if only this had been a lovers' quarrel. Sibongile allowed herself a gesture from some television serial repertoire, straightening his black bow-tie with an appreciative expression as they entered the residence of the ambassador recently arrived from the Far East. How confidently and attractively Sibongile, in African robes and turban she wore for such occasions, picked up whatever conventions of ceremony and protocol came from different cultures! The kind of contacts they had had in exile around the world as obligation and privilege of various positions he held there might have been more important but were less social; a liberation movement in exile may be received secretly by foreign ministers, commissars, army and Secret Service generals whose self-interest (shared ideology, future access to raw materials, trade privileges, military co-operation, expansion of spheres of influence) in the defeat of a particular regime offers support to the liberation movement, but neither supplicant nor donor, for reasons of security or their other alliances, had ever wanted these deals displayed in the disguise of full dinner dress Didymus wore now.

Sibongile was the one more suited to present roles. Moving from group to group about the room, she paused with equal amiability among members of the white Government, comrades from the Movement, and a loud huddle that included the sometime apologist for having sat in a white's seat in a train. Now Didymus heard her familiar singing rise of voice as she joked with the man, drawing attention to his resemblance to the huge ink-and-wash panel of a Chinese sage on the wall behind him, his wispy beard and straggle of hair over his collar therefore referred to without offence, flatteringly. Delighted, taking the reference as to his wisdom, he was making some remark Didymus could not catch, and put his arm in avuncular flirtatiousness round her bare shoulders, half-complimenting, half-patronizing femininity.

While Didymus stood talking to others, in his mind he walked across the room and pulled her away, punched the face with the smile that had forfeited self-respect in apology for what should have been taken as right, and slapped the woman who tolerated his touch. Slapped Sibongile. As if Sibongile were a woman craven as the man, and would accept restriction on her actions; as if he, Didymus, belonged to the tradition of men who took it as their right to hit their women. Sibongile had been, was his comrade-in-arms, something along with and beyond his woman. The fantasy enacting within him had no sense or usefulness in real time. Sibongile was on a mission, in action suited to particular circumstances, as often he had been. He said nothing to her of the incident. He was tender to her when they got home that night. Sibongile had the feeling he thought he had to atone to her for something—something that had been said to her or about her? That she had been wounded—had a wound of public life (by now she knew well enough about those) she herself was not yet aware of, but that would evidence itself, throb in harm, in time, sometime? —What did you think of it?—

—Of what?—

—Well, the ambassador, the evening, the whole do—

He answered in her language, that they used in intimacy.

—Just like all the others now. Exchange compliments with foreigners for trade deals, alliances, maybe arms if we should need such things again. Eat and drink with friends and enemies even if once they drank your blood. Our fathers did it under a tree but they had their impis ready. (In English:) *Public Relations.*—

She unwound the turban, feeling through her freed hair as if for some inkling of what he saw had happened to her. Nothing; one of his mysteries. —I knew you were bored.—

•

But the fantasy sprang from convictions, however unreasonable and inappropriate, outdated, they might be, that could not leave him. He had lived a whole life by them; whole lives, different personae. Traitors come large and small, and those who commit petty treachery, apologizing to the enemy, abasing, licking backsides, are no more fit company than the informers who infiltrate a liberation army and are confined in camps where no one may admit to being an interrogator, no one may admit to knowledge of what that meant. What has to be done in war is terrible and if this is to be forgotten then so has that committed by traitors—that's it? Yes, that is it.

This was Didymus's mystery. His moods, the contradiction he could not speak of, turning inside himself without the acceptance that is resolution. The old silences that were necessary between him and his wife when he came back to their exile home from a mission, the weeks and months he could not speak of, had returned between them although now they were really at home, together.

And then something happened. Human affairs move in natural uncertainty always, deaths and lives and eras end in illness, old age—and accident. And accident is exactly that: something unplanned, unforeseen by anyone.

Assassination is planned. Assassination is determined. There is no uncertainty; pure intention. Assassination axes jaggedly through the fabric of life, the bearable and borne, tears the assuaging progression of past into present and future. Murder strikes the lives corollary to an individual; assassination rips the life of a country, laying bare ganglia that civil institutions have been in the process of covering with flesh. Assassination is a gash.

The death of an old leader can be understood and taken into continuity in the sense that his work was done. The assassination of the young leader, outside his gate, that day like any other—there's no sense to be made of it except in the mind of the one who held the gun, no sense although the priests and ministers may speak of commending him to God's keeping, the prayers speak of laying him to rest, and the funeral orators assure that his spirit lives on. His place and work was on earth, *here, now*, not in God's keeping, wherever that might be situated; he was for action, not rest, and the survival of his spirit is claimed in many distortions to the purpose of the crazy pleasure of looting, burning, and killing, licence taken in the name of revenge for his death.

But the irreplaceable, no matter how obviously so, must not be so, even in the confusion of loss must be replaced. With his assassination the meaning of the position of the young leader in negotiations becomes clearer than it has ever been; his presence carried the peculiar authority of the guerrilla past in working for peace. If men like him wanted it, who could doubt that it was attainable? If a man like him was there to convince his young followers, could they fail to listen to him?

Didymus was one of those who put on again the battle dress he had worn in the camps and the bush, a persona that was no disguise but his ultimate self, and bore the weight of the coffin on his shoulder. He had read in the paper that morning a letter signed with a white man's name that rejoiced in revenge that the man being carried to his grave had lived by the sword and deserved to die by the sword. He had been angered by the letter, but now, with sorrow palpable on his shoulder, he felt peace in himself and for the man he carried, at having had to accept the necessities of living by the sword prepared to die, as he had been, by the sword.

In the days following the assassination of the young leader, when the gap left by it had to be closed and a successor chosen, he and his kind were sought out and consulted.

Didymus had worn the battle dress again, emerged out of his past. The day had come—aborted from the logic of history by the intentions of tragedy—too soon.

Empty houses. FOR SALE. Estate agents' portable signs propped at corners, arrows pointing: ON SHOW. Clues in the paper-chase of flight. On Sunday afternoons the cars clustered at an address are not the sign of a party but another form of diversion, curiosity to see what other people are abandoning— not all who follow the estate agents' signs are prospective buyers.

It has happened a number of times in the neighbourhood where Vera Stark has continued to live in the house that is one of the only two evidences of an early alliance. The Sharpeville massacre in the Sixties, the black student uprising in the Seventies, now the assassination; although all these dire events did not lay a hand upon the occupants of the white suburbs (only the violent robberies against which they try to protect themselves with walls, alarms, dogs and revolvers do so), these events literally send them packing. In commercial indices in a time of recession, the international movers' firms report unprecedented growth, their competitive advertising campaigns include jingles on television and radio.

FOR SALE. ON SHOW. Are these suburban museums, exhibiting a way of life that is ended? Is that why the once house-proud occupants are leaving? Or as they flee do they really have to fear for their lives—in the constitution, Bill of Rights, decrees that are going to change life?

Vera and Ben Stark drive past the signs on their way to the airport, not to see someone go, but someone arrive.

•

Several months before, there was another letter from Ivan in London. One unlike the short notes and postcards which supplemented phone calls and kept awareness of one another's existence, the slack familial liens, hooked up. After the first page the letter broke off and had been continued under a new date: a letter the writer did not know quite how to write, whose reception he was unsure of. It was addressed to them both, this time. Vera handed it to Ben. A gesture to how much Ivan meant to him.

—I'll read it out.—

—No don't—I can wait.— She was opening other mail, tearing up pamphlets, putting aside bills, but as he read he put a hand out to her. In response, she moved to read over his shoulder as he sat.

—Oh my god.—

—Ben wait, let's get the whole picture.—

But he was drawing breath through pinched nostrils, he held his hand, stayed, at the page.

The boy, the son Adam, had been arrested for drunken driving, suspended sentence, but only after Ivan had made representations to the magistrate, and then the boy had been arrested again, his third offence for speeding, and lost his driver's licence.

Vera did not find it such a tragedy . . . she spent every day with people in great anxiety whose youngsters threw stones, couldn't be got back to school, defied the police in marches and sit-ins, and risked being shot dead. Thinking of what sort of hazards were likely in London streets, she offered —At least it isn't drugs.—

They read on. Ivan put the blame 'mostly—I'm aware I'm a weekend father, and sometimes not even that' on the boy's mother. *To put it bluntly, Adam is too intelligent for her. She can't meet him on his own ground and so he does what he likes with her—and for himself. She makes scenes. She phones me around the world, always these urgent messages to get in touch with her at once. I think god knows what's happened to Adam, and then it's the same tears on the phone, he won't listen to her, he came home five in the morning, he won't bring his friends in for a meal, he wears jeans torn over the backside, what must she do. And it's finally not a matter of what she must do, it's what I must, I see that more clearly every day, if Adam isn't to become at best a drop-out and at worst land in jail.*

Here the letter had been put aside, like Vera's bills. Three days later, Ivan began again. *I said I must do something. Of course it's obvious—you'll be thinking. I should try and get custody for myself. (She has it until he's eighteen.) There's the strong evidence that the mother is not a fit guardian—the arrests testify to that, eh, Vera, you're the lawyer in the family, but of course this kind of case, divorce wrangles, are not quite your thing. And these days the preference of the youngster himself for one parent counts, in the courts; I'm pretty sure he'd want to come to me, though not for the best reasons, I'm afraid. He's bored with her nagging, with being expected to bring his friends home to chat with her over tea (that's what she really wants, she has never got over her girlishness, sees herself as one of them, and you know how the young hate that—you never did, never, Vera, a great advantage of the little time you had for us when we were adolescent). He knows I'm away a lot, and he'd be on the loose. And he's old enough, worldly enough to see that as I live with a woman I'm not married to I couldn't very well make some big moral stand over his relations with girls—and he seems to have many.*

Which brings me to a tremendous worry. The usual. AIDS. He's had all the information and warnings (they educate even small children as well as adolescents at schools here) and I've added mine, told him that as he never goes out without his credit card he must never go out without his condom—but . . . What I'm getting at I'd better come right out with. If his mother is not fit to look after him at this stage in his life, neither—and it's hard for me to admit it—am I. I think he needs time to mature, away from both of us, before he goes to university or trains for whatever else it is he wants to do (as yet undecided, of course; that's part of the trouble). Once he's in training for a career and living independently—I'll set him up in a flat or something—I'm sure he and I will get on and become closer. (It's not that we don't get on well now, it's that I know I can't give him what he doesn't know he needs.) So I'm going to ask you if he couldn't come to you, to the house at home, our old place that doesn't refuse anyone or anything, not that I know of, Ma. I have a feeling his mother will consent, though she'd raise all hell if I wanted to move him in with the Hungarian and me. If Vera and you, Dad, would let him live with you for, say, a year, I think he'd gain a new perspective on his life. If Ben could find him something to do, some work—no offence, Vera, but quite honestly I don't want him getting out of one kind of mess here and getting into another kind because of becoming involved in politics. Anything you'd offer him wouldn't be without that risk. One bullet in a leg's enough. So no good works, please, no brave works. He doesn't belong in that country, he

doesn't owe it anything. He did fairly well in his A levels and,
at my insistence, is taking another at a crammers to be sure
he'll be well qualified to get into a university eventually. This
course will be over soon. Ideally, he should go to you then. The
handwriting became larger and wide across the page. *No im-*
mediate hurry. Think about it. Do it for me. I can ask you
because I love you, Ben, Vera.

We can talk now.

This is something they can talk about. Now; any time. What
concerns Ivan occupies Ben's attention and energy openly. He
remembered Vera's dismayed silence when—some time ago, he'd
been thinking about this solution for the boy even then—there
was the divorce and he suggested they might take the boy for a
while. Ben rose, turned her to him and with his index fingers
lifted her short hair where it lay behind each ear as if it were
the long tresses he used to loop back to study her face when it
was new to him. He kissed her, one of his long embraces, sensuous as they always became at any contact with her, the letter
hidden in one hand of the arms that held her. —It'll be like
having Ivan back again. It'll be all right.—

They talked many times, many nights. Ben's practical prop-
ositions of how they tactfully could take care of the boy for
Ivan—

—He's not a boy—

—how they could make arrangements for his needs and
anticipate his preferences—

—Arrange our lives.—

Vera's sense of resentment. Half-defiant, half-ashamed, she
had never realized how much her (what was it?) sense of privacy
had grown. How could someone like herself whose preoccupations of work were so public, so intertwined with other lives,
have at the same time this sense? She did not know, could not

decide whether it was protective, necessary (she saw how those who, unlike herself, really were public figures, were surrounded by piranhas of public adulation), or whether it was the early sign of some morbid onset, like the first unnoticed symptom of a loss of physical function. It was linked in an obscure way—she chased it in random dissociation down labyrinths of the subconscious—with the voice that had come up in her several times, the impulse she had had to ask: What am I to do with this love?

Ivan, Ivan. Her double (how Ben loves them both, her in him and him in her); her invader. He had germinated in her body, interloper from an episode into her definitive life. And now he sent his representative, his replacement, for her to 'make arrangements' for in that life, over again.

Her *daily life*. This became the irritable obsessive expression of her emotions; *daily life*, she challenged and argued with Ben over details that astonished him, housewifely niggles of anticipated disruptions of petty routines she had no more thought worth discussing than she would have needed deliberation about brushing her teeth. Young men always dumped bundles of dirty clothes about; Esther Dhlomo, who came to wash and iron once a week, would have to be engaged to come twice. The kind of simple meals Ben was satisfied to eat and Vera quickly cooked when she came home from the Foundation; a young man would want red meat. And the telephone? He would be on the phone for hours, no one would be able to reach her. It would be necessary to apply well in advance for another line, have a phone installed in the room he occupied.

Ben countered all these problems and was only occasionally impatient. He smiled, offering Vera the bonus, in the life of parents of adults, of what was surely an empty space in that life about to be filled. —He'll have Ivan's old room.—

What pleased Ben as a destined occupancy, a heritage bind-
ing son to father, Vera recoiled from. With a sudden switch of
her emotions in an insight: she had been seeing the son as the
father, but Ivan was what Adam was being rescued from.

Ivan's room; yes, because it had become the room of Annick
and her woman lover. A room that imposed no succession upon
a male. So there he could be himself, whatever that might turn
out to be.

·

Past the signs.

A powdery Transvaal day at the end of summer drought
rested the eye. Pale friable grass flattened at the highwayside,
fine dust pastel upon leaves and roofs pressed under the sky
night had breathed on and polished. Driving in quiet to the
airport together, something more than a truce in their opposing
anticipations of arrival came upon Ben and Vera. He put the
seal of his hand in her lap; upon not only the contention that
set them one against the other in acceptance of Ivan's proposal—Ivan's blackmail, for Vera; his right, and proof of love,
for Ben. Also upon all that had broken between them over their
years, and hairline cracks where the impossibility of knowing
another being had impacted, despite confidences, the exchange
of the burdens of self Vera put so much value on in entry to and
acceptance of the body they had experienced together countless
times since initiation in the mountains. She, who had been hos-
tilely apprehensive, was serene; Mrs Stark of the Foundation
had trained Vera that once a circumstance has no chance of
avoidance it must be accepted without further capacity for conflict and loss of energy. Ben was the one whose eager anticipation
of receiving Ivan's son had become apprehension. Yet there was
an atmosphere between them as if they were sharing one diastole

and systole in existence that may come briefly between people who have been living together a long time, and disappears, impossible to hold on to or recapture by any intention or will. This bubble of existence was trapped within the car's isolation—air-conditioning, locked doors and closed windows—from the landscape they could see: that landscape was not innocent. There were shootings along the highways and roads every day, attacks like the one that had killed Oupa, shots in the cross-fire between rival political groups, ambushes by gangs representing themselves as revolutionaries. Vera had said to Ben, when final dates for the boy's arrival were being discussed, that Ivan should be told of the risks his son would be subject to, the ordinary risks of every-day in this country, this time. Ben was ashamed of distrust of her motives. To him it was unthinkable that Vera, who had chosen him so openly, could ever be devious, but he had written soberly to Ivan, a constriction in his fingers at the idea that this might mean the boy would not be sent, after all. Although Ivan must have known that, unlike any risks he admonished his mother not to put his son to by finding him employment in her circles, these risks were not ones that anyone could arrange to avoid, he replied he was sure his parents would take good care of the boy. *I only hope there won't be a last minute objection from his mother because she hears something . . . But then she never did take much interest in what was going on in the world.* Whatever Vera's motives had been, at this reply she was concerned that Ben (his dark head bent, considering) might not become aware of how determined Ivan was to get rid of the boy. She somehow owed Bennet his illusions—thought of him as Bennet again, when seeking to honour this debt.

As they walked from the parking ground to the airport

terminal he laughed jerkily with nerves and remarked it was a
pity it was too early for a drink.

—Well, why not? Let's have one anyway. D'you think the
bar'll be open? Yes!—what d'you feel like?— She laughed with
him while they suggested to one another what it was appropriate to drink at eleven in the morning 'like a couple of alkies'.
—Gin and tonic?— —No, that'll make me have to go and pee
just as the plane lands.— —Sherry, brown sherry, when I was
a young girl that was regarded as a suitably mild tipple and I
don't remember it being diuretic.—

No prancing, singing, ululating surge pressing to the barriers for the appearance of these tour groups arriving and trav-
ellers returning from sightseeing holidays and business trips
instead of exile. No banners; travel agents listlessly holding cards
with the names of Japanese, Germans, French and Taiwanese
they had come to escort to their hotels. No children conceived
in strange lands, tossed home from hands to hands; only small
Indian boys dwarfed in men's miniature suits and little white
girls wearing the duplicate of their mothers' flowered tights,
chasing about families patient as cattle, chewing their cud-gum
while waiting to greet grandfathers back from Mecca and fathers
back from business deals on the other hemisphere. Ben and
Vera's passenger came out among the first to emerge. There he
was, guiding a trolley unhurriedly while others urged past him,
a tall boy with a bronze ponytail switching as he casually looked
around. Ben did not move, taking in this first moment, first
sight, in emotion. It was Vera who rose on the balls of her feet
to wave and smile. Now the boy steered, careening the trolley,
for them. They had seen him only less than a year before, in
London, he couldn't have changed much, the same—it seemed
to Vera—outdated Sixties style, the ear-ring, the long hair; ap-

parently the hippies had retreated sufficiently far in history to
inspire a revival of the way they looked even if their flowered
path had become strewn everywhere with guns, their pot-
smoking dreams had become Mafia drug cartels, and their sexual
freedom had been ended, more horribly than any conventional
taboos ever could have decreed, by a fatal disease. Only his jaw
had changed. Facing them now, he had the squared angle from
the joint beneath the ear of a handsome adult male, it was only
with his back turned that, ponytail curling on his shoulders, he
could have been mistaken for a girl. When they embraced there
was the snag of a night's beard on his skin.

He leaned forward from the back seat of the car chattering
in a London accent, well-educated but slightly Cockney, telling
them of the enormously fat man who had overflowed the arm-
rest in the plane, and how in the middle of the night he'd chatted
up the cabin attendant, not the steward who'd said he couldn't
do anything about it but the girl, to find him another place—
and bumped up to business class it was, too! With his air of zest
and confidence it seemed he was arriving on holiday. He had
never been in his father's home country before; the woman beside
him in business class was going all over the show, Kruger Park,
Okavango, the Cape—he was certainly looking forward to getting
around a bit. The mood prevailed among the three of them while
he was shown his room and Ben opened a bottle of champagne
before the special dinner Vera had prepared.

After dinner there was the first of the awkward hours that
were to follow each night in the next weeks. Vera customarily
went to her private place, the enclosed stoep which was her study,
in the evening, and Ben read in the living-room. Although the
young man had just spent thirteen hours in a plane he was not
tired, he would never be tired at night, he wandered about the
living-room looking at books and pictures, picking up newspa-

pers and the art journals Ben subscribed to, the Foundation's
pamphlets and offprints of articles about land laws and removals
that overflowed from Vera's study; he walked out into the night
and rounded the limits of the garden. Vera at the living-room
window saw him standing at the gate before the streetlights
webbed in trees, the blur of an all-night neon sunset burning,
away over the city, with the stillness of one listening to the
turbines of life sounding distantly: a captured animal pacing its
new enclosure, seeing and hearing an unknown freedom, out
there.

•

Kruger, the Okavango, the Cape. —Of course we'll do some
travelling together—naturally—but first I have to find you some
sort of work. Have to be a responsible grandfather . . . What
would you like to do? I can't promise to come up with it exactly,
but I'm prepared to try.—

—D'you notice how the people we meet think I'm your
son—you don't look much like my grandfather, Ben!—

Vera broke in with a cry. —And me? I suppose I certainly
look like a grandmother!—

—Well, do you dye his hair for him? How come it's still
black?—

This kind of light sparring was the initial communication
between Vera and the boy, Adam. —It's always been black,
black, never changed. Just as it was when I first saw him.—
The boy doesn't ask where that was, the youth of someone who
is a grandmother is something unimaginable. But her remark
succeeds in bringing a smile to Ben. —There are white ones if
you look closely enough.—

—What'd I like to do? Now what would I like to do? Vera?
Ben? People are always telling me what I ought to do, I'm not

used to these big decisions.— The three were sitting in the garden; he was at the age when he could sprawl in the sun for hours, perhaps just growing, completing the physical transition to adulthood, his penis secretly stirring under the warmth.

—That's why I'm asking.—

—But I really don't know.— Useless to tell them, hitch the road to Kruger, the Okavango, the Cape; even she, who was holding him in a look as if she knew, smiling with a quirk to the side of her mouth, would not let him go. She might have: but she wanted to please her husband. He had been quick to see that his own presence in this house was some sort of gift to his grandfather, she didn't really want this grandson there. Yet he'd taken a liking to her; their sparring was an admission that she liked him, too, while both were aware he was not welcome. —Maybe I could do something at Vera's offices, what she tells about the place sounds quite interesting. I'd meet people.—

—That's out.—

He looked from Ben to Vera. She stirred in don't-ask-me amusement.

—Ivan specifically didn't want that.—

—Ben, surely Ivan's told him.—

—No I swear to you! He told me nothing.—

—Because I got shot in the leg. He thinks anything connected with the Foundation's likely to put you in danger.—

—What crap! I could be blown up by an IRA bomb in London, couldn't I?—

—The incidence isn't quite the same. Vera escaped with her life. Living here is dangerous, even this garden, this house, if people come to rob they shoot or knife as well, if you walk up the wrong street and there's a demonstration on, you can get tear-gassed or shot; you'll learn all about this, why it is like that—

—I'm streetwise.—

—No, much more than streetwise—you have to be. You have to accept there are risks you can't do anything much about. Certain aspects of Vera's work simply add a few more. Ivan wants to avoid them.—

—Well, anything. Anything. It's not meant to be a career for life, is it?— He hid in sulks his irritation with his father, with both of them.

—All the same— Ben paused, to reject the too emotional 'unhappy'. —I don't want you to be bored.—

He didn't answer, sat there sucking at the hollow inside his lower lip. He knew they wanted him to get up and go into the house so that they could discuss him. He didn't move. Vera rose with a leisureliness that challenged him, touching a plant, wiping greenfly off its buds as she left.

—See you later.— Ben followed.

In the bedroom she stood by while he changed into jeans and running shoes. Ben had always liked to run when something was troubling him; a good household remedy. Each has his or her own. Standing in underpants taking the jeans from the generous wall-cupboards the parents of her first husband had fitted, he still had beautiful, strong legs, the ankles and knees perfectly articulated, the thighs—so important if a man is to be a good lover—frontally curved with muscle under smooth black hair. She regarded him as if he were a statue; one of the works of limbs and torsos he used to sculpt.

—He doesn't really mean it, about working at the Foundation. He's not disappointed at all, I assure you.—

—Well, it's the one positive answer he gave me.—

—He wants to show he doesn't take this whole mock exile seriously, whatever we do. It's a kind of flirtation with us.—

Adam went to work at Promotional Luggage. Profits were

steeply down, with the recession and labour disputes, travel costs rising with the devalued currency, it wasn't the time to take on unnecessary staff. But Ben knew he couldn't hope to find anything else for the young man; his A-level achievements didn't qualify him for something above the rank of junior clerk anywhere else, and where that kind of opening did happen to exist businesses were finding it expedient to Africanize. No one wanted to be seen to employ a white foreigner on some sort of sabbatical, even as a favour to a friend.

Adam was too young to be a salesman—who would give orders for expensive briefcases to a boy with Pre-Raphaelite locks, Ben was amused to think.

—Let him start at the bottom. Messenger and tea-boy. Like any black boy.—

That's Vera, of course.

—Fax and automatic coffee dispensers now. You know that.—

A place was made for him that hadn't existed, in design and production, he could learn something there. Ben had an arrangement with his partner, to which Vera was not privy, to pay the salary himself. Apparently Ivan had not provided for Adam to receive any allowance in his banishment; he couldn't go about penniless and it would have been humiliating for him to have to accept what would have looked like a schoolboy's pocket-money from Vera and Ben. He spent most of the first month's salary on compact discs for the player that was in his luggage. Vera's house was filled with the one intrusion she hadn't thought of complaining of in anticipation, to Ben. Many desperate voices, accompanied by a heavy beat that she heard without distinction as Michael Jackson, resounded from what had been Ivan's room.

Zeph Rapulana dines on board the Drommedaris now.

·

He has moved more or less permanently from Odensville,
where he built a home for his family in the temporary settlement
area secured, and, leaving the backyard cottage, has taken a
house in a modestly affluent suburb vacated by a white couple
who have left in the latest count of emigration to America or
Australia. What has been abolished along with the laws of segregation is the law and custom, more deeply entrenched than
any law, that only white people could live in these pleasant areas.
Anyone who can afford to pay the rent or buy property may do
so now. Many whites who want to see racial prejudice abolished
and have applauded its passing nevertheless comment high-
mindedly whenever a black man or woman is successful enough
in their—the whites'—world of professions, finance and business
to move into one of the formerly white compounds. There are
so many blacks living in degrading poverty, how can a black
man live it up with a tree-filled garden, lock-up garage for his
car, and neighbourhood security watch? For one to want justice

for black people, they must all qualify by being poor. He ought to be living a dozen to a shack without light amid shit running from broken drains. He ought to be standing before a farmer's door shut in his face, saying without menace, non-violently, we won't harm you. Not you or your wife and children. Never. Whatever you do to us. Never. And we'll never penetrate your boardrooms, we'll never enter and take the place behind the desk in the chairman's office, don the robes of the judge, fit the uniform of the commander-in-chief.

When Vera comes to have coffee with him they sit and compare notes. Vera is sharp-tongued about the patrons of the Drommedaris, teases him a little, in his position as an infiltrator of a new kind. He's calm as the old kind. —Of course, underneath that smoked salmon stuff and the wine they keep pouring I understand they're having problems in taking a black man seriously. Of course I understand that.— He is neither sarcastic nor facetious.

Vera smiled. —'I know the white man'.— And they laughed.

—Well, I've been learning about him a long time.—

—But you get on with them—not just amiability; I mean you get them to take you: seriously. Have your say in decisions.—

—Slowly, slowly—yes.— He is a director on the boards of several finance companies, a development foundation, two banks. —I think I'm not decorative enough to be put in the window.—

—Oh *I* don't think so! My bet is they certainly counted on you being decorative enough, with your credentials from the housing commission, they thought that looks good, you don't need to say anything round the boardroom table, you'll lend them enough credibility for progress just by being there, and then they find they haven't got a dummy, they've got *you*. I could have warned them.—

—I'm just a schoolmaster who's trying to educate them to diversify their excess profits into enterprises that will benefit our people whose labour made those profits. That's all. Cheap bonds for housing, technical training instead of casinos, backing for blacks to get into setting up our own financial institutions—and the right kind of co-operation to make sure we don't fail while we're gaining experience. It's like everything else with us blacks, Vera; fail, and it's proof you can't succeed because black can't succeed. It's a trap; give us funds and no access to expertise along with them. 'See what happened? They can't do it'.—

—Probably we're going to nationalize banks—and then?—

He bent towards her with a gentle smile. —I think your politics are a bit different from mine, Vera.—

She was sitting back in her chair with the coffee cup on the arm, legs stretched and crossed at the ankle. With him there was no haste in communication; in every encounter between human beings there is a pace set that belongs to them, and that will be taken up in its own rhythm whenever they are together. —Private enterprise . . . I think you're getting me to see it your way, sometimes.—

—The banks we've created will have belonged to our people already. Only the private aspect will change—there'll be government men on the boards, some of the directors will go.—

He? He'll move on, as he did from the way he found to emerge from the Odensville affair, doing what was to be done when it had to be done.

—I wonder what you really think of them. When you're with them.—

—People. Human beings, men like any other.—

—Oh come on. That's the 'politically correct' reply. And women? The few women I've met in that circle are not what I'd call like any other.—

—Can't think of any women . . . yes, there's one.—

—Poor thing.—

—Well, yes, I suppose so. But I have to admit I didn't notice it, how she was treated. Among us black men, too, it's been usual. I suppose I've been conditioned from boyhood. Although I like to think I've resisted all that!—

—You're the least conditioned person I've met. I was quite wrong about you when I first saw you, hat in hand. I mistook dignity for servility. I can tell you that now.—

He avoided personal references by withdrawing to himself. He filled his cup. —And you?— She put her palm over hers. —I mean would you say you are conditioned?—

She knew he was saying he didn't believe it was so, while he didn't think they needed to be personal in this way; such a level already existed differently between them.

—I find at the moment I need to be, more than I am. I have my son's young son living with us.—

Correcting the awkward definition: —Your grandson.—

—Grandson. I'm unsure—of our position—you know? I don't know what he expects, the right thing.—

This was how he listened in boardrooms, waiting to unravel speakers' motives, giving them time.

—What I should be to him.—

—You're Vera.— His, the last word, no qualifications.

She laughed and pulled a face.

—What about the other children?—

They had been thinking aloud over the news that pupils at black schools were out in the streets again, this time in refusal to pay examination fees. He took up in doubt: —I wonder why we call them children. Eighteen, nineteen, sometimes more than twenty years old, and that's part of what's gone so terribly wrong in our times. If the parents weren't too poor to keep them in school when they're small, if there had been enough schools to take them all in at the right age, as white children start their schooling, if they hadn't been chased here and there, everywhere, all over the country in removals—if they'd really had the chance to *be* children like other children—they wouldn't be young men and women treated like children now. They wouldn't be doing the things that scare people so much, the things that young men and women do when they're angry. This country got it all wrong.—

—And we have to believe we're going to get it right.—

—A piece here, a piece there. It's all broken up. You do what you can, I do what I can. That's it.—

Vera was looking at the palm of her right hand as if (to him) seeking to divine something there; but she was turning to the distraction of some blemish while dealing with uncertainty; she picked at the tiny grains of a couple of warts that came and went, from time to time, in that palm. —So it's some sort of historical process in reverse we're in. The future becomes undoing the past.—

—You still believe history will do it through us. I believe we act through God's will.—

—I know. I know you do.— It was an atheist's declaration of faith: in a man.

They sat in unnoticed silence for a while, closer in their difference than they might have been in agreement, with others.

When politics turns to gangster methods the vocabulary that goes along with these is adopted. The slang of the TV crime series people amuse themselves with night after night becomes the language by which planned killing of leaders and those close to them is termed. There is a hit-list, there are hit-men. Just like the movies—but these tough guys are not actors behind the get-up of balaclava helmets they wear, they are individuals convinced by others that they have a mission: to save this or that political ideology, racial or national formation, religious belief.

It is only after an assassination of a leader has successfully taken place that the hit-list is released to those whose names it comprises. No one gives a ministerial or official police explanation for this, so that an explanation offers itself out of the very circumstance: those in officialdom who kept the list to themselves had among them some who were involved in compiling the list and providing the hit-men. But there are so many formations, so many intrigues, so many messianic claims for exclusive destinies not provided for by any Bill of Rights, that there could be any one of these responsible. If there is an arrest—and most times there has not been—the unlikely individual seems a strange being (produced in an unlikely period in the sense that nothing is like it was for so long) who could have served any of them. For although they squabble solemnly among themselves their yearning is the same, they yearn for the impossible (escape from history, Vera Stark would call it), the reinstatement of life as it was before. They are prepared to kill for that, although nothing will bring it back; assassination is an offering for which there are no gods left.

Sibongile Maqoma is on a hit-list. A telephone call came while she was turning over some chops under the grill. Mpho, who always rushes to answer a ring in the evening in the certainty calls are for her, yelled through the sizzling to her mother, and Sibongile picked up the mobile phone she has resorted to, like her beeper, to make her life manageable. When she heard the slowly emphasized voice of an Afrikaner speaking English she quickly, with the free hand, signalled to Didymus, who was opening a bottle of beer, to go and listen in on the receiver in the living-room.

There had been one or two abusive calls since she had become a member of a multi-party commission in negotiation talks. Pushed under the front door, a note written in straggly capitals called her a black bitch who should keep her cunt out of politics—but to be told over the telephone in that steady monotone (the man might have been reading a grocery order) you were listed to be murdered! If the Colonel had sent someone to talk to her, to tell her; but a telephone call!

She rushed to the living-room giggling on a high note, shaking. Didymus and Mpho stared as if the threat must somehow show on her. —It was so casual, I felt like just saying thanks but my chops are burning—

Mpho flung herself on her mother and started to cry. Sibongile struggled to lift her face and chide her lovingly, don't be silly, nothing's happened, I'm all right. —But he said they're going to kill you— Didymus took over, his arm round her. —You've got it all wrong, he said her name is on a list, a whole list of other people, some names jotted down, that's all. Your mother's not a real target, she's not one of the top leaders, is she.—

—But she's up there, isn't she, she's sitting there, she's part of the discussions those awful people want to stop. They hate us! They hate her!—

Mpho had not been told about the note under the door; but they could not fob her off again by telling her, don't be silly, it's nothing. She sat with her head on her father's shoulder; Sibongile repeated exactly what the police officer had told her. She had at least resisted her disbelief sufficiently to ask where the list had come from: it was not in the interest of certain investigations to reveal. That's all. They calmed the girl, Sibongile taking her hands, turning the silver and elephant-hair rings on her fingers, Didymus stroking her hair, while they talked, as of commonplaces in their lives, of the possibilities: which group might be responsible for the list and how the police found it. In someone's house, office—where? But Didymus was experienced in these matters. —It's come from the cells. They've got someone to sing.—

Under her fear, Mpho was taking the opportunity for regression, becoming a little girl again. —Daddy, you must get the police to guard us, you must.—

—My darling, you couldn't be sure that'd be the best thing . . . But we'll be careful.—

—But how can you be careful! You can't stay inside all the time. Look what's happened, if you go to the corner shop just to buy a newspaper, just down the road, they can drive past and shoot you as you come home, right at the gate. I'll be like the other girl at her father's funeral—I saw her on TV—seeing my mother put in the grave—

The phone rang again and she jumped up in reflex to answer it while Didymus called after her. —Don't tell anything to your friend, whoever it is.—

There were no gods for them to turn to, either. No new state, not yet; no Security that was not at the same time part of the threat. The feel of the house, that was home at last, changed. The dimension of rooms stood back, fragile. The painted burglar bars that had come along with the house were toys to keep out petty thieves. The locks on the doors—nothing, to a force that had the keys to everything in everyone's life, that had sent them into exile and let them in again. They carried on with routine lives during the day and at night sat on the furniture Sibongile had bought, as in a waiting-room.

Adam's and Vera's approach to one another came about through faulty objects. She did not know how to make real contact with him, nor he with her (if he bothered to think about it at all); and it happened of itself. Fixing things. As if some side of him he wouldn't have wished to admit to, hidden under the boldness of getting drunk and losing a licence, there was the guilty pleasure of tinkering, of making objects other than souped-up motorbikes work. It started with the washing machine, from which water wouldn't drain after the rinsing cycle, and now it was the computer in Vera's stoep-study. They were before it together, she on her swivel chair and he crouched beside her. She showed him how the machine either did not respond to or disagreed with her instructions, he watched and tried it for himself. It seemed as if the two of them, beginning to laugh at their own frustration, ganged up in argument with a third person of stubborn obduracy. —Let it cool off a bit. I think I'm getting the idea.—

—But what makes you think you can put it right!—

—Well I'm coming to something . . . we'll start over again

in a minute.— He went to the kitchen and fetched two cartons of the guava juice he had become addicted to in his father's country. They sucked at it through straws.

If machines were the train of thought in which they best met it was easy for her to maintain it. —Wha'd'you think makes my car suddenly begin to stall instead of idling? It's really annoying, yesterday every time I came to a traffic light: engine dead. I suppose I'll have to go to the garage and they'll expect me to leave it there for half a day, a whole palaver, I'll have to arrange to borrow someone else's at the Foundation . . . what a bore.—

—Sounds like something to do with the feed.— She saw how he liked to be consulted. —If you give me the keys I'll take it out this afternoon and see what's what. Could be just a small adjustment, you don't need the garage charging you through the neck.—

Give him the keys; he was devious, this boy, taking advantage of the ease between them at this moment to suggest he should be allowed to drive again. She smiled on closed lips, in doubt: *we understand each other*: —And if you bump into someone? Insurance won't pay and you'll be charged with a criminal offence.—

—Oh how could anyone know about the licence business, back in Britain!—

—Because you'd have to produce it. Wasn't it confiscated? Or if you have it, isn't there an endorsement?—

—I've got an international one they didn't ask about. I've got that right here with me!—

Vera did not want to lose touch, be punitive, the lawyer too correct to be amused in recognition of shady initiative. —Compounding your culpability, man!—

—I wouldn't fail the Breathalyzer, would I? You and Ben

never offer me a drink, do you? I'm going to turn into a guava.—

Vera was still laughing. —No, Adam, no, whatever contingency plans you have . . . it's not a good idea.—

He was looking at her openly, so young, beguiling, set aside as a nuisance by those other adults—his parents, her son; knowing how to make himself irresistible. —Vera, I want to take somebody you know and like very much to a jazz festival out of town, what's the place called, Brotherstroom—

—*Broeder*stroom?—

—Well whatever. I need a car to take Mpho there on Saturday, you don't go to your office that day, Ben's home and you could use his car?—

He was amazed at the change in her face and the disposition of her body in the chair.

—Where have you seen her?—

He laughed in deliberate misunderstanding, as if at her lapse of memory. —In your house. When she came with her parents.—

—I mean since then.—

—She came into the shop a couple of weeks ago. Turns out she's keen on the same groups I like.— Adam had found a job for himself and left Promotional Luggage. The knowledge of all the variations of pop music he showed as a customer led to his being offered a place at the CeeDee Den. He believed, quite correctly, that Vera privately approved the move towards some sort of independence, a freeing from the authoritative chain father-grandfather, while Ben's acceptance was an unexpressed sense of desertion.

Vera appeared to be struggling with some formulation, whatever it was she wanted to say. He watched with impatience. Who could understand people as they leave youth further and further out of sight. He and she were getting on so well, and now she had disappeared before his eyes into some domain he might reach in fifty years or so.

—You should keep away from her—Mpho.— After all that preparation what came out was blunt.

—But why? She's a damn nice kid. We have a good time together, what's wrong with that? Why keep away, all of a sudden?—

—Because I ask you.—

The lame reason lay between them.

There must be something more to it: his look interrogated her, without response. Suddenly, he was again amazed: —Because she's black. Because she's black!—

She lowered her head and looked up at him from under her brows.

Then what was it, what was it, Vera knew as well as he that she would not and he would not accept 'Because I ask'.

—Because she's trouble. Yes I'm very fond of her and she's a particularly attractive girl, a charmer, but it's better not to get mixed up—not to be involved there.—

—Better for her, for me? Who?—

—I don't know how well you know her, how much she may have told you about herself—

—We've been out a few times, a disco and club, we don't have any heavy sessions *explaining* things.— He had had enough of his own family problems; couldn't older people understand there were other interests in life if you were young.

—Her parents have been my friends for a long time and I was drawn into some trouble they had with her. Over a man.— No point in treating him like a child; he's also a man. —It was a painful business for everyone. The young man was a close friend of mine, too. He's dead.—

Dead.

A death, the idea, so distant from any sense of it at seventeen, drew him level with Vera's interpretation of the significance of his going about with Mpho, even if he did not understand this. —She hasn't said anything. I mean she's such a great girl, happy and all that.—

—It's just that her parents had a bad time as much as she did, and they're people with all sorts of special responsibilities, any more personal trouble is something they shouldn't have on top of everything else. You know that her mother's on the hit-list. There are people who want to kill her.—

—Is that really true? My God, I can't imagine knowing anyone at home in London who was being shadowed by hit-men. It's something out of a movie.—

—It's not a movie, here.—

—I see.— A confusion of dissatisfaction came over his face; perhaps he was wondering what he was doing there. Why he was sent by the collusion of adults.

—If you were to start something with her, Adam. If you were to sleep with her. I have to tell you, Sibongile and Didymus would hold me responsible—for having put her at risk again, emotionally—and in every way. I know you're grown up, you have to live . . . but this would be a drama you shouldn't get into. And if you have—if you're sleeping with her—

The frankness drew some sort of clandestine confidence between them. To him she was not so old, after all; to her, he was not so young.

—Not yet, but I can see she'll go along with it, I mean she's ready for anything. She rather likes me . . . of course I'm keen on her. Who wouldn't be.—

He began touching the keys of the computer again as one might run a hand over a piano.

His apparent submission affected her, she began further explanations. —You know I'd never have done this if it had been any other girl you want to sleep with. It's not that I'd be blamed, it's not that which matters. It's the Maqomas.—

—What complicated lives you people lead.— The curiosity and superiority of distance, youth.

Vera was watching the screen with him. —And in London?—

—Oh in London there's only my mother and the Hungarian to worry about—for Dad.—

—Look, it's doing that same thing again . . . !—

Their eyes moved in duet across acid-green signals glowing and disappearing on the screen. Meanwhile he began to chat. —D'you know, I've been meaning to ask and I always forget, did Dad ever remember to tell you? He bumped into the man you were married to before. He was in Sydney at one of those business conferences where everyone wears dog-tags with their name, a man came up in the bar and said, you're Vera's son, aren't you. It was crazy—he said like he was introducing himself, I'm her husband.—

Vera's eyes did not leave the screen but he felt her attention there cut out, a current suddenly switched off.

—Well he was.—

And then the boy began to see with fascination something he didn't think could still occur in—ever be needed by—older people, real adults, who had no need to fear the power of authority: an instant alert wariness quickly dissembled into indifference. Without that recognition of a route of escape he knew too well, he never would have had the nerve to press her. —Must be ancient history.—

Her shoulders lifted and fell.

—How old were you when you married him?—

—Your age.—

—God, how awful.—

—Well, it was the war. It's a hothouse for that sort of thing. Falling in love or rather thinking that's what it is. People are getting killed so nature advances the mating age to replace the dead with children—something like that. Same sort of thing among young blacks in the violence of the townships now; life's cheap, sex tricks you into breeding.—

—When you were young sex meant getting married.—

—Generally, yes. Certainly for girls. If you wanted the sex you thought you wanted the marriage.—

They contemplated, a comfortable pause between them.

—I can't imagine it. We've got the sex, now. And we've got AIDS . . . so?—

—Looks like there's no such thing as sexual freedom. Well, perhaps one generation, at least, had it—Ivan and Annie. Between the end of the necessity to marry and the arrival of the disease.—

—Doesn't seem to have helped much. Dad got divorced, same as you. When I'm with him, and when I'm with my mother, I wonder why on earth either of them married the other. And what about Annie?—

—How d'you mean?— So Ivan must have related as a disaster Annie's choice of alliance.

—You know what I mean.—

—That Annie's a lesbian.—

There was a slight waver of embarrassment on his face before he pursued. —So that's part of freedom.—

—I suppose so, Adam. Yes.—

—But when d'you think it happened? When she was my age? What about boys?—

—Of course—she's beautiful. Like Ben; people fall for that kind of beauty. There were boys, men, but they somehow couldn't strike the right response in her.—

—But another woman could. Why d'you think it was—that she went that way?—

Their attention met and turned aside like the flick of a page, several times. For his part, he was giving her space to reflect, to offer him something he could learn from. She almost said it, shed on this unlikely confidant, Fear of men because her mother was 'taken away', the nest of home broken into by a man. But she answered with an assumption of careless self-deprecation. —Sometimes I think I know, but of course it's nonsense. Maybe the 'cause'—can you call it that, gays themselves are furious if you suggest it's an abnormality—maybe it's physical. Maybe psychological. There are many theories. But Annie would say: choice. Free choice.—

Then he said what Ben had once said, perhaps the question all heterosexual men ask of a woman when considering the rejection of their gender. —Could you sleep with a woman? I don't mean now (she smiled as he respectfully absolved her of any survival of sexuality, as if it would have been a disgrace), when you were young.—

And she turned Annie's accusation to advantage. —I've loved only men.—

—Some people say to try it . . . I don't know. Doing it— or something like it—with my own sex, the idea turns me off. I mean, once you've done it with a girl, how can you think of any better way. I love girls.—

—You don't have to apologize for that!—

—The idea of the war, your getting married to that chap. But you didn't have any children, did you?—

—No.—

—Before Ivan.—

—Before Ivan, no.—

—Did Dad really not mention that he's met him?—

—You know how his letters have been preoccupied with you.—

The gentle reproach had him deflected, smiling in a different direction. But he fingered along his jaw a small lump where a shaven hair had burrowed into the skin. —Not just the meeting at the conference. The man took him snorkeling with him, he flew him to the Barrier Reef.—

There was the waiting silence that comes between two people when one is confronting thoughts the other does not know of, but an instinctive inkling, a kind of prickling of the nerves, is being conveyed.

—They seem to have had a great time together.— His curiosity grew; it secluded Vera and him closely.

—I've heard the Barrier Reef's wonderful.—

—Oh he says it was the time of his life. Dad as a pick-up! It's sure out of character.—

—What do you think of as Ivan's character?—

—Well he's not—spontaneous (pleased at finding the right word), like you must have been. He weighs things up. Look how long it took him to make up his mind between my mother and the Hungarian. But maybe it was because of the man knowing you. Not just any stranger in a bar.—

—Maybe. We never know what a son or daughter understands about us; what we think of as ourselves.—

—Well old people are so cagey! . . . d'you ever tell Ivan what you've just said, about the war and sex and everything?— He slowly moved his head in certainty of her joining him in the denial, and she did, the two of them smiling at her compliance.

They returned to the computer. —It's really bombed out. I'll see if I can recover the data, try the back-ups.—

She said she'd leave him to it. He sensed that he had gained some advantage over her: she was at once Vera, to him, and his grandmother. He turned. —I'll take some other girl—you'll lend me your car for Saturday?—

•

Consequences.

Father and son.

Vera sees them. They swim towards each other through ruined palaces of coral, flippered feet undulating, ribbons of current and light passing, and, magnified by water: recognize. Ivan's face is the face of the young woman on the bedroom floor, the wriggling sperm magnified by time out of sight and mind into the man picked up, tagged, in a bar. Without the tag, he might have been taken for one of those coincidental likenesses that share no blood: at one side of the ocean and another two beings happen to have been born with the same conformation of features. Vera, that wilful sexy bitch Vera, had to transform fertilization into parthenogenesis, the proof of her deceit being that she reproduced herself, only herself, in male form, for her new lover. And Ivan is drawn to the man never seen, never talked of, who once was married to a girl who became his mother; such attraction is a kind of recognition. The time of his life, together.

Father and son. No end to consequences. This consequence is that the seventeen-year-old boy has become one of Vera's confidants. He knows there is something about herself she conceals, making other confessions round about it. He does that kind of thing himself, to protect himself from adults. In recognition—another kind of recognition—of this, she lets him drive without a valid licence, and both of them, as friends, are concealing this from Ben.

She has a need to redefine. Friends. Friends are differing individuals who are the repositories of confidences and confessions. The act of these friendships, in which the various aspects of self cannot be placed all upon one person, is the equivalent of placing the burden of self within the other by which she used to define the sexual act.

Ms Vera Stark, Deputy Director of the Legal Foundation (in the end she has not been able to avoid a title), is among the faces in the newspapers captioned as nominated to serve on the Technical Committee on Constitutional Issues. Vera had heard that her name was being considered, but had not taken the possibility seriously; there were so many commissions and committees sitting, more set up every day either to pass the heat of change from hand to hand or keep an ethos of democracy evolving while the set of the old hegemony theatre was being struck, its now incongruous flats still lumbering people's lives. Some groups wanted to keep them in the way, hoping that an ivy of acceptability might be able to be painted over them; others wanted to cart the junk off to live by in some enclave of a single skin colour or language, and pranced the streets with guns in mounted commando to make their Nazi neo-Arcadian cause a threat. Some enterprising adapters to a coming order where it might be possible still to make money while losing political control, wanted to lease the ultimate relic of the dead regime's power, Robben Island, to a resort developer. A former political prisoner whose people the Foundation was representing in a land dispute made to Vera the counterclaim: *We spent our lives there. We earned it. The Island is ours.*

Vera was cautious not to decide at once on what the nomination meant. Not in terms of how she was favoured publicly: with committees on all questions—and what was not in question now?—there was surely a desperate search for people even marginally qualified to deliberate them.

Ben looked at her with admiration, seeing the light of others playing upon her and taking pride in it. He chided her hesitation. —You don't refuse an honour! And you damn well deserve it. Your qualification as a lawyer is as good as any of the others— better. None of them has your experience. What do they know about rural communities and squatter camps, all those constituencies to be considered?—

They had met for lunch at his suggestion, the new development providing the occasion to take up again what once had been a means of seeing one another during the separation of the working day. She went on picking olives out of her salad. He watched her. —You're not thinking of turning it down, are you, Vera.— She did not know what she was waiting for him to say, what it was she wanted from him. When the coffee came she sat over her cup, dragging the skin of her cheekbones under her fingers towards the temples. All she received from Ben was distress at her indecision, and her apparent lack of ability to explain it. Then she had to get back to the office; there was the awkward fact that he was in no hurry, unfortunately his business was doing poorly and there was no urgency or incentive to cut short the distraction of lunch. She touched his hand in acknowledgement and left, not looking back at him sitting there, alone.

·

She sat at her desk gazing at the door so familiar she no longer saw it, following the gauze of an after-image, the old entry of Oupa with his papers for her and his plastic tray of curried chicken and pap. If he was no longer there, neither was she. When did she first start suddenly seeing a familiar scene (bedroom at night, the level of a glass of water, the abandoned clothes) as if she were describing to herself something already past? It was when she had beside her in One-Twenty-One, so real, a young lover. The Hitler Baby. Long ago as that. Her sense of her existence was as if she had entered someone's house and seen a letter she had written, addressed in her own hand, lying there, delivered and as yet unopened: the impulse to gather it up, gather it in.

One by one her colleagues finished the day's work and left the offices. She could hear the cleaner emptying paper baskets with a slap on the base accompanied by singing in the strange soprano, almost atonal, of black women, the Greek chorus to their lives. They passed one another in the corridor on Vera's way out, Vera prompted to come up on cue with the usual enquiry for Bella's *amour propre*, how was the Dobsonville Ladies' Choir doing in competitions lately, and Bella responding with the appreciation expected of her in return —Oh very good, very good, just won second place.

The lopsided Stop sign at a crossroad, the splendid purple bougainvillaea espaliered on a wall, the fence where the black-and-white mask of a Husky was always pressed yearningly against the lattice, the place at which the elephant's-foot roots buttressing a belhambra tree had raised the tarmac of the pavement like the bedclothes of a restless sleeper; the turn into a side street where these signals reached a destination. She picked up the evening paper at Zeph Rapulana's mail-box and took it with her to the front door. Rang; stood there patiently. The silence of an empty house where his electric wall clock (a stickler, he says, no African time for him!) whirrs on the edge of audibility, and documents shift under the current of air from a fanlight left open. After a while she turned and went into the garden where a neat arrangement of two plastic chairs and a table was kept under the jacaranda. There she sat reading the paper. She did not find it difficult to give it her full attention. The dimension of awareness she had inhabited at the office had closed away. Vera was not even waiting for the owner of the haven she occupied to come to his home. If he had not, she would simply have stood up and left, when she was ready, refolding the paper and placing it carefully on the doorstep. But his car was heard slurring into the garage, and in a few moments he came through a side gate into the small garden claimed with palms and tree ferns he had brought from some ancestral home in the Lowveld that was not the Odensville squatter camp which for her was his place of origin.

He smiled without sense of surprise, as if he always expected to find her there; or more likely because the African characteristic that rather exasperated her, in her house, of arriving at any time without a telephone call in respect for privacy, worked appealingly in reverse, where in African homes it was taken for granted that people walked in whenever they wished. He wore one of his Drommedaris suits, an elegant grey, but they exchanged the usual bobbing embrace of greeting appropriated by the liberation movement from the dictators. He took off the jacket and settled down in shirt-sleeves.

—It's an honour.— She tried it out on him.

—Oh certainly.—

—But is an honour the most useful. For me.—

—Now what are you thinking of, Vera?—

—Aren't I better off, isn't it better for me to be doing my job at the Foundation—the work you know I do well, don't I— than putting myself in the position of making terribly important decisions, conditions for other people—the whole country. Putting myself way up there, above them—

—Isn't an honour as useful as you can make it? You know you always remind me I'm not against what people think of as honours. Some of our people even think of going to a board meeting as an honour, but you and I know it as something else. What did you once say?—infiltration.—

—But this's different. It's setting oneself up to decide power, in the end. What's a constitution but the practice, in law, of a Bill of Rights? The practical means of achieving all our fine phrases, The People Shall Have . . .—

—It's only the draft you'll be dealing with. Something for the transitional council. It's not final, all-out responsibility our grandchildren will blame you for.—

—Ah but it's the draft that will have to reconcile everything, so that the final constitution will have coherence, at least, to go on. Think of regions, alone; the passions of disagreement over regions, everyone with his own home-drawn map and the powers he wants there. The Odendaals, the Buthelezis and Mangopes all shouting and stamping their feet for the right to do what they like with the people in this part of the country or that, no power of interference from a central government.—

—But that's exactly where the last battle's going to be fought! There where the Committee sits! That's the last gasp of the old regime, we'll hear it there! There's this one breath left in it. Go for it!—

She swayed uncertainly, half-smiling; his usual manner was not vehement.

The schoolmaster in him spoke as if he were back in his rural office and had called her in. —It's your duty.—

But she couldn't see herself as self-righteous.

—All right. It's power. And power scares you.—

—I don't know.— She feels vaguely aggressive. —Yes it
. . . I'm not like you: I've belonged so long to a people who used
it horribly. I distrust it.—

—For yourself. But if this Committee does the job, it'll
mean real empowerment for our people.—

It was accepted tacitly that when he spoke of 'our' people
it was as a black speaking for blacks, subtly different from when
he used 'we' or 'us' and this meant an empathy between him
and her. They continued to accept one another for exactly what
they were, no sense of one intruding upon the private territory
behind the other. It had come to her that this was the basis that
ought to have existed between a man and a woman in general,
where it was a question not of a difference of ancestry but
of sex.

—It's a matter of degree, whether I sit on boards or you
get to be part of the Committee—that's something more urgent.
You've never shown any doubts about where I sit.—

—Ah no. Who could have anything to say about that. You're
making a place for blacks in the money world. Even the ex-
Stalinists among us want it. There's no millennium; only the IMF
and the World Bank—

—There are plenty who do say! I'm in it for the directors'
fees. I'm living in the Northern Suburbs instead of Alex or
Soweto.— He was smiling at her certainty.

She had teased him about that fancy restaurant. She released her tongue sharply against her palate and jerked her
head in dismissal of herself and his detractors. To believe in
him was to accept that the Left, as expressed in the living conditions of the majority rather than in ideology, can find its
solutions to those conditions by using some of the means of
capitalism. Looking at the neighbouring countries of the con-

tinent, what other solution was there to try, for the present?

—So I should set myself up there among the little gods who are deciding what the country will be. Proportional representation, regions . . . And what about the Foundation? I'd be away for months, you know. We're always short-staffed. There's going to be so much work, things hotting up before a new government comes. People fear the old boundaries will stick unless you can get back your land first. Places on the borders of homelands that are resisting incorporation with the rest of the country— we need successful court action to claim them quickly, and you know what a wrangle that can be. Problems like Zevenfontein —who, black or white, wants those poor people squatting next to them in a middle-class suburb? And Matiwane's Kop, Thembalihle, Cornfields—they want their land back. Yesterday I was in Pretoria—again—the Advisory Commission on Land Allocation—

—The old battlefield.—

—Mogopa this time. A hearing we'd prepared for the Mogopa delegation. You know what one of them said to the Commission? 'The Government is a thief who's been caught but returned only half he's stolen.' The application we'd made for the restoration of those two farms taken from them in the mid-Eighties has resulted in them getting back only one, and it's Swartrand, the one with less arable land. So we're contesting. The man burst through our legal jargon like a paper hoop. 'Now that the land is supposed to be given back to us, there are a lot of talks, talks . . . the Government is having the power to steal people's property and afterwards set up commissions.' And there was one old man, Abram Mabidikama, I can't get him out of my mind—he said that watching white farmers graze their cattle on Hartebeeslaagte was like watching an abducted child labour for someone else's profit, 'while I have nothing'. And then he stood there and he told them, we are going to struggle to get our land back 'up to the end of time'.—

Zeph echoed quietly, for himself and them. —To the end of time.—

The old man hadn't said what rally crowds were chanting, *kill the Boer*, *kill the farmer*; but like Odendaal when this man sitting opposite her in his cuff-linked shirt-sleeves had said *Meneer, we won't harm you. Not you or your wife and children*, the Commission fingered their pens, hid behind their bifocals from the menace as Odendaal did behind his slammed door.

—What piece of paper that's going to be disputed by the gang of the white Right and homeland leaders is more important than the chance to make sure, now, people have somewhere finally to *arrive*, for god's sake—to end being chased from nothing to nowhere. At least I know I can do something about that. Someone else can sit on the Committee? It's easier than to replace me at the Foundation.—

—Many things seem not to make sense because we're rushing ahead, we have to, and this gets pushed aside for that, gets knocked over so something bigger can go forward.—

—But nothing measures up.—

—No. We have to leave the old standards of comparison, what's important and what's not. We're not just weighing a bag of salt against a bag of mealies, Vera.—

—I'm supposed to sit quietly on an electoral committee while down the road someone watches Sally and Didy's house, waiting the chance to kill her.—

—Have you seen her?—

—I took a bunch of flowers, and that was all wrong—as if she were sick, or the way we do when someone's died. She took them from me with a peculiar expression.—

—You should go often. When something is threatening people need to have others coming round. I've known that in my life.—

—She and Didy won't come to our house. It is as if it were a disease. Or a curse. They don't want to involve anyone else in the risk. Sally's all bravado, of course, says you never know whether the man knows how to shoot straight, he might hit someone else by mistake.—

The sun had set and the underlit sky was pearly with cloud. She stood up and stretched towards it. They walked together to his gate, sharing the end of the day without domesticity, he did not ask what she was going to do, she gave him no decision. He twisted a yellow rose absently off the bush beside the gate; and then handed it to her. She rolled the stem in her fingers.

—Mind the thorns.—

—Empowerment, Zeph. What is this new thing? What happened to what we used to call justice?—

Didymus accompanies Sibongile everywhere with a gun in the inner pocket of his jacket. On his political record he never would have been granted a licence to carry a firearm had he applied for it; the Movement supplied one, asserting its own form of legality. Not only the State, but those factions within it but out of its control, rebelling at the State's even reluctant concessions over power, had the whole arsenal of army and police force to seize upon. What were a few caches of smuggled arms— symbolized by the AK–47, mimed, chanted, mythologized— against that? When police protection is blandly offered, behind it is this reality: the bodyguard itself may include in its personnel an assassin. To have that one patrolling the street outside the house, the first home back home, where Didymus and Sibongile and their daughter are eating the evening meal, to have that one sitting behind her head as she drives into the city!

Sibongile looks at the thing, the gun, with distaste, and constantly asks Didymus if he's sure the safety catch is on, there against his body. But he is no white suburban husband, needing to be instructed how to 'handle' a gun—as the professional-sounding phrase used by amateurs as a euphemism for learning how to kill, goes. And he will not, he assures, hit anyone by hazard, the wrong one.

And they both know that if the hit-man acts it will not be while presenting a target. It will be, as it has been for others, a spread of bullets from a passing car, or through a window where she and her husband and daughter sit at table. Didymus will not have time to see a target or fire. The gun is a pledge that has little chance of being honoured. Didymus has long been accustomed to heavy odds in his way of life and all he can do is lead Sibongile through them.

Suspicious-looking individuals hang around the house but they are only journalists; the assassins will not arouse suspicion, or if they do, it will be after the event, as when neighbours remembered that a red car circled the block a few days before the last assassination. Failing to get to the prospective victim or her husband, journalists manage to waylay Mpho, who is quite flattered to be asked how she feels about her mother being under threat, and appears in a charming photograph which she cuts out of the newspaper and puts up in her room. The distraction makes her feel less afraid.

No one can say when again it will be safe. Safe to do what? Move about freely. Leave the gun at home. At the Negotiating Council sessions Sibongile and others on the hit-list are at least conveniently gathered in one place. Young men from the liber- ation army are on guard; grown plump and relaxed after the austerities of years in bush camps, they stand close among them- selves, like schoolboys at lunch break, when their share of the refreshments provided for delegates is handed out to them. To be accustomed to precautions may be exactly what the hit-men are waiting to happen to their targets. Any routine, even that of watchfulness itself, becomes absent-minded: once you get used to being at risk that is when you are most at risk. That is when the opportunity arises for you to be taken in a way not foreseen. A surprise. Those singled out on the hit-list remind each other: go out to the corner shop for a newspaper on a quiet public holiday morning, there's nobody about so early, it's not a movement habitual to you that anyone could predict, just to the corner, that's all, and when you come back you get a bullet through the head, not once but three times, to make sure. The last surprise of your life.

Sibongile has the compulsion to leave nothing half-done. The most trivial task; before she leaves the house in the morning she goes from room to room, putting things in place, fitting new batteries in the cassette player Mpho has left empty, sorting the disorderly files Didymus piled on the kitchen table, as if these tasks will otherwise never be completed. She is agitated at any disagreement left unresolved when Mpho closes the door behind her on the way to the computer course she now attends, even at the casualness with which such daily partings take place. She will rush to snatch a kiss on Mpho's cheek and watch, from a gap in the blinds supposed to be kept drawn so that movements inside the house may not be followed, while the girl's high little rump pumps under her scrap of denim skirt as she hurries. Didymus finds notes in various places. He sees they are not Sibongile's usual reminders to herself but instructions for others that would keep continuity in life if she went out, like the one who bought a newspaper at the corner, and did not get back. He says nothing. Crumples the notes and aims them at the kitchen bin. He himself had never succumbed to the temptation of rituals of this nature; but then he had had the talisman of disguise.

They continued to sit in the house in the evenings, he reading or at the computer making notes for the book he was expected to write and she studying documentation from various committees who reported to the Negotiating Council. Would it happen when she went into the kitchen to make herself a cup of that rooibos tea which in her old fussiness about her health she thought was good for her? Or when she said, I'm off now, and, on the way to bed, in the bathroom would have time only to turn the taps on? The slam of a door or the crack of gas exploding from a car's exhaust in the street made them both swiftly look up; then Sibongile assuming careless haughtiness, and Didymus wryly smiling to her. Mpho sat with bare feet up on the sofa arm, little mound of well-fed stomach showing in her slouch, rustling a hand into a packet of her favourite cornflakes as she watched the TV parody of their lives in simulated violence and shootings.

Sibongile and Didymus went about as a team, and with others on the list were the initiated, set apart from people who had not been singled out, even close comrades and friends. These did not seem to know how to deal with the situation, though the victims appeared to be managing the unimaginable well enough. Vera Stark came to the house fairly regularly with silent Ben. What was happening in the Starks' lives? At least this was one way of getting friends off the subject of the List, away from the endless going-over who was behind it. Vera is battling with the Advisory Commission on Land Allocation—'as usual', she dismisses. They talk of the first sitting of the Technical Committee on Constitutional Issues due soon, assuming she is going to be part of it. Didymus is not resentful at himself being passed over; the threat of death, close by, drains ambition of all importance, for the time being. —You'll be taking leave from the Foundation next week, then.— He grins and gives a tap on her hand; wonderful she's been chosen. Vera glances at his assurance, a moment of exchange between them.

—Yes. Next week.—

It is the first Ben has heard of a decision to accept. He

studies her in his silence, he is alone in the room among the others. She doesn't look at him and he sees that her profile—thumb momentarily tested between her teeth—asserts that her life has no reality for her in the context of the situation of Sally and Didy, this stage-set on which, in a dread adaptation of Chekhov's maxim for the theatre, a gun whose presence is unseen but everyone is aware of may go off before the end of the act, before the Technical Committee makes its measured deliberation and a new constitution is created under which—it is the only hope—assassins come to realize that the gods to which they sacrifice have abandoned them.

Ben half-believes, has to believe, Vera has spoken only to ward off further questioning about the Committee, she doesn't want to discuss her indecision. For these old friends, Sally and Didy, he is coaxed out of his preoccupation by a sense of Didy's need for distraction, for a show of normal interests, and he offers that his business is in trouble. Faith in the promotional value of Zairean crocodile, South American lizard and Cape ostrich skin luggage with gold-leaf initials and logo was low in these times of recession and political uncertainty. The sanctions-busters who liked to travel equipped this way had had their day, and the succeeding affluent class who would come when sanctions were lifted and unemployment dropped, were not yet in place. He joked dryly against himself, for diversion; the irony of his attempt to secure the old age of his Vera, a woman like Mrs Stark, by profiting from the vanity of the Government's officials, expressed in contrast with the distinction of his face, his black eyes deep as the eyes of antique statues suggested by dark hollows. —The regime's ambassadors know they'll soon be recalled for ever, no more boarding for London and Washington with a dozen matched pieces.—

—Well if you're selling off stock cheap, I wouldn't mind a

smart new briefcase. Doesn't matter if it has some Pik Botha or Harry Schwarz initials and the old coat-of-arms, I don't care even if it's embossed with a *vierkleur*,* I can always stick one of Mpho's decals over it.— Sally matched the spirit. —And maybe if you've got any off-cuts handy we could order a nice holster for Didy. Something cowboy-style, you know. The lining of the pockets in his jackets is getting worn from the weight of the damn gun carted around all the time.—

—Some people wear buttons on their lapels, I wear the gun, that's all.—

—At least you're not the only one. Everyone carries guns about these days . . . without your reason.— Vera turned to Sally. —Ben even wants me to keep a gun in my car . . .—

But Vera is small fry. A terrible privilege to which Sibongile and Didymus belong changes and charges everything about them, to the outsider; the sound of their voices in the most trivial remark, the very look of their clothes, the touch of their hands, still warm. When every old distinction of privilege is defeated and abolished, there comes an aristocracy of those in danger. All feel diminished, outclassed, in their company.

The Island is ours.

---

* Flag of the old Transvaal Boer Republic.

Vera's house is empty.

Promotional Luggage closed down, bankrupt but honestly so; Ben paid out creditors, owed nobody anything. He did not know what to do next and to disguise this went to fill the interim with a visit to Ivan in London. Ivan had parted from the Hungarian; a treat offered, Vera anticipated for Ben an interlude of male companionship between the generations without the intrusion of women. What would Ben do, around the house, while Vera was occupied and preoccupied, every day, every hour, between the Technical Committee and her attempts to keep in touch with work at the Foundation? Shop in the supermarket? Bennet? Regard himself as retired? Take up as a hobby, like joining a bowling club, the sculpture whose vocation he had given up in passion for Vera? Vera was his vocation; Promotional Luggage had been intended to provide for Vera.

Adam stayed on for a while in Ivan's room. He and Vera had the curious loose accommodation of individuals who, though vastly divided by age, by the commitment to ideals in one and the lack of ideals in the other, are at some base alike in following their instincts and will. His grandmother did not give him advice (the one occasion on which she had done so was to protect her friends rather than himself), make his bed, sew on his buttons or supervise his activities, so she was no grandmother. They took telephone messages for one another, ate independently at no fixed meal times whatever was in the refrigerator or each left for the other in the oven, sometimes met up late at night and chatted like contemporaries simply sharing a convenient roof. At one of these incidental meetings he remarked that a friend had found a cottage in Bezuidenhout Valley and wanted someone to share it. A week later he moved out in a party atmosphere, borrowing Vera's car to make several trips with the possessions he had acquired, helped and hindered by the to-and-fro of volunteers among his friends. There was fondness between Vera and him but both knew they would see one another rarely once they did not sleep under the same roof. The family roof: it was that, the house built in the Forties in the style of whites of the period, half colonial bungalow and half modernist with a split-level living-room and coloured slate stoep they called a patio, the house provided for the young bride and their soldier son by people who did not know what they themselves were, part of Europe or part of Africa; the house that was Vera's loot by divorce, the roof under which she took her lover home, where her children were born, where the 'patio' meant for white tea-parties had been converted to a study where strategies for restoring blacks to their land were worked out. In every room the house retained the life lived there. Scratches and stains, makeshift (bookshelves built of planks mounted on bricks) the newly married lovers, caring only for love-making, nothing for material things, had made do with. A sculptor's chisel among counters from a children's game and someone's collection of labelled stones, rose quartz, crystal, geode. Clothes hanging limp, lost the shape of the body that wore them, never given away because someone (Annie?) once had had the intention to pick them up some time. Boxes that hid the remains of Promotional Luggage, 'vanity' cases and elephant-hide wallets nobody wanted to buy. The scent—her own particular body-smell of the house, independent of the perfume she used—of the documents and newspaper cuttings she hoarded, a calendar of her days and years, live as paper in its organic origins is, secretly wadding together in damp and buckling apart thinly in heat. Broken pottery, a Mickey Mouse watch stopped at some hour in childhood, postcards and photographs. It is impossible for anyone, tidying after the departure of a sojourner, not to stop as Vera does and look through photographs come upon. It is then that she turns up, once again, the postcard photograph sent to Egypt during a war. She had not thrown it away, torn it up; only slid it back under all this other stuff.

And who was that?

I'm the one in the photograph whom no one remembers.

·

It was within this calm that she worked with the Technical Committee on Constitutional Issues. What came out of the Committee would be anonymous in its effect on millions, only a small sample of whom she had known and knew, and whose lives she had affected personally, the people of the Mogopas and Odensvilles. She and Zeph Rapulana talked together under the jacaranda as perhaps they would not, elsewhere. It was necessary to believe that elections and the first government in which everyone would have a vote would stop the AK–47s and petrol bombs, defeat the swastika wearers, accommodate the kinglets clinging to the knobkerries of ethnic power, master the company at the Drommedaris; no purpose in giving satisfaction to prophets of doom by discussing with them the failure of the mechanisms of

democracy, of elections 'free and fair', in other countries of the
continent.

—At last—a year, a month, an actual day!—our people
are coming to what we've fought for. They can't be cheated! It
can't happen! Not to us. We can't let it! What a catastrophe if
people started thinking it's not worthwhile voting because whatever they do the old regime will rig the thing.—

She took his determination as a reviving draught. —But if
we're going to deliver the goods there has to be a real anticipation
of what could happen, Zeph. How to deal with the Homeland
blacks who'll still want to keep their petty power even if their
territories have been reincorporated into the country before the
elections. What if their alliance with the white right-wing holds,
grows? What if the white generals become *their* generals? And
the regular army becomes their source of weapons?—

—They have to be shown—absolutely, no other possibility—they can't win. After all the years with their guns and their
armies, after all the thousands they've killed, all the laws they've
made, all the millions they've robbed of land and chased about
the country to take it for themselves, they had to let Mandela
out of jail and sit down and bargain with him. Didn't they? They
must know they can't win! Not even if they do what UNITA did
in Angola and refuse to recognize election results when we win,
not even what Babangida did, and declare elections null and
void. They can't win.—

—So somehow they must be convinced to take what's offered
them. But this has to be done *now*, they have to be accommodated
somehow, *before*. And that may betray everything.—

—How everything, Vera?—

—If we have to give in to that crazy idea—the white
extremists—the bit of the country they want exclusively for
themselves! The ultimate laager. What corner of the country

doesn't also belong to others? What about the blacks who live there, or once did? The land, Zeph, the land. You know all about the land. We promise redistribution of the land to the people and then we so much as consider giving even a metre to those who stole it in the first place? Are we going to start endorsing people out again, this time in the name of the good of unity, one South Africa, one people? And are we going to have to settle for federalism, or some sort of regionalism that's a disguise of federalism, so the old power blocs of whites—maybe with some black satellites, or their alliance with ethnic ambitions—remain?—

—We'll deal with that with regional powers, that's being tackled. The regions aren't going to be a disguise for anything. It's a difficult game, but it'll come off.—

—But the other! Those whites we laughed at until they drove an armoured car into the negotiations building.—

—That track goes nowhere. They'll run out of steam. You and I can't tackle that one, Vera.— He was kindly amused at consideration of the presumption. —We have to trust the leaders to find the right signals to send them on their way. We can only stick to what we're doing. Each of us.—

Chill comes quickly these afternoons. The last light intensifies evergreen foliage to black, with a brush of thin gold across the fading jacaranda that will shed only when winter ends. In pure radiance far off a plane floats silently, linking their vision as their eyes follow it. The presence of shrubs rises. And then the incineration of the vanished sun blazes a forest fire behind blackened trees.

In some eras what would seem the most impersonal matters are the most intimate. Becoming part of the massed design of the dark, there was nothing either felt more intensely than these political fears and exaltations, no emotion that could draw two individuals more closely than this. A strong current of the present carries them headily: this is the year when the old life comes to an end.

.

Ben and Vera exchange regular telephone calls. Tacitly they were supposed to alternate but if a week passes in silence when it is Vera's turn to call, he will call instead.

When the phone rang late at night she knew it was him.

He heard the rings and followed them through the empty rooms of the house to find her: the stoep-study under the gooseneck lamp, the piece of fruit she had beside her when she worked at night, the kitchen where she would be squeezing a lemon to make herself a hot drink, the bedroom where her body emerged from her clothes in an unconscious ritual he could have described.

Usually she was in bed, her arm went out for the phone. Each gave an account of those of their activities they thought the other would like to hear. There were pleasantries, small anecdotes. Ivan had had a party and one of the guests had brought a two-year-old boy who had been put to sleep on Ben's bed and wet it. Vera had been driven round the block on the back of the motorbike Adam had acquired and brought to display. Ben asked, with in his disembodied voice the assumed concern of one to whom such things are a story in the foreign news pages of a daily paper, how the negotiations, committees and commissions were going, and whether the killings were as bad as it seemed on TV flashes. She asked if Ivan was away in some other capital or at home with Ben. He reminded her of routine obligations she might forget—he knew how little time Vera had to think of such things. Licences to be renewed, tax returns—although she was the sole earner now. She passed this over quickly: another kind of reminder, one she wished to avoid, for him—the failure of Promotional Luggage to provide for her as he wished. This was the progression to the moment when there was nothing left to say. In a pause before goodbye—she was lying looking at the ceiling as if she were a stray fly walking there in the silent room—his voice reached her. —Are you lonely.—

—No.— A laugh. —No.—

After she had dropped the receiver she cringed with remorse. She must pick up and call him back, call Ben, Bennet. Say what? If she could lie to him before, times before, why couldn't she find it in herself to give him a lie to grasp at, now. She turned out the light and slept, her empty house drawn up around her.

Forgive me, for I know quite well what I do.

·

Ben and his other beloved, Ivan, were having a good time in London as bachelors together. Ben was in a rage of sorrow no one knew of. A rage of sorrow for all Vera has done and will never know. And if she had? Would things have been different, better? If he had told her that he had felt another man on her, in her, those years, he knew that she was enjoying two men at once, she was capable of it then, he knew there was a flat or a hotel room somewhere she came from, back to him—would she be lonely without him, need him now? Oh not as in the mountains, the delicious and wonderful seduction of him by someone else's wife. But as the husband he became. He saw that Vera never ever really wanted a husband—only for a time, when it excited her to have her lover domesticated, a kind of dressing-up in other garments, perversely, looking after babies together, telling each other confidences, having friendships as a couple, tandem in political beliefs even if she lived them in her work, risked herself, while he built the beaver dam to shore up, provide for her . . . the dam that breached, wrong enterprise for the wrong era. Not that she cared about that; it was part of her not having wanted a husband, ever, not the first or the second: not needing security, which he supposed is what a husband represents to most women. She's getting old and she understands something about security, down there he's far away from, he can't fathom. She's getting old, even his Vera's ageing; and she's not lonely. He searched himself for the bitter comfort of her inadequacies, the things in her that irritated him. She had no plastic, tactile feeling—except for flesh, of course, fondling him, making him rise in terrifying excitement, stroking his lips and eyes, she used to, telling him how beautiful that face of his, that he still bears with, was. A mask for a performance he can't take off. He has all the time he's always needed for reading, now. There is exegesis in everything he reads. Going back to the books that had been the essential texts of his youth, rereading Rilke, he seems sought out, signalled to: Vera is Malte Laurids Brigge's 'one who didn't want to be loved.' 'That inner indifference of spirit': it was written of Vera. And he was reading an Irish poet—not Yeats this time—he wanted to let the words tell her that although he'd failed to share the credo with her in the end, he understood: *What's looked the stronger has outlived its term, / The future lies in what's affirmed from under.* (But it's the beauty of the assonance, perhaps, that holds the meaning for him.) She had listened in his arms when he read poetry to her, Yeats and Lorca, in the mountains, she had said she was entranced. Entranced! Vera never read anything but newspapers and White Papers, Blue Papers, a house full of Reports. For her the condition of existence was what happened in the power of politics, while the very power of life itself, the all-beneficent sun, god-symbol eternally of a future rising, was turning out to be the source of death rays humans are letting in upon themselves by tearing their only shelter, the atmosphere. She nagged him to 'keep up' sculpture in his spare time of being a husband; she didn't know volume, shape, the smooth skin of wood and the grainy one of stone, and the full time these needed. She favoured her daughter openly, cold Annick, and seemed, even when he was a baby, her first-born, to have some kind of unexplained resentment against her son, perhaps because Ivan was formed in her image—did this mean Vera did not like herself? God knows. Lover, husband, you never know the one to whom you are these. He wanted to call out, call out to her—Yeats again—lines that came back to him as a blow: *What do we know but that we face / One another in this place?* He hated—not Vera, but his dependency on loving her. He has gone away knowing that he does not know how to carry on his life alone.

·

Didymus gave evidence about the camps. It became necessary, for the cause, to go further than a report. He was to speak in open inquiry of what he had had to keep to himself. A change of self-discipline; in a career of exile, infiltration, guerrilla battle, spy and spied upon, he was accustomed to such switches. The Movement itself announced to the press and conducted the investigation.

What is the difference between a criminal and a hero? He had thought about this with the particular form of revolutionary sophistication—the nearest to irony a revolution may allow itself to get, because irony is distancing, a luxury, like expecting a soft bed when waiting in ambush to kill. While standing 'trial' before his comrades instead of the last white government's courts, it's hardly a matter of justifying his actions in the name of a just cause, the end against the means. It's a matter of fulfilling whatever is needed by the Movement to show its integrity to the truth, its capacity for self-examination and condemnation because it is strong enough to survive these, a capacity others dare not attempt. He tells as much as is needed to demonstrate that the Movement may emerge with a cleansed conscience. He tells himself it is a mission like any other, suited, as all have been, to a particular stage in liberation.

When the press badger him with questions contrived to make him express bitterness etc. so that they may have a sensational story about divisions within what they call the 'upper echelons' of the Movement, he disappoints them effortlessly with a well-worn formulation, one of the printer's lugs of rhetoric.

—I'm in complete agreement with the principle of accountability we have always rigorously followed.—

They scamper after him with the weapon of their microphones. —You don't feel you're the fall guy? You've been victimized?—

—How?— He appears indulgent of stupidity. —After more than three hundred and fifty years of victimization by one white power after another, I should feel 'victimized' by a normal process within my own liberation movement?—

And afterwards, although there's now no possibility of concealing his involvement with the camps, there is also no need for this in order to ensure that Sibongile's advancement will not be prejudiced. The death threat provides the highest proof of political correctness of the potential victim. Paradoxically, the reputation of Sibongile is unassailable.

Vera and Didymus suddenly caught sight of one another as each was approaching the pay booth in an underground parking garage. He walked with Vera to her car and at a gesture both made at the same time, got into the seat beside her. There was something clandestine about the vast dim cellar of a place, evil-

smelling of fuel fumes, and cold; as if the context of their encounters, just as some people are likely to meet at concerts, bars
or libraries, was set when the *umfundisi* stepped into her house
and she kicked the door shut behind him. They didn't talk of
the inquiry; if Vera was curious she knew enough about him to
keep her curiosity to herself. They talked of Sally. She was the
one on missions all about the world, now, delegate to this country
and that in search of funds for the election campaign. She was
tipped for a portfolio in the cabinet when it came. There were
newspaper photographs in which she could be picked out among
Japanese and German dignitaries and Scandinavian politicians;
Vera saw that the Portobello Market boots and African robes
had been succeeded by a wardrobe of suitable international
elegance for her position. The two in the car were proud of her,
as if from the same perspective; when someone becomes a public
personality and gains an image distinct from an intimate one,
he or she regains the remove of being 'someone else'; Didymus
spoke of her as of a stranger rather than one whose being is
dulled by familiarity. —At least she's safer when she's overseas.
And she's doing so well! She has this way of getting to people
and dealing with these institutions—you can tell she does her
homework, when she meets them she knows exactly what their
resources are, their pet prejudices, what they like to fund. And
tough! No pledges, she says: cheques, not promises. And she
gets them, too. How she can charm . . . just watch her, sometimes . . .—

—She's always been beautiful, that helps.—

—But now!— The two words are almost a boast. Vera
understands something else about any kind of public distinction:
the individual with such an image remains sexually tantalizing
despite the passing of years. Ben beckons distantly. She catches
at a disembodied wisp of telephone voice, words that are going

round lost in her space. —Ben saw her in the foyer of some hotel. One day in London. He said she was splendid.—

—Ben in London? When did that happen? When'd he go?—

Neither he nor she was prepared for the strangeness into which his cheerfully ordinary remark had fallen.

—He'd already been gone a long time.—

Didymus did not want to be drawn into confidences with this woman, old friend from the days across the colour line. The private relationship of his secret visit in one of his revolutionary personae was not licence for her to speak to him of that other privacy, between husband and wife. It was something only a white woman would have expected. Yet he understood what she was telling him; understood out of the balance and imbalance of withdrawal and closeness experienced between himself and Sibongile. But in their case it was surely all due to factors outside themselves, to the struggle and what that meant in all its phases. Whites, even Vera and Ben, surely had at least some intimacy safe from these things? If he had allowed himself to say: I'm sorry—that would have acknowledged he understood, and burst discretion for her to pour out God knows what, Ben with another woman, the usual story. In and around the Movement there were many such; when political action is the only imperative, the sexual emotions rebel.

—Ivan's still over there, isn't it? Big boy in banking, man, that's really nice. We must get together and hear all the news when Ben gets back. I'm expecting Sally next weekend, with luck. She's in Los Angeles and coming via Bonn. You know that Mpho's got a scholarship to study drama at N.Y.U.?— Here was an area of confidence to which both belonged since Vera had taken responsibility for a mishap in the girl's life, along with her parents. —Much better, for a girl like Mpho, than computers

—she'd never have stuck with that, hei. Not with her temperament. Sally fixed it.—

•

Vera returned to the empty house at night in complete self-forgetfulness; and met herself. The curtains she went about drawing across the windows, the angles of walls she followed, the doors she closed as she passed from room to room sheltered and contained only her. Her house, acquired dishonestly, that she never should have kept; that house was still with her, it was, in a sense, her sole and only possession, the only one she had carried with her through everything that had come and gone within and around her, Mrs Stark and Vera; men, the children she bore them, the communities she saved or failed to save from removal, the deaths of and the death-threats to companions, the terrified traipse of squatters from hostel attacks to refuge, the return of faces from prison and exile, the last white parliament that would ever sit, the swastika rising from the bunker to blazon, with a new twist, on the arms of white vigilantes; the abstract of words, power struggling with the unfamiliar ploughshares of negotiation, the committee she came home from where the needs and frustrations and ambitions of more than three centuries were meant to be reconciled and achieved on paper in some immutable syntax.

Old partners in crime (so long ago it had become respectable, a family home) she and her house were alone together. Ben had put in an alarm system. Like every other dwelling that could be called a house, whether in the city suburbs or the black townships, it was a cage outside which prowlers cruised in their cars or loped along the gutters waiting for a way to get in and take what they wanted. She was not afraid because she reasoned that a house with such a shabby exterior would tempt no one to

believe there was much worth taking, inside; and that belief
would be correct: her files were priceless to herself and would
rouse only disgusted disappointment in anyone expecting valu-
ables; the furniture supplied by parents-in-law for the war bride
was worn and abraded.

She would pour herself a stiff vodka with a prickle of tonic
water and put up her feet on the coffee-table elevated with
stacked newspapers. She watched the news on television and
then listened to every other version of it, switching from station
to station on the radio. Events were in the house with her,
nothing else. The voices of events peopled it, speaking to the
preoccupations of her day, and the responses she made mentally
were as if she were answering. The evidence of personal life was
around her; but her sense was of the personal life as transitory,
it is the political life that is transcendent, like art, for which,
alas, she'd never had time after Bennet read wonderful poetry
to her in the mountains. Ben himself had so easily given up what
had attracted her to him along with his sexuality—his artistic
ability, his sculpture. Politics affects and is evolved endlessly
through future generations—the way people are going to live,
the way they think *further*. She had no illusion about politics;
about her part in it. People kill each other and the future looks
back and asks, What for? We can see, from here, what the end
would have been, anyway. And then they turn to kill each other
for some other reason whose resolution could have been foreseen.

Yet there's purpose in the attempt to break the cycle? On
the premise that the resolution is going to be justice?—even if
it is renamed empowerment.

Sometimes, after a second drink, when the news gave way
to some piece of popular music revamped from the past, Vera,
too old to find a partner, danced alone, no one to witness, in
the living-room of her house, the rock-'n'-roll and pata-pata her

body remembered from wartime parties and the Fifties in the Maqomas' Chiawelo house. That was the time, she accepted, tolerant of her young self, when all other faculties of judgment were blinded by sex. She would stop: laughing at herself giddily. But the dancing was a rite of passage. An exaltation of solitude would come over her. It was connected with something else: a freedom; an attraction between her and a man that had no desire for the usual consummation. Ben believes their marriage was a failure. Vera sees it as a stage on the way, along with others, many and different. Everyone ends up moving alone towards the self.

After Vera signed the deed of sale of her house she went to spend a week with her daughter Annick in Cape Town. As she was leaving she stood a moment in the doorway and looked at all that had been there over decades, in place still. Buildings, rooms, witness; the inanimate stand outside time.

Lou came to meet her at the airport. Annie had taken the baby to her surgery for routine inoculations; Annie and her lover had adopted an infant. It was female, like themselves, and black, chosen whether as their form of political commitment against that of sitting on commissions and committees or in their concern for one of the abandoned children of adolescent schoolgirls Annie came upon in her round of clinics in the squatter camps and black townships outside the city.

Annie and Lou were in the state of distracted preoccupation of new parents. Lou called to Annie to listen to the infant's breathing or sniff at its stool in case there was something to be worried about her professional skill would detect; Annie summoned Lou all through the house to witness that she was the first to get the little creature to smile. The room that had been a Victorian nursery and was converted to a lovers' retreat where

Annie and Lou had kept to themselves was restored to a nursery with the door kept ajar so that the baby's summoning cries could be heard. The baby girl was not beautiful. It had feet and hands too attenuated for its body, wavering about like the legs of an insect trapped on its back. Its sad oil-yellow face crowned with hair like a black sponge bore the aspect of something unloved and unwanted in the womb.

—Here's your grandchild.— Annie placed the baby in Vera's arms. She had sensed Vera's reaction; perhaps because it was her own, that in her case moved her to love and protect. —They're all a rather pale muddy colour when they're new. But her mother's a beautiful Xhosa from the Transkei.—

Annie and Lou had rearranged their working schedules so that one stayed at home to take care of the child on alternate days. All such arrangements were discussed, told to Vera in the conviction of parents that every detail concerning the conduct of life around a child is of the same interest to others as it is to themselves. —We tried turns taking her with us to work, Annie to the hospital and I to the lab, but the one who was without the baby always got so worried about what was happening—we were phoning each other madly all the time! Hopeless! When she's a few months older we'll get a good day-care woman in.—

Annie and Vera sat in the sun on the verandah. Tea and scones under the valance of white wooden lacework. Annie with Ben's beautiful face, the black eyes lowered, the fine nostrils white with concentration, fed the baby from a bottle, but it kept nuzzling towards her breast, pushing up the cushiony flesh above the open neck of her shirt. There were clean cloths handy in case the baby should regurgitate and one of the cats, adjusted to banishment from the lovers' retreat, lay bubbling a purr, a kettle coming to the boil, in appreciation of having a household where now there was always someone at home. Vera watched

Annie listening to the other rhythm, the infant sucking, Annie's breathing becoming adjusted to it, as if she would fall asleep; it had been easy to fall asleep while giving the breast, yes. The baby might have been Mpho's if the old *gogo* in Alex had had her way and it hadn't ended in a bucket at the abortionist fortunately procured. So often Vera had felt like this, far removed from what was steering her daughter's life, further and further, unable to check the remove.

Grandmother and daughter and baby; appearing so natural to anyone passing in the street. A squirrel gibbered in one of the old oak trees carefully tended in the garden and Annie looked up—the closed circuit of infant, Annie, Lou, broken by Lou's absence at work—realizing her mother's presence, Vera's presence, having time for it for the first time. —Dad wrote a few weeks ago. I'd written about our acquisition . . . Perhaps we should give him a call, while you're here? He seems quite happy with my rich brother. But what about you? Couldn't that kid Adam at least have stayed until papa comes home? Are you safe in that house alone?—

—I've sold the house.—

Annie was instantly, frighteningly indignant: home, the old home, it must be kept intact even if one never sees it again, doesn't want to. —You've what? For God's sake! When? And what about Ben, when he comes back? Where'll you live?—

Vera let her lift the baby against her shoulder, patting it in the ritual of aiding digestion, before she spoke.

—Ben won't come back.—

Annie did not look at her mother. —And when was that decision taken.—

—There's no decision, but he won't come back.—

—Don't tell me you and he are getting divorced at your age.—

—No, not divorced. No. I'll go and see him and Ivan when I'm overseas.—

She was amazed to see Annie's face reddening as it did when as a child she was about to lose her temper. The black eyes hostile behind a thick distortion of tears.

—How nice of you. What has he done?—

—Done. Nothing.—

So now she—Vera, the mother—who came home to him fucked out from another man, was abandoning that home, nothing for her father to come back to. Shut out.

—For Christ's sake, why do you do this?—

Vera was looking with incomprehension at something else before her, the baby back at the breast of a woman who wouldn't have a man. —Because I cannot live with someone who can't live without me.—

—That's right. Answer in riddles.—

—When someone gives you so much power over himself he makes you a tyrant.—

A few tears fell on the baby's spongy filaments, glistening there, Annie brushed off the contamination fiercely. —Like the penis business. You and the penis, I couldn't understand that, either, could I.—

Vera wanted to bow her head, walk indoors hangdog, and despised herself for it. Always she had had a masochistic need to be chastised by Annie in expiation of the times when, loving her, she had neglected her by having her *out of mind*, that most callous form of neglect; while caring for nothing but making love in One-Twenty-One Delville Wood. She resisted the need by coldness. —By now we ought to have accepted there are things about each other neither of us understands.—

Above the head of the baby Annie screwed up the left side

of her face as if to focus better, ward off. —And what are you
going to do?—

—When the Committee's finished, I'll be back at the Foundation of course.—

—You know I don't mean that. Where're you intending to
live? You're not going to buy another house, are you? A flat? I
can't see you in one of those buildings where you have to sign
in and out every time with some security thug in the foyer.—

—I'm moving to the annexe of Zeph's house.—

No recognition of the name.

—Zeph Rapulana. You know him. He was at the party we
gave when you and Lou were staying with us.—

—When my grandfather died.— A reproof asserting the
order of events in better proportion to their significance.

—I think you and Lou talked to him for a while, in the
garden that night.—

—The man who sits on boards and is a director of banks
and whatnot, you told us? The smooth-talking representative of
the new middle class?—

—The squatter camp leader I've known for a long time. A
good friend.—

Annie was looking at her in sour derisory disbelief. —You've
always dominated in your own house. You're going to share with
someone, now? Why?—

—It's an annexe. Quite separate, own entrance and so on.
There's no question of any intrusion, either way. We respect
each other.—

—But how did this decision come about? Not out of thin
air! Not because you answered an offer of accommodation in the
newspaper!—

—We talked about it together.—

—So you're such great friends.— No reaction: something else Annie sees she is not expected to understand. —And how will you get on with his family. The wife? D'you at least know her? All very well your professional friendships, Vera—

—She lives in the house he built in an area the Foundation fought a successful action over. She doesn't like the city; the children are all away, grown-up—like mine.—

Annie's body began to rock gently back and forth, soothing the baby to sleep, and, as if with the movement, her sense of her mother changed, she felt that her mother needed protection from herself—her headstrong naïvety. —Ma, so you're virtually moving in with a man. What will people think?—

From Annie! Vera laughed. What a consideration, from a lesbian, a lesbian parent—Annie! —D'you mean a black man, then?—

—I mean just what I said: my father's gone to live in London, you move in with another man.—

—I don't think anyone could think *anything* about someone my age, and a man.—

Vera had her palms raised in a steeple against her mouth in her familiar attitude of obduracy. Annie seemed to have to capture her attention against the fascination with which she was following the darting ballet of the squirrel approaching and retreating near the verandah.

—Ma, you're wrong. They'll think.— She continued to rock, in embarrassment at what she was about to deliver. —And they'll laugh at you.—

Vera was deeply curious rather than hurt in some residual sexual vanity. —Do you think so? That's interesting.—

And this roused Annie's curiosity, or wonder. —What are you experimenting with?—

—Not experimenting.— Vera kindly, but to the point.
—You're the one who's doing that.—

—We're doing what we know we want, Lou and I. Simple.
I don't know what it is you think you want. *Still.* Oh I know—
your work, what's coming for the country—but you? What have
you wanted?—

Only someone young could ask this as the single question.
Yet she was forced into response. —Now. To find out about my
life. The truth. In the end. That's all.—

—Oh Vera!— A gesture with a hand free of the baby,
flourishing the size, the presumption of the answer. —And have
you?—

—I'm getting there.—

—'The truth about your life.' But that's not the question.
Was it worth it?—

—What?—

—Everything. All that you made happen. The way you're
suddenly making something else happen now.—

—But *that's* not the question. It's not a summing-up. It's
not (Vera has the expression of someone quoting) a bag of salt
weighed against a bag of mealies.—

—And so? You're not obliged to answer because I'm your
daughter. I'm not looking for a guiding light . . .—

But a key opening a door they had looked for entry to only
once before, they were in some place of confidence.

Vera searched there for something partially, tentatively ex-
planatory that would not make some homely philosophy of a
process that must not be looked back upon with the glance of
Orpheus. —Working through—what shall I say—dependencies.—

—What a strange way to see life. Yours, or others on

you?— But the sound of Lou's third-hand Karmann-Ghia (relic of the days when she was a carefree bachelor, so to speak) braking at the gate made Annie forget about an answer. Lou was coming with a smiling here-am-I stride up the path. A cancelled appointment had given her the chance to slip home for lunch—she brought it with her, a hot loaf and a tray of avocados. She dumped these and kissed Annie, was kissed back while she caressed Annie's nape and both hung over the padded basket where their baby slept.

Home.

Vera is the onlooker to domestic serenity.

Somehow, she and Annie have exchanged places. She has left home, and Annie is making home of a new kind entirely.

Perhaps the passing away of the old regime makes the abandonment of an old personal life also possible.

I'm getting there.

Proposals to the Technical Committee on Constitutional Issues come from all groups and formations. And the groupings scarcely can be defined with any accuracy from week to week. Wild alliances clot suddenly in the political bloodstream, are announced, break up, flow in and out of negotiations. Everyone wants their own future arranged around them, everyone has plans for a structure of laws to contain their ideal existence. It is the nearest humans will ever get to the myth of being God on Creation Day. Vera Stark and her colleagues sit week after week, sometimes into the night, considering the basis of proportional representation, parties qualifying with five per cent or ten per cent, consensus in Cabinet decisions or on the vote of a two-thirds majority; the percentage by which the President should be elected, the percentage by which amendments to the constitution could be made, the percentage by which the Bill of Rights could be amended, the extent of powers and duties to be assigned to regional legislatures. And on and on. The principle of each proposal is almost without exception the same: every cluster or assembly of individuals wants to protect itself from the power of others. The fallible human beings on the Committee are occupied with the task of finding a way through this that would protect all these without danger or disadvantage to any. Politics began outside the Garden; the violent brotherhood of Cain and Abel can be transformed into the other proclaimed brotherhood only if it is possible to devise laws to bring this about.

Zeph found her in the garden where a place seemed to have been ready for her for some time. He had dinners and evening meetings and she often was in late session with the Committee, so they seldom coincided on working days. But on Sundays they were there. Vera had pensioned off her three-times-a-week maid with her house, but Zeph had an old woman brought in from the country, perhaps a relative, to whom he referred as his 'housekeeper' since it was delicate for blacks to admit to employing servants. The woman went to the all-day open-air gathering of some religious sect on Sundays, as Zeph went to early service in an Anglican church: Vera cooked breakfast and set it out under the jacaranda mid-morning. He was used to being waited on by women but did not expect it of her, always thanked her as if it were a surprise, and carried the dishes with her back to her small kitchen when they had eaten. They read the papers, passing particular pages to one another without comment; each, out of their particular activities and connections, had knowledge to exchange in private of what was omitted there, not for publication. —No one'll trust we're impartial, whatever we put forward to the negotiations, every day when I get to that chair where I sit I have to remind myself of this. And perhaps they're right? I know, for myself—I'm influenced by the land, at the back of my mind I'm seeing every possible check and balance in terms of how it might affect the question of land distribution. It comes from all my time at the Foundation, it's been the perspective of my life for so long.—

—I don't think *everyone* thinks the Committee isn't impartial. I wouldn't say that, Vera. Just a few who don't understand what impartiality tries for, because preventing 'abuse of power' only means to them they haven't a hope in hell of succeeding with their own kind of domination.—

—But that's just the problem. You and I, here, we can see those people for what they are, and dismiss them. We know what they are, we've decided they're a dangerous hindrance. But the Committee has to consider all submissions, has to take every one seriously, there we have to correct in each other any personal judgments. Remember I once said to you, a constitution's the practice in law of a Bill of Rights? Well I've found impartiality really means listening to the most obvious contrivances thought up by people who don't care what they'd do to claim legality to hang on to power, finagle power. The use to which they'll put beautiful legal formulations! We're caught up in a jungle of our own negotiationspeak.—

—'Technical Committee' . . . yes . . . sounds so simple . . . Like knowing how to wire up some lights or keep the air-conditioners going . . . They could have called it something else. But that's a hangover from all the names we had, nothing to do with the circumstances we were supposed to believe were described by the names—remember Separate but Equal, Extension of Universities Act, Immorality Act, whatnot . . . It's a habit we took over.—

They laughed, matching alone together in the winter sun many of the curious aspects of the changes of which they were part, the time through which they were moving.

If she was grappling in difficulty with what were supposed

to be the technicalities of people's future lives, he had no such officially defined euphemism to protect him. There were scandals in the financial enterprise of empowerment. His face appeared among others in the newspapers they opened. A tangle of loans, debts, transfer of funds from one company to another, and accusations of these being fronts for the Movement. —So are they going to ask you to write into the constitution that no one in a political party can have business interests? That's something, after the way big business and the mines kept the old regime in place since our grandfathers' days!—

—How did it happen? Is there really embezzlement somewhere, people you thought you could trust?—

—I don't like to think so, straight off. We have to sort it all out. It began to get too big too quickly, out of hand. Some sectors—I told you when the figures came out last month how well the insurance company's investment in housing is going?— they're doing well, but the papers don't make much of it. Blacks can't succeed. They mustn't. The old story.—

—Wish-fulfilment rumours. But the figures they quote?—

—I wish it was just rumours. Other things are shaky. We haven't kept strict enough control! . . . when we've seen some of our brothers heading for trouble we've baled them out on their assurance it was temporary, we believed them, they believed it themselves! We haven't learned yet to be ruthless, and that's the first rule in business, make no mistake; we did.— There came to him the jargon that had entered his vocabulary from the Drommedaris. —Not a question of anyone's hand in the till. I'm prepared to stick by that. It'll be a terrible thing for me, Vera, if it is.—

Her eyes moved in resentful alarm. —You wouldn't be involved directly.—

—No.— His hand blotted the photographs spread across

three columns. —But I'd be seen, for good, as being among those who were.—

She took an orange and separated its sections. He was looking at her indulgently, carefully, from the very limit of trust between them, testing if he could even accept, from her, that she might think him capable of theft—for which 'unacceptable practice' was simply the Drommedaris name in the world where he risked himself now.

—What would my tenant do? Move out?—

She dropped pips from her lips to her cupped hand and looked down as she ate, as if all she had to do to find the answer was finish a mouthful. —I'd know it's sometimes necessary to do things now we wouldn't do in another time. That it was done for a reason, someone, something else.—

He smiled. —Ah no. Be careful. We have to make a lot of new rules but that's not one. A thief is a thief, Vera. You and I cannot be exceptions.—

—You'd be offending God, wouldn't you. Yes. But Zeph I'm not so sure about myself; that consideration not coming into it for me. I might decide money would achieve more for the people, in one place rather than another. I might cross funds . . . A good thing I don't sit on your Boards.—

—Well if you did, at least you couldn't be accused of being predictable. Black.—

·

The scandal died down; or was averted by reorganization. Zeph had many discussions with business colleagues at his house. Of course she was not present, kept to her annexe. Sometimes he talked to her later as a consequence rather than a direct account of these discussions. —Can you imagine, there's the example of a factory that regularly produces nearly double the amount of each order because the workmanship is so sloppy, there are so many items that come out not up to standard that only half the number can be used to fill the order. The waste! The cost! In money, in man-hours! Low productivity can sabotage completely our hopes of raising living standards in the long run. Our talk all these years about redistribution of wealth and land—when we've done that with what was stockpiled for themselves by white regimes, we'll still be unable to compete in world markets if we don't raise productivity. We're far behind successful countries, far behind Korea, Taiwan, China . . . countries with cheap labour. They produce better goods than we do and on a scale that makes our productivity chicken-feed. We've blamed exploited cheap labour and lack of skills training for our failure. And that's been true, far as we could judge, because we've never had anything else but an exploited labour force. But when our workers are no longer exploited, will they produce more and better? What about the old ways? What are we counting on? That when you have black management, a black executive director, if in some cases the State you voted into power is your boss, you'll put enthusiasm into your work? Motivation. I worry. It won't be a form of protest against the white exploiter to be caught skimping on the job. No more fifty per cent rejects. We need black management that knows how to make people work.—

Vera watched his face, his manner; smiled. —On board. No avoiding it.—

If she happened to encounter his colleagues in passing he introduced her, hand on her shoulder: —My tenant.— If anyone showed curiosity about this tenant, the ageing white woman who lived on his property, he was pleased to have the opportunity to inform them —Mrs Stark is on the Technical Committee. She is one of the people drafting our constitution.—

The tenant. The designation, for the public, suited her well.
It was a kind of private play on words, between Zeph Rapulana
and Mrs Stark, linking their present arrangement to Odensville,
the matter of land, over which they had come to begin to know
one another. It was a consequence in which there were loyalties
but no dependencies, in which there was feeling caught in no
recognized category, having no need to be questioned. On the
home ground of the present—violent, bureaucratic, shaking, all
at once, expressed in burnt and bloodied bodies, in a passion
of refusal, revulsion against institutions, in the knowledge of
betrayal by police and army supposed to protect, in the anger
turned against itself, in the prolixity of documents—there manages to exist this small space in existence. Yet Vera felt it open,
to be traversed by herself: *herself* a final form of company discovered. She was able to do her work on the Committee with
total attention, she wrote letters filled with news of it regularly,
addressed jointly to Ben and Ivan, she telephoned Annie to
enquire after the progress of the baby, she visited the Maqomas
and marked off in silent apprehension the passing of another
week, another month that perhaps meant Sally, alone in her
danger, would survive.

Vera's annexe was really too small for her to have visitors
there; only Adam, on his motorbike, occasionally arrived at a
weekend, and once took her with his girl-friend to hear a jazz
group from what he thought must be her era, in a café crowded
with young blacks and whites to whom the music was quaintly
new.

Perhaps he had had a request from Ben. Ben was reassured
(guilty, somewhere unacknowledged in himself, at leaving her,
even if this was for her reasons) that at least she was living on
what must be the safest kind of premises, in present conditions,
the property of a prominent black man not overtly involved in

politics. But he worried about her way of life, apparently so completely involved, in public, always part of group thinking, group decision, and so withdrawn outside that. Ben searched for her in her letters without success. Ivan, just to satisfy him, suggested she might have taken up some mysticism or other, Sufi or something. No, no—how little could a child know of its own parent! Ben at least had gone far enough with her in her life to know that, wherever she was now, it was not a form of escape. He was diffident to explain to this being who was so much like her in the flesh (the face he addressed himself to made it seem to him it was her he was talking to) that she belonged to the reality back there as he himself never had, never could try to, except through her. Ivan occasionally wondered why it was apparently impossible for Ben to go back; but it was a bargain he made with himself that if he didn't pry into the parents' lives they wouldn't pry into his own. He and this sometimes strange father were close on their own terms; there was no financial burden, he was making plenty of money; so long as he himself didn't find a woman he really wanted to marry they could go on perfectly well living together in odd bachelordom. His colleagues rather admired him for his affection for this handsome ageing parent they encountered in the Holland Park house. Evidently he had been an artist of some kind. According to Ivan, he kept himself busy going round the exhibitions.

One winter night in that year a pipe burst, flooding outside Vera's annexe, and she put her leather jacket over pyjamas and went to turn off the main water control in the yard. The tap was tight with chlorine deposits and would not budge in hands that became clumsy with cold. She quietly entered the house. Vera always had access, with a second set of keys Zeph had given her; she kept an eye on the house while he was away on business trips or spent a few days with his family in Odensville. The keys were also a precaution Zeph insisted on for her safety; if anything or anyone threatened her, a woman alone, she could come to him. The disposition of rooms in his house was familiar under her hands in the dark. She would not disturb him by turning on lights. She was making her way without a creak of floor-boards or any contact with objects to the cupboard in the passage between his bedroom and the bathroom where she knew she would find pliers.

Without any awareness of a shape darker than the darkness she came into contact with a warm soft body.

Breathing, heartbeats.

Once she had picked up an injured bird and felt a living substance like that.

Through her open jacket this one was against her, breasts against breasts, belly against belly; each was afraid to draw away because this would confirm to the other that there really had been a presence, not an illusion out of the old unknown of darkness that takes over even in the protection of a locked house. Vera was conscious of the metal tool in her hand, as if she really were some intruder ready to strike. For a few seconds, maybe, she and the girl were tenderly fused in the sap-scent of semen that came from her. Then Vera backed away, and the girl turned and ran on bare feet to his bedroom where the unlatched door let her return without a sound.

Vera came out into the biting ebony-blue of winter air as if she dived into the delicious shock of it. She turned off the tap with the satisfaction of a woman performing a workman-like task. Instead of at once entering her annexe she went into the garden, the jacket zipped closed over live warmth. Cold seared her lips and eyelids; frosted the arrangement of two chairs and table; everything stripped. Not a leaf on the scoured smooth limbs of the trees, and the bushes like tangled wire; dried palm fronds stiff as her fingers. A thick trail of smashed ice crackling light, stars blinded her as she let her head dip back; under the swing of the sky she stood, feet planted, on the axis of the night world. Vera walked there, for a while. And then took up her way, breath scrolling out, a signature before her.